I0763371

Loving the Prophetess

Anna-Stacia Haley

Anna-Stacia Haley

Loving the Prophetess

Published by: Grace Affirmed Publishing Services, LLC

Text Design by: Anna-Stacia Haley

Cover Design by: Leah Haley

ISBN-10: 1-7334636-0-7
ISBN-13: 978-1-7334636-0-7

Distributed by:

Ingram Sparks
1400 Broadway #520
New York, NY 10018

DEDICATION

For my Heavenly Father, my mother, and my grandmother. Thank you for your faith in me, and the gifts you've helped to cultivate and grow. I love you.

CONTENTS

ACKNOWLEDGMENTS

I wanted to take this time to first honor God. I'm thankful that He never left my side throughout this journey. I also want to thank everyone that has taken the time to read this book before its publication. A special thank you to my Grandmother and Tytianna Wells, who have been instrumental throughout the editing and revision process. You have helped me ensure that this book would be ready for a larger audience. I also want to thank my sister, Leah, for her photography and cover work. You're awesome. You have no idea how much I appreciate all of you.

PROLOGUE

Four years ago:

Micah pulled back the sheets on his queen-sized bed. When he finished he stood paralyzed by the feelings that washed over him-- the guilt, the hopelessness, the fear, the anguish. How was he supposed to take care of his younger sister? They had all they needed financially and then some, but well-off or not, he didn't know anything about parenting. Was it selfish of him that he wanted to live his life? Was it selfish of him that he wanted to be young and have fun?

How could his parents, who loved God more than anyone he knew, not have been spared from a car accident? In the hands of the Almighty, protection shouldn't be listed among the things that God was incapable of. Couldn't God have told them not to go out? Of course He could have, but why didn't He? God was loving, kind, merciful...this didn't seem to fit the description of the God he knew—unless there was no God. That was the only explanation that made sense to him. Why would God who was supposedly so loving and so merciful do something like this?

He knew that his parents weren't perfect; they had their fair share of flaws. But in spite of those flaws, they were faithful to God and to their church. The members of that hypocritical, greedy church didn't deserve them--all that hard work and time that they put in. Nothing ever seemed to be enough for them, never enough time, never enough money. They wouldn't have been satisfied until his parents gave up the very blood from their veins. Maybe that wouldn't have even been enough. They would always tell him that they weren't doing it for the members of the church, they were doing it for God.

Although the idea that there was no God hurt him, the idea of serving a God who would do something like this hurt him more. This was deeper than a flesh wound. This pain ran deep. Not only had grief overtaken him, but the bitter sting of betrayal took root in his heart.

What does this make me? He thought. *I'm just a stereotypical character from one of those stupid inspirational movies. If I stop believing does that mean I never really believed in the first place? No, not possible,* he thought. *There is no God. There is no God.*

The anger and misery he felt within began to increase as tears spilled down his cheeks. Micah wrapped his arms around himself, fingers clawing at the bare skin of his arms.

"It was supposed to be me and You! That's what You told me!" Micah shouted finally.

His words were suspended in mid-air by the thick and palpable streak of disappointment that ran about the room. Fear surrounded him, suffocating him. All that he'd endured, all that he'd suffered in his eighteen years of living proved to be worth nothing. Every time he wanted to walk away from that hypocritical, judgmental church he came running back, and it wasn't because his parents forced him to, it was because he felt that God told him to, or maybe it was his own guilt. Regardless of his reasons for staying, he was done. In Micah's eyes, this was God's last chance.

"Prove to me that You're real. Prove it! Right now, You're looking like nothing but an empty room, full of air, that doesn't talk back! I stood for You! I stuck it out for You! I proved to You that I was in it for the long haul! So now it's Your turn to prove it to me! Prove it!"

Silence.

Nothing but absolute, ear-shattering silence followed and that was enough proof for him.

That night he dreamed of a young, brown eyed girl. She looked to be about his age. Her brown curly hair looked like wildfire as it danced around her face like flames. She held up four fingers, then waved. The dream remained with him for the next four years.

ONE

Micah Williams bolted upright in bed, sweat pouring from his body like heavy rain. His eyes were wide, searching about the room for a single ounce of familiarity.

Again, he thought bitterly. Micah covered his face with his sweaty palms and rested his elbows against his knees. His failed attempts to banish the images from the dream he'd just awakened from created a desolate feeling within him.

Will the dreams ever stop?

These dreams had plagued him for four years. Sunlight streamed through his large window, muted slightly by sheer curtains. In the light, he could see his blue and gray plaid comforter and sheets strewn about on the floor. The fitted sheet had released its corners of the mattress and was now bunched around him. He clenched the sheet tightly in his hand, so much so, his knuckles started to hurt. His heart raced and his breathing became uneasy as the sound of bare feet against hardwood fell upon his ears. He jumped as the door to his room creaked open. When he saw who was in his doorway, he relaxed. He released the sheets and forced a smile on his face. It was his sister--ReAutumn.

"Hey Rea," he said.

"You were screaming," she murmured. "Are you ok?" She watched him through her large emerald eyes, frightened.

He beckoned her closer with one hand.

"I'm fine," his voice cracked despite his best efforts, causing him to grimace. She propped herself up on one elbow as she lie on her side next to him.

"Just a bad dream that's all," he continued.

She didn't respond.

He sighed, "I mean it. I'm ok."

She didn't say anything else. She simply sat up and wrapped her arms around his torso, hugging him tightly. Micah held her closely as he rested his damp cheek upon her mess of brown ringlets that were similar to his own. She was the best thing in his life. Every time he looked at her, he saw *them*-- his mother's ivory skin and bright emerald eyes and his father's tawny skin and sharp angular face. She was the perfect blend of their parents. He himself had similar traits-- golden-brown skin and emerald eyes. His tight curls were a pale honey color that had grown past his shoulders.

"You stink," she murmured. He guffawed. "And you're all wet." He squeezed her tighter, making her squeal and wretch with laughter.

"Let me go, Micah!" She complained, struggling to escape his grasp. He kissed her forehead and let her go.

"Get ready for school," he ordered gently. This time a genuine smile lit up his countenance.

"Ok," she grumbled. He shook his head at her endearingly as she left his room.

That night he fell into a deep sleep but it was far from peaceful. He was trapped in an endless cycle of dreams. *Her* face flashed in his mind. Her wide brown eyes bore deep into his soul. She'd been appearing to him in his dreams recently with that unforgettable wild, curly hair and beautiful brown skin. He'd only dreamed about her a few times over the years, but now the dreams of her were occurring more frequently.

Despite having convinced himself that she was only a character in a dream he'd subconsciously created, there was something about her that drew him in. *Bewitched*, that was the term that he used when he told his best friend Jay about her. Jay had laughed it off, consequently causing Micah to do the same, even if it was only for a little while. He'd never admit it out loud, but he wanted to know her. He wished she was real. But it wasn't the mystery girl that made him hesitant to pursue sleep again, it was the dreams themselves. They felt so real, so real that he hardly knew reality from fiction when he awoke.

She wasn't the only thing that he dreamed of, although at times he wished she was. He'd dreamed of getting his acceptance letter into college, and a few days later he received it in the mail. If he dreamed it, it was going to happen and he had no control over it. These dreams began after his parents passed away in that stupid car accident. No, not passed away—*died.* They died. Micah hated the phrase "passed away".

What did that even mean?

They were dead. They didn't pass anywhere. He could feel the bile rising up in the back of this throat as he thought about it. He should have died in that accident as well. Immediately, he chastised himself. Had he died he wouldn't be there to take care of Rea. The thought of his younger sister in foster care made his skin crawl. He'd heard the horror stories--the sexual abuse, physical abuse and starvation; he would buy his own one-way ticket to hell before she got put in the system.

After his parents died, he and his younger sister Rea had been left a large sum of money, a trust fund for each of them. Micah had gained access to his only a year ago and until then, he'd been living off of whatever money was left in his bank account and whatever their grandmother had. It wasn't long after they'd moved in with her, that she'd died as well.

After she passed, Micah and Rea moved out of their grandmother's house and got an apartment in the city they'd grown up in. Their complex was one of the more moderately priced, and contemporary apartment complexes in town. Because of the pricing and how close it was to campus, a lot of college students lived there. There was no need to get a house with a lot of room or space, as it was only the two of them, and with him starting college, the more money he could save the better. Micah didn't believe in wasting money and he didn't want Rea growing up with the "silver spoon" mentality. He wasn't raised like that, and she wouldn't be either. They'd only lost their parents four years ago, and he was confident that they'd sown some excellent moral seeds into her, but he also knew how quickly that could change, especially with her only being fifteen and in high school.

Micah stretched his arms above his head and threw his feet over the side of the bed onto the plush carpet. Slowly, he made his way to the bathroom. He leaned down to grab a fresh towel from underneath the sink and when he arose, he caught his reflection in the mirror. His jade eyes were bloodshot and expressionless with bags beneath them. He was taken aback.

The four years of wear and tear covered him-- four years of grief, torment, and wearing that stupid smile to cover up all that had gone wrong in his life. He quickly turned his head away. He placed both hands on the sink, leaning against the granite stone for support. He hung his head, chin to chest. He *would not* go there, not today. This time when he gazed up at his reflection, he was smiling. The bags were still there, his hair was still wild, his eyes were still emerald tombs, but he could still smile. He could smile and that was all he needed to do to ensure that no one would ask him any questions. He quickly showered and dressed in straight leg jeans and a t-shirt, then waited on the couch for Rea to finish getting ready.

"I'm ready," Rea said as she walked into the room. "You sure you're ok?" She leaned against the wall next to the front door for support as she put on her black and white converse. Micah stood up, grabbing his keys off the coffee table.

"I'm fine," he slid his feet into his shoes as Rea grabbed her backpack. He paused before opening the door, but when he finally did, he smiled-- sunlight. It flooded the room and filled him with warmth. He inhaled deeply--there was nothing like the lingering smell of cannabis in the morning. He could often smell his neighbor before he saw her. Today was no different.

Micah and Rea both stopped briefly to wave at their blond and curly haired neighbor, Carol, as she walked out of her apartment. The smell was of course from her apartment, apartment 23B. She and her husband Dave had been their neighbors for a few years now. They were kind and they stayed to themselves. They were also hardcore stoners. Directly across from his apartment was where Rea's best friend, Mallory, lived.

Micah and Rea made their way down the set of rickety metal stairs, from the second floor to the first. As Micah strapped himself into the front seat, a strange knot of anticipation began to form in his stomach.

"I had a dream too," Rea said quietly.

"Hmm?" He glanced over at her.

She didn't look at him, she kept her eyes on her cell phone as she scrolled through her social media page. It wasn't uncommon for his sister to dream, and sometimes he thought that they shared a similar gift—except, she *knew* things. He would dream events; his sister simply knew them.

"I had a dream," she repeated.

"What happened?" He asked as he backed out of his parking spot.

Rea fiddled with her fingers for a moment. "I'll tell you later."

"Um, ok?" He gave her a strange look.

The remainder of their ride to Bryant Wilson High School was silent. When they arrived, Micah finally broke the silence.

"You'll tell me later won't you?" He asked. He gave her a one-armed hug.

She nodded.

"Ok. Have a good day. Love you," he said as she got out of the car.

She put on her backpack, paused, and then smiled at him. "Love you too."

When Micah arrived at the university's campus, he parked his car in a dimly-lit parking garage. Putting his earbuds in, he began the trek across campus. He began to scroll through his playlist, eventually deciding on Beethoven's "Piano Concerto No. 5."

As he walked, he surveyed his surroundings. He took in the tall green leafed trees, the sunlight that shone through the spaces between the tree branches, and the people—the people that were scattered everywhere, moving to and fro like ants. They were always in a hurry, always consumed with anything apart from their current circumstances. He snickered when he saw a student nearly trip and fall.

Serves him right, Micah thought confidently. His mind filled itself with incoherent thoughts as he walked to class.

Everything was attracting his attention. He was fascinated by the Greeks strolling in their park and the huddles of students talking loudly.

The campus itself was huge and practically ancient. Different buildings—some more modern than others—sat tall and daunting over the eight-hundred and sixteen acres they occupied. Micah continued walking until he arrived at a faded red-brick walkway. On either side of the walkway were small, well-manicured shrubs.

In early August, the trees—as they usually do—that stood right beside the old building ahead of him, bloomed with small white flowers. Their petals littered the stairs of the large edifice. He made his way up the large granite staircase into a tall old building. The awning, large and made of contrasting and cracked stone, was suspended with large alabaster columns, slightly faded from years of nature's antics.

He was the first to arrive at the lecture hall, and took his seat in the middle of the row closest to the back of the room. The lecture hall was large, and resembled an amphitheater. The farther *back* he sat, the farther *up* he sat and he wanted to be as far away from the professor as possible. He was perfectly centered, so it would be easy to see the large white board in front of the room and the two large flat-screened monitors that were placed on either side of it.

It was eerily silent, not that he minded. Silence meant that he could enjoy his musical selections in peace. He paid attention to every note and every chord. For the first time in a very long time, Micah wished that he had his notebook of sheet music. He burned it and any plans he had of continuing to use his musical gifts after his parents died. Honestly, he was surprised he hadn't destroyed his Yamaha.

When class started, he did his best to pay attention but his phone kept buzzing. He glanced down to see who messaged him and smirked. It was Sheba, his ex. His phone buzzed again, he now had two messages. The first message was a lewd photo of her, the second message was it's caption.

`Come thru- ;-) -Sheba`

`Bet.` He replied.

She sent a winking emoji in return. As much as he knew he needed to break things completely off with her, he couldn't. This was too easy for him. He didn't have to worry about the relationship problems or the emotional attachment. They swore to each other that it would be nothing more than convenient sex—no feelings involved, no strings attached.

He tried his best to pay attention to the professor's lecture on mitochondria, but he was bored. If there was nothing else he'd learned from his public-school education, it was that the mitochondria was in fact the powerhouse of the cell. What else was there to know? And besides, Sheba's text had sparked a stream of thoughts that he wasn't apt to ignore. His eyes roamed about the room, but finally settled on the young woman in front of him. Micah snickered when her laptop screen. She was watching some cheesy soap opera. He took to watching that until the end of the class period.

After class, he began grabbing his belongings. He threw them in his bag quickly and carelessly.

"Hey man."

Micah looked up in response to the greeting, and grinned.

"Tony!" He said. "I didn't know you were in here!"

In a lecture hall with a little over two-hundred students, it was difficult to find anyone. Tony shrugged his shoulders.

"I just got in this class today. I dropped my physics class to get into this bio class. Eight a.m. classes just don't work for me," he admitted while shaking his head.

"Ah. Gotcha," Micah nodded his head in understanding and slung his backpack over his shoulder.

"I just wanted to say hey and see if you wanted to hang out on Friday." Micah's face contorted into an apologetic expression.

"I would bro, but I have some things to do." Tony smirked at his friend.

"You mean you've got a *Sheba* to do." Micah merely shrugged, a stupid grin plastered on his face.

"You need to let that go man," Tony continued.

"All in good time my friend," Micah assured him. He threw an arm carelessly around his Tony's shoulders. They began walking toward the exit, dodging fast paced students as they went.

"She's an ex for a reason. It's good now, but just wait," Tony said.

He was never a fan of Micah's exploits with Sheba, or any other woman for that matter. Micah had once wondered if he was secretly jealous, and wanted Sheba for himself. However, when Tony met Denver—his now fiancée—his suspicions were assuaged.

"I know you don't like her, and most of the time I don't either, but trust me on this one," Micah pleaded.

"I'm just saying, there's no way you two could have broken up and still be messing around for this long without one of you guys still having feelings for each other. You remember when y'all broke up? Y'all stopped talking for a few weeks and she slashed your tires, dude. She's obsessive *and* vindictive," Tony said.

"I know you're looking out for me, but I've got this handled. She knows what's up."

Tony gave a swift nod. Moments later he was sporting a crooked grin.

"Yeah, we both know you're heartless."

Micah's short outburst of laughter caused a few other students to look their way.

"You know me so well. This is why we're friends man. This is why we're friends." Tony pushed Micah away playfully and the two began roughhousing on the lawn outside of the building.

"Ok, I give!" Micah said breathlessly. "I gotta get to work or I'm going to be late." They parted ways and Micah began his walk to the parking garage on the other side of campus. He reached into his pocket to pull out his phone and cursed when he couldn't find it.

"For the *love* of all that's *holy*..." he grumbled.

He turned around abruptly and headed back to the classroom in search of his lost phone. If he didn't get there soon that phone was as good as gone. When he made it to the doorway, he paused upon hearing the voices of his professor and a young woman. There was something familiar about her, as if he'd met her before. Her dark curly hair was pulled up into a bun, and her back was to him. He couldn't see much of her. Her oversized backpack nearly covered her entire body.

Quietly, he teetered in and immediately retrieved his phone from his desk. From what he could hear of their conversation, the girl had just enrolled into their class and was asking questions about the homework that would be due in a few days. Micah rolled his eyes. *Kiss ass,* he thought disdainfully. He swiftly left the classroom, this time he was sure not to leave anything behind.

TWO

When Micah awoke Friday morning, the overwhelming fear that usually assaulted him wasn't present. As he sat on the couch waiting for Rea to get ready, he propped his feet up on the coffee table and gave himself over to his thoughts. The dream he'd had a few nights ago had stirred him awake, and chilled his body to the core. In the dream, he'd sat beside his best friend, Jay Emmanuel's hospital bed. It was clear to him what had happened--Jay had been shot, and in the dream, Micah knew who'd shot Jay, but when he woke up he knew nothing. Rea's voice pulled him from his thoughts,

"Ready!"

Micah jumped at the sound of his sister's voice. Her voice was a warm soprano, like tinkling bells. He feet fell to the floor like heavy weights. He turned around and smiled gently at her.

"Let's go then," he said.

She nodded in response and turned toward the door. Micah opened it, expecting the smell of Cannabis to greet him as it usually did but the air was fresh. No one was there.

Maybe she slept in, he thought. That was odd. Come to think of it, he hadn't seen her at all in the past few days. Every now and again when he went outside on the balcony, he would find her out there on her balcony smoking. They would make polite conversation for the most part and other times they'd have some deep conversations. When he felt inadequate as a guardian to Rea, and he felt this way often, Carol was always one of the first people he'd go to. Sometimes he'd go to Jay, but Carol wasn't religious. He could be himself with Jay, but Carol truly understood him. But he hadn't had a conversation with Carol in a while. Rea didn't seem to notice the woman's absence, at least If she did notice, she didn't comment.

The two made their way down the stairs. Rea's steps were light as she looped her arm through her brother's. The two got into Micah's car just as a medium sized U-Haul truck pulled up beside them. A young, darker skinned man, was in the driver's seat. From what Micah could see, he was on the phone, grinning widely. He got out of the truck and when he noticed Micah staring at him, he waved. Micah nodded back. *Hm.*

As they pulled out of their parking spot, Rea fiddled with her purse straps. Micah glanced over at her, concern clouding his face.

"What's on your mind?" He asked quietly.

She refused to meet his eyes but opened her mouth to speak.

"Nothing," Micah's eyebrow lifted, showing his disbelief.

"Stop lying," he chastised jokingly.

The corner of her tiny mouth lifted slightly. She shrugged and shifted uncomfortably in her seat.

"What's a prophet?" She whispered.

Micah shrugged his shoulders and gripped the steering wheel a little tighter.

"I don't know. Isn't that like Isaac or Jeremy or something in the Old Testament?"

"Oh," was her only response.

Immediately she went back to playing with the straps on her purse.

"Ask Siri, I'm sure she knows. Why do you want to know anyway?" He asked.

"I just wanted to know."

Micah pulled up to the school and stopped next to the curb. He put a hand on her shoulder and squeezed gently.

"Hey, I love you. Have a good day at school and don't think too much about it, ok?"

She gave him a small smile.

"Love you too," he murmured as he watched her make her way up the stone pathway to meet her friends.

The instant she was in their presence, her downcast expression morphed into a large smile. Her friends bought into it and soon they were walking away laughing, probably about some boys or shoes or whatever it was that girls their age talked about. Micah was torn from his musings by the sound of a horn blaring. He cursed the offender under his breath and drove away.

Since when did Rea ask *him* questions about the Bible? She knew that he didn't know a dictionary from a Bible anymore. Sure, he used to be interested in that poorly crafted entertainment show called church, but he grew out of it and he knew that she would too. He shook his head.

She was going to get hurt.

He knew his little sister liked going to church. She liked learning about the Bible, but perhaps it wasn't the best thing for her. He was allowing her to get her hopes up and build up her faith in something that didn't exist. While he knew that she'd find out soon enough on her own, he didn't want to have to pick up the broken pieces of her heart when it happened. She'd already suffered too much loss. She'd lost her parent's, her grandmother, and now she was stuck in his care. That was hard enough. He knew that he was a mess. He did his best, but no matter how hard he tried, he'd never be what she truly needed. He was still trying to figure it out as he went along. She was eleven when they'd lost their parents and now she was becoming a young woman. He'd read parenting books, books about teenagers, anything he could get his hands on to help him, but it wasn't enough. Rea was still different, at least in his opinion.

Often times, he let her go to youth group on Wednesday nights with her best friend Mallory. He also dropped her off at church every Sunday— sometimes he even stayed. But lately it seemed that this was no longer enough for Rea. She was asking more questions, asking him for money to get more books like: *Prophetic Intercession for Beginners* and *The More of God.*

How heartbroken would she be when she found out that there was nothing more?

He wished that he could say she began her pursuit of the religion when their parents died, that way he could have some confidence in the idea of her devotion being a simple phase. Despite his hopes, her desire to learn more about Christianity had only intensified after their passing.

Maybe it was guilt.

That had to be what it was. He'd felt that way for a while too, feeling compelled to continue going even if he didn't believe in it, to honor the memory of his parents. In a way, he felt closer to them by going. Sometimes, he could still picture them sitting on their row in the sanctuary. It was the third row from the front as his father never liked to sit too close. Micah and Rea would sit between the, Micah closest to his father. Now Micah sat in the back when he visited, but Rea kept to the family tradition and sat in the third row.

Maybe that's why she was so into the whole church thing. Perhaps she felt the same way he did. If that *was* how she felt, they could work on rectifying that. Micah no longer felt guilty though; he simply went because Rea asked him to. Well, that and because there were few things more satisfying than making fun of the *idiots* in the pulpit.

Unlike most young girls, Rea's make-believe world wasn't of knights, princesses, and dragons. It was of saviors and steeples, sin, and sanctification. The happy ending was the only aspect of a fairytale that was remotely normal. Should it have bothered him so much that his younger sister wanted to be a Bible thumper? Probably not, but it did. A small part of him felt reassured that the only man she'd be chasing after would be one that was dead…or alive…or whatever it was those freaks believed.

I need a drink. It's too early in the morning to be this deep, he thought.

Micah soon found himself parked outside of a large, dull brick building with seven floors and large glass windows. He knew she'd be mad at him for arriving so early, but he was bored and needed something to do. He didn't have work until later on that evening and his brain was too active to simply go back to his apartment and sleep, so he did the next best thing.

After all it *was* a Friday, he had one class and didn't have to work. Sheba didn't have class on Fridays so everything would work out perfectly. He unplugged his phone from the charger cable and dialed Sheba's number. She answered on the third ring. He wasn't sure if she'd actually answer, especially since he didn't show up on Monday evening as planned. Whoops.

"Yes?" She snapped.

Yep, she's mad.

"Let me in. I'm outside."

She was yawning and he imagined her stretching on the other side of the line.

"You actually showed up huh? Couldn't wait til tonight?" She teased.

He rolled his eyes sighed into the phone.

"Hurry up."

"What's wrong?" A beat of silence passed between them. "You know what? Never mind, I'm on my way," she sang before hanging up.

Micah quickly stepped out of the car and headed into the lobby.

"Hey Chase!" Micah said as he clasped hands with another man about his age. Chase was tall, and mirrored Micah's broad shoulders.

"Sup Micah? What are you doin' here?" Chase asked.

As if on cue, Sheba made her way into the lobby. Micah's eyes shifted over his friend's shoulder and landed on the fair skinned woman clad in black yoga shorts and a white tank top. Tony's eyes widened in realization.

"Oh, that's why. Well, I'll see you at work tomorrow?"

"Yep."

They hugged briefly before Chase made his way out the door, laughing quietly to himself as he did so.

***

Micah awoke in Sheba's bed, dazed. Fidelity wasn't a concern for him, as he was a single man, but even *he* felt it was a little wrong that he'd dreamt about the brown-eyed girl while being in Sheba's bed. She'd appeared, cross-legged on a floor in a dark room. Had it not been for the bright spotlight illuminating her form, he wouldn't have even seen her. She'd smiled softly at him, and for the first time, he actually heard her voice. It was vaguely familiar and painfully out of reach, the ghost of a memory. He was certain that he'd heard something similar once or twice before but he was unable to place it. The words she spoke were simple and haunting:

"It's time."

He lie back down and closed his eyes, trying to block out that growing feeling of discomfort.

What is wrong with me?

"You're uncomfortable because you shouldn't be here." A still small voice whispered to him.

"Did you say something?" Micah asked aloud. He looked over at the sleeping woman beside him and waited to see if she would give some sort of response. She didn't. Of course, The Voice was a little too deep to be hers, but he figured he'd check just to be sure. The alternative wasn't exactly better.

"You're more than this. I created you for more than this."

Oh my god I'm hearing voices…I knew this was going to happen one day. I knew that I was going to go crazy.

Clearly that wasn't Sheba. Micah sat up suddenly, both hands grasping the closest thing in reach. His left hand gripped the sheet, while his right hand held onto Sheba's leg. Startled Sheba sat up quickly. When she realized that it was just Micah, she stared at him with half open eyes.

"What's wrong with you?" Sheba yawned.

"Nothing. I gotta go," he said hastily.

Sheba watched him from the bed as he searched for his clothes, her hazel eyes following him as he forced his shirt over his head. She sat up, the sheet still wrapped around her body, watching as he nearly fell over trying to get his pants on. To her, he seemed dazed and confused; he blew about the room like a violent wind. He patted his pockets making sure he had his keys, phone, and wallet.

"You know I'm always here for you right?" Micah rolled his eyes.

Right…

"Yup. Thanks."

"What's the rush?" She asked.

"Booty call--not a hangout session. I don't owe you any explanations," he replied as he made his way to the door. Sheba sucked her teeth.

"Man, whatever. We still on for tonight?" She asked. She flipped her ebony hair over her bare shoulder and began playing with it. He paused in the doorway.

"Um…I don't know."

"But we always hang out on Friday nights."

"Yeah, I know," he said. "But I may or may not need to get drunk tonight."

He gave her a lazy military salute and left. He made his way home quickly but was hesitant to get out of his car. The moving van was still there. Well, he'd only been gone for a few hours. The young man he saw earlier was walking up the stairs with two large boxes in his hands. Micah watched him as he made his way up the metal rickety staircase, onto the second floor, and into apartment 23B. Micah furrowed his eyebrows, his face scrunched in confusion.

"Neighbors? Like *neighbors* neighbors? When did the stoners move out?" He wondered aloud. The man returned to the truck and leaned against it. The shrill sound of a ringtone startled him. He pulled his phone from his pocket, looked down at the screen, smiled, and then answered it. Micah rolled down the window of his car slightly to see if he could hear their conversation better.

"Yep, I have a few more boxes and then some pieces of furniture left," He paused. "Oh, you're on your way back now?"

He briefly paused again. Micah wondered if the person really had time to answer.

"Well, take your time I'm fine. Mark is supposed to be over later to help me with the couch and stuff. ok, love you too. Bye." He hung up as he shook his head endearingly.

So there's two of them…hmm. I should have come back here in the first place. This would have been a hell of a lot more interesting.

Micah opened the car door. He decided that it might be a good time for introductions. He approached the truck slowly at first, but then quickly ran to the stranger's aid when he saw him struggling to grab more boxes from the truck.

"Need some help?" Micah asked.

The man smiled. "I think I can manage. Thank you for offering though."

He seems friendly enough.

"You sure it's no problem?" An awkward silence passed between them. *Might as well play nice, we* are *neighbors now.*

His friendly demeanor diminished as his eyebrows rose to his hairline.

Micah extended his hand for the man to shake.

"Micah Williams," he said.

The man sat the boxes down, then grasped Micah's hand firmly.

"Thomas Crowder. I'm not actually the one living here. My friend is moving in here, she just asked for my help." Micah nodded and shoved his hands into his pockets. "I thought I saw you guys this morning. Was that your sister?" The amber colored bun on top of Micah's head bobbled as he nodded.

"Yep. That's her. I had no idea that our previous neighbors had moved out," Micah said.

"This might seem like a weird question, but did they smoke by chance?"

Micah laughed loudly.

"Dude, all the time. I would go out to the balcony in the back and they would be out there *super* high."

"Yeah? We were wondering about that."

"Yep, mystery solved. Well, I'm gonna get out of here. It was nice meeting you… Tony?" Micah's voice rose in pitch as he spoke the name with uncertainty. Thomas looked down at his feet momentarily and then up at Micah again.

"It's actually Thomas, and it was nice meeting you too."

Aww, true.

"My fault. See you around, man."

Micah jogged up the stairs to his apartment and headed straight to the shower. He hoped that the hot spray would not only remove the evidence of his earlier deeds from his body, but that it would rid his mind of the thoughts and questions that plagued him as well. Briefly, he wondered what his new neighbor would be like.

What strange timing! He hadn't even noticed that his neighbors were moving. The week had passed by him in such a blur, it truly was possible that he hadn't seen Carol since Monday. No, he could have sworn he saw her Wednesday when she was out on the balcony smoking. Or was that last Wednesday? Micah dressed quickly after realizing that he'd stayed in the shower a bit too long. Despite his racing and confused thoughts, Micah was sure of one thing, something strange was about to happen.

***

Micah sat in the parking lot of Rea's school patiently, his eyes sifting through the hordes of teenagers in search of Rea. He finally saw her weaving through the students, down the concrete pathway leading to the curb with two girls flanking either side of her. Mallory he recognized, but the other girl he didn't know. Mallory was a short, thin, red-headed little thing. She had way too much energy for Micah's liking, but she had always been a good friend to Rea, so he liked her. The other girl, a golden skinned brunette, was brand new. The three girls laughed as they made their way to the car.

I know they are not all getting in this car…Oh my--yes they are. Do I look like a taxi service? ReAutumn Marie Williams…

Although he was irritated, he plastered on a fake smile as the girls got into his car.

"Hey, Micah," Rea said as she climbed into the front seat.

"Rea. What are they doing in my car?" Micah whispered through clenched teeth. Rea smiled apologetically at him.

"I meant to ask if they could come over, but I kind of forgot," Micah rolled his eyes. "I'm sorry," she continued.

"Yeah, yeah, yeah," he sighed.

I am such a pushover, he thought.

This wasn't the first time she'd picked up a guest without his consent. He cleared his throat and glanced in his rear-view mirror to look at the girls he'd been forced into toting around.

"Hello, Mallory, and Rea's friend that I don't know," he greeted.

"Stephanie," the girl supplemented quietly.

"Hello, Stephanie. I'm Micah, Rea's *amazing* older brother," Stephanie giggled and sat back against the seat.

"Hi, Micah," she said.

"We have a project due in a few days, so would it be ok if they came over so we could all work on it together?" Rea asked.

"*Now* you ask me," Micah muttered to himself. "Sure, why not. I'll get pizza on the way home."

"Yes! I love you, big brother." Rea turned to Stephanie, her angelic and soft features were alight with triumph. "See, I told you he was cool."

Micah's heart warmed at his sister's words and he smiled. It was nice to receive some sort of appreciation. It reassured him that he wasn't completely failing at taking care of his sister.

"I never said I didn't believe you," Stephanie said.

"He's hot too," Mallory whispered.

Micah was positive that he wasn't supposed to hear that comment, but he did. He bit his cheek to hold back his laughter.

"So how did you and Stephanie meet?" Micah asked.

"Church," Rea said. Micah raised his eyebrow.

"Vernon Rush?"

Stephanie nodded before responding,

"Yep,"

"Since when?" Micah asked.

"Since, two weeks ago when my church visited yours. I recognized Rea and Mallory from my English class," Stephanie said.

"She's been my bestie ever since," Rea said, grinning from ear to ear as she bumped Stephanie playfully with her elbow.

Micah briefly glanced in his rear-view mirror, and saw Mallory staring out of the window with her arms folded, a stony expression on her face.

Hm…guess Mallory doesn't like this new friendship too much. This just screams high school drama--not my area of expertise.

He couldn't care less about the beef between the two girls, he just hoped that whatever Mallory's problem was, wouldn't create any problems for Rea.

***

"Micah?" Rea asked as they stepped through the front door. They'd just finished dropping Stephanie off at her house. Rea had failed to mention that it was across town.

"Yes Rea?"

"Don't forget about next Wednesday," she said.

Wednesday? Wednesday? Nope. I got nothin'.

"Wednesday?" He asked.

Rea glared at him.

"Church? You promised you'd go?" She reminded him as she took off her tennis shoes.

"Oh yeah, yeah, yeah…I didn't forget. Psh, I just…misplaced the event in my mind," he joked.

Rea didn't find it funny. She ignored it and continued.

"Yeah well, me and Mallory are going to Stephanie's church to visit."

Stephanie's church?

"And where does this Stephanie girl go to church?"

Rea shrugged.

"I dunno. She invited us and we said we wanted to go."

"Is this your way of asking my permission, or what?" He asked.

She shook her head in exasperation as Micah put his hands on his hips. He couldn't blame Rea for not taking him seriously in moments like that. He wouldn't be able to either.

"I'm going to bed now," she waved and kissed his cheek before heading back into her room, leaving Micah alone in the living room. His phone buzzed in his pocket. A text from Sheba:

`Coming back tonight?`

He didn't respond. He wasn't going to do either-- he wasn't going to get drunk and he wasn't going to meet up with her. He was going to stay at home and try to pretend like he hadn't had such a strange day. First, he got new neighbors, and then, he started hearing strange voices in his head.

On second thought, a drink does sound pretty good.

He'd only have one. If he planned on getting wasted, Rea would have to be out of the house or simply not around. He checked on Rea first to make sure that she was ok and actually in bed. Once he saw that she was asleep, he went to his room and got a bottle of beer from a hiding spot in his oversized closet. He opened the patio doors and stepped out onto the balcony located in the rear of their apartment.

Frankly, it was strange not catching that familiar scent of weed when he stepped outside. He was saddened by it. It meant that his neighbors were truly no longer there. He liked Carol and on days like this, he would have appreciated someone like her to talk to. If he talked to Rea or Jay about his problems he knew that it would only lead to an argument about the Bible or God or both. He'd read the Bible backwards and forwards before he gave up on the whole thing. They couldn't tell him anything that he didn't already know. He could probably tell *them* a few facts that would make their religious house of cards come tumbling down. The idea of having to believe in something that he couldn't see, irritated him. And how could he believe in, or worship a God that was good but allowed evil things to happen? Ah yes, free will. *Tell that to starving children and to the mothers who buried their still-born babies*...Micah cleared his throat and rubbed his hands down his face.

He leaned against the thick metal railing of the balcony and stared out into the night sky: a dark blue tarp with little spots of light shining through.

Looks a lot like life to me, he thought, *mostly dark days with a few sunny ones every now and again.*

He took a sip from the bottle just as the patio doors to the adjacent apartment opened. Traces of white curtains blew in the cool night breeze.

I'm about to meet my neighbor, he thought. *Great first impression.* He took another sip. *Well, I'm not so sure I'm making the best one myself.*

The alcohol burned his throat as it went down and he imagined that burning as a consuming fire that would burn away his anxieties. Patiently, he waited for his new neighbor to come out so that he could play the part of the welcome committee. No one came out. He only heard the sound of music. He recognized the song immediately as one that he used to do with the worship team when he was in youth group. It felt so long ago. He was glad that he left that bunch of hypocrites behind. And just like that, he was irritated by the sound of the music. The song itself was beautiful, the musician in him couldn't deny that fact. However, the memories it stirred in him were ugly. He placed his bottle on the balcony. His mood shifted from bad to worse and the night was officially ruined. Desperate for an escape, he retreated to his bedroom, thinking nothing else of the nearly full bottle of beer that he left sitting on the balcony.

THREE

As Micah walked into the red and white 50's style diner on Saturday morning, he was determined to put on his best face. The smell of greasy burgers and fries made his stomach growl. There were people in just about every red leather booth in the small diner. His co-workers couldn't bus the tables fast enough—typical Saturday morning. Just as he made it through the double doors leading to the kitchen, a long arm was tossed around his shoulders. Micah's eyes followed the arm to its owner—Jay Emmanuel.

"You're late," Jay chastised.

"Sorry," Micah said as Jay herded him through the frantic servers, and steaming stove tops to his office.

When they were safely inside the small, cluttered office, Micah took a seat. He fixed his eyes on the plain white walls that had grown dingy from the diner's aging. The diner was established in the fifties and had been running in Jay's family for years. It was now Jay's responsibility. Jay shut the door behind them, then leaned against his desk.

"You look terrible," Jay said.

Micah scoffed.

"Thanks for the compliment."

Jay shrugged nonchalantly and laughed.

"You know I keep it real. For real though, what's up? You've got bags under your eyes, and you look like you hate the world more than usual."

Micah leaned back in his chair. His long limbs were sprawled out over the arms of the wooden framed seat. He blew out some air and looked up at the ceiling.

"I couldn't sleep," he said.

"Dreams?"

"No. I was just restless. I was up literally all night. I finally fell asleep at about five thirty."

Jay moved some papers around on his desk. Without looking up he asked,

"Any idea why?"

"We got a new neighbor."

Jay's eyes enlarged and he waved his hand, expectantly.

"And?"

"I haven't met her yet, but I was out on the balcony before I went to bed and she opened the backdoor to her balcony and had her worship music playing. It was kind of loud."

"Did you recognize the song?"

"Psh. No."

Jay's eyes narrowed and he crossed his arms.

"You didn't?"

Micah shook his head and began tapping his fingers rhythmically on the arm of the chair.

"Nope."

"Liar," Jay said.

"So what if I knew the song? What does that have to do with anything?"

"I'm trying to help you buddy," Jay held up his palms, up against his chest. "Chill."

Micah's phone vibrated once, signifying that he'd received a text. He groaned when he saw who it was from.

"Is that your woman of the night?" Jay asked. He already knew what to expect.

Micah glared at him. In response, Jay lifted up his hands in surrender again before continuing,

"I'm just saying," Jay said, cutting his eyes at Micah.

"Whatever. She wants to know why I didn't come by last night."

"Why didn't you?" Jay crossed his ankles.

"I don't know. I guess I just didn't feel like it."

"That's a first."

"Whatever man," Micah said as he ran a hand down his face.

He thought about it for a moment. *Why didn't I want to go?*

He was tired from hanging out with Rea and her friends, but that usually never stopped him from doing what he wanted to do and last night wasn't the first time Rea had surprised him with her little girl group. "I just want to get through today and go home and go to sleep."

Jay nodded.

"Cool, but one more thing. You already know what I'm about to ask you."

Micah placed both hands over his face, then quickly pulled them away. He was already losing his patience.

"I'll be there Wednesday, ok? Rea's making me go. I barely make it to church on Sunday mornings, I'm not tryina' go on Wednesday night too. It's boring as hell, and a waste of my time."

Jay rolled his eyes.

"My church is not boring. Yes, that's what Rea invited you to. She's been hanging out with my little cousin Stephanie."

"So that's *your* church?" Micah pursed his lips when Jay nodded.

"Yep and it's supposed to be a really cool service. We're gonna have dancers, spoken word and I'm kinda excited to go."

"Well that makes one of us." Jay rolled his eyes at Micah's interruption. He gawked as Micah continued, "If the dancer don't require me dropping some ones, I'm not interested."

Jay threw his head back, and groaned. "Grow up. Man forget all that, I think you're actually going to like it."

"And why is that?" Micah had better things to do than listen to some dusty old man getting up to talk about the *power of the gospel.* Nope, he'd pass on that one.

"You'll just have to wait and see."

Micah tilted his head back, stared up at the ceiling and said, "I hate surprises. You know that."

"You'll like this one," Jay said tapping his fingers on the desk. "You won't regret going."

"Right. Anyway, I have work to do--tables to bus, orders to take--you understand," said Micah as he rose to his feet. He stretched, his long arms nearly hit Jay as he did so. Jay ducked away from him just in time. "Whoops." Micah smiled cheekily at his friend. Jay rolled his eyes and threw his arm around Micah's neck, effectively putting him in a headlock.

"I give! I give!"

"Now go do ya' job boy!" Jay said as he pushed Micah toward the door. Micah walked out of the office, laughing loudly as he went.

***

Micah walked through the front door of his apartment that evening beyond exhausted; all he wanted to do was eat and go to bed.

"Rea, I'm home!" He yelled. The lack of response unnerved him. "Rea?!" He yelled again.

The layout of their two-bedroom apartment was spacious, and open concept, so she obviously wasn't in the living room or kitchen area. He walked back to her room. The room itself was large with a nice sized closet, queen sized bed and personal bathroom. Her bed was well made--the white bedspread laid flat and unwrinkled. It seemed she hadn't been in there in a while. He checked her bathroom. It was void of any human presence. He then made his way to his room.

Maybe she's with Mallory, he thought.

He pulled out his phone and called her. On the third ring, she answered.

"Yes, I'm with Mallory," she said. Micah sighed in relief.

"You couldn't have told me that before you left?"

"I left a note on the fridge because my phone was dead when I left and I couldn't find my charger."

Micah scratched his head.

"No, you didn't." He hadn't seen any note. Quickly, he strode into the kitchen and when he reached the refrigerator he grimaced. On the stainless-steel surface of the refrigerator was a pink post-it note with her perfect cursive script on it. "Oh."

"Yeaaah. I'll be home later."

"Ok. Do you have your key?"

"Yep. Love you."

"Love you too."

The moment he hung up, loneliness washed over him.

In the presence of this new feeling he'd forgotten his hunger, and despite his exhaustion the wheels in his head turned. He untied the black work apron from around his waist and laid it on the sofa. Just as he was about to sit down, he heard voices. No, not *voices*—a single *female* voice and it was loud. He stood to his feet immediately and followed the sound to the back of the apartment, out to the balcony. He threw open the doors and peaked out.

"…in the name of Jesus. You've got to go. I come against every unclean spirit in the name of Jesus: every spirit of addiction, every spirit of depression, every familiar spirit, you've been evicted you've got to go right now."

His face contorted in confusion as he listened to her pray, beneath the sound of her voice was a familiar song. Micah hated the fact that he actually recognized it as Jekayln Carr's "Bigger."

"What in the hell?" He murmured to himself.

When he stepped out fully onto the balcony and looked towards origination of the sound and saw, his new neighbor's doors were wide open, just like they had been the other night. Following the commands that his new neighbor was giving to these spirits, she released a garbled and unknown tongue.

Oh great, a Bible thumper and not just any Bible thumper—a sanctified and Holy Ghost filled, skirt to the ankles Bible thumper. Just what I need.

He rolled his eyes. These were purely assumptions of course, as she still hadn't shown herself.

"Hey!" He exclaimed. There was no response apart from her loud music. "Hey! You!" Still no response. "Keep it down!"

Frustrated, he stormed back into the apartment, slamming the balcony doors behind him. Moments later he heard his neighbor's doors shut, and the music was replaced with silence. Still frustrated and cursing under his breath, Micah walked back to his bedroom, slammed the door, threw himself on the bed, and huffed.

I should go knock on her door and tell her to keep the freaky Christian voodoo to herself.

He looked down at his arms, chill bumps had risen on them. The temperature wasn't even close to being cold in their apartment, nor was it chilly outside. Her words were stuck on repeat in his mind. There was something so striking and so familiar about it. Her words…her voice. *Her voice*!

No way. Not possible. This is me, trying to make something out of nothing. This is definitely me, trying to make up some sort of exciting end to my crap day. He groaned. *But it is possible, wouldn't be the first time my dreams came true…NO. NOPE. This is not a fairytale, this is the real world.*

Between going to this stupid service with Rea, and becoming indirectly acquainted with his new Spirit-filled neighbor, he was positive that he'd be going insane soon.

By Wednesday, his attitude on life had taken a turn for the worst. He didn't want to sit amongst a bunch of Bible thumping lunatics, and hear of the miracles of *their* God which included, but were not limited to: receiving cars that they'd worked hard and saved up for, being able to get their money back on a store return, and the infamous waking up that morning, clothed in their right mind--although to him that was debatable. He'd heard it all before. When would *their* God ever do a new thing? Same old parlor tricks, no real power. Same old sayings, songs, and spirituals. He was tired of the cycle and he was proud of himself for getting off the crazy train.

Why had he let Rea talk him into going? He loved his sister, but *dang.* After classes he went straight home, sending Sheba's phone calls directly to voicemail. He'd seen her around campus a few times that day, but his foul mood kept him from having any dealings with her. He didn't feel like dealing with people.

Micah strolled into the kitchen in search of a snack.

"Micah."

Micah immediately recognized the voice as the one that had spoken to him when he was with Sheba a few days ago.

Oh hell, Micah thought. *Just when I thought this day couldn't get any worse. I'm hearing voices again.*

"You're not going crazy."

La la la, Micah sang mentally.

"Really?"

La la la. Micah would have put his hands over his ears, but Rea would have noticed and he was *not* in the mood to answer questions. Then again, how much would that have actually helped? It was clearly not an external voice, Rea didn't hear anything. At least, if she *did* hear something she wasn't acting like it.

"How is it, that you demanded proof from Me four years ago and yet, you've denied every single sign I've sent you?"

I'm assuming You're supposed to be God, right? So how about You tell me? What signs are You talking about?

"You're supposed to be the human that believes he knows more than Me, so what do you think?" Micah pursed his lips in response.

Touché.

"The proof I'm sending you, tonight will be something that you can no longer deny Micah. You can clearly hear the sound of My voice and still deny Me. You never stopped believing, you just started ignoring, but after tonight, you no longer will be able to."

Oh? And just what is that supposed to mean?

Silence.

Of course, sure…let's get cryptic and then abandon the conversation. Abandonment seems to be Your specialty!

If Micah didn't want to go to service before, he certainly didn't want to go now. He would bet his left arm that the freak next door was *His* doing. What exactly did He expect to happen? Was she supposed to cast the devil out of him? Micah laughed out loud at the thought.

Rea stopped her work in the kitchen and turned to him with a raised eyebrow. She'd been cleaning for the past half-hour, not because he'd asked her to or because the house was dirty, but simply because she wanted to. The smell of Mr. Clean and Comet assaulted his nose.

"What?" She asked, taking the yellow cleaning gloves off of her hands. With pursed lips, Micah shook his head. She huffed. "Yes, something. Tell me. I wanna laugh too." She smiled slightly at him.

With a thoughtful look on his face he replied, "Have you met our new neighbor yet?"

Micah began rummaging through the refrigerator in search of some grapes. He found them stashed behind a gallon of milk. He took a few grapes from the bag and walked over to the sink to wash them off. He put one into his mouth as he leaned against the counter.

"Yeah," Rea said.

Micah choked on his grape.

"What?" He asked, as he gasped for air.

Rea leaned back against the counter,

"Yeah. She's pretty cool--" Micah scoffed, causing Rea to pause with a puzzled expression on her face. "What? Have *you* met her?"

Micah shook his head. "No, but I've heard her. Definitely heard her."

Rea turned around and opened the cabinet above her head. With her slim fingers, she touched every glass before finally grabbing one from the back. She filled the glass with tap water then turned back around and leaned her head on Micah's shoulder.

"What do you mean you heard her?" She asked.

She took a sip from the glass. Micah sighed and put another grape in his mouth.

"Every time I go to the balcony out back, I either hear music or like last night--I heard her out there praying,"

Rea nodded.

"Sounds like her," she said. She polished off the water in her glass, then placed it in the sink.

"Ha."

Rea turned to face Micah and their jade eyes locked.

"What's wrong? You're more broody than usual," she asked. Micah looked away, toward the refrigerator and sighed. Rea stepped to her left, effectively blocking his view. "Talk to me."

Begrudgingly he met her eyes, his curls falling about his face. A silent argument passed between them-- him telling her that he was fine and her telling him that he was lying.

"I'm fine," he smiled, despite her annoyed glare.

"You're lying," she said as she crossed her arms.

"Nope, I'm just not in the mood for talking. I'm gonna go out for a bit. Is Mallory home? You guys can hang out while I'm gone."

Rea shrugged.

"I'm old enough to be home alone, and I don't know. I'm here with you." She pulled back when Micah glared at her. "Relax, I'm joking. I hope that wherever you go gets you into a better mood."

She kissed him on the cheek and then walked out of the kitchen area. She paused when she reached the door to her room. "And one more thing. Don't be late getting home big bro, we still have a service to go to."

"Right."

God's words echoed in his ears-- *"The proof I'm sending you, tonight will be something that you can no longer deny Micah. You can clearly hear the sound of My voice and still deny Me. You never stopped believing, you just started ignoring, but after tonight, you no longer will be able to."*

"We'll see about that," Micah whispered.

He snatched his keys from the countertop and made his way to the door. *Let's see how much debauchery I can get into in three hours…*

FOUR

His plan was simple: Do just enough foolishness, get into just enough trouble, and God would put up a fire barrier around the perimeter of the church—he wouldn't even be able to get in. But his plan failed; clearly, God had a lot of patience. That much had been made certain when he pulled into the church's parking lot--no fire. No brimstone. He'd missed the *parking lot ministry*, but that was his only consequence; not having someone to direct him to open parking was the least of his worries. He'd even had Rea ride with Mallory just in case he got a little too carried away with his wicked fun. If he was being honest, he shouldn't have even been driving. He knew he was a little messed up, and God knew that he'd *just* had a few drinks and hit a blunt once or twice, but he didn't want anyone else to know that--especially Rea, that's why he showered, brushed his teeth twice, and put on his favorite cologne before coming to service.

Rea was gone when he'd arrived at home after his *activities*, something about getting there early to eat or meet friends. She'd instructed him to text her when he arrived at the building so that he didn't have to go inside alone. He knew she'd be fuming, he was late. He was only fifteen minutes late, but late nonetheless. He'd texted Jay the minute he left Sheba's place. Sheba had rushed him out of her dorm so quickly, she'd angered him.

To ease his frustrations, he went to smoke with Tony. He didn't smoke too much, as he didn't want to be totally faded. The last thing he needed was a lecture from Rea. However, at this particular moment he was willing to risk that lecture for another blunt. He'd acquired a pleasant buzz--a slight high, but it wasn't enough. He was still aware of where he was, and was still just as uncomfortable with being there as he would have been entirely sober. Not only was he now terrified to walk into this building, but he was also irritated. He stared at the building in front of him--it was massive, had a cobblestone exterior, and a large white steeple.

He pulled out his phone and sent a text to both his sister and to Jay:

`Here.`

Hair up? Or hair down?

He *wanted* them to see how long his hair was and he *wanted* them to judge him for it. Their judgement would only further prove his point that all church people were the same. After all, it wouldn't have been the first time that he'd been judged by church members.

Five and a half years ago:

Sixteen-year-old Micah Williams stood in the hallway as he listened to his parents argue. His mother Lyla, stood with her arms crossed over her chest. His father, Theodore had one hand on his forehead, rubbing the wrinkled skin.

"She's out of line, Theo and if you don't say something to Pastor, I will!" Lyla said.

"I have talked to Pastor and you know how that went."

"That's because you haven't let me talk to him yet!" She insisted, "The way they're treating him isn't right."

"I know that," Theo sighed. He placed his hands on Lyla's shoulders and gently rubbed them up and down. His calloused hands, over her smooth skin caused her position to relax a little. Her crossed arms fell to her sides.

"I'm just tired of this. If it's not one thing it's another. I'm starting to think that Mother Wilks just has it out for our son," Lyla said. "First, she didn't like the way he sang the Doxology, then she freaked out over his arrangement—which I thought was pretty good—and now she's flipping out over his hair. His hair has always been long." Micah sighed and tore his gaze away from the pair. So that was the reason Mother Wilks had been giving him the evil eye on Sunday. Anger blazed through his veins, but quickly left.

"Ok, God," he whispered to himself. "I'm not going to give up. It's

me and You." He went to the bathroom and stared at his reflection in the mirror. Long bronze curls and large emerald eyes stared back at him.

Micah's upper lip curled in anger, and embarrassment. A few weeks later he cut his hair to appease Mother Wilks so that he could continue leading the church choir. He stopped cutting it when he turned eighteen, as he was officially done with conforming. A knock on his window startled him. He rolled down the window and blanched when he saw who was standing on the other side.

"Sheba," he said, before clearing his throat. "What are you doing here?" She placed her hands on her wide hips, sheathed in a burgundy skirt. He'd been holding those hips not too long ago.

This night could not possibly get any worse.

"I go here. What are *you* doing here? Lose a bet?"

He laughed bitterly before responding, "Yes, actually."

She placed her hands in her pockets. "I didn't know you went to church," she murmured.

He snorted. "Only on Sundays and not because I want to, trust me." He glared at her as she raised her eyebrow at him. "Oh don't give me that judgmental look, you are the last person to be saying anything about church. After what we did earlier, I would have never even known you were *saved*."

He winked at her, grinning. Sheba crossed her arms again, her hazel eyes stinging with tears.

Here come the tears... Micah thought as he looked away. *Why is she crying? What part of that was a lie?* He thought as he squirmed in his seat. He couldn't deal with girls that cried, it made him feel awkward--especially when it was his fault, and he wasn't the best at comforting people. He could barely handle it when Rea cried, and he loved her with all his heart.

"Whatever," said Sheba, tightening her crossed arms. She blinked back tears and looked down at her feet. "Are you going to come inside or are you going to sit out here all night?"

Micah leaned back in his seat and smiled.

"I think I'm gonna stay out here all night." She sucked her teeth at his response and looked towards the church. "What are *you* doing out here? Shouldn't you be inside receiving from the Lord?"

Sheba made a disgusted face and he laughed at her frustrated expression.

"I left my Bible in my car," she said as she held up the black leather-bound book. The gold letters that indicated its title had long since faded. "Are you buzzed?"

Micah nodded and glanced over Sheba's shoulder. Maybe he could walk in there with her, but he didn't really want to. The last thing he needed was for anyone to think they were together, or that he was her new convert or something ridiculous like that. He knew how much church people *loved* to assume. He also didn't want Rea to know anything about her.

I'll just wait for Rea to respond, he thought. But who was he kidding? Rea probably wasn't even paying attention to her phone and therefore probably didn't even know he was there. He was better off just walking in there alone. At least if he walked in without her, he could pick where he wanted to sit, and that was as far away from the front as possible.

"You're for real about to show up at church after—never mind." She waved her hand in annoyance. "I'm going back inside, you can either come with or not." She shrugged and turned to walk away.

Sheba's high heels clacked against the pavement as she made her way through the parking lot to the church. Micah huffed, before getting out of his car and slamming the door behind him. He paused when he reached the front doors of the church. They were made of glass and the church's name, in white letters, was printed on them. Through the glass double doors, he could see the spacious, white-tiled lobby. Three people stood outside the actual doors to the sanctuary. He couldn't see beyond the double doors, and he couldn't hear any music.

They must be praying, he thought. *That's probably why the doors are closed.*

He'd been stopped from re-entering the sanctuary quite a few times by the usher board at his home church. It didn't look like there were any ushers on the door so he made a split decision. Steeling himself, he grabbed the metal door handle and took a deep breath.

Why was he so nervous?

He walked into his church every Sunday as if he owned the place, and plopped down on the back row completely, unbothered. Sure, he hated every second of being there but he didn't hesitate at the door. So why was tonight any different? Micah took another deep breath—in through the nose and out through the mouth, his nerves slowly starting to settle with each breath. Squaring his shoulders, Micah made his way into the lobby. He looked around, taking in the high ceilings and consecutive portraits of who he assumed to be the church's former pastors. The walls themselves were a bright white color. To his right was a receptionist desk, and to the left of that desk was a long hallway. Micah straightened his shirt, then clasped his large hands together. His gaze shifted around the room as he nervously hastened to the wooden double doors before him. The other three people in front of him greeted him with small smiles and soft "hellos." One of them was an elderly lady, the other was an elderly man with extremely long nose hairs. Micah found it extremely difficult to return the smile and tried his best to contain the disgusted look on his face as he observed the elderly man.

Good God that's nasty. That ought to be a sin. Micah thought as he gagged. The older man didn't seem to notice Micah's reaction. After smiling at Micah, he'd turned away. The third person in the lobby, was of course, Sheba.

"Finally decided to join the party I see," she whispered as Micah came to stand beside her.

Sheba crossed her arms and smirked. The usher—a short woman with a pixie cut, wearing a black skirt and white blouse—opened the door. With her white-gloved hand she beckoned them inside. The sanctuary was large with red carpeting and padding on the pews. The pew's frames were light brown, and large lantern-like chandeliers hung from the high ceilings of the church. It was packed.

Micah greeted the usher with a nod, grimacing as her nose crinkled up when he passed by her. *Perfect*, he thought.

Micah began to straighten his shirt once again but was stopped when Sheba's arm wrapped around his. An elderly usher from the corner saw them come in and huffed in distaste. When Micah realized that the usher was trying to find Micah a chair to put along the back wall, he quickly stopped him, insisting that he wouldn't be there long and that he'd be fine to stand. Sheba rolled her eyes at Micah and took the chair that Micah declined.

Micah should have known better than to be concerned about getting there on time.

They clearly run on CP time, he thought.

They had just finished the devotional and the choir was preparing to sing their first selection. Micah's eyes roamed about the room, searching for his sister. She was on the third row with Stephanie and Mallory. Beside them, sat a young woman whose wild, curly hair brushed her shoulders. The woman leaned over to Rea and whispered something in her ear. He hoped to catch a glimpse of the woman's face, but her countenance was concealed by her hair.

Rea glanced behind her, and upon scanning the room she saw Micah in the back of the sanctuary, pressed against the wall with his arms folded. She waved and he waved back with his lips, tightly drawn up into a bitter smirk. With Rea's attention being drawn to the back, the people around her also turned to face him. After giving him a disapproving once-over--a look that said he didn't belong in their church, they turned back around and began their gossip. Micah had seen that look many times before, but that didn't make it sting any less.

Damn heathens. Micah thought to himself. His smirk grew wider at his own joke.

The smirk dropped as he listened half-heartedly to the song that the choir sang. They were easily one of the worst parts of the service. His tender, musician's ear was honed in on every mistake. To the average listener, perhaps they were pretty good. The congregation seemed to enjoy them at least as they stood to their feet, shouting statements of affirmation and praise.

Micah cringed when their notes clashed, or someone was a little under pitch. He thought that simply having to be in attendance was torture, but he changed his mind; listening to that choir was the true torture. The Mistress of Ceremonies tootled her way up to the podium that had been placed before the congregation. Her suit— a two-piece jacket and skirt, complete with an ostentatious church hat—was pink with cheap, plastic clear jewels. He felt his stomach churn in disgust He couldn't stand those flashy suits.

She looks like a bottle of Pepto Bismol….

Her country accent was thick, making her nearly impossible to understand. All he heard was a name—Esther Wickers. The girl sitting beside Rea stood to her feet. She was about Rea's height, closer to 5'6, with wild curly hair and golden-brown skin. Micah's eyes raked over her petite form, thoroughly impressed and now effectively distracted. Despite the tempting thoughts that crossed his mind, his distraction stemmed from that unusual feeling of familiarity. It was the same way he felt when he saw that girl in biology class the day before. He knew her from somewhere, he just couldn't put his finger on it. Esther, was dressed in a pair of skinny jeans and a nice light blue flowing blouse.

She slowly made her way to the front as the audience applauded. He made a move to clap, but stopped when he felt someone's hand lock with his. The hand was soft, smooth, and familiar.

What the hell? He looked down to see Sheba at his side. She was glaring at the girl before them who was making her way to the podium to stand by the Emcee. Quickly, Micah tried to pry his hand out of Sheba's. He stared at her in wonderment as her grip tightened with pythonic strength. Sheba's face was expressionless as she stared ahead, blazing eyes fixated on the young woman up front.

"Hello everyone," Esther said as she took her place in the front of the church.

Micah looked to the front of the church and immediately stopped breathing. He gave up on trying to let go of Sheba's hand and squeezed it tighter. The action was counterproductive, because the longer his eyes rested on Esther's face, the more uncomfortable he felt standing in front of her with his hand clasped with Sheba's.

This can't be real, he thought as his hands grew hot and slimy--a phenomenon that hadn't happened since his parent's funeral. *Those eyes.* Esther had those same brown, doe-eyes, curly hair and brown skin as the girl from his dream--the same angled features and full lips; the same ability to possess both the innocence of a child and the strength, grace, and beauty of a woman.

"Esther, here, is going to read us one of her spoken word poems. She's also going to be ministering to our youth down stairs while this service goes on, alright?" The Emcee. said. "Go ahead baby."

There was a chorus that followed from the crowd, of "let Him use you baby" and other encouraging statements.

"Go 'head baby," the Emcee repeated.

Esther took a deep breath and closed her eyes as the Emcee took a seat on the front row.

"*I thought I knew me, but I didn't know until I knew You,*" she began. Her voice, though obvious that it was small in nature, trembled with an unseen force. That same force moved across the pews delivering chill bumps and an inner stirring to those sitting there. The entire atmosphere began to shift.

"I didn't know that in order to get to know me, I'd have to get to know You

Becoming me, Esther.

Becoming Esther

Would require one of the toughest battles of my life

The most tears shed in my life

The loneliest times of my life

But You knew that

Tried to save me from that

But I fought You

I thought if I bought You

Going from prophet, to prophet who was only interested in making

profits off of the money in my pockets

Dockets upon Dockets

Of names, people giving their hearts and sometimes their very souls away

To these phonies

These fools

These underestimated, looked over and generalized satanic tools

To come through and destroy the kingdom of God

My responsibility was to stop it

But I didn't

I bought into it,

Boy did I pay for it

Boy DO I pay for it.

What need could You possibly have of me God?! I cried

How could You possibly use me, one who was addicted to porn

And once before then sworn

to have nothing in this life or the life to come to do with You

Then You said to me,

My darling child

Though You want nothing to do with Me

I want everything to do with You

You knew Me once and you strayed

As long as you have breath in your body you can be saved

I

am not going to stop pursuing you

I

Am not through with you

I

Am not going to abandon you

Like they did.

I am like no one else who has ever lived

Because I am That which causes you to live

And if you think that your purpose is forfeited by mistakes or failures

You clearly don't know Me

If you think I'm going to abandon you because you simply hurt My feelings

You're wrong about Me

I don't leave

Where in Heaven or earth would I go

Everywhere that I could go, I created a pathway for you to follow

My world is about you

How could I create you and then abandon you

When the reason that I made you was to spend eternity WITH you

Yes, the journey to becoming you was hard and left you bleeding

But I can tell you that the moment you say yes to Me,

Will be the moment that you start healing

I had to strip away the old so that you could become new

I had to pull those friends away

They were weights that were easily besetting you!

I could not lose you

I will not lose you

I made you to be Esther

And that is exactly who you will be

For I created you to not simply make it through life

But to live gloriously

In eternity

With Me."

Silence.

Had he not been so surprised, with his mouth agape and eyes wide, Micah would have dropped a pen in the quiet, just to test the old cliché. The fire of her words, the passionate expression on her face--perfectly manicured eyebrows scrunched in concentration, her lips holding a perpetual soft snarl as her words flowed from them like a rushing river, her voice just as soothing as one. Esther's eyes remained closed the entire time, scrunched together in the passion of her words. She'd grow louder in some areas, and in others--the ones that seemed to portray the deepest emotion--she grew quieter, falling into a harsh whisper. The scariest part about it all, was that not only did he hear the words she said, but the music behind them. While she spoke, unfamiliar melodies flooded his ears. He wanted his music notebook. No, he *needed* his notebook. When the applause finally started, Micah broke out of his stupor.

"Well, I'll be damned…" Micah whispered.

Four years. *Four years.* For *four* god-forsaken years this girl had been haunting his dreams and she just shows up out of nowhere? Why here? Why now.

"Did not our hearts burn?" The Emcee said as she regained her spot behind the podium. She paused and waited for the crowd to quiet down after their shouts of approval and roaring applause. "Ok, we're going to separate into classes now. Youth from fifteen up to the age of eighteen, go with sister Esther down stairs into the fellowship hall."

If they thought that he was going to stay up there with some dusty preacher, they were dead wrong. He was torn between the intense desire to talk to her, and the desire to run as far away from the church as possible and never look back. God's words from earlier echoed again in his mind.

"This can't be happening," he grumbled. He caught onto the tail end of the line of young people who were exiting the sanctuary. Sheba quietly called after him but he ignored her. Hopefully, she'd stay upstairs with the other adults.

He followed the youth down a small flight of stairs and into a spacious, brightly lit room with round tables. The sound of heels clacking against the tiled floor behind him caused him to stop in the doorway, allowing the hoards of teenagers to pass by him and fill the room. Micah braced himself for an argument, already knowing who was behind him.

"I'm not in the mood," he murmured as the sound of the heels came to a halt.

"What is with you? You saw her and completely freaked out." Sheba's voice was higher in pitch, signifying her annoyance.

"Oh like you didn't?" He shoved his hands into his pockets and then finally turned around. "What was all that about anyway? Since when was PDA apart of this agreement? We're not together and my sister's here, not cool." Sheba rolled her eyes.

"Ugh, Micah. You act like she's five. That girl is fifteen-years-old. She's probably got a boyfriend of her own. She's not worried about what we're doing." Micah's glare sent her back tracking. "I'm sorry. I didn't mean that," she said, looking down at her black patent leather stilettos.

Micah shrugged.

"Yeah, you did. Don't you have friends here or something? Go find them," Micah snapped.

He walked away, uninterested in her response, his hands in his pockets as he tried to calm himself down. He took a seat at an empty table and leaned back in his chair. Why was he still there? Oh right, he wanted some answers. Was this really the best place to get them though? He could always ask Siri, that usually worked out pretty well for him.

"Hey! Micah, right? I think I see you in church on Sundays sometimes. You sit in the back, right?"

He looked up and found himself face-to-face with a blond-haired girl who had her hand extended to him. She had pale skin, ice blue eyes. He stared at her extended hand, until she slowly retracted it when she realized he wasn't going to take it.

"Yes," he said. His response was short and sweet, just like he hoped this conversation would be.

"I brought some of the youth from our church here."

"Oh," he murmured as he turned his attention back to the table.

"Yeah so--"

"And you are?"

Unable to take a hint apparently. Micah thought as he studied her. She didn't even bat an eye when he cut her off.

"Crystal," she said with a smile. "You seemed kind of lonely, so we figured we'd come sit with you."

Oh great, I'm the weird loner guy, he thought as he acknowledged her with a nod. Deep down and maybe at a later date, he was sure that he'd appreciate their thoughtfulness, but for now he was content to sit alone.

"This is my brother Cody," she continued. The burly blond-haired male to her right greeted Micah with a nod and Micah returned it. "That's Alice," Crystal said, gesturing to a petite girl with a large afro. Alice smiled at him flirtatiously. Again, Micah nodded in greeting.

It wasn't his intent to be mean or rude this time, it was just that he *knew.* He saw straight through the façade; he knew they didn't really care about him. They just wanted to earn brownie points with their youth leader by stepping up and helping the lost sheep assimilate back into the group.

"It's a pleasure," Micah drawled sardonically as he looked around the room. Maybe he was being a bit rude, but so what? They'd forgive him for it. They had to--forgive or not be forgiven, right?

It was quiet for a moment before Crystal spoke. She was a ball of energy. In a way her energy was refreshing, but in an even larger way it was very annoying. She spoke very quickly, and excitedly. What was she so excited about all the time? It was like she was constantly moving and buzzing. Micah rubbed his forehead; she was giving him a headache. Relief flooded him when Crystal was interrupted by a tall, lanky, brown-haired man taking the stage.

"Praise the Lord everybody," the man said.

Amidst the echoes of that sentiment Micah scanned the room for Rea. He found her at the table next to him situated between Mallory and Stephanie. Rea and Stephanie were bouncing in their seats in excitement.

"Well, as you know we have a very special guest tonight," he continued, "She's one of our city's own, and she came here for free. We didn't pay her a dime, so we thank God for her giving heart. Please, give her your undivided attention guys and without further ado, let's welcome her. Esther, please."

When Esther reached the stage, she embraced the lanky man. Micah had heard someone refer to him earlier, as Brother Jim. Brother Jim whispered something in Esther's ear and her face lit up. He handed her a wireless microphone as she scanned the room, almost as if she was looking for someone.

"Hey, everybody," she said.

There were various responses to her greeting, some of them more humorous than others.

"Like Brother Jim said, I live here. I'm not some upper-level, out-of-town evangelist. I'm very grateful to be here with you all tonight and to share with you what God has given me. The gospel isn't meant for you to keep to yourself you know? Anyways, I'm a student at the university here in town. I'm an anthropology major and religious studies major and I'm currently a senior. If you don't mind, before we get started I'd like to pray. But before I do that, I'd like to encourage you all a little bit, get some faith rising in here. Jesus is about to radically change some lives in here tonight. You don't have to leave the same way that you came." Applause broke out. She began pacing the floor, with her eyes closed.

Micah wasn't sure what he'd been expecting when she began to pray, but he knew he hadn't been expecting what actually occurred. The moment she began to pray he was floored.

"Abba God," she began.

Micah had never heard anyone address the Man Upstairs as "Abba God." He knew it was possible, as he knew the scripture that told Christians that they could call out to Him as such, but he'd never heard anyone *actually* call Him that. Even more than what she called Him, *how* she called Him really confused him.

There was such longing in her voice, such desire and intimacy, it was as if she were in love with Him. She reminded him of one of those cheesy romance movies that Rea forced him to watch from time to time. The way that she called out to her God reminded him of a woman beholding the face of her love.

He craved a love like that. There was something about the way she prayed, the fierceness, the boldness, the absolute power and confidence in her God that called to his very core, to his innermost being. He wasn't interested in church; he wasn't interested in God but he *was* interested in Esther Wickers. He'd never seen anything like her before. She was different. She was quite literally the girl of his dreams, with some added oddities. Those things he was sure would fade with time, well maybe. She was a rare gem indeed.

"Amen," she said. "Mycah. Who is Mycah?" She kept her eyes closed, and rested her arm against her forehead. With her other hand, she held the mic tightly.

The room was silent. He looked around, hoping that she was talking to someone else. Everyone in the room, was perched at the edge of their seat, their eyes boring into her. How did she know his name? Was she really about to call him out in front of all those people? There was a weightiness in the room that caused the hairs on the back of Micah's neck to stand at attention. The goosebumps on his arms to rise. It was a familiar feeling, but he hadn't felt it in such a long time, it surprised him.

What the-?

"Which Mycah?" A curly-haired boy asked. He couldn't have been more than ten. Esther opened her eyes and smiled sweetly at him.

"You," she said.

Relief washed over Micah and yet, so did disappointment leaving him confused. He raised his eyebrow curiously at her. How did she know the young boy? Rea had never mentioned anything about this Esther person before. He looked to his sister. She sat beside Stephanie, with that knowing and anticipatory look on her face. Although he wasn't sure of what was going on, it seemed that Rea did.

"How do you know my name?" The little boy asked.

Esther motioned for him to come up and he did so without hesitation. She knelt down so that she was at his height and looked him in the eye.

"I don't know your name, but God does."

Great, she's beautiful and schizophrenic. She hears voices in her head and she thinks it's God. Boy can I pick 'em. Micah thought begrudgingly. Well, then again, he was hearing voices too. Pot, kettle.

The little boy's eyes grew large.

"Wow!" He yelled, his eyes wide with excitement and wonder. Esther laughed.

"Yes. Amazing, isn't it? He knows everything about you Mycah Joseph Straders. He knows that your favorite color is blue," she continued.

Anyone could guess that a ten-year-old boy's favorite color is blue. Micah reasoned. In his heart, he knew that his attempts to discredit her were going to end up futile. She was too strange to be a woman of chance. As much as he wanted to disprove her, there a certain element to her that seemed unnatural. Was she a psychic? Clairvoyant? If so, why did they let her into the church? He'd never seen anything like her, and yet, he wanted to see more of her. He had so many questions, and none of this made sense.

I thought Christians didn't believe in witchcraft.

"He knows that you've been praying really, really hard for a big red fire truck for your birthday next week and He knows you've been praying for your Auntie Sarah."

The little boy nodded. How did she know that? Micah stared at Esther in wonderment. He had never heard of such craziness in all his life.

"God wants you to know Mycah Joseph Straders, that Auntie Sarah is going to be ok. God says that He heard you. As a matter of fact, He always hears you and He is going to make her well."

A brilliant grin lit up the boy's face and he took Esther in his chubby arms. Pure joy was painted upon her gorgeous features as the little boy embraced her. It became apparent to Micah, in that moment, that this was what she lived for. He couldn't help but think that perhaps she'd gone too far though. Rea said that the little boy's aunt had cancer.

She should know better than to give that little boy false hope ...but what if it isn't false? Micah wondered.

"What about my firetruck?" He asked suddenly, his wide eyes were hopeful. Esther stared at him for a minute, then laughed obnoxiously.

"Oh Lord," she whispered after she'd calmed down. "You'll have to wait and see. Go have a seat, and don't forget to thank God tonight, ok?"

Esther held up her hand for a high-five, and Mycah happily high-fived her back before running back to his seat. She scratched her forehead and paced.

She spoke softly, "I don't want anyone in this room to think that what just happened was me," she paused, "How many of you have ever seen anything like that happen?" Micah glanced around the room. Rea and Mallory had their hands raised as well as a few others that he didn't recognize. The majority seemed to have no idea what she was talking about. "Hmm, ok," she said, nodding. "Well, that's not what I'm here to talk about tonight. Maybe one day they'll invite me back." She smiled at Brother Jim. Micah followed her gaze over to the older man. He wasn't smiling back.

What's his problem? Micah thought. To his surprise, the older man's sour expression, *irritated* him.

"I believe that tonight God wants me to talk about His faithfulness." From the corner of his eye, he could see Rea pulling out her journal. While he was glad that the girl had taken an interest in something, he couldn't stop his stomach from turning because she'd chosen this particular interest. Why couldn't she have just had Bieber fever? That he could handle.

"Here's what you need to know. No matter what you do, God is always faithful. What does that mean? That means that if anybody is going to give up in the relationship between you and Him, it won't be Him." Esther paused to survey the room. "Let me clarify. There are times when God will turn you over to a reprobate mind. He will let you have your way at times. What I'm referring to currently, is the fact that when you get tired and you feel like you can't take this Christian walk anymore, God will not abandon you. I repeat: God will not abandon you. Ever. How many of you were here in time for my spoken word poem?"

She paused and glanced around the room.

"Ok, a few of you. You should know that the journey that I was talking about, was not just for me. There's a journey that we all have to take and a process that we all have to endure. We may have different tests and circumstances than each other but we all have one thing in common--we have God on our side and He is faithful…"

Yeah, faithful to screw me over. Micah zoned out as she continued talking about the faithfulness of *her* God. By the time Esther finished talking, she was nearly in tears. Micah almost felt bad. She was about to cry and he had no idea why. Well, if the chill bumps on his arms were indicative of a shift in the atmosphere, he did have one clue.

Ok, God. If this is Your life changing proof, I am not impressed. He folded his arms and leaned back in his seat.

"I just want to open up this altar," she said. Her voice was confident, but cautious. "Brother Jim is that alright?" He nodded back, his earlier disapproval now untraceable. "If we could have someone start playing some worship music in the background, that would be great," she said as she looked back and gestured to the keyboard behind her. She inhaled and exhaled deeply before continuing, "I feel this spirit of heaviness. Some of you have been walking with God for a while, since you were a kid even, and now it's hard to navigate your walk with Him" The room was silent, apart from the soft piano playing behind her. "You're contemplating walking away, some of you contemplating suicide—Jesus." She stopped and took a deep breath in an attempt to contain herself as tears began to fill her eyes.

What just happened here? Micah thought as he looked around the room at the tear-stained faces. From the tables beside him, he could hear sniffling and from somewhere across the room, he heard someone begin to weep. It was the kind of cry that came from deep within.

"Jesus is saying that now is not the time to quit. Now is the time to dig your heels in and keep going. It's you and Me. It's you and Me."

Micah's blood ran cold. His mind fell backward through the scope of time, back to the argument he'd had with God four years ago.

You're gonna have to do better than that, he thought indignantly.

"If that's you, come to the altar. If you need a fresh start with Christ, you need to rededicate, or you need some prayer, come on. If you need to be saved, come on." She laid the microphone on a nearby table.

Brother Jim came to her with a glass oil cruet and poured some oil into her awaiting hands. He drizzled some of the oil into his own hands as students flocked to the front. Micah expected to see his sister's face in the crowd but he didn't. Esther, again, reached for the mic. She didn't put it to her mouth immediately, as it seemed she was murmuring something under her breath. He caught a few sounds, but none of them appeared to be any words he knew. He recognized this from YouTube videos that Jay had made him watch one day at work--she was praying in the Spirit. The difference was that she wasn't joking like they were. She was serious. Finally, Esther put the mic to her lips,

"Rea. Rea, short for ReAutumn."

Micah's heart dropped into his stomach. What would she say? He glanced at his sister, whose face had lit up like the dawn. Rea rose from her seat quickly and bee-lined to where Esther was standing. Esther embraced his sister instantly.

"Hey Prophetess," Esther began. Rea's smile grew as her eyes gleamed with excitement. "You knew that already though, didn't you?" She continued. Rea nodded.

"Yes ma'am," Rea said.

Micah couldn't help but marvel at seeing his sister so happy, but again that worry plagued him. *Prophetess?*

"God's been speaking to you, hasn't He?" Rea nodded. "It's important that you do exactly what He tells you to do, ok? Even if it's scary, and even if it doesn't make sense. If God didn't think you could do it, He wouldn't have asked you to. You are beautiful, and you are favored and anointed by God. It's time for you to start walking in what God has called you to be. Don't ask yourself why. Just know that God has kept His eye on you. He trusts you and He knows what He's doing. He just wants you to trust Him." Esther's face took on a look of awe and solemnity that he recognized on the faces of many ministers while preaching—furrowed eyebrows, scrunched up nose, tightly pressed lips. She paused as if she was listening for something.

Yeah, to the voices in her head…

"And that thing you've been praying for. I won't say it out here in front of everybody, but there's something you've been praying about for almost two years, and God says He's going to do it for you."

Rea's eyes filled with unshed tears as she embraced Esther again, sobbing into her shirt. Micah felt the urge to run up and tear his sister from Esther's arms, but he resisted. Esther was only making things worse. The more Esther spoke, the stronger Rea's faith was becoming. Esther was promoting and affirming the very thing in Rea's life that Micah was trying to eradicate. That was the last thing Micah needed. As his little sister sobbed with tears of joy, Esther's eyes roamed the room.

They stopped when they landed on him. For the first time, brown met green. She didn't sport any new expression. Instead, she kept that serious expression that was beginning to grow on Micah.

"They said she was a prophetess and I didn't believe them," Cody whispered to his sister. "I wish I would have known what we were about to walk into."

From his peripheral vision Micah could see the two of them huddled closely together, deep in discussion.

Prophetess? It was all he could do to keep his mouth off of the ground. She certainly didn't fit the description of a prophet that he'd been used to--long beard, angry, old… Not to mention that, Esther had called his little sister a prophetess. Was he to believe that his sweet, sassy, annoying little sister was going to be like Esther? Some sort of Jesus loving fortune teller? He shuddered at the thought. At least she'd stay out of trouble with boys-- she'd scare them off with all of that prophecy mess.

Before he knew it, his sister was back in her seat. He watched as people flocked to the altar, each wanting to hear a word from God.

"There's someone here tonight who to hear this word. I'm not sure who you are exactly, but I'm pretty positive you need to be at this altar. God says, 'It's always been Me and You. Nothing that happened in your life, happened simply to cause you pain. You know Me better than that.' God says, 'I cannot, I *will* not, forget about you. I will never leave you, nor will I forsake you. You were brave. You stood your ground.' He says that 'you held your tongue when people came to start trouble, you cut your hair just to keep from being a stumbling block. My Sampson, you didn't just cut your hair, you tried to cut off your ties to your purpose because accepting the pain was easier than rejecting the lies of the enemy. The enemy, through the people around you, told you that you weren't good enough, that there was something wrong with you. But you were uniquely made. They weren't rejecting you, they were rejecting Me. I love you, I have always loved you. I never stopped, and I never will."

Micah couldn't breathe. His entire body, locked up in absolute disbelief. Before he could stop himself, he felt his hand reaching up to touch a lock of his hair. *No way…*

"Yes way," she continued. "And yes, I'm faithful but not to screw you over. *This* is My proof. Are you impressed now?" Esther shrugged on the last bit, clearly not understanding exactly what she was saying.

He was both intrigued and afraid. He could not allow himself to fall for this. This was a trap, this had to be some sort of scam. She had to have gotten that information from somewhere. No one knew about that conversation he had with God, and she was reading his thoughts!

"I know you're in here. Come. I can assure you that running is a waste of your time. You'll get tired of it and then where will you go? If you're being honest with yourself, you're already tired of it." His wide eyes, met her tear-filled ones, emerald against brown.

This can't be real life, he thought.

He could prove that this was false. He could disprove this. He could—all he had to do was go up there. If she didn't pick up on the fact that, that *word* was for him, then he knew she was faking it and he had nothing to worry about. Besides, how many other people have had that conversation with God? She'd already said that a lot of people in the room were ready to give up. That was a generalization. She was *reaching.*

Some damn proof.

The closer he got to the altar the more his palms began to sweat. He spotted Sheba on the opposite end of the crowd of students. He couldn't help but snicker to himself as he watched Brother Jim pray over her.

She needs it, Micah thought.

He turned his attention back to Esther.

What would she say to him? Moreover, what would the voices in her head that she claimed to be God, say about him? That he's devilishly handsome? He knew that. A nasty sinner? He was proud of that. He hung near the back, watching as some kids, from a light touch of her hand, fell onto the floor with a thud, out cold. Dozens of kids were at the altar still and there was Esther, praying with each and every one of them. He wondered then how she came to do what she did. Was she born with this ability? Was it a skill she learned?

He waited patiently as she went from person to person until she was standing right in front of him. Fear and anticipation formed within him. He wasn't sure what he was anticipating. He could just tell that something was about to happen. Yep, the buzz was officially gone.

"You should know," she whispered. "That word was for you." She looked him directly in the eyes. Immediately, he looked away. She—*He* would not get to him, not tonight. "Is it alright if I lay hands on you?" She asked. His mind immediately formed an innuendo as a response, but a wave of unfamiliar fear coursed over him—almost reverential, and he dared not speak it.

"Sure," he said and cleared his throat.

His voice came out about an octave higher than his normal tone. She was half his size. What was the worst that could happen? There was no way she could push him down. He smirked at that thought. This was all smoke and mirrors.

"Brother Jim, could you get behind Micah please?" She asked sweetly.

Micah's smirk remained intact. The moment she laid her hand on his head, the room changed. Before him was a bright light and it nearly blinded him.

"Micah." A soft voice protruded from the light. It was gentle, but strong and sure and in the presence of the light he felt unworthy. He fell to the ground, unable to speak or move. He was rooted to the spot by his intense feelings, and despite his unworthiness, he felt loved. He'd never felt anything like it. *It can't be,* he thought.

"Micah," the Voice called again. Micah wanted to respond, but couldn't. He waited for the voice to continue. "Even though you hate Me. I love you."

Unworthy. Unworthy. Unworthy. Not real, not real…

"I love you and I will not give up on you," the Voice continued.

Micah's eyes opened and closed rapidly like the fluttering of hummingbird wings. The fluorescent lights hurt his eyes and he was vaguely aware of other voices, and weeping. Where had he been? Where was he now? Something cold was pressed against his back side. He used his hands to feel it out and was confused to find the cool tiles of the fellowship hall. He sat up slowly, expecting to be dizzy or have a headache from his fall. He had neither. He was merely disoriented. He looked to his right and saw that Esther was making her way down the line of people. She still had a few more left.

She just laid me out, he thought in amazement. *She's half my size and she laid me out. How is that possible?*

He shook his head and walked back to his table. He sat down and studied Esther's every move, not wanting to miss how she did what she did. He watched in wonderment as another person fell backwards into Jim's arms. She'd barely touched the poor girl, just as she'd barely touched him.

"Amazing, right?" He turned his head in the direction of Alice, the curly haired girl from earlier who'd just spoken. He nodded, unsure of what to say. "Just think, she's in my biology class. She sits two rows in front of me. This must be what she does on the side," she chuckled. She wiped her face, removing the remaining tears from their steads and sat in the now empty chair next to him. He spotted Crystal and Cody somewhere near the front line of the altar.

"You don't say much do you?" Alice asked.

He shook his head. He didn't really want to talk, despite having a thousand questions. He knew there was only one person that could answer them, and she was a bit busy at the moment. It was getting late and he needed to get Rea home. Service ran longer than usual, he realized. It was almost ten o'clock. Praying for that many people and giving them life changing words, *would* take up some time, he supposed. He glanced at Rea who was now also watching Esther's every move. The feeling that coursed through him was strong enough to tempt him to stay a little while longer but he knew he had to be responsible and take her home and make her go to bed.

"Rea," he called softly.

Immediately, she looked over at him, and the light in her eyes dimmed a little when he motioned for her to come over. She knew what that meant--it was time to go. She said goodbye to Mallory as she grabbed her belongings and headed toward the door. Micah stood, and followed without bothering to say goodbye to anyone. He was relieved to be out of their presence.

The ride home was quiet and uncomfortable. Micah spent the whole fifteen minutes lost in thought. What he'd seen as he was lying on the ground troubled him. *Who was that?* He wondered. He'd never been made to feel like that by anyone, especially not by a stranger. In the presence of the light he'd felt so unworthy, so *unclean.* It was as though everything he'd ever done was brought to the forefront of his mind and while the guilt for these things consumed him, it was as if it didn't matter. It was as if his uncleanness didn't matter, the words spoken to him from the light consumed every thought of his shortcomings and replaced it with that overwhelming love.

And just like that, he knew.

He knew and he was furious. Micah was well aware that most people who would have had that experience would have appreciated it, or may be even been confounded by it, but after the initial shock wore off, he was annoyed. Micah had claimed for the past four years to be an atheist, slowly turning his back on the belief of God that he once held dear to him.

In truth, though he'd never admit it to anyone, he never stopped believing. His heart simply filled with bitterness, and his faith decayed over time as anger overtook him. Yes, he was angry; angry that the one Person he thought was going to help him in his time of need abandoned him, and now, he was angry that the One he'd sworn off forever had the gall to reappear in his life like that. *God never can do anything that I need Him to do.* Micah thought as he chuckled bitterly. He supposed that expecting anything good or decent from God was expecting too much. He'd expected Him to protect his parents—clearly that was too high of an expectation. Now, he just wanted to be left alone and it seemed that God couldn't even do that.

"What's funny?" Rea asked.

"Nothing."

They stopped at Jay's diner to pick up some food to go. He wasn't going to lie, he was upset that Jay hadn't shown up that night and that was partially the reason that he stopped by. That really wasn't like Jay. When Micah walked in, one of his co-workers informed him that Jay hadn't been at work either. He called in sick. Micah sighed. *Of course.* When they arrived back at their apartment, he allowed Rea to go up before him and took his time getting out of the car.

What a night. He trudged up the back stairway, vaguely registering the sounds of footsteps going up the front stairway. When he arrived at the top, he blanched.

"You," he muttered. He took a step back and gripped the railing to steady him. There, standing at the door of the newly occupied apartment, was Esther Wickers…slipping her key into the door.

FIVE

Esther's hand froze on the door knob. Very slowly, she turned around. Despite the darkness outside, and dim lighting of their apartment complex Micah was certain that this was the girl who'd just ruined his entire night. His disdain and fear was evident in the tremor of his voice when he said,

"You're that girl from service."

Esther rendered a half-smile.

"That would be me," she sighed and extended her hand, "I'm guessing that you're either here because you live here, or because you're stalking me." He glared at her. "Ok, then. Not in the mood for jokes. I see. I get it." She retracted her hand.

"Why are you so nonchalant about all this?"

Her eyebrows knitted together in confusion.

"Umm…this?"

"Whatever the hell you just did to me back there?"

Esther placed her hands in her pockets and exhaled through her mouth as her face scrunched up in confusion.

“Should I be upset about it?”

Micah took a deep breath, unsure of how to answer her question. It was bad enough that she’d shown up in his dreams, then shown up at the service he’d all but been dragged to, but then she’d gone and basically called him out in front of everyone and laid him out. His cheeks burned with embarrassment.

“Listen, you tell your God to mind His *damn* business.”

Esther smiled a little. Did she *ever* stop smiling? What was so funny all the time? Why was she so happy?

“I don’t have to tell Him. I’m sure He heard you just fine. Fortunately for you and well, I guess all of us, He’s God and you’re not. Your demands don’t move Him, and they certainly don’t scare Him.”

Micah’s fists clenched at his sides as anger seeped from every pore in his body.

“He’s not real.”

That sent Esther into a fit of giggles. She quickly covered her mouth.

“I’m sorry, that was rude. But you mean to tell me that after all that happened tonight, you can confidently stand here and deny Him?” She paused, giving him a moment to respond. When all Micah did was stare, she threw up her hands in exasperation. "Ok, whatever. Believe what you want,” she said. The sureness of her belief pushed Micah into a full-blown rage.

"You Christians think you're always right huh? You expect someone to believe that some supreme being had a son, sent the son to die for—what? *Sin*? Get out of here with that bull crap. Even if all that was true, your God is so cruel that I question the morality of just about anyone that claims to follow Him." He stalked past her, his eyes never leaving her tiny frame until he got to his doorstep.

"Wait."

Micah huffed.

"What?"

"No one *expects* you to believe that some supreme being had a son that was sent to die for your sins. I *hope* that you will believe that *the* Supreme Being, sent His Only Son to die for your sins, and then rose again for your justification."

"He's still cruel."

Esther craned her neck, staring at him incredulously. "By whose standards?"

"The World's!" He exclaimed, throwing up his hands.

"Oh so, the same world that's broken and full of imperfections and limited knowledge has the right to decide the morality of a perfect and limitless being?" Silence passed between them. "I don't know what god has been shown to you, but this cruel god that you're talking about is not the same one that pulled your card tonight."

"The God that's been shown to me is one who allows children to starve, people to die--"

"Who allows man to decide. Who gives man the tools to rectify these problems. When's the last time you gave food to a homeless person on the street? But that's God's fault that you're not willing to help another person? How many times did He instruct man to feed the poor, take care of the widows--"

"Yeah, great God," Micah said.

Esther squinted her eyes for a minute and placed her hands on her hips. "You have no interest in really finding an answer to these questions, do you? You've already made up your mind."

"You're damn right."

If she had more to say, he didn't hear it. Micah threw open his front door, stepped inside and slammed it behind him. He leaned against the door and allowed his guard to fall. The distress on his face became visible, the tears began to pool in his eyes.

"Micah? You ok?"

Rea's room was visible from the front door. She appeared in the doorway of her room already dressed for bed, with a makeup wipe in her hand. He nodded. She opened her mouth as if she were going to disagree, but the pity she felt for him caused her to do otherwise. Her brother's sweaty, broken down form, resting against the door of their home was enough to silence her. Instead, she ran to him and embraced him. His arms immediately wrapped around her tightly.

"I love you," she said.

"I love you too," he whispered as he buried his face in her curls.

"It's ok to believe," she murmured. "You don't have to keep trying to fight it, you know."

Micah sighed. He kissed her forehead, squeezed her for a moment, then released her from the encirclement of his arms.

"There's nothing to believe," he whispered hoarsely, "And therefore, nothing to fight." He got up from the floor and made his way to his bathroom to shower.

"The worst feeling in the world, was knowing the truth and denying it, in a desperate attempt to have control," Esther had said during service. That was one of the things he remembered the most. He wasn't after control though, or was he? What would it cost him to let go of the anger? What would it cost him to believe?

He ran through the service on repeat as he showered. Every time he saw her face in his mind, more questions arose. How did she know all that she knew about him, and all of those other people? And what on earth was so funny about what he'd said outside?

When he finally stepped out of the shower, the water was

freezing. There was definitely some substance to what had been said that night. His argument with God four years ago, in his anger, had caused him to bring up the words that God had spoken to him so many times before that night, "It's you and Me." That sense of oneness that he once felt with God, that sense of never being alone, all of that was obliterated when his parents died. For God to speak those words through Esther was more than mind-blowing, it was wall-shattering.

"This can't be happening," Micah whispered as he towel-dried his hair.

He knew in his heart that God did exist, and after declaring the opposite for so long, he was just now getting to the point where he was finally believing it. Well, just because he might have recently acquired a little proof of His existence, didn't mean that he had to have anything to do with God. That ship had long since sailed.

But if he truly believed that, then why couldn't he be content with being semi-certain? Because *now* he had to know. He would ask. He would find her tomorrow on campus, and he would ask her exactly what happened; and if he couldn't find her on campus, he'd knock on her door and demand that she did.

***

He eyed every student that walked into the lecture hall. Every time the door opened, he jumped a little. He couldn't stop fidgeting; no position in his seat was comfortable enough for him. She came in about ten minutes before class started with her earbuds in. Her curly hair was tied up in a messy bun and she was dressed in gray sweatpants and a black t-shirt. If last night hadn't occurred, he would never have guessed that a woman, *this* laid back, and *this*...normal, wasn't truly normal. He started to rise from his seat, but stopped himself. How was he going to approach her? She was unmoved by his outburst from the night before and even though he meant most of what he said, he felt bad for taking out his frustration on her. She was just doing what she believed was right.

He sighed and glanced down at his phone. He'd already called Jay ten times, between last night and that present moment. He'd sent him numerous texts. It was official--Micah was worried.

He tried his best to pay attention to the lecture, but his phone kept buzzing. However, all his text messages were coming from the wrong person--Sheba. The person he needed to hear from wasn't returning his texts or calls but the person that he wanted to talk to the least was blowing up his phone.

Speaking of the wrong person…what was Sheba's problem last night? She'd looked at Esther as if she'd run over her cat or something. Micah scratched his head as his professor went on about microorganisms and cells. The piece of paper he'd pulled out to take notes was completely blank.

I'll look up the slides online, he thought.

Esther's seat was in the center of the third row from the front. She was fully engaged and scribbling furiously in her notebook. How studious of her. He watched her intensely, wondering what in the world could have caused Sheba to hate her so much. Micah pulled out his phone and sifted through the various text messages he'd been receiving.

What was last night about? -Sheba

What are you too good to answer people now? –Sheba

Really? –Sheba

We need to talk -Sheba

Micah rolled his eyes. He was in no mood for her melodramatics. These text messages had been sent not even a full five minutes apart. She must have been really bored. He had bigger things to worry about, like whether or not his friend was dead or alive, and figuring out a way to talk to Esther. She seemed like—no he *knew*—that she wasn't the type of person to take anyone's BS, certainly not his. He'd have to be straight forward with her, come out of the gate swinging. *Maybe* an apology would help.

His professor dismissed class early. Micah figured it was because the man was boring himself with his lecture. He watched Esther gather her things and make her way toward the door. She was going to have to pass by him again, and that gave him the perfect opportunity. He gathered his belongings and stood to his feet. He was about to step out into the aisle when another body blocked his path.

"Sheba," he groaned. "Why are you here?"

Sheba stood with her arms crossed, glaring at him.

"Why haven't you been responding to my texts?" He shrugged. His fingers gripped the straps of his backpack tightly. He looked over her shoulder, searching for Esther. He spotted her talking to someone, a girl he recognized from the night before as Alice.

"I was in class, clearly," he said off-handedly. She moved to block his view, standing on her tiptoes just to grab his attention.

"I wanted to know what happened last night," she said. "What did she do to you? Who are you looking at? Micah?" She waved her hand in front of her face. Finally, Micah turned his head sharply so that he could look her in the face. She followed where his gaze had been and bit the inside of her cheek in disbelief and anger when she saw Esther and Alice walking out of the room.

"I have to go," he said. When he looked around the room again, Esther and Alice were gone.

"Listen," Sheba said. Her voice was low and dangerous, indicating that a warning was about to follow. She put her index finger in his face, a sign that she was serious. "You need to stay far away from her. She brings nothing but trouble wherever she goes." Micah's eyebrows knitted together in confusion. "When you're done trippin' you know where to find me." She ran a hand down his arm before sauntering out of the lecture hall.

He now had new questions and he still hadn't found the answers to his old ones. Adjusting his backpack, he made the hike across campus to the parking garage. He'd just put his backpack in his car when he saw her. Esther was walking away from a light blue sedan with her headphones in. Afraid that he'd think too much and talk himself out of going, Micah quickly ran to her side. She jumped at his sudden presence but otherwise said nothing. Their eyes locked immediately.

Micah always liked to look people in the eyes, but he could never hold their gaze for long as they always looked away. Most people felt uncomfortable, but she didn't. She held his gaze confidently. It was as if she was declaring to him that she had nothing to hide, and it became abundantly clear to him that she wasn't intimidated by him. Seeing her stirred up the emotions from the night before, the fear, the worry, the annoyance, and the anger.

"Hi," he said.

"Hi." She took one ear bud out then clasped her hands together, letting them fall together in front of her. Micah opened his mouth, then closed it again. "Is there something you wanted?" She asked.

"Yeah, just…why did you tell that little boy that his aunt wasn't going to die? You don't know that. No one knows that, my sister told me that his aunt has cancer. You're going to get his hopes up for nothing."

She laughed. He found nothing funny about his question.

"What is this a joke to you? You like playing with other people's lives?" He asked, his tone rising in volume.

“You’re projecting again, and it’s not cute. Listen, the reason that I told that precious little boy that his aunt would live is because it’s true. I told him what God told me to say and God doesn’t lie. It’s only a matter of time before that woman gets up and walks out of the hospital.”

Micah took a step back and looked around the parking garage, dumbfounded.

“Projecting?”

“Yeah, pushing your past church hurt on me. I didn’t do it,” Esther said as she crossed her arms.

“You don’t know anything about me,” he challenged.

“You’re right I don’t, but I’m going to need for you to change your tone. My own mother doesn’t even talk to me like that, so I definitely will not allow you to. ok?” Her tone was no-nonsense and her eyes silently dared him to push back.

"Ok, but I’m just saying—” He pinched the bridge of his nose trying to get a handle on all of his emotions. He’d never been this out of control before, never fallen apart like this before—at least not in front of anyone else.

"Ok. I apologize for coming at you sideways.”

“No worries,” she said, her tense and defensive tone returning to its normal, sweet one. “Listen, how about we start over. Sound good?”

"Ok." He extended his hand to her. "I'm Micah Williams."

She took his extended hand in her tiny one.

"Esther Wickers, and apparently, I'm your new neighbor."

With her hand, she gestured for him to follow her. Evidently, she didn't want to miss her twenty seconds of crossing time. It was a cloudy day and apart from the background noise—the people passing by and cars racing up and down the street—there was a thick and uncomfortable silence between the two. He rubbed the back of his neck, trying not to get his fingers tangled in the mess of hair that he'd worn down that day.

"You know what your name means?" She asked.

"Who is like God?" He was embarrassed by how quickly he responded, so he added, "Or something like that."

"Exactly," she said, her slender lips turned up at the corners. "Your name is a very praise unto God, there's a little fun fact. How's that for irony?"

"Listen," he began cautiously. When he took too long to continue Esther glanced at him briefly.

"I'm listening." Her voice was soft and inviting.

"I really am sorry."

He wasn't sure why he kept apologizing. He offended plenty of people on a daily basis and he didn't care. He had a daily quota that he needed to reach. A brilliant smile broke out across her face.

"I already told you that your apology was accepted. You should really work on your social skills though," she said.

Was this really the same girl he'd seen the night before?

"I'm conflicted," he confessed.

Her smile dwindled until it became a light and playful smirk.

"Sounds like a personal problem," she quipped, causing Micah to roll his eyes. "Sorry, I'm extremely sarcastic at best. I'm working on it. Still human you know? What exactly are you conflicted about?"

"You called my sister a prophetess," he began. His tone wasn't accusatory, but inquisitive. "You're one. You expect her to be like you."

Her posture grew rigid as she looked around frantically, as if she were checking to see if anyone was close enough to hear what he'd said.

"Listen, I don't throw titles on myself ok? I call out what God shows me, but you're going to have to be a bit more specific. Who is your sister? Was she the girl I hugged?" She asked.

Micah stopped walking, and looked at her in confusion. Why didn't she want anyone to know who or what she was? Was she afraid that people would judge her as he had? *But she didn't even know that I was judging—well, the first thing I ever said to her was a bit judgmental.* He conceded.

"And additionally, Micah Williams, I don't expect her to be like me."

Her statement jarred him from his thoughts and he began walking again. He sped up to keep pace with her.

"You know that's not what I meant. You expect her to be some sort of sanctified psychic."

This time, Esther stopped and looked at him incredulously.

"You believe in psychics, but not God?"

Micah shrugged. He stopped to face her, his hands were tucked away in his pockets as he toyed with the stitching in the bottom of them. He was glad that she couldn't see how nervous this was making him.

"I never said I don't believe in God, but to answer your question…more or less." She shook her head at him as he hurried to explain himself. "Either that, or this is some sort of scam." Her silence made him uncomfortable, so he continued, "By the way, has anyone ever told you that you're really judgmental?"

"A few times and a *scam*? Really Micah?" She laughed at him, her eyes widened in shock. "I'm not gonna beg you to believe in what you saw last night; that is something that you will have to work out for yourself. But if you legitimately want answers about last night, my answer will always refer you back to God. I'd love to stay and talk more about this but I have to get to class. It was a pleasure." Her voice, though firm and passionate, was soft.

To Micah, it seemed that she was determined not to lose her temper with him. Did she have practice doing this? She began walking again, leaving him behind. He jogged up to her side.

"Will you stop walking away from me?" he asked. "I didn't mean to offend you." Her smile rendered him breathless.

"I'm not offended Micah. I'm just telling you the truth. I honestly don't mind answering your questions Micah, but they're questions you already have the answers to. I think you just don't like the answers and you're hoping they'll change. They won't. What you saw last night was real. I'm not trying to pull one over on you Micah, nor am I purposely trying to offend you. If you did get offended and last night made you feel some type of way, I can't control that."

Micah nodded. He believed her, well the part about not wanting to offend him. That awkward silence appeared again as they walked.

"How about we just agree to disagree?" He offered. Esther nodded in agreement, so he continued, "What did you mean when you said that you call out what God shows you?"

Esther shrugged and grasped the strap of her purse with both hands.

"I see things about people. Sometimes I hear things about people—"

"From the voices in your head?" He interrupted, smiling coyly.

She rolled her eyes and waved him off, exhaling agitatedly.

"Whatever, Micah. If you're going to make fun of me then you can go look up your explanations on Google."

He was finally beginning to break through her patient exterior, and it was a lot more satisfying to him than it probably should have been.

"Google might make more sense."

"Then ask Google. It will give you plenty of answers. You don't really want to hear any explanation that doesn't fit into your 'anything but God is responsible mold' do you?" He glared at her as she continued on unapologetically, "I'm just saying, I mean I've seen some pretty weird conspiracy theories and things on there." He was quickly beginning to lose his patience.

"Do all Christians do what you do?"

"No. You're born a prophet or prophetess, the difference in title obviously being gender. All believers are able to have a prophetic gifting. Visions, dreams, and hearing from God are not subject only to Prophets."

"Hm. Did you want this?"

"You ask a lot of questions," her answer was sharp, leaving a jagged silence between them. "I did at first," she murmured.

"Why not now?"

"Why do you think?" She quipped. "I was afraid of what people would say about me."

"And you're over that now?" Esther rolled her eyes, but otherwise didn't answer. "What did you do to me?" He continued. Esther snorted obnoxiously. He didn't find anything amusing about his question.

"Prayed the hell out of you."

"Ha. Ha."

"Seriously, what are you asking me?" She placed a hand on her hip.

"When you touched me, I…felt--something happened…" His voice trailed off as he remembered that strange and overpowering feeling. He shook his head, hoping he didn't sound too weak, or helpless. "I don't usually let women just touch me like that."

"You say that like I was trying to caress you are something, boy *please*. You are not that pretty," she sassed.

His smile grew as the tense atmosphere diffused. "But you do think I'm pretty right?" He ran his fingers down the side of his face and paused to give her his best model pose. She quirked her eyebrow at him. As ironic as it seemed, her dry humor was refreshing to him.

"You are so full of yourself. Pride cometh before a fall."

"And you are churchy. Do you have a response that, you know, isn't a Bible verse?" He responded quickly with a laugh. She laughed a long with him.

"I *am* churchy. Can't help it--either love it or hate it."

"I haven't decided yet, but I guess we'll find out *neighbor*," he countered. "Am I making you late for class?" He asked. She smiled at him sheepishly.

"No. I get to class super early, just because. I like to be settled before the other students come in." His eyes widened at her response.

"Oh so, you *were* trying to get away from me."

Esther laughed and fidgeted a bit.

"Maybe." Micah's mouth dropped as Esther hurried to defend herself, "Hey you were pretty aggressive. I'm not scared of you or anything, I just—"

"I just make you uncomfortable." He took a step closer to her.

What was he *doing*? She was *not* his friend. She wasn't like Jay; Jay could be his friend and be a Christian because Jay didn't take things to the extreme the way she did, but he couldn't deny that despite her strange nature, she was fun to be around. She didn't suffocate him with Bible scriptures and yet she exuded that ethereal presence he felt the other night--the same presence that he felt as a child and when he used to lead the choir. He shook his head, he had to get focused--back to the original goal:

"So if you're not in danger of being late for class, then you have time to answer my question about why I fell. I mean you barely touched me and then…"

"Micah, that was the Holy Spirit. I touched you for like, half a second while I was praying for you and you went down."

"So that was all God?"

"Yep." She popped the "p" and then smiled at him.

"That's your final answer?"

"Yep."

"Hm. So you definitely believe in God?" He asked, scratching his chin.

"And you don't?"

"We've been through this."

Esther nodded. "Well, you're entitled to your opinion."

Micah tilted his head to the side, puzzled. "You aren't going to try to convince me otherwise?"

Esther shook her head and paused before responding, "Mm. Nope." She began walking again.

"You know, you told me what my name means but I never told you what yours means," he yelled, causing her to stop dead in her tracks.

"Oh? And what does my name mean Mr. Williams?" She asked, spinning around on her heel to face him.

He looked down at his feet, then released a breathy chuckle as he walked towards her.

"Esther is that little girl from the movie *Orphan*—"

Her eyes grew wide as she smacked him on his shoulder.

"Oh *my* gosh!" She exclaimed through her horrified laugher.

Micah laughed at her expression. He didn't think it was possible for her almond shaped eyes to have grown in size, but they grew exponentially at his comment. He studied them for a moment after his laughter had subsided.

"It's true. You know it is," he continued.

She shook her head in a resigned fashion; she couldn't deny that fact.

"Yes, it is true, but I'd rather think of the biblical significance of that name."

"And that would be?"

"Look it up," Micah said grinning.

"Can we agree not to speak of that ever again? That movie gave me the creeps." She shuddered. Micah laughed.

"Ok, agreed as long as we do get the chance to speak again. Aside from your whole sanctified psy—" Her reproachful glare gave him pause. "Prophetical thingy, you're pretty cool." He scratched the back of his neck.

"And aside from your whole ignorance thingy, you aren't half bad yourself. I suppose you can't help it though, bless your heart." She retorted. Micah scowled.

"Aren't Christians supposed to be nice?" Esther snorted at his question.

"Have you *been* to church lately?" She asked.

"You got jokes," he murmured.

She nudged his arm with her elbow. "Yep, I've got a ton." She smirked.

"I'd like to hear them sometime."

"Oh really?" She asked.

"You didn't see that coming?" He smirked at her.

"Not a psychic remember?" He smacked himself on the forehead playfully.

"Oh right, excuse me."

He found some satisfaction in the fact that this girl was not only giving him the time of day, but seemed to be enjoying his presence. Esther pulled her phone from her pocket and glanced at the time.

"I have to go," she said.

"Wait, I have some more questions."

She shifted her back pack.

"Ask me later. You know where I live," she said. And she walked away from him, leaving him conflicted once again.

***

He arrived at work that evening, drowning in thoughts of what he could have done better. Those thoughts soon gave way to re-runs of their earlier conversation.

"Listen the reason that I told that precious little boy that his aunt would live is because it's true," she'd said.

She seemed incredibly confident and sure of herself, or rather her God. She was so confident that she didn't have to argue with him, bait him, or force him to believe that her God was real. She walked around campus like she owned the place. *It's probably the whole 'cattle on a thousand hills mentality.* He figured. The thought of it had him reeling at work that evening. When Micah walked into the diner Jay was the first person that he saw. He was hollering at some other worker for God only knew what. Micah speed walked over to him and grabbed him by the arm.

"What in the—oh hey, Micah," Jay turned quickly to see who'd come to his side. When he realized that it was only Micah, he turned back to the other worker. "Next time I catch you sneakin' cornbread off the tray, you're fired. Got it?" The worker nodded, then scurried away. Jay turned his attention back to Micah. "What's up man?" Jay asked.

"*What's up?* Seriously? You had me worried to death about you."

Jay placed a hand over his heart and rendered a large toothy grin. "How sweet! You were concerned about your best friend." He paused, allowing his smile to fall. "I'm fine though," he said sharply before turning around. Micah gripped Jay's arm, forcing him to turn back around.

"Where were you?" Micah asked.

Jay snatched his arm away from Micah's grip.

"Handling some business." The steel in Jay's gaze and voice warned Micah to leave well enough alone and he did. Micah followed Jay to the back of the dining room toward the kitchen.

"Just wanted to make sure you were ok," Micah said. Jay nodded, then pushed open the double doors that led to the kitchen.

"I appreciate it, but I'm good. I swear."

"Ok then." Micah clocked into the employee computer, then went off to find his bussing tub. Jay followed him back out onto the floor. He leaned against an empty booth as he watched Micah buss the table.

"I'm still mad at you," Micah said.

“For what?”

“Ditching me the other night. You completely bailed on me.”

Jay folded his arms.

“Told you I had business to take care of. Anyways, how was it?” Micah shook his head. "Ok, next question: still pining over that mystery girl from your dreams?” He teased as he clasped Micah’s shoulder.

Micah shrugged his hand away and went back to putting dirty dishes into his bussing tub.

“No,” he lied.

When the table was cleared of dishes, he wiped off the table with the rag he’d slung over his left shoulder. Afterwards, he moved onto the next table, in hopes of getting away from his best friend’s teasing.

“You’re lying, man,” Jay said.

“Jay.” Micah glared at him. Jay threw his hands up in mock surrender, but couldn’t help the laughter that escaped his lips.

“Micah,” he mocked, replicating Micah’s warning tone. “Quit lying to me, brotha’. I know something’s up. You come in here all pensive and brooding and stuff. You clocked in and went straight to the tables, no sarcastic comments, no nothing. I mean I’ve been waiting for you to see Chase’s new haircut. I just knew you were going to have something smart to say about it, but I can honestly say that I’ve been thoroughly disappointed by your actions today. I mean I know you were upset and worried about me, but I don't think that's all there is to it." Jay folded his arms and shook his head in amusement.

Micah was never one to come in or leave quietly. He always had a joke or a snarky comment that filled the break room and kitchens with laughter. There was no appearance of that kind of Micah today, and that was unsettling.

"Maybe it is her. Ok?" Angrily, Micah grabbed the plates and very nearly began throwing them in the tub.

"Careful with my plates playa' those are expensive!" Jay exclaimed.

"Sorry," Micah grumbled. "It's just, she's so weird and she's so…" He struggled to find the right wording. "So cocky." Jay raised his eyebrows.

"I take it you spoke to her?" He asked. Micah nodded. Jay stood up straight as the realization dawned on him, "Wait she's real?"

"Yep."

"And you talked to her? How did that go?"

Despite how uncomfortable their conversation made him at times, he'd loved every moment of speaking to her and looking into her deep brown eyes. They were so expressive and honest. All of the passion she put behind her words when she was speaking her mind to him, reflected back into those shimmering pools of brown.

"I did not. Maybe cocky is the wrong word for it, she's…she's confident. Very confident."

"Is she fine?" Jay asked.

"She's beautiful man, but that's not what she's confident about," Micah murmured. "She's humble in that aspect, doesn't seem to care much. What gets me is that she's so confident in her God."

"And that's a problem?" Jay asked, bewildered. Micah raised his eyebrows at him, exasperated. "What man? Everybody needs a good church girl. You know what they say about those church girls…." He trailed off and wiggled his eyebrows suggestively. Micah rolled his eyes.

"It's not even like that. She's a church girl alright, but not like any I've ever seen. She's like, she's like…some Jesus-y psychic or something? She tells people their own personal business without knowing them. Or at least she claims not to know them. I think it's a scam. When I saw her in my dreams, I didn't think she was going to be some freak," Micah said.

Jay laughed.

"But we like freaks," Jay teased. His eyes were wide with feigned innocence.

"Really Jay?"

"She's got you sprung huh? Normally you'd be gushing about tapping that, but it looks like you've been tamed," Jay said. He looked down at his cell phone and frowned.

"Jay?" Immediately Jay looked up from his phone,

"Huh?"

"Shut up."

Jay glared at him. "I'm the boss remember?" He joked.

Micah rolled his eyes and pressed on as if he hadn't heard that comment. "I've wanted to make some jokes, but every time I get ready to open my mouth, it's like…"

"You feel convicted."

"She demands that I respect her and she doesn't have to say a word," Micah murmured.

"And let me guess, you like that? Don't answer, of course you do. You've managed to get every woman you've ever wanted—at least that's what you tell me—and now here comes a P.Y.T that won't give you the time of day."

"It's not that. I don't even like her like that, she's too weird for me. I can't have her knowing all my personal business and stuff. Like what if I told her I was going to hang with you, and I was really at the bar. She'd know that. That's not cool and the worst part is that she gets her info from the little voices in her head. She says it's God. Pfft." Micah jeered. Jay rolled his eyes. "She could be like some kind of uncover FBI—" Micah cut himself off. Even he knew that he was beginning to sound desperate.

"Alright," Jay laughed. "What did she say to you?"

"Who said that she said anything to me?"

"Tell the truth. Shame the devil."

"Shut up."

"Whatever. We got one of those type of people at my church, Prophetess Rita Clark and my God is she good and fine—I mean good and anointed. Bless His name." He bowed his head to conceal his laughter. Micah laughed along with him.

"Don't you have a wife at home? How is Sherry by the way?" Micah asked. He listened intently as Jay talked briefly about his wife, Sherry, and how stressed she was about getting her master's degree.

"You're coming to her graduation, right?" He asked. Micah nodded.

"For sure."

"You know I love you man, right?" Jay asked as he began to stand up. He walked over to Micah and put his hand on his shoulder.

"For sure," Micah responded again. "Love you too man."

"You know, I know you only asked about Sherry to change the subject right?"

"For su—wait no I didn't!" Micah protested.

"Micah, that stuff ain't no joke. You know I play a lot about church and I know you ain't into all that stuff, but make no mistake about it. That stuff is real." The seriousness in Jay's voice was enough to silence him, if only for a moment.

"Sure," Micah murmured. His mind went back to the word that Esther had given him the night before, the word about the little boy's aunt, the word that she gave his sister. For just a moment he allowed himself to admit that maybe the night before was real; maybe there was something to it.

"What was that?" Micah sighed and tore the dish towel from his shoulder, he then tossed it onto the table.

"Hmm?"

"What did you say? What exactly did she do that's got you so messed up, Micah?" He hesitated. Should he tell him about the word she gave him, or should he keep her weirdness to a minimum?

"She laid me out Jay." Jay raised an eyebrow as Micah continued, "She touched me and I hit the floor."

Jay fell backwards into the booth seat howling with laughter.

"She laid you out? You mean you were slain in the Spirit? Tell me exactly how it went," he said after he'd composed himself some. "Wait a minute." He burst out laughing again, pointing at Micah and repeating Micah's earlier disgruntled statement. "Ok, now. Go ahead. I'm ready."

"It's not funny."

"Yes it is. It's hilarious. The great Micah Williams falls at the touch of a woman. Oh how the mighty have—too soon? Speaking of women, how's your woman of the night?" Jay folded his arms, a smirk on his face. Micah made a face at him, voicing the fact that he was definitely less than amused.

"Who?"

"Sheba?"

"Don't even get me started about her. I think we're done."

"You've been done for over a year but you still manage to get along well enough to hit that."

Micah dropped another plate into the busser tray.

"I'm tired of her," Micah said. He hoped that his lie would pass undetected. It didn't.

Jay gave Micah a knowing look.

"Sure…or you just found a new toy."

Jay patted him on his shoulder and walked away, yelling at another employee who'd just dropped a glass on the floor. Micah shook his head at his friend's antics and returned back to his work.

***

"Micah is that you?" Rea asked. She was standing in the doorway of her room. Her hair, dripping with water, was pulled on top of her head as she tried to finish tying her fuzzy teal bathrobe together.

"Who else has a key?" Micah asked as he shut the door behind him. "Nice PJ's," he said, gesturing to the Sesame street pajama pants she had on. Elmo's face was plastered all over them. Rea walked to him and hugged him. He returned her embrace quickly and kissed the top of her head. "Everything ok?"

Rea nodded against his chest.

"Can we talk?" She asked. "I know you just got off and you're probably really tired." She pulled away from him. He untied the apron from his waist and threw it over the couch. With one hand, he beckoned for her to follow him. He plopped on the couch, put his feet up and sighed.

"Let's hear it," he said.

Rea timidly took a seat next to him. She fiddled with her fingers, took her hair down and then put it back up. Eventually she turned sideways to face him. She positioned her elbow on the back of the couch and curled up on the leather seat.

"You sure?" she asked, her voice quiet and timid.

Micah gave her soft and encouraging smile. She exhaled.

"You know I'm here for you, Rea. I always have been, always will be," he murmured.

Rea went back to playing with her fingers.

"I've been thinking about last night." The words came out loud, almost as if by accident. Her now widened eyes clearly confirmed that her words had in fact come out accidently.

"What about it?" Micah asked. His entire body tensed up and he tried his best to keep his voice as nonchalant as possible. It was already clear that she was nervous to talk to him. He didn't want to make it any harder for her.

"Well…" Micah turned to face her, copying her position. "I've been thinking a lot about what Esther said…about me being a prophetess."

"Listen, Rea, don't let anybody tell you who or what you are. That girl has some mental problems. She hears voices in her head." Rea looked down at her fingers.

"You don't really believe that," she whispered. Micah rubbed his forehead.

"Here we go again," he muttered.

"Well what *do* you believe then?" She asked. "That last night was some weird coincidence? How could she know all that stuff about all those people?"

"There's a logical explanation for it."

"Spell logical," she snapped. "Never mind I'll do it, G.O.D."

"Actually, that spells illogical."

“Whatever.”

“The girl hears voices in her head and she’s probably taken a class on how to read people. I bet she’s a psych major.”

“She told us that she was an anthropology major Micah,” Rea said drily.

Micah shrugged.

“People lie, or have two majors. You know, either option is plausible. Hell, anthropology, psychology-- whatever it is, she still studies people.”

Rea rolled her eyes and shook her head.

“I just wanted to get your take on last night.” Micah squinted his eyes at the young woman before him. She was squirming in her seat.

“That’s not all.”

She glared at the hard wood floors with disdain.

“Yeah, it is.” He rubbed a hand over his face. Whatever she’d wanted to tell him, he now realized, he’d just made it impossible for her to share. Again, God had driven this wedge between the two of them. To push or not to push? That was the question.

“I’m sorry.”

“Don’t be. You still didn’t answer my question.” She picked up a throw pillow and squeezed it tightly to her chest.

“It was freaky,” he admitted with his eyes wide.

“I saw you get slain.”

His mouth hung open slightly.

“Excuse you?”

“Slain. You know, like slain in the Spirit?” Micah shook his head. "Ok, maybe you don’t know then.”

“Why would I?” He smirked.

Rea stood to her feet and threw the pillow on the couch.

“Because, as much as you want to forget, you used to know God. You think I don’t remember? I was eleven when they died, not *two*. I remember what you used to be like. I remember how much you used to love God, and how you used to sing. I’ve stood idly by, watching your pain eat you from the inside out. Last night was the first time I’ve seen you cry in years,” she paused and composed herself. “I refuse to continue to watch you push this away, to watch you push *Him* away.”

“I get that you think that you’re helping me and I appreciate the thought. You know I love you Rea, but I think that you might be the one out of us that needs help. This isn’t healthy. You’ve gotten too deep into this. Now, I was fine with you going on Sundays and Wednesdays because you know, that was somewhat normal but now…not so much. You think that last night was some sort of God ordained act? That stupid church we go to down on the corner wouldn't tolerate half of that and you know it. Now, you're stepping into something dangerous."

She didn't respond, she made her way back to her room and slammed the door behind her.

"Rea!" He yelled. No response. "ReAutumn Marie Williams!" He couldn't let her go to bed angry at him. She was right. She'd watched him spiral for four years and never said a word apart from her invites to church. He got up and knocked on her door.

"Rea, please. I'm sorry." He leaned against the door as he waited. There was still no response. "You know I'm not trying to hurt your feelings." He put his hand on the door knob and hesitated before trying to open the door but it was locked. "I just want what's best for you. I know it seems like it's real right now, that it'll last…but I'm telling you, one day you'll realize that this was just a fairytale with no happy ending. I don't wnat to see you hurt. I love you."

He placed his hand on the door and stood there, staring at the wood for a moment longer. He sighed, and then slowly walked away. He walked back to the balcony. Maybe he shouldn't have said that to her. She wasn't ready to hear it, *but* she was fifteen-years-old, and although she was pushing him, she didn't deserve what he'd said. These thoughts consumed him as he went to his room, grabbed a bottle of beer, then headed back to the balcony. He sat in the patio chair and put his feet up on the railing.

"She'll be ok," he whispered to himself as he put the bottle to his lips. “I turned out fine. Just look at me.”

“Hey neighbor.” His head snapped to the left, and his eyes widened when he saw Esther leaning on the railing of her balcony.

“Um...hi,” Micah replied.

Esther’s hair was pulled into a bun, and she was smiling widely at him. All of her perfect, teeth were showing.

He took another swig of his beer. That was the only response he could muster. He partly wanted to put the stupid thing away because he was sure she’d lecture him. On the other hand, maybe it would make her go away. After his argument with Rea, he didn’t want to be bothered.

“Whatcha drinking?” She sang.

“Sunny D.”

“Hmmm. That’s what I thought.” She smirked. Micah scoffed and looked away.

“It’s beer.”

“The good stuff.” She chuckled.

His eyes widened. *What did she just say?*

“Excuse me?”

“Yeah, I used to drink too. I couldn’t do it without getting drunk so I had to stop when I got saved.”

"Mm. If you came out here to preach to me, I'm not in the mood."

She snapped her fingers and sighed.

"Dang, seems like I'm fresh out of 'Jesus is better than beer' sermons. No, I came out here to think but when I saw you out here I felt that a little friendly conversation might be nice." Micah eyed her warily, his eyebrows knitting together in interest.

"Well, hate to break it to you but I'm not really in the mood," he said, turning away from her. She nodded.

"Ok, understandable." Micah watched her, with slight disappointment as she went back into her apartment. She returned moments later with a chair, a book and a journal.

The distance between the two balconies wasn't far. He could probably step from his railing onto hers, albeit it would be a large step, but he could make it. He was close enough to see that she'd now placed a mechanical pencil in the bun on top of her head and put a pair of black, square framed glasses. Quietly, she took a seat in the chair, and opened the small thick book. Micah took another sip of his drink.

"So..." he began.

"I thought you weren't in the mood for conversation," she said. She didn't look up from the book she was reading. Micah shrugged.

"I'm not, but I do still have some questions for you." He waited for a few moments, she still didn't look up. "What are you reading?"

"Shakespeare's plays."

"Which one?"

"*Othello.*"

"Hmm. Can't say that I'm not surprised."

"And why is that?" She asked. She was smiling now, but still refused to look up at him. "Did you think that only I read the Bible?"

Micah laughed.

"Well yeah."

Esther giggled. Micah stood to his feet and looked out over the parking lot. It wasn't the best view, but it wasn't the worst. He took another sip of his beer then walked over to the side of the balcony railing that was closest to Esther.

"Hate to burst your bubble Micah, but I don't know about every other Christian in the world. I simply know that I, Esther Wickers, like to read other books besides the Bible."

"You know technically the Bible is not a book."

"It's an anthology. I'm well aware. Thank you." She took the glasses from her face. "Is there something that I can help you with Micah? You're blocking my moon light."

In the moonlight, the ineffable glow on her face gave him pause. *I can think of a few things that you can help me with,* he thought.

"You know if you weren't so weird I might ask you out," he said finally. Esther rolled her eyes.

"You mean if I wasn't a *Christian* you'd ask me out."

"No, I've dated Christians."

"Hmm." She shook her head. The smile of her face was indicative of the laughter that was about to burst forth from her lips.

"What?"

"Nothing."

"If you say so." There was a moment of silence before Esther quickly and suddenly closed her book then looked up at him.

"Why would you ask me out? We're not exactly friends."

"Maybe I like your attitude."

"Who's to say I'd even go out with you if you asked?" She smirked.

"Trust me, you'd date me." She shook her head.

"Believe what you want, you're good at that." He laughed.

"Oh I will. Will you go out with me?"

"No. You're not my type."

His eyes widened. *Ouch.* ok, so maybe he hadn't been entirely serious when he asked her out, but there was a part of him that was. *If* it was possible to get past her oddities, he'd have given it a go. After all, Sheba claimed she was a Christian and getting with her had been just as easy as *one*, *two*, *three*.

"Damn."

"Told you so," she laughed.

"I thought you were joking."

"Clearly," she snorted. Esther reopened her book, the smile still planted on her face.

"Why not?" He asked. Esther sighed.

"I thought this was a joke."

"Just answer the question."

"One, I just met you and two, I'm not sure if I like you yet. Three, as I just told you, you're not my type."

"Ah, I'm not a Bible toting church boy. You're one of those equally yoked people."

She turned the page in her book.

"Yup."

"Well that's a simple fix. I'll go buy a bible and keep it in my car. I'll get one of those Jesus t-shirts and wear a cross around my neck. Would that satisfy you?"

"First of all, if you were to touch a Bible it would probably burn you."

Micah threw his head back and laughed.

"True."

"And I'd need for you to have the Word in you, and not just on you."

"Judge not, lest ye be judged."

"Mmm, would you look at that? You want a cookie for knowing that verse?" She said teasingly.

He rolled his eyes.

"I'm just trying to show you how spiritual I can be."

"Demons are spiritual. Next."

Micah's mouth dropped at Esther's comment.

"You're so mean," he said laughing. Esther laughed.

"Relax, I'm kidding. What is it that you want from me Micah? I know the mood didn't just suddenly strike you to be sociable." Micah scratched the back of his neck.

"I need some answers. Let's start with this question: how did you know all that stuff about me last night?"

"I didn't, God did."

"Rea mentioned something about being slain in the Spirit? What is that exactly?" Esther dog-eared the page of her book, and closed it.

"I'm going to give you a challenge."

"That's not an answer," Micah sang. He wagged his finger at her. "No challenges, just answers."

"Actually, it will help you find answers for yourself. Ready?" He nodded but kept a skeptical eyebrow raised. "You'll love this answer." She paused. "Go pray." He scowled at her. "I'm being serious Micah, go pray and here."

She opened her journal and pulled out a piece of paper. She handed it to him and smiled.

"What is this? A diary entry?"

"It's going to help you get the answers you need."

Micah looked over the paper. It was a list of spiritual terms, books, Bible verses, and sermon titles. As much as he hated to admit it, some of the verses he recognized immediately. He knew them without even having to look them up.

"How is this supposed to help me?"

"Categorize every question you have by the terms on that sheet and if you still can't find the answer then come talk to me. I keep telling you Micah, you know the answers. And judging by the look on your face when you started to read over that paper, you already know half of those verses on there. You want me to give you a different answer. I can't give you anything contrary to the Word, otherwise it wouldn't be God, it'd be me. It wouldn't be holy, it'd be witchcraft." Micah wrinkled his nose.

"Witchcraft? That's a teensy bit over dramatic don't you think?" He asked.

She smirked.

"I wish."

Micah's mind drifted back to the conversation, or rather argument that he'd had with Rea earlier. Now more than ever he wanted Rea out of that madness.

"What's that supposed to mean?"

"I'm only twenty-one but I've encountered a lot in the past few years, witchcraft being one of them. There are leaders with ulterior motives in the church, but I'm sure you knew that, huh?" She chuckled. Micah nodded as she continued. "They want to be worshiped, rather than worshipping God. They look so convincing you know? You really think they have a heart for God, but really all they have a heart for is power, and worshipping themselves. They tend to identify themselves as being the absolute liaison between you and God. If God didn't tell them something then, then He wouldn't tell you."

"Do these people by chance tear people down in the ministry that don't do things they want them to do?" Micah asked. He already knew a handful of people that would match that description. Esther nodded.

"Yep. You might know it by another name."

"Oh?"

"Jezebel spirit. It can manifest in both men and women. Witchcraft goes hand in hand with it." Her eyes were unfocused, although they appeared to be fixated on a piece of his balcony. He eyed her cautiously. What did she know? What had she experienced? Was that what made her so reserved about her calling and her experiences? The serious atmosphere was becoming too much for him, so he decided to draw her attention back to the initial topic.

"Well from what I've seen of you so far, you're not like those people. With that being said, I don't see why I need this list when you could just tell me the answers."

"The last thing that either of us needs is for you to look to me rather than looking to God. Don't get me wrong Micah, I want to help but you have to want to help yourself too. If you have any more questions after reading, or need some help navigating, I'll be happy to lend a hand."

"Yeah, well, is the reason why you and Sheba McGruer hate each other on this list? " He said as he folded his arms, a smug expression on his face.

Esther put her glasses back on.

"I *don't hate* Sheba McGruer. What made you come to that conclusion?"

She redirected her gaze to the book in her hands.

"She did. She told me to stay away from you. Any idea why?"

"I'm not sure Micah. Why don't you ask her? I haven't done anything to her, bless her heart," she said nonchalantly as she turned the page.

"You really don't care?" Micah asked, tilting his head to the side as he studied her. The glasses were sliding down to the tip of her nose. A few loose strands of hair framed her face. "You're not like a lot of Christians, are you?"

Esther shrugged.

"Define that please. That could either be an insult or a compliment."

She flipped another page. He looked down at his feet.

"You're not trying to shove your religion down my throat."

"You're the one who brought it up," Esther said laughing.

Micah nodded.

"I guess you're right. I feel bad for you. You know, eventually you'll see that this is just an illusion, a dream, a crutch." He took a sip of his drink. "I'm trying to get Rea to understand that," he whispered.

"Leave that girl alone. Just because you don't believe, doesn't mean you should try to force other people not to," Esther said sharply.

"One day, she'll thank me for it. You know the little *word* that you gave her last night, has now taken root in her brain?"

"Good."

"Good? What do you mean good? That's not good Esther. You're setting her up for failure."

Esther huffed and slammed her book shut.

"I'm setting her up for victory. Maybe if you'd try to understand instead of fighting with it all the time, you'd get a little bit further. You know that saying, you see what you want to see? People use that a lot to talk about us but, honey, it works both ways."

"Did you just call me honey? Cute."

Esther rolled her eyes.

"Did something happen between the two of you?" She asked softly.

His automatic response was to deflect, to tell her that nothing had happened, but there was a part of him that wanted badly to trust her. Although she scared him periodically, although she challenged him, she was safe. Dangerous and safe all at the same time; she was the perfect paradox.

"You could say that," he said as he leaned against the balcony, holding the bottle with both hands.

"Wanna talk about it?"

"We don't know each other enough to be divulging each other's personal business, but given the fact that you clearly already know mine—"

"Actually, I don't. Stop assuming that I know your whole life please. It's really annoying. I am *not* a psychic. I don't even remember whatever it is that I said last night."

"Right. God knows. You said that."

"It's ok if you don't want to talk about it," she said. "I get it. Just know I'm here."

"Ok," he conceded. "Ok."

"I'm gonna finish this chapter or whatever, and then I'm gonna go to bed," she said.

"This early?" He looked at his watch. She shrugged. "Right, right. The whole 'Children of the day' thing…gotcha." Esther rolled her eyes.

"Goodnight, Micah. See you around."

"Probs not," he joked.

She smiled softly at him, then returned to her book.

He turned around and headed toward the back door. With his

hand on the handle, he turned to look back at Esther, who sat cross-legged in a patio chair, reading. His lips turned up gently at the corners. The piece of paper she'd given him was clenched tightly in his hand. When he got inside he laid the paper on the coffee table and slumped down on the couch. What was he going to say to Rea to make this better? Was there anything he could say? Should he just wait it out? He ran his hands over his face. This had to come to an end and soon. He'd prove to them, both Esther and Rea, that their pursuit of God was pointless. He'd figure out the mystery behind Esther's strange gift, his strange dreams, Rea's strange gift of knowing. He'd find out about the beef between Esther and Sheba, he'd find out who Esther Wicker's truly was, why Jay had gone all M.I.A on him the day before and he'd justify it--all of it-- without God.

SIX

The sun's rays washed over Micah as his eyes fluttered open. As he looked at the alarm clock on the bedside table, he realized that he woke up earlier than he was supposed to. It was only when he looked at the date on the digital clock, that he realized that it was Saturday. He didn't beat his alarm; it simply didn't go off. He rolled over and rubbed his eyes. He grunted in annoyance when he checked his phone and saw a text from Jay asking him to come into work. He didn't want to. The text was simple,

`Bring ya ass.- Jay`

Micah threw the pillow over his face and huffed. Eventually, he got up and padded down the white carpeted hallway to his little sister's bedroom. She was awake, as he suspected. Micah leaned against the door frame as he took in the scene of his sister sitting on her bed with her Bible in front of her and a notebook on her lap. The Bible was worn and tattered. It's pages were falling out, and there were, what appeared to be a hundred different color tabs sticking out of them. Her face was scrunched up as she read it, a sign to him that she was confused.

"What's wrong?" Micah asked as he folded his arms. She didn't look up at him as she responded,

"Nothing, I just…I can't understand the King James Version of the Bible. I think need a new translation." Micah nodded in understanding.

"Well, I don't understand any of it, King James Version or not so you're doing better than me," he joked. She glared at him icily. "Ok, Ok. What are you reading?"

"Multiple scriptures," she said quietly. "'For the preaching of the cross is to them that perish foolishness; but unto us which are saved it is the power of God.' That's 1 Corinthians 1:18."

Micah pursed his lips and nodded. "And the other one?"

"'The natural man does not accept the things that come from the Spirit of God. For they are foolishness to him, and he cannot understand them because they are spiritually discerned.' 1 Corinthians 2:14," she read quietly.

How convenient… Micah thought as his eyes drifted to Rea's perfume, and lotion covered, dresser. His eyes landed on the last family photo they'd all taken together. Seeing his mother's face was enough to draw back the smart aleck comment he wanted to release about the scripture.

"Listen," Micah began with a sigh, "I'm sorry about last night Rea. I just worry about you," he murmured.

Esther's words from the night before rang in his ears. *She was right...*

Rea shrugged her shoulders, and rolled her eyes. "I don't know why you do that Micah. You used to be into this stuff," she said quietly. She picked up the pencil next to her crossed knees and began writing something. "What happened to you?" She asked.

Such a loaded question. He wasn't even sure of how to answer it. As he thought of how to respond, he grew more and more uncomfortable. He had to figure out a way to change the subject, or at least fix the heavy and uncomfortable vibe in the room.

"I woke up. Stay woke!" He laughed nervously. She glared at him, causing his discomfort to grow. "I was joking."

"You always joke. Don't you get how serious this is?" She asked, throwing her pencil down, onto her journal.

Micah huffed and stood up straight, he unfolded his arms.

"How serious what is?" He asked.

"Your soul," she said evenly, as she stared into his eyes.

He held back a snort. He'd committed to be understanding about his sister's infatuation with all of this churchy mumbo-jumbo, and until last night he had been. But now she was pushing the limits on his patience. Ever since the night that Esther came, it was as if a fire had been lit under her butt.

"My *soul* is just fine," he began.

He broke his sister's gaze and walked over to her bed and sat down next to her.

"Look, I won't stand in the way of you doing your whole Jesus thing. I love you and if you're happy then I'm happy, but don't try to force me into it. I already go to church with you on Sunday's Rea, what more do you want?" He continued.

"I just don't want you to go to Hell Micah," she said.

Her last words pierced him clean through. He stared at her for a moment and she didn't waver under his gaze. Had it been anyone else, he would have told them off, but this was his sister. In her eyes there was no judgement, only love and concern for him. He sighed, and decided to do what he did best, brush it off.

"I'm not going anywhere but to work Rea. Are you going to hang out with Mallory today?" He asked.

Rea's expression hardened, but he knew this conversation was far from over. She nodded. Micah stumbled backwards when his little sister shot towards him. She wrapped her thin arms around his waist and held him close.

"Hey, I'm gonna be fine alright? I pay my tithes, so I'm pretty sure I've stored up enough money in heaven for a little shack outside of the gates ok?" He joked.

Yes, he did pay his tithes--he knew that's what his parents would want. He didn't pay his tithes *all* the time, but he paid them often enough in his opinion.

Rea didn't laugh.

Micah arrived at work heavy in spirit. The conversation from earlier rested upon his shoulders. He tied his apron around his waist and clocked in, only pausing to greet his friend Jay with a small, "Hey." That one word, left several confused men behind him.

"Micah? Man, bro—you've gotta stop coming in with this whole depressed vibe. You're worrying me man. Is it that girl again?"

"No, it's not Esther," Micah snapped.

He leaned against the door way of Jay's office. Jay stood in front of him with a hand on his shoulder. His eyes showed true concern, rather than the usual playfulness.

"Then what is it? Something wrong with Rea?"

"She's concerned about my soul. We fought last night and had a discussion about it this morning." Jay shrugged his shoulders.

"Ok…you know baby girl is a Christian, what's the big deal?"

"It's just…"

Micah waved his hands around wildly as if he were trying to conjure up the words.

"Just what?" Jay asked.

"I don't know, I feel guilty for making her worry about me so much," he confessed. "At the same time, all of this could be solved if she would just realize the truth." Jay reared back and placed his hands on his hips, preparing himself for whatever Micah was about to say.

"Oh, and what would that be?"

"That there is no God!" Micah fumed angrily. "I mean think about it Jay. There's no proof, no evidence all you people can say is: 'You have to know Him for yourself.' The whole idea of Him has done nothing but cause division in my family."

"Your parents were Christians." Micah cut him a dark look, one that suggested that Jay drop his case.

"I know that," Micah said darkly.

It wasn't as if he didn't know that his own parents were Bible Thumpers. He saw how well that worked out for them. Heck, everybody at their funeral could attest to how well it worked out for them. Both men stared at each other, a silent argument passing between them. Neither of them noticed a fellow server approaching them.

"Micah you're down," Julias said as he clasped Micah's shoulder. Micah didn't take his gaze away from Jay. "Table three." Julias looked between the two of them then quickly walked away.

"Listen man, I'm sorry," Jay said. "I wasn't trying to offend you." Micah's glare softened at Jay's words.

"I know you weren't. I'm just—"

"I know. You're worried about her. Don't be. She's going to be ok and who knows, maybe the God thing will work out for her."

Jay rubbed his hands together as his mien transformed into a much lighter expression. He had been serious for far too long.

"Now, what you're going to do, is go serve those girls at table three," Jay ordered evasively.

Micah stared defiantly at his friend.

"How do you know they're girls?" Micah asked.

Jay shrugged.

"Saw them when they came in and they are *cold* man. I mean *fine*. Go get you one."

He smacked Micah on the back of the head and laughed when Micah punched Jay's shoulder in return. The two friends grinned at each other, their earlier tension forgotten.

"Go." Jay pushed Micah out of his doorway.

Micah walked through the kitchen trying to change his thoughts and attitudes. Jay was right, he was at work, he shouldn't be thinking about his problems, he'd do that later in his statistics class. It's not like he paid attention in there anyway. He grabbed a black circular serving tray on his way out of the kitchen, then pulled out his server's pad. He clicked his pen as he scanned the room for his table.

There were three girls seated in a booth on the far side of the restaurant just as Julias and Jay described. He inhaled and exhaled slowly on his way over, thankful that the booth was across the room from where he'd been. It gave him adequate time to right himself.

He put on his best smile as approached the table only to have it fall instantly when he caught sight of who was with the group. Her wild curls were flying loose, and her eyes were bright with laughter and mirth. Beside her was a blond girl and across from her was a red-headed girl that he'd seen Esther talking to in her biology class.

"Esther, hey." Her laughter died down as she turned to face him.

"Micah, hi."

"So what, you're following me now?" He said.

The girls immediately paused their conversation. The one farthest away from him, in the corner of the booth smirked at him. Esther placed her hand on her chin, resting her elbow on the table.

"That's a little conceited don't you think?"

"Esther, just admit it. You like me."

"The Lord hates lying lips," she jeered.

Micah rolled his eyes. "Not my problem," he said.

"You guys know each other?" Esther's blond-haired friend asked.

"Unfortunately," Esther joked.

"Well introduce us Esther. You're so rude!" The red-headed girl insisted. Esther rolled her eyes.

"Why?"

"Yeah, go ahead, introduce us Ess," said Micah.

He smirked at her; any chance he got to get under her skin he'd take it, hands down, and without hesitation.

"Ugh. Ok, so goldilocks here is Emily and my favorite ginger across the way there, is Fallon," Esther said.

Fallon gave him a small wave. Emily merely stared at him. Micah shifted his weight from one foot to the other.

"It's a pleasure ladies."

"Mhm," Emily said, turning her nose up as her eyes ran over his body.

Micah raised his eyebrow in return, slightly annoyed by her attitude but otherwise unfazed. Fallon and Esther shared a pointed look. *Is this Emily's normal behavior?*

"Nice to meet you," Fallon said. Her eyes kept darting to Emily, almost in warning.

"I honestly didn't know you worked here," Esther added. "Otherwise I wouldn't have come," she said, smirking.

At the sound of her voice, Micah's discomfort began to evaporate slowly. Micah shrugged, and stared deeply into her brown eyes, anchors holding him in place while the rest of the world faded away.

"Yeah, part-time. My buddy, Jay, owns this place," he said jabbing his thumb over his shoulder. Esther nodded.

"Can you point him out so we know who to complain to if your customer service sucks?" Esther joked.

Micah cracked a smile.

Fallon looked back and forth between the two. She'd heard Esther talk about this Micah before and while she'd said that he was good looking, she didn't realize he was *that* good looking. Esther had also revealed that Micah had asked her out, and she'd turned him down. It had made her laugh at the time, and she'd admonished her friend, telling her that one dinner wouldn't hurt. Esther agreed to take the idea into consideration although she was sure he'd never ask again after how she'd acted. Now, Fallon wasn't sure it'd be long before they not only went to dinner, but were dating.

Micah cleared his throat, then took their orders. When he'd confirmed that they were correct he headed back to the kitchen area. He leaned against the computer screen as he put in their order, fighting desperately for focus. At this rate he was never going to get the order in correctly--he kept pressing the wrong buttons. He kept glancing back over his shoulder at the girls, one in particular—Esther.

He didn't know much about her, apart from the fact that she was sarcastic, grounded and that she was in fact a "sanctified" psychic. *Prophetess.* He corrected himself. He sighed in agitation and ripped the receipt from the printer. This wasn't him! He wasn't supposed to be fawning over some weird girl he barely knew. He was Micah Darnelle Williams, and he was not about to let some girl come in and mess up his flow. *But she's not just some girl...*

"So, how did it go?" Jay asked, dragging out every word.

Micah rolled his eyes at his friend. Jay couldn't seem to be anything but comical most of the time. Micah didn't answer but instead walked past his friend with his serving tray clenched tightly in his right hand.

"Hello? Anybody home? Micah?" Jay waved his hand in front of Micah's face.

Micah leaned over the prep cook's counter with a flirtatious smile on his face.

"Hey, Penny," he said, ignoring Jay's huff of irritation.

A woman appeared at the counter with a mother's kindly expression. She was a copper-skinned woman in her mid-thirties, and her dark curls were pulled away from her lightly wrinkled face with a hairnet.

"Hey baby. What can I do for you?" She asked brightly, her southern accent hanging off of every word she spoke.

"I need three strawberry milkshakes please. Oh, sorry I mean two strawberry, one vanilla."

He shook his head. Esther just had to be the odd ball. That seemed to be the girl's M.O. Did she wake up in the morning and ask herself: How can I be weird today? Or did it just come naturally?

"You got it, Micah."

"Thanks, Penny."

"I know you heard me, boy," Jay said.

Micah propped himself up against the silver-plated counter and smoothed his hair down.

"Don't you have managerial stuff to do?" He asked flippantly.

Jay smirked sardonically.

"Managerial stuff. Funny, I like that. Listen, just make sure you wash your hands before you touch anything else. We both know you don't wash that mop on top of your head," Jay joked.

"Jay—"

"And another thing, boy you better answer me when I'm talking to you. Respect your elders, youngin'. Now, I'm gonna ask you one more time. How did it go?"

"It went," was Micah's response.

Jay rolled his eyes as he continued to prod Micah impatiently. "Get a phone number? A date? Anything?"

Micah narrowed his eyes at his best-friend who, at the moment, was starting to feel like more of a nuisance than a friend.

"I couldn't get it the first time, what makes you think I will the second time?" he asked.

Jay's eyebrows knitted together in confusion.

"Whatchu' mean the first time? Oh-oh, oh ...oh lawd, that's that gal ain't it?" He exclaimed.

Jay's exaggerated expressions--wide eyes and such, reminded Micah of a cartoon character. *Oscar Proud...that's it!* Micah thought.

"Esther?! Ain't that her name?"

Micah put his hands over his friend's mouth to shut him up, as he looked around. Jay was a loud mouth, and the last thing Micah needed was for Esther to know that he was having conversations about her. Jay pushed his hands away.

"What did I tell you about washing your hands? Here." Jay pulled some hand sanitizer from his pocket and squirted some into Micah's awaiting hands. "Now, nasty, you approached the situation all wrong the first time. Plus, you didn't have me to help you."

"Oh God—" Micah groaned.

"Thought you didn't believe in Him?" Jay said. As Micah glowered at him, Jay raised his hands in surrender.

"I'm just calling it like I see it. Everybody wants to call on Jesus or God or whatever when they want something, but any other time He doesn't exist. You in pain it's: *Oh Lord, Oh Jesus, Oh God!* Y'all pitiful. Just straight pitiful."

"Jay!" Micah exclaimed just as Penny slid the first milkshake out on the counter. "Point. Get there. Please!"

"Don't listen to that fool," Penny said.

"I know what I'm talking about. I am married you know. Where's your man?" Jay quipped.

Micah's mouth dropped. He closed it and then opened it again as he struggled to find the right words to say, but nothing came out.

"Now listen here, the Micah I know can talk a woman out of her good sense and her drawers." Micah nodded in agreement as Jay continued, "this Micah right here, is a punk. Channel your inner Stella and get your groove back. *But*, I should warn you that from what you told me about this girl, she ain't gonna be like any other girl you've ever hit on before Micah. She's one of those real church girls and you are going to have to be either a really sexy bad boy to pull her or you're gonna have to be a really, *really* good church boy. You're neither one of those. So with that being said, good luck. May the Lord watch between me and thee while you get turned down once again," Jay said as he patted Micah on the shoulder.

Micah stared at him incredulously.

"Was that supposed to be advice?!" Micah exclaimed as he grabbed the three milkshakes and placed them on his tray.

"Yep. Go get 'em or die trying. Probably won't get *her*, so I say, go for the friends. I saw how that blond one was looking at you. She don't look too saved. Try her."

He began to push an anxious Micah out of the kitchen door. Micah straightened his posture, deciding *not* to take a majority of Jay's advice. He could do it…he could at least get her phone number he supposed. *If not, then who needed her anyways right?* Micah strutted over to the table, nearly tripping over a chair on his way there. *Damn. Really Micah? Channel Stella, Channel Stella.*

He interrupted Fallon mid-story with his arrival.

"Here you go ladies," he said as he placed their milkshakes on the table. "Two strawberry milk shakes and one vanilla for Miss Difficult here in the corner." He flashed Esther a smirk as she stuck her tongue out at him.

"Thanks Micah," Fallon said quietly. Emily simply nodded.

"Yes, thank you Mr. Williams," Esther said as she eyed her bronze-haired friend.

"It's my pleasure," Micah said earnestly.

Esther's eyes flickered to him as he spoke and the two locked eyes. "You're so much nicer when you're on the clock."

Micah shrugged and looked away. "I try, have to make money somehow."

"I'm not tipping you," she said with a smirk. He rolled his eyes.

"Maybe you could repay me in another way. Since I work here, I get a discount on meals. Maybe you could join me some time."

Esther's mouth dropped.

Emily scoffed. "Are you asking her out? Seriously, *discounted* dinner?" She wrinkled her nose.

Esther elbowed her friend

"Micah--" Esther began.

"Therein lies a loophole. *Because* it's a discounted dinner at my place of employment, it cannot be considered a date. I would never take my date out for a discounted meal. This would only be a cheap dinner or lunch or breakfast—whatever you prefer—between two friends." A vague sense of pride well up in Micah. Esther leaned back against the red cushioned booth seat and crossed her arms, a playful smile on her lips.

"So now we're friends? Ow, Fallon!" She shrieked as she grabbed her knee. She glared at her friend from across the table and then threw Micah a smile. "Alright, Micah."

Micah could barely contain his mirth. The grin that was struggling to break free upon his face morphed into a small smile, but his emerald eyes were shining like jewels.

"Just as friends though right?" She confirmed.

Micah nodded and tapped the back of the tray with his hand.

"Just as friends. I'm going to go check on your food." As he began to walk away he smirked as he heard Esther question her friend's behavior.

"Fallon, what was that?"

"You were about to turn him down. You know better than to turn down someone who looks like that and plus, isn't he the guy from your dream?" Micah stopped mid stride, and turned around. Without thinking he blurted:

"What dream?"

Emily instantly turned her nose up at him. "Wow, you're rude. No one was talking to you," she sneered.

"Emily, stop it. It's nothing," Esther replied as she shot her a dark look.

Esther and Fallon shared another look. Esther finally broke their staring contest by smiling nervously at Micah. He didn't return it. He wanted to press the issue further. Although he knew it wasn't the time or place, to talk about it he was burning with the desire to know exactly what Fallon was talking about. He couldn't respond audibly. His mouth was dry, his palms were sweaty. All he could do was begin walking again. He hurried to the back, with his heart pounding and mind racing. *Dreams? Was she really dreaming about me? Couldn't be.* Hurriedly he scanned the back of the kitchen area for Jay. He found him at the server's window, yelling at the grill cook.

"Where are my wings, Jordan? Customer has been waiting for fifteen minutes man. Get me my wings!" He slammed the wall next to the window.

"Coming up, boss!" Jordan, the six-foot- five grill cook, exclaimed. He huffed in agitation and slid a plate of barbeque wings through the window.

"Jay!" Micah exclaimed. He slammed his tray on a nearby table and then proceeded to grab his friend by the arm.

"Terry," Jay said. A blue-eyed teenager came to Jay's side. "Take this tray to table thirteen." Jay told her quickly. She nodded and took the tray immediately. He then turned to his wide-eyed friend. "What, Micah?"

"Please tell me what the hell is going on!" Micah exclaimed.

The servers around them who'd been busy readying their trays and drinks paused and stopped to look at the pair. Jay's face became serious and he searched his friend's eyes, concern seeping through every feature on his face.

"What do you mean? And lower your voice." Jay stood to full height and then looked around. He sighed and ran a hand down his face. "My office. Let's go kid."

Without hesitation, Micah shot off towards Jay's tiny cluttered office, leaving Jay in his trail of fire. Micah plopped down in the cushioned chair in front of Jay's desk, but then quickly stood back up and began pacing, nearly knocking the chair over in his haste. He wanted to sit down; he felt like he *should* sit down, but he couldn't. His mind was being pulled into too many directions. Again, this woman had managed to throw him into a tailspin.

"What's going on Micah?" Jay asked, he closed his office door behind him.

"I don't know. I don't know." Micah pulled the elastic band from his hair, freeing it from its ponytail and allowing it to immediately revert back to its wild natural state. He began pulling at his curls as his chest tightened and the anxiety began to set in.

Jay took a seat and watched his friend pace. He hadn't seen Micah this frantic before, not even when his parents died. When Micah's parents died depression set in, but it left quickly when he realized that he needed to stay functional for Rea. Yes, Micah grieved in his own way. Sometimes he became angry, seemingly for no reason at all, and sometimes when they hung out he drank a little too much and cried, but never this.

"Dreams," Micah whispered. "Her friend said that I looked like the guy from her dreams. She's been dreaming about me, just like I've been dreaming about her," Micah muttered.

Jay shrugged as he leaned forward, putting his elbows on the desk. "That's a good thing."

Micah stopped pacing and stared at Jay, his eyes wide.

"No, it's not a good thing Jay. Do you wanna know why this isn't a good thing?" He didn't wait for a response. "If she's dreaming about me then, that means that these dreams might mean something and if these dreams mean something Jay, that could change everything." He thought back to the dream he had of her while he was with Sheba, a mere few weeks ago. Was that his warning that she was about to enter his life? Was Esther responsible for making these dreams happen? *There's just no way… This doesn't make any sense...*

"Coincidence?" Jay asked again. He crossed his arms over his chest, staring at his friend. "Sit down, you're making me tired just looking at you."

"I can't. She's like…like a witch Jay. That's what she is. She's put some sort of spell on me. It's making me crazy."

"You and your dumb explanations," said Jay. "Listen, she's not a witch."

"How do you know? The name fits perfectly. Sounds like it belongs to some decrepit old lady with a bunch of cats! I'm waiting for the wart to appear on her nose."

"Sometimes I wonder about you. This clearly isn't about Esther, Micah." Jay stood to his feet, arms still tightly folded.

"Then what is it about? Please enlighten me, because it looks like she's been planting dreams of her in my head! She's dreaming about me, I'm dreaming about her…"

"I think that you're freaked out, because you're scared that all this God stuff might be real," Jay said. His voice was light, playful even.

"No, I'm not. This is not even about God," he argued. "That's the problem with you Christians! You always make it about your God. There's more to life than God!" Micah hissed.

Jay lifted his hands and took a step back. Rather than seeming afraid, Jay's demeanor took on a smugness that Micah found irritating. "It's not about God, huh?"

Silence.

"Look bro, I'm not trying to attack you. Stop being so defensive. You need to calm down. Maybe you should take the rest of the day off…" Micah placed his hands over his face and plopped down in a chair. "It could be a coincidence Micah, or it could be that God is using this girl to change your life. If I were you, I'd stop resisting." Jay waited for a response, but got none. "Wait, you're not on that stuff, are you?" Jay, looked into Micah's eyes carefully. What he was looking for, Micah wasn't sure of. Micah sucked his teeth in aggravation.

"Man, nah."

"Just checking. Stick to weed. C'mon, you go home, get some rest and think. I'll set Tabitha up with your table ok? Do you think you can at least take their food out without having a meltdown?" Micah nodded.

"That was the part where you deny that you ever had a breakdown. You know! Denial? Typical Micah behavior?" Jay paused briefly for a response. When he didn't receive it, he sighed. "Whatever, I'll come with you. You better be glad you're my friend, or I'd fire you," Jay said. "You need to get your life. I think it'd be good for you to take the next few days off to get your head together ok?" Micah simply nodded again. "C'mon."

"And you're sure you're not on drugs?" Jay asked as he put his arm around Micah's shoulders. Micah pushed him. Jay removed his arm and stumbled away from him. "Dang man, I was just asking," he said as he laughed.

Numbly, Micah followed him back out into the kitchen area. He was no longer frantic, as his anxiety had left him tired.

I don't understand this. Micah thought as he took the tray from the server's window. He put the necessary condiments and furnishings on the tray before following Jay and Tabitha out onto the floor. The moment he saw Esther again, his heart picked up the pace. With every step he took his heart rate increased. Micah held the tray while Tabitha issued the plates of food. He told her which plate belonged to which person, and when they were done, he tucked the tray under his arm.

"Micah here isn't feeling too well, so Tabitha is going to take over for him. Tabitha will take good care of you." Jay placed a hand on each server's shoulder respectively as he said their names.

"That stinks. I hope you feel better Micah," Fallon said. As if realizing that she might've offended the other server she looked at Tabitha and said, "No offence Tabitha." Tabitha smiled in response.

"I'm sorry you're not feeling well," Esther added. "Rain check on the friend outing?" She asked. Micah nodded stiffly.

"Yeah, rain check. Don't come up with an excuse to get out of it either." He half-heartedly joked. Jay squeezed his shoulder. "It was a pleasure serving you ladies. I'm going to get my things from the back," he said. "I'm sure I'll see you tonight Esther."

Micah didn't give her a chance to respond, and disappeared to the back and hung up his borrowed apron, as he'd forgotten his at home. He'd only made it to the front door of the restaurant when he heard Esther's voice calling out to him,

"Micah, wait!"

"What's up?" He asked. His eyebrows knitted together.

"I don't want to keep you, but I'm sorry for being so harsh towards you," she said. He raised an eyebrow and waved his hand, urging her to continue. "I can be a little judgmental at times."

"No kidding?"

"And weird."

"Do tell." Micah folded his arms.

"And self-righteous."

"Please go on."

Esther sighed gave him a withering look. "I'm trying to apologize here."

"No need. I know you're weird, judgmental, and self-righteous and rude—"

"Micah!" She slapped his arm playfully.

"I'm kidding. Esther you haven't done anything wrong. I know I'm not all that easy to deal with, you can ask Rea." Esther smiled reassuringly as he continued, "What brought this on?"

"Well, you asked me out on a friend date and I was kind of rude."

"Did Fallon put you up to this?" Micah asked as he pointed over at Esther's friend.

"Nope." She paused. "Well, kinda…"

"Why? I thought you hadn't decided if you liked me or not." He laughed.

"You're kind of growing on me like…fungus."

"Fungus?"

Esther thought about it for a moment and then nodded.

I'm growing on her? Boy has she got it backwards…

"Fungus," she said with a swift nod.

"I'm the sexiest fungus you've ever seen though, am I right?" He joked.

"That's so gross." She laughed. Micah looked down at his feet. Their banter nearly made him forget the reason he was trying to flee the diner. Nearly.

"Wanna make it up to me?" He asked.

"Depends on what I'd have to do," she said.

"Smart girl. I'll let you know."

Esther huffed and looked away as she shifted her weight from her right leg to her left.

"Listen, about what Fallon said…"

"Yes, let's talk about what Fallon said." *Be cool Micah.* "I knew you had a thing for me," he teased. *Keep it light, don't freak out.* She rolled her eyes. "Dreaming about the sinner boy. Isn't that a sin?" He continued.

"Someone's conceited. Don't pay Fallon any mind Micah."

He frowned. His jokes weren't getting any of the information he needed.

"So you didn't dream of me?"

She rubbed her arm. "Define dream?"

Micah rolled his eyes. "It's a yes or no question."

"Yes, I did." He took a deep breath at her response. "Why does it matter?" She asked. She stood up straight, that inner confidence began coming out. *Uh-oh psychic witchy prophetess mode…*

"It doesn't," Micah lied. She crossed her eyes and tilted her head to the side, studying him.

"You're lying. If it didn't bother you, you wouldn't be asking about it. Something is clearly bothering you," she murmured.

"Stop it," he ordered, taking a step back.

"Stop what?" Genuine confusion was etched upon her face. He sighed and let go of the door handle.

"That witchy mind-reading thing." He waved his hand at her as if shooing her away.

"Witchy mind-reading thing? First, I was a psychic, now I'm a witch? How original. Neither of those things are what I told you I was."

"You didn't tell me," he said off-handedly.

"I guess you're right. You figured it out," she admitted ducking her head. Micah shrugged.

"Even if something was bothering me Esther, why would I tell you?" She didn't respond, so he continued, "Didn't see that one coming did you?"

"Micah. You're the one who said we were friends and *friends*, look out for friends. *Friends*, can talk to each other. Here's my number." She slid a tiny piece of paper into his open hand. "If you need anything, I'm right next door but…just in case, you can call me."

"Right. Thanks." He held up the number between his pointer and middle fingers.

"And by the way, I didn't have to peep that in the Holy Ghost. It was written all over your face."

Micah smiled crookedly at her then placed a hand in his pocket.

"Peep that in the Holy Ghost huh?" He rubbed his chin with his free hand.

She nodded. "Go get some rest or something," she said.

Without warning, she threw her arms around him and brought him into a hug. He stepped backwards, startled. It took him a minute before he fully registered what was happening. He put a free arm around her waist. She pulled away from him and gave him a comforting smile. It was small, barely noticeable but still warmed his entire body.

She walked away from him, her curls bouncing as she went. He watched her take a seat next to her friends, who'd been staring at them unabashedly the whole time. He shook his head, then exhaled deeply. *Go home, think about it later.*

***

Micah stood, leaning against the railing of the balcony as he waited for Esther to come out. Rather than a bottle of beer, he held a bottle of water in his hand. He sat back in his chair, with his feet propped up on the balcony. Micah raised the bottle to his lips.

"Hi, friend." Esther's voice was chipper and pulled him from his thoughts.

"Hello…friend," he replied.

"Eiw you said that all creepy-like," she said, wrinkling her nose.

Micah laughed. "How was I supposed to say it?"

"I don't know, just not like that," she said as Micah sniggered. "No Sunny D tonight huh?"

Micah smirked, then took a sip of his water. "Nope, not in the mood."

"How are you?" She asked as she leaned against the railing.

Micah shrugged.

"I'm making it. You?"

"Same." She smiled. "Milkshakes were good. I left your tip with Jay." Micah quickly turned to face her.

"You did what? You didn't tip Tabby?"

Esther snorted.

"Of course I did, but you did some work too. I felt like you should have gotten some."

"Former server?"

"Is it obvious?" She asked with a laugh. He nodded and laughed as well.

"Yes. Very."

"Well, whatever." She waved him off with a flick of her wrist. "I'm technically still a server."

"Oh, so you know the struggle?"

"I know the struggle. Trust me." She smirked.

"Where do you work?" She turned her lips up at him.

"Why? So you can come stalk me at my job? No thank you."

Micah rolled his eyes and took another sip of water.

"Says the woman that showed up at *my* job today."

She shrugged her shoulders.

"I honestly didn't know," she said. "I didn't even suggest the place. Fallon did." Micah stood to his feet.

"She's the red-headed friend that doesn't hate me, as opposed to your other friend that hates my guts?"

Esther nodded. "That would be her."

Micah walked towards her. He put his water down on the floor, then grasped the railing with both hands.

"Why does your other friend hate me?" He asked.

"Emily doesn't hate you. She just doesn't like you. She doesn't like very many people."

"She likes you."

"We've been friends since we were three."

Micah nodded.

"Ah. I see." He said, drawing close enough to see her face.

Her hair was confined to a bun on top of her head, like the one that he himself was wearing. She was clad in a dark colored hoodie, the night wouldn't permit him to see the true color of it. Her tiny hands were gripping the railing, just as his were. She was smiling at him, clearly unbothered by the loose strands of hair that curled up around her face.

"Yeah. She's one of those kinds of people that you have to grow on. So, did you get some rest? You look better."

"Yeah I did. Listen, Esther, that dream you had about me—" Esther sighed.

"Micah, it's nothing. No big deal ok?"

"It's a big deal to me because you're not the only one who's having dreams."

Esther's eyes widened, her eyebrows shooting to her hairline.

"Woah there, what are you talking about?"

Now he understood why Esther didn't want to talk about it. His palms began to get sweaty as he took a deep breath.

"You're right we should leave this alone," he said.

Esther crossed her arms. As he watched her, the inner battle she was having was becoming more and more evident on her face. Her forehead creased and she placed a hand on her chin. Micah didn't know what he was afraid of. How bad could her reaction truly be?

"We're always stuck at an impasse when we're on this balcony. You know that?" She asked. He nodded and scratched his head.

"You're right. We usually are."

"Did everything work out with Rea?" Micah nodded and looked down.

"I think so."

"Good. From what I can see, she's a pretty cool person. You should invite her out to the balcony with you sometime."

He nodded.

"I'll think about it. She's usually in bed around this time."

"It's only like, ten o'clock."

"I know. I think it's because when she was little, I used to tell her that if she didn't get enough beauty rest, she'd be ugly when she woke up."

"You're such a jerk." She laughed.

"I own that."

"Hey, did you take a look at the paper I gave you?" She asked.

"Nope."

"Ok."

"That's all you're going to say?" She stood up straight and stretched.

"Yeah. You're grown, I can't make you do anything and I just gave it to you like…last night. You have a life, I'm sure." Micah's phone began vibrating in his pocket. He pulled his phone out. Sheba's name and face flashed across the screen. "In fact, I'm positive that you do." Esther murmured.

"I don't have to answer it right now. I'm sure it's not important," Micah said as he declined the call.

"No, you should answer. Call her back. You never know."

"Nah. I'm good."

Esther nodded.

"Ok..."

"Are you going to ever tell me what happened with you guys?"

"I already told you, I didn't do anything to her," Esther said nonchalantly.

Micah put both hands in his pockets and looked around.

"Ok then, what did she do to you?" Esther smiled and Micah's smug grin appeared.. "I see. Ok yeah, I definitely asked the right question."

"Yeah, you did," Esther said as she folded her arms. "We go back a few years. She was my friend in high school. When I first moved here to go college, we were roommates. And suddenly, everything kind of changed. Sheba kind of came off as this super spiritual person that I kind of viewed as an accountability partner. You know, she had my back in the spirit."

"I actually don't know, but please continue."

She rolled her eyes at his sarcastic tone but continued, "I did everything I could to help her. I overextended my resources, time, and energy for this girl. She screwed me over in the end." She looked down at her feet. "I've forgiven her for it. Had to."

"When you say she screwed you over…"

"I mean that the first chance she got she threw me under the bus, ruined a couple of relationships I had in the church and tried to drag my reputation through the mud. I soon became known as the church *thot*." She sighed.

"I have a question," he said.

She nodded, giving him permission to continue.

"Were you a thot?" Micah asked. He'd meant for her to laugh at the joke, and she did. Her mouth flew open.

"Do I look like a thot to you?" She asked incredulously.

"You know what they say 'bout them church girls."

Micah immediately felt a pang of correction. *Ughhh*, he thought in disgust.

"Sorry," he said begrudgingly.

Esther waved him off without another thought.

"Don't apologize. Even if I was a thot, I wouldn't tell you."

Micah stuck out his bottom lip and pouted.

"Why not?"

"Because that's none of your business."

They both erupted in laughter. Soon the laughter died down, leaving them in a comfortable silence.

"I'm guessing you guys are pretty close huh?" Esther said finally.

"If you call sleeping together being close then, yes," Micah said with a shrug.

Esther nodded. "Just be careful ok?"

"I think we're about done anyway," he said. "How long ago did you say this happened?"

"About three years ago."

Three years ago? Micah's entire body tensed as his mind raced with possibilities. He folded his hands in front of him, and kept his gaze centered on them. Without looking up at her, he asked, "How old are you?"

"Twenty-one, I'll be twenty-two in November," she said, picking at a piece of lint on her pants.

"So you're a senior."

"Yeah."

"I am too."

Esther tilted her head to the side and pursed her lips.

"Um…that's great."

"I was with Sheba about three years ago, we only recently broke up…like a year ago."

"Are you telling me that you were involved in that whole mess?" Micah shrugged his shoulders.

"I don't remember hearing anything about it, but if what you say is true, I'm like the third guy in this equation. She never mentioned you. Like I said, I didn't realize that she was actually a Christian. My best friend claims that she's been going to his church for a long time."

"That's good," Esther whispered. "Maybe things have changed."

Micah's eyes, wide and alarmed bore into Esther's. He shook his head quickly.

"No. *No*, they haven't. The sad part is that I believe all of this. Before you say anything, I know you're not trying to set her up to look bad. I've *been* knowing that the girl had issues."

"Amazing what sex can blind you to, huh?" Esther said softly.

Micah shrugged.

"I don't know that I'd say that it blinded me. Dating her was like hell on earth towards the end though. Now we just screw for the fun of it. No strings attached."

"Except the ones that she attached to you," Esther murmured.

Micah's eyebrows once again, threaded together in confusion. Micah's phone buzzed.

"Ever heard of a soul tie?" Esther asked as he checked his phone.

Micah declined the phone call.

"Listen to me Micah, I'm not judging you. I'm just telling you, as your friend, be careful."

"Noted," Micah said with a nod.

"Alright, enough of this heavy talk. I have to get my beauty rest, don't want to be late for Sunday school. I'm teaching."

"Wait, you teach Sunday school? Of course you do. Why not?" Micah took down his bun.

Esther nodded, her face lighting up slightly at the mention of teaching.

"I'm actually filling in for someone. I have the middle school group."

"How unfortunate."

Esther laughed loudly; it took her a moment to catch her breath.

"No. It's actually fun," she said finally.

"If you say so," he said with a sly smile.

"And I do. Goodnight, Micah." She gave him one last coy smile before making her way back into her apartment.

"Night, Ess."

SEVEN

Micah didn't know that he could stand to look at himself in the mirror on top of his dresser but he had to; he had to straighten his tie. The last time he'd been staring into the dresser mirror, looking this nervous, his life had changed forever. He'd become an orphan.

"Rea! Are you almost ready?!" He exclaimed.

She poked her head into his bed room, fully dressed but clearly not ready. Her hair was half flat ironed. The other half was a curly mess. He laughed at her appearance. Rea's presence was enough to gain the courage he needed to look into the mirror. Micah straightened his tie quickly and pulled his hair into a bun on the top of his head.

"Do I look ready?" She asked.

He shook his head as he admired her sweetly.

"You look like her," he whispered.

"Mom?" Rea asked, her angelic face darkening with sadness. She wasn't a child anymore, but her soft eyes and round face, often made her appear younger than she actually was.

"Yeah. You look just like her," he said softly, his eyes moistening.

"Thanks," she whispered, her tear-filled eyes mirroring Micah's own.

Micah held up both of his hands, "No, thank *you*."

"Are you alright?" She asked him.

His furrowed his eyebrows.

"I'm fine," he said. "Just thinking about mom, why?"

Rea shrugged, disbelief was apparent on her face. "I don't know. I just feel like something's going on with you."

He emitted a nervous chuckle. "Is this your prophetess thingy kicking in?" He expected her to roll her eyes again or sass him back, but she just stared at him instead.

"Maybe," she murmured.

His face hardened. All signs of his earlier playfulness, gone.

"God told you something is wrong with me?"

She didn't respond.

There was a heavy silence that passed between them. He'd hoped that they were past this point, that she was moving past this new idea of being a prophet. Why couldn't this God just leave him alone? Why was God so interested in him? Better yet, why was everyone so interested in this "spirituality"?

"How about you tell God to mind His own business?"

"You are His business."

"No. I'm not. I come to church on Sunday, I pay tithes to the church—"

"Not all the time."

How would she know that?

"How do you—It doesn't matter. I uphold my end of the bargain. He needs to stay out of my head, out of my wallet, and out of my business!"

Rea opened her mouth to say something, but thought better of it. As she left the room he heard her murmur, "Why would He uphold a bargain that He never agreed to?"

It happened almost too fast for his own mind to comprehend. He grabbed the first thing in reach and threw it at the wall. Satisfaction began to set in as he saw the webbed crack in the plaster. Neither said a word.

The ride to church was quiet; the silence, deafening. He was positive that he'd hurt her feelings. Rea looked out of the window the whole ride, no sarcastic comments or jokes. *Damn.* Micah thought.

They'd never fought this much before. He now had another thing to thank God for.

When they arrived, he took his usual seat towards the back and bent over at the waist, resting his elbows on his knees, waiting for service to start.

"Hey."

Micah didn't look up at the sound of the female voice. *Maybe if I ignore it, it'll go away,* he thought spitefully.

"Remember me?" The voice continued, "Crystal?"

He turned his head slowly, to see the girl had taken a seat next to him. *Go away.* He almost felt bad for the girl. *Almost.* It wasn't her fault he was in a bad mood, but she didn't seem like she was able to take social cues very well. If she were able to, she would have realized that he didn't want to be bothered.

"Yes, I remember you."

"I figured out where I know you from," she chirped.

Inwardly, Micah rolled his eyes.

"And where is that?" He asked, sitting up.

"You dated Sheba McGruer."

What?

"What?" He asked monotonously.

"Yeah, you dated Sheba. She's one of my good friends. We met this one time at a party." Her head bobbed excitedly as she talked.

"Oh." There was an awkward silence. He knew he was going to regret his question but he asked it anyway, "Is that all you wanted?"

She looked thoughtful for a minute. *If you didn't know what you came over here, then you shouldn't have come over here, and why the hell are you asking me about my ex?* Micah thought disdainfully.

"I think, I just wanted to talk to you," she said. As she spoke to him, he could feel his face contorting.

Is she trying to hit on me?

"Wanted to talk to me?" He asked.

She batted her eyelashes.

Yep. She's hitting on me.

"Yeah. I really like you Micah," she stated honestly. "And, I think you're cute."

Forget hitting on me, this girl is kick-boxing.

"Well, thank you."

"That was really forward wasn't it?" She gushed, blushing.

"Kind of," he replied, an annoyed expression settling on his face.

"I'm sorry."

Micah shrugged his shoulders. "No big deal. It's just my mind is someplace else," he admitted.

Crystal nodded. "I understand that feeling."

Micah eyed her skeptically. *Do you really?*

"Wanna know what that girl said to me that night?" Her eagerness returned.

In his mind, Micah rolled his eyes again.

"What girl? What night?" He asked tiredly.

"That one service I went with you to two weeks ago, when that girl from our school came to speak."

"Esther?"

"Yeah, that's the one. Wanna hear what she said?"

No. Well kind of. I guess it would be interesting to hear what other 'words' she gave to people. I wonder who else's life she's screwed up.

"Sure," he conceded.

"She told me to write the vision. She told me that I needed to record my dreams and ask God about their meaning. I dream a lot you know." She sat up straight, seemingly proud of herself for having caught his attention.

"Do you?" He asked, suddenly interested.

Alright. I'll play along.

Crystal nodded.

"And has He—God—been giving them to you?"

"Yes, He has. It's amazing really. I'm like Joseph or something…or Josephina…or Josephine…or—"

"You interpret dreams?" He interrupted. She nodded. *Hm, maybe she might be good for something.*

"Well, God does," she amended.

Of course, He's always taking the credit for something. Micah thought cynically. He turned to face her.

"Why? Got some dreams?"

Micah nodded once. "You could say that."

"Lay it on me," she said. The deacons stood and began a chorus of "Walk with me Lord." Crystal groaned quietly. "Well, maybe later. My brother and I are going out to eat after church, wanna come? We could talk about it then?"

Brother? He wasn't so sure he wanted to share his dreams with random people. He barely trusted Crystal. He *was* curious though, he just wanted to see what she would say.

"Sure. Rea and I would love to come."

Crystal's face lit up.

"Ok great, just meet me back here after church and we'll go."

"Great."

What am I about to walk into?

During service Micah could barely keep still. His eyes were darting around the sanctuary and his hands were clasped so tightly together in his lap that his knuckles were turning white. He tried not to focus on how dead the church was. He couldn't understand why Rea loved it so much. Maybe it wasn't the church. Maybe it was simply the idea of coming to church? Maybe it was her friends…

He listened as the choir sang the words to "Glad to be in God's Service One More Time" and found himself annoyed with them for singing it for various reasons. For starters, different individuals were singing in different keys. Then, there was also the fact that *none* of them looked like they were glad to be this service.

Bunch of liars. All of y'all are going to hell for lying in church. He thought it was funny. Esther would have probably laughed at it too. He couldn't imagine her going to a church like this. The youth from his church had been so on fire when they saw Esther at Stephanie's church, but as he looked around seeing them huddled together in the pews in one area of the large church, he was disheartened. *Fairytales don't last.* He reasoned.

The preacher preached to the best of his ability. He hooped and hollered, he broke down the Hebrew and Greek meanings of words and phrases, but Micah couldn't stay focused. What was Crystal going to say when she heard his dreams? Should he even be telling her? Maybe he should've talked to Esther first. He pulled out his cell phone and scrolled down his contacts list.

His thumb hovered over the message button. Should he text her? What if it wasn't even her number? What if it was the number to the rejection hotline? It would be childish yes, but it would serve him right. He used to give out that number to the girls who'd been bold enough to approach him, and those who, instead of giving him their number, asked for his. He thought it was funny. In his mind, it still was. Suppose it was her number, would she even respond? How quickly should he respond after she texted him back? He didn't want to look thirsty.

This is dumb. She gave me her number, why wouldn't she respond?

It was simple with Sheba; every time he saw her there was one goal in mind. Esther, wasn't like Sheba and although the goal was on his mind constantly, he could it push to back burner when he was in her presence. She didn't exactly give him a choice. When they were around each other, he didn't have time to let his mind wander--they were always engaged in some sort of interesting conversation.

"And one day y'all, I just got tired of running," the preacher said. He was a tall, graying man with a beer belly that Micah believed was evidence of his "sinning days".

It's obvious that you haven't been running anywhere lately buddy.

Micah smirked. The preacher looked nice enough and seemed kind-hearted, but Micah wasn't fooled. Given that he'd known the old man for a while, Micah had come to form a pretty solid opinion of him. That opinion could be summarized in one word--hypocrite.

Micah's gaze kept flickering to Crystal, watching as she wrote in her journal and hung on the Pastor's every word. When he'd been thoroughly sickened by Crystal's attentiveness, he looked away. His eyes landed on a woman on the front row--Ms. Mayes. His stomach turned as he remembered overhearing a conversation that he wasn't supposed to have heard between her and the Pastor. How cliché of them--a pastor and a member of his beloved congregation having an affair.

And that right there is why I hate coming to church, bunch of damn hypocrites.

"Jesus offers salvation, but there is a place for those who won't accept His free gift," the preacher continued. *Yeah buddy, I'm sure there is a place for you too. I'd probably get in to Heaven before you do, just by being honest.*

The service seemed to drag on for hours. Micah was bored and was desperate for a distraction He took to looking at the ostentatious hats that church members wore and mocking them. After he'd finished ranking them in terms of stupidity, he began making correlations between the members and characters from some of Dr. Seuss' books.

God might be good after all. Micah thought as the service came to a close. When service ended, he stood to his feet and stretched, issuing out tight smiles to the people that greeted him. He put his hands in his pockets and when his fingers brushed against his cell phone, he made a split decision.

`Hey. It’s Micah. -Micah`

Almost immediately after he sent the text, his phone buzzed.

`Hey Micah, got you saved now (: -Esther`

A small smile graced his lips. *I have Esther Wicker’s phone number saved in my phone.*

“Micah.”

He placed his phone in his pocket before he answered his younger sister, “Yeah?”

“Can I go with Mallory to dinner today?” She asked this question often, and he always agreed, but today was different. He needed Rea there with him. Even though they’d had a falling out earlier, she was still his baby sister and having her present alleviated a lot of his stress.

“Not today. We are going to dinner with Crystal.” She wrinkled her nose in distaste.

“Crystal?” Micah raised his eyebrows at her reaction. He hadn’t expected that from her.

“Yes, Crystal.”

“Why?” She asked, folding her arms.

"Micah has some questions." Crystal's voice startled them both. "I'm more than happy to answer them," she said as she smiled at Micah. She was standing a little too close to him, her brother, Cody, stood on the other side of him.

"Why don't you just talk to Esther? I know you talk to her anyways. I ask her questions all the time," Rea suggested, she froze, then covered her mouth quickly with her hand. With his eyebrow raised, Micah opened his mouth to question her but Crystal beat him to it.

"You talk to her?" Crystal asked. Her face was incredulous.

"And how do you know we talked?" Micah added.

"It's not like I call her all the time or anything. I just called her once, and we talked. We're neighbors remember? I hear you guys out there on the balcony sometimes when you think I'm asleep. At least I hear *you* laughing," Rea said with a shrug. Micah's disbelieving eyes bore into his younger sister as he tried to form a coherent question.

"Is she super deep outside of church?" Cody asked.

Rea shrugged.

"*I* don't think so. I think she's actually pretty funny. Anyways, where are we going to eat?" Rea said digging in her cross-body bag.

"Applebee's sounds good," Cody said nonchalantly. Micah nodded. He didn't care, he wasn't even hungry. He just wanted answers.

“Sounds cool,” Micah said.

“So it’s settled then,” Crystal mused.

They parted ways after agreeing to go straight to the restaurant rather than going home to change clothes. Micah supported his head on his hand, as his elbow rested on the door of his car. The windows were down as they drove, one of his favorite rappers was blaring from his speakers. Micah sang along loudly to “RGF Island.”

“Really, Micah?” Rea reached over and turned the music off. “We just left church.”

“You know, if you read between the lyrics this could qualify as a church song.”

“I am not entertaining this,” she said, refusing to look up from her cellphone.

“No, just hear me out. You know, when you die you can’t take any money or anything with you. He’s telling the truth.”

“Shut up, Micah.”

“Ok.”

Silence. Awkward silence. He glanced at her from the corner of his eye then sat up straight, both hands gripping the wheel.

“I’m sorry about this morning,” he said finally. “I didn’t mean to snap at you. I was frustrated."

Rea shook her head.

"Don't worry about it." She glanced at her phone and began typing out a text message. Feeling slightly relieved, he nudged his sister with one hand.

"Who are you texting? Your boyfriend?" He smirked.

Rea stuck her tongue out at him, before responding snarkily with, "Wouldn't you like to know?"

Better not be.

They arrived at the restaurant laughing at each other. The moment he saw Crystal and Cody in the waiting area, his playful demeanor dissipated. He then remembered why he was there and the cloud of confusion returned.

"Hey," Rea said as she linked her arm with his chiseled one. "It's going to be fine." He patted her hand on his arm and led her inside. After they were seated, Micah kept his eyes trained on the door. Questions were forming and then falling apart in his mind. He didn't even know where to begin.

"So tell me about your dream," Crystal said. Micah tore his eyes away from the door to meet her sapphire eyes. *Here goes nothing.*

He told her almost everything. He told her multiple dreams, leaving out the identity of the woman he'd been so enamored with in his dream. He even shared his dreams about Jay. Crystal and Cody listened intently. Rea maintained a smug look throughout his narrative, almost as if she knew something that everyone else didn't.

"Did you know who the girl was?" Crystal asked.

Yes.

"No," Micah said.

"Hm." She pursed her lips. "She could be your future wife." Crystal cringed at the word "wife."

Wife? Esther, my wife? Micah shook his head. *Nah.* She was cute, but not that cute.

"I don't think that's possible. She didn't seem like the type to be interested in me," he admitted. He began fiddling with the napkin and eventually began tearing it up into tiny pieces. Crystal raised her eyebrow.

"Why is that? How would you know?" Micah sighed.

Time to come clean.

"Because, I do know her. I said I didn't, but I mean…" Micah sighed. "I've seen her around a few times but I don't really *know* her. We're cool. I hadn't even spoken to her when I started having these dreams."

"Not all dreams are from God," Cody interjected. "Some dreams are just created by our subconscious. Do you find her attractive?"

Hell. Yes.

"Kinda, but I didn't even know who she wasn't til a few years after I had the dream, like four years after," he admitted. She was more than attractive to him. She was mentally stimulating and beautiful. She was slightly insane, possibly schizophrenic, but still beautiful. Cody shrugged.

"You could have created some subconscious dreams; however, I don't believe that's what these are Micah," said Cody. "I personally, would ask God and not my sister. No offense, Crystal."

Yeah, see, I don't make it a habit of talking to myself.

"None taken. He's right, Micah. I think I'll stand by what I told you earlier, she could be your future wife or someone that will turn out to be very special in your life." Micah leaned forward on his arms, disappointed.

I was expecting some sort of spiritual juju. I want answers, not possibilities.

Everyone jumped at the sound of the server's voice. No one had noticed her approaching.

"What can I get you to drink?" She asked.

Micah grimaced.

"I'm not thirsty. Thanks."

The dinner didn't last very long. After talking about the dream, they struggled to find genuine topics of conversation. Rea saved the day by stating that she had homework that she needed to do. Micah was more than happy to take that ticket out of there.

"Feel accomplished?" Rea asked. She turned the radio down in the car as they headed back to their apartment. Micah snorted.

"Not even a little bit."

"I think we need a brother and sister day. We haven't talked in a while. How about you take off work and don't go to class and I don't go to school and…." Micah stared at her, wide-eyed in disbelief.

"Um...you're going to school. I can sense the trickery from a mile away."

Rea tried to hold back her laughter, but failed as she replied, "Pft. You can sense the trickery…"

Micah pulled into the parking lot just as Esther was getting out of the car. She wasn't paying attention to them, as she was talking to someone. Micah recognized him immediately as the guy that he'd seen with the boxes the other day—*Tobias...Trae….Thomas! That's it.*

Esther spoke to Thomas as he got out of the car. "That's crazy," she said laughing. "Why in the world would you want to do that?"

"I dunno," Thomas said with a shrug. As Esther made her way to the trunk of her car, Micah's eyes briefly traveled from her smiling face, down her body, and to the high heels she had on. He caught Rea's eyes for a split second, and he saw Rea's knowing smirk.

"Hm," Rea said.

"Don't say it," he warned. She nodded.

"Just get over there already, and profess your undying love to her ok?" Micah glared at his younger sister.

"Oh please, I barely like her."

"Right…" Rea opened her door, drawing Esther and Thomas' attention. Esther waved happily when she saw Rea and darted over to hug her. Micah observed the scene with awe. Esther's excitement upon seeing Rea was genuine.

"Hi, neighbor," Esther greeted.

"Hey!" Rea said. "I like your outfit," Rea said, referring to Esther's yellow dress and white shrug. It made her look young, as it was tight about the bodice and flowed out from there. It stopped just a little bit above her knees. He liked the dress too, the color was an excellent match for her skin. She was glowing.

"Thanks, Rea. I like your skirt." Rea twirled around in her long indigo skirt.

"You know I try," she said flipping her hair.

"Well slay then!" Esther said as she snapped her fingers. Both girls laughed. "You've gotta come over for dinner soon, ok? I just went grocery shopping today."

"Absolutely. But right now, I'm going to head on up. I have a lot of homework to do," Rea said, casting a mischievous glance at Micah.

"Alright, see you later!" As his sister began walking up the stairs, Micah opened his car door.

"Hey, stranger," Esther said with a wave. Micah flashed a smile at her and locked his car doors.

"Hey, Esther. Hey, Thomas," Micah greeted.

"Good to see you again, Michael."

"It's Micah," Micah corrected. "But you knew that."

"Sorry," Micah shrugged.

"You guys know each other?" Esther asked as she put a hand on both Micah and Thomas' arms.

"We met briefly before you moved in. He offered to help me carry some boxes upstairs," Thomas said. Esther nodded in understanding.

Micah could feel her eyes on him, but he refused to look at her. Something about Thomas made him uncomfortable. Was it how closely he was standing next to her? Was it the way he'd made her laugh when she was getting out of the car? Was it the fact that wherever she'd just come from, she'd been there with him? In reality, Micah had no reason to be jealous. He had no right to be--they were barely friends. Maybe it was the fact that Thomas was her type that irked him. The silver cross around his neck and the Bible in his left hand gave it away.

Thomas put an arm around Esther's shoulders. A scowl appeared on Micha's face instantly, but he quickly schooled his features as he tried to talk himself down from the irrational annoyance and anger he was feeling.

"Where are you guys just getting in from?" He asked. His eyes traveled over Esther's body again, his eyes pausing at her legs. Thomas cleared his throat. When Micah looked up at him, Thomas gave him a pointed look. Micah rolled his eyes, *Hypocrite. It's not like he's never looked before.*

"Church," Esther said.

"Oh, you guys go to the same church?" Micah asked.

"Yeah. You should come some time," Thomas said. "Probably need to." He murmured the last bit to himself, but Micah heard it, and if Esther heard it as well, she didn't react.

"Excuse me?" Micah asked.

"I said that you should come visit sometime. It's a nice little church." Micah nodded and bit the inside of his cheek. It seemed that Thomas had a thing for Esther too, and if Micah maintained his distance they could be cool. Unfortunately for Thomas, Micah didn't care about the prospect of friendship between them. His eyes were on the P.Y.T in the yellow dress. He knew that he didn't stand a chance against a *Man of God.* Micah snorted. The snort was in response to both his own thought, and Thomas' invitation.

"Doubtful," Micah sneered. Esther hit his shoulder lightly.

"Be nice," she reprimanded. Micah shrugged. "Thomas is visiting. He doesn't live here, but he wanted to see how I was settling in." Esther said. Micah nodded.

"So, he's leaving?"

"Micah!" Esther exclaimed, her doe-eyes, which had widened in mortification reflected her horror.

Micah shrugged unperturbed, with pursed lips.

"I am leaving," Thomas admitted pushing his hands down into his pockets. "But I visit often," he finished smugly. He looked up at Micah and smirked at him, as Esther checked her cell phone.

"I invited Rea over for dinner sometime, you should come too," Esther said, putting her cell phone back into her purse.

"Umm...yeah, sure," Micah said, staring back at Thomas.

Oh he might catch these hands before he leaves town. Micah thought angrily.

"It would be nice to have a conversation from somewhere else besides the balcony," Esther teased.

Thomas looked between the two of them and then cleared his throat. “Speaking of dinner. I’m hungry,” he said.

“Sorry, Thomas.” Esther said as she darted around to her open trunk and pulled out some grocery bags. “That’s what your problem is, you’re hangry.”

“That’s his only problem?” Micah muttered.

“What was that?” Thomas asked, taking a step forward.

“You gonna help her with those grocery bags? *Man?*” Now, it was Micah’s turn to smirk. Getting under Thomas’ skin was proving to be a lot more fun than he realized. See you later, Ess. Nice seeing you again, Timothy.”

Thomas narrowed his eyes. “It’s Thomas.” He paused, then chuckled darkly. “You’ll be seeing more of me. I’m sure.” Thomas turned on his heel and walked over to help Esther with the rest of the grocery bags.

“Right.”

Micah kept his tone sharp and didn’t give Esther the chance to really respond. The last thing he wanted was for Thomas to see him sweat. Micah walked away from the pair, being careful to take light and nonchalant steps. As he walked, he heard Esther questioning Thomas about his behavior. Micah wanted to stay and hear more of what was being said, but he didn’t want to stir up any more trouble. When he got to the top of the stairs, Rea was waiting for him with her arms folded and a smirk on her face.

"I know what you're thinking," Rea said. "And that's not bae." Micah put an arm around her shoulders and herded her inside the apartment.

"What, did God tell you that?" He asked with a small smirk.

"If I say yes, are you going to throw another hair brush?" He looked down.

"Listen, I really am sorry. Lately it's just been--it doesn't matter. There's no excuse." Rea walked to the couch and sat down. She patted the spot next to her and waved him over.

"Come sit on my couch and talk to me."

"What are you my therapist now?"

"Dr. Williams at your service." Micah took a seat on the opposite end of the couch, took his shoes off and placed his feet in her lap. "Eiw," was her only response.

"My feet don't stink," he protested. Rea held up a hand to stop him.

"What seems to be the problem?" She asked as she leaned back against the couch cushions.

"I have Bible bangers in my face, a very hot psychic as my neighbor who, by the way happens to proudly profess being a Bible banger, and as if that wasn't enough, she's the girl I've been dreaming about for the past four years."

"What?" Rea sat up immediately, incredulity blanketing her face.

"You heard me. I dreamed about her four years ago. She started to appear in my dreams again recently, and then she appears at the stupid little service thing the other night." Rea's mouth was agape as she stared at her brother.

"No wonder you've been so on edge."

Micah threw his hands up in the air.

"Thank you!" He exclaimed, relieved.

"So, she's like the girl of your dreams and the bane of your existence as a fraudulent atheist, all at the same time," she said, rolling her wrist.

"Fraudulent atheist? What the hell is that?"

"Someone who says they're an atheist but aren't really, but I'm going to leave that alone." Micah glared at her. She returned his glare with a smile.

"Anyway, please continue."

"She's hot."

"You've said that."

"She's funny, and strong, and she reads!"

Micah could feel Rea's judgement as she stared at him.

"Sheba doesn't read?"

Micah sat up abruptly. "How do you know about Sheba?"

Rea shrugged. "I've *been* knowing about her. I've known about her since you guys started dating Micah. I had a theory that you two were still messing around but you didn't confirm it until just now." She paused for a moment and put her finger on her chin, in a thoughtful manner. "Well, and the other night. So, thanks for that. I definitely saw her holding your hand the other night and boy did you look mad." She chuckled.

He frowned. Well, that wasn't good. Rea wasn't five anymore--he knew that. She didn't need to be protected from his life and it wasn't like he was truly doing anything really bad--he also knew that. Still, he wanted to keep her as far away from potential trouble as possible. Sheba was potential trouble. Sheba was *sure* trouble. By acknowledging this, he was forced to answer a newly formed question: Why did he keep messing with her if he knew that she was dangerous? If he knew that she could cause problems in his life, why would he continue to put himself in that predicament?

"Hello? Micah, you still in there?" Rea asked as she snapped her fingers in front of his face.

He shook his head back and forth, trying to bring himself back to the present.

"Y-yeah. I'm here."

"I'm not judging you if that's what you're worried about." Rea sat back against the couch cushions.

"I'm not," he murmured as he shook his head.

"Alright. You said she reads? What do you mean?"

"She was reading *Othello*."

"Oooh I have to read that for my literature class in school." Rea scrunched up her face in disgust and stuck her tongue out. "Sucks."

"Well, she loves it. She reads it for fun." Rea's jade eyes grew wide with excitement.

"Maybe she can help me."

"I don't know that that's a good idea," he said.

"And why not? Scared she's gonna brainwash me?" Rea sighed.

"More or less," Micah said, shrugging.

"Wait, you want to be around her but I can't?" Rea put her hand on her hip. "Micah, based on what I've been studying, a prophet is not a fortune teller. Sometimes they tell you things that you don't know, but most of the time it's just confirmation," she paused, her eyes roaming her brother's face. Whatever she was looking for she didn't find, as with another exasperated sigh she continued, "She doesn't read—*we* don't read—palms or anything like that. Everything she told me, I already knew."

Micah listened carefully to what Rea was saying. It took him a moment to realize that she wasn't fussing at him. He weighed his possible responses carefully. Before him was an opportunity to have a real conversation with her, not just an argument.

"I just needed some confirmation. She gave me what I needed, actually God, gave me what I needed. There's nothing you can do to stop this Micah, I'm sorry. Go pray the serenity prayer or something, 'cos this is out of your control fam."

EIGHT

`Gold. -Esther`

`Gold isn't a color. :P-Micah`

Micah snorted at her response.

`Yes, it is. -Esther`

He could imagine her being completely straight faced as she responded it to his comments.

`We still on for 7:30?- Micah`

Micah bit his lip as he put his phone back into his apron pocket. It had been four days since he'd had his break down at work, and his talk with Rea. His strategy had been to block everything out altogether--it wasn't working. During the day, he could push it to the back of his mind. At night, well that was a different story. He could hear Esther and Thomas laughing through the open balcony doors. So instead of going outside he sat on his couch, sour-faced, angry, and annoyed with the world as per usual.

The more Micah thought about Esther and Thomas, the more his skin began to crawl. He turned his thoughts toward a more pressing matter: his recent dreams. These dreams, weren't of Esther. They were dreams of his own death. In the dream from the night before, he'd seen himself laying in a casket. Esther was holding his weeping sister and Jay was standing by their side with his head bowed and tears rolling down his cheeks. These dreams would wake him up in the middle of the night and when he went to wipe his face he found that the moisture wasn't coming from his forehead, but from his eyes. He was crying. He'd been texting Esther since the second night he'd dreamed of this, hoping that building a relationship with her would be somewhat of a distraction. It was, until night time when he heard them laughing. She'd invited him to come over and hang out with them, but he wasn't interested in being in Thomas' presence. Esther probably already knew that he couldn't stand Thomas. Anyone could see that.

Of course. Am I driving or you?-Esther

We can ride together. -Micah

He followed up with the winking emoji and waited for her response.

Be there on time, friend…make a good impression. -Esther

As if he could be late picking up the girl who lived in the apartment next to him.

He rolled his eyes and put his phone away again. He busied

himself with rolling silverware while he waited for Jay to come out of his office. He'd barely said a word to Micah all day. Micah wondered if it was their last encounter that made him so stand-offish. He seemed more on edge, cracking down on other workers, yelling at them for small mistakes. After finishing his last set of silverware and clocking out, he went to Jay's office door and knocked.

"Hey Jay, I'm leaving," he said loudly.

"Bye."

Confused by Jay's frigid response, Micah opened the door and walked inside. Jay was on the phone, arguing with someone in a hushed tone.

"I just need a few more days…no you don't understand…." Jay's wild and frightened eyes met Micah's questioning ones. Jay cursed, something he seldom did, and slammed his cell-phone on the desk. Whoever he'd been talking to had hung up on him.

"Jay, what's going on?" Micah asked as he took a seat in the chair in front of Jay's desk. Jay shook his head back and forth furiously.

"Nothing."

Micah shot him an exasperated look.

"Nothing? Do you really expect me to believe that?"

Jay sighed and stood up from his desk. He walked over to the door and peeked out to see if anyone was around. When he was satisfied with his search, he shut the door and locked it.

"You remember Dupes?" Jay said.

Dupes…Dupes…Do I know a Dupes? Finally, it clicked.

"Shawn Dupes?" Micah asked. "The drug dealer?" Micah's eyes grew wide. He didn't like where this was going.

"Yeah. That's him. Well, I owe him some money," Jay confessed. Micah leaned forward in his chair, his eyes cautiously watching his friend.

"Is that why you went missing the other day?"

"Yes, I was trying to lay low."

"How much?"

"What?"

"How much money do you owe him Jay?"

Jay sighed. "Twenty-five thousand dollars…"

"For what?! Jay what did you do?" Micah yelled. He'd seen several people meet their end on account of their debt to Shawn Dupes.

"I got into a bit of gambling…"

"You have lost your damn mind," he hissed. "Gambling with Shawn Dupes…Oh my god!"

"I know. I know. I don't know what I was thinking," Jay said, rubbing his hands over his face.

Micah placed his hands on his hips and stood to his feet.

"Nothing! That's what you were thinking." Micah paced back and forth, rolling possibility after possibility around in his mind. If Jay didn't come up with that money, there would be a funeral soon.

"When do you need the money by?" Micah asked.

"Tomorrow."

All Micah could do was stare at him. No sounds were made, neither of them seemed to be breathing. Micah's face was contorted into a disbelieving expression--eyes wide, eyebrows raised, and mouth agape.

"I'll go to the bank in the morning," Micah said.

"No," Jay interrupted. "I have it covered."

Micah scoffed.

"Didn't sound like it to me."

Jay narrowed his eyes. "I've got it covered."

Again Micah, was rendered speechless.

"What are you gonna say? The *lawd* is my shepherd? The *lawd* will make a way somehow? Screw all of that. You don't have twenty-five thousand dollars! Even your genie in a bottle god, can't get you that much in a day."

"Micah--"

"It's already eight o'clock at night!"

"Micah--"

"You're going to get yourself killed. You've got a family Jay."

"Don't you think I know that!" Jay exclaimed. "I know what's at stake here Micah! Trust me when I say that I've got this." They glared at one another.

"Fine. First sign of trouble, you call me," Micah said. Jay nodded. Micah didn't believe that he really would call him, but he had to at least put forth the effort to trust his friend. "Shake on it," Micah commanded. Jay agreed.

"Be safe going home Micah," he said softly. Micah nodded in response.

"No, *you* be safe. See you later?"

"Yeah."

Without another word, Micah turned and walked out of Jay's office. As he got into his car, his phone rang. He answered the call through the Bluetooth system of his car.

"Hello?" He said as he began backing out of the parking lot.

"Micah?" At the sound of her voice, he felt as if his heart had stopped.

“Esther, hi,” he gushed.

“Hi,” she said. Esther chuckled softly.

“What’s up?” He asked. She exhaled loudly as she answered him.

“Well, it’s nothing serious. I just needed somebody to talk to. I’m walking home.” Micah pulled up to the traffic light, and rolled to a stop slowly.

“And you decided to call me?” She was quiet for a minute.
“Esther?”

“Yes, I guess I did huh?” She almost sounded amazed. “How are you holding up?”

“What do you mean holding up?” He imagined her rolling her eyes.

“I haven’t really talked to you since Thomas came to town. You’ve been avoiding me.”

“I text you.”

“But you never want to hang anymore. Are you jealous or something?” Micah’s mouth dropped.

“I don’t get jealous,” he quipped, fiddling with the change in his cup holder.

“Whatever you say.”

“I don’t!”

"You're in denial," she claimed as Micah pulled into his parking space, ironically, again he found himself right beside hers.

"Denial is not just a river in Egypt."

"You couldn't resist, could you?" She asked. He could practically hear her smiling on the other end.

"Nope." He shut his car door loudly and bounded up the stairs leading to his apartment. "Why are you walking home? You have a car." He stopped and leaned over the railing to look out into the parking lot. "I actually parked right beside you."

"Don't think I don't know you're trying to change the subject. Yes, I do have a car but I wanted to go walking. I stayed out a little longer than I'd planned," she explained. Micah shook his head as he unlocked the door to his apartment.

Micah didn't like that. She shouldn't be walking alone, especially not at night. Now, not only was he flattered that she'd called him, but he was also relieved.

"Well that wasn't the smartest thing you've ever done."

"Oh please. If that isn't the pot calling the kettle black," she snorted.

"I can come get you," he said, his hand still poised on the door knob.

"It's fine. I'm coming up the stairs now, so you can go back to your life." Micah rolled his eyes and took a seat on the couch.

"What if I don't want to?"

"Then don't." The door to the apartment next to him, slammed shut. "I'm home," she chirped.

"Is Thomas still here?" He asked. Esther giggled.

"Told ya' you were jealous. He left yesterday."

"I'll be right out."

Esther laughed again.

"I'd love that, but I have some cleaning to do. If and only if you're that bored, you can stay on the phone while I clean up my kitchen." Micah sighed, a large grin on his face.

"Sure."

***

Micah woke up the next morning on the couch with his phone stuck to his face. He'd slept soundly, and dreamlessly. *Maybe I need to fall asleep on the phone with her more often.* He thought. He made sure that Rea was up and moving before getting dressed himself. He didn't have anything to do until the evening, so he decided to spend the day catching up on homework. He wanted to stay as busy as possible so he didn't have to think as recently, it always got him into trouble. But if he absolutely had to think about anything, he wanted to think about

Esther.

He'd found so much about Esther from their conversations. He found out that she was funny, and spoke four languages, loved to read and loved Disney movies. Her favorite movie was *Brother Bear.* They'd planned to watch a few Disney movies together one day. Actually, she'd planned it. Micah had no real interest, but any excuse to spend time with her would work for him. The more he thought of Esther, the more he talked to her, the more he realized that she wasn't always so deep. She was a real human being, a beautiful human being. That was the side of Esther that he wanted to see more. It was the side of her that added pure gasoline to the already raging bonfire of emotions he felt towards her.

"Micah."

He glanced up from his laptop and looked around to see who'd called his name.

"Hello?" Silence. "Rea?"

"Micah."

Now, he was sure he was going crazy. *Great, now I'm hearing things.* The Voice was soft, yet commanding. It didn't force his attention, but drew it. It was familiar, the Voice. He'd heard it somewhere before…

"I'm hearing stuff," Micah concluded. He got up from his perch on his bed and walked through the house, looking for Rea.

If he found out that somehow his sister was home, when she was supposed to be at school he would be angry yes, but he would also be relieved. Micah's distress only grew when he found his sister's room empty. The Voice was deeper than his sister's no doubt, but it was worth a shot. He opened the front door and looked around. *Please tell me this is a joke. Please be an extra loud neighbor…*

"*You're not hearing things*," the Voice whispered.

Wait a minute ...this is the voice from that vision I had when Esther laid me out. The Voice chuckled.

"And the voice you heard when you were lying in Sheba's bed."

"Who are You?" Micah asked aloud.

"I am."

Oh yeah, let's be cryptic. Micah thought sarcastically.

"Micah, why are you running from Me?"

If I hear voices in my head does that make me crazy, or do I only become crazy if I respond to the voices in my head?

"I'm not running from anybody," Micah said.

"No? Is that why you always ignore Me? Was our encounter not clear enough? Even though you're angry with Me, I love you more than you could ever imagine. I love you more than you could ever love yourself."

Micah could no longer deny who he was speaking to.

"God."

"I am He."

"I thought God was supposed to be all, Thee and Thous…this doesn't sound like God."

"Well then who do you say that I am?" That statement gave Micah pause.

"I don't know."

"Micah, I want you to understand Me. I will speak to you in whatever way is easiest for you understand."

"What do You want from me?" He asked, bitterly. "I don't even know why I'm talking to You. You aren't real."

"If I'm not real, then why are we having this conversation?" The Voice replied softly.

"Because I'm either dreaming or crazy," Micah replied.

"Now that is crazy. Keep in mind that I know you, there is no point in lying to Me, to Esther, to ReAutumn, or to yourself." Micah rolled his eyes.

Part of him was overcome with fear, the other anger. Why couldn't God just leave him alone? He'd already taken enough from Micah, now he wanted to take more. Micah didn't respond to the question.

"I love you, Micah," the voice whispered.

"Have You ever considered that I may not be running from You, maybe I just don't *want* to choose You?"

"Yes, and I still love you."

Micah's eyes pricked with tears, as he thought about God's words. If God loved him so much, then why did He let his parents die? There was silence. *Ha, finally a question that He can't answer.* Micah waited for a few more moments.

"If I told you the answer Micah, would you listen? Would it matter?" Micah was taken aback by His question. Would it really matter? No. They were still gone. Would he listen? Maybe, but no excuse would be good enough. No excuse, no reasoning would bring his parents back. So no, nothing that this God would say would matter to him. That didn't stop his curiosity though.

"Maybe not," Micah said aloud. "Regardless, I'd like to know Your excuse."

"I answer to no man," He began. *"No reason I give you will meet your standards. You have made up in your own mind to blame Me and hold Me responsible for the decisions and outcomes of others, but consider this Micah. I didn't kill your parents. I allow, you and everyone else in this world to choose their way. The world that you live in, is a fallen world. I will not accept blame for the things that I have not done. I've done it once, I won't do it again."*

Once?

"Yes, once. The cross." Micah wanted to come up with a smart comment. He wanted to have a snippy response, something—

anything—to render Him speechless, but it was Micah who was speechless. *"Even in your hatred for Me Micah, I am still desperately in love with you. You are mine. Just like your parents are mine."*

Micah sat back down on the couch and gripped the arms with tears in his eyes. He began blinking rapidly, trying to hold back his tears. He felt his very soul tearing in two as the war within him began to intensify.

"I can't," Micah murmured, nearly choking on the words.

If he accepted this love, he'd have to revert back to his old views. He'd have to give up everything he knew, everything would change. He liked his life how it was. He liked going to work just because. He liked going out with his friends when he wanted. He didn't want to go to Bible study, he didn't want to go to that hypocritical church every Sunday and pretend to be interested. He didn't want to become a hypocrite himself. He didn't want to be a Christian, that would mean that he would have to hand over his life to someone that He couldn't even see.

But Esther's not a hypocrite and Rea's a Christian. He just felt tired. A heavy weight rested itself upon his shoulders. He was tired of reasoning, tired of running, tired of ignoring but rather than use the last of his strength to let it all go, he pushed all thoughts away. He stuffed his feelings inside a box, just like he always did. He'd patiently wait for it to blow over.

"What you feel now Micah, is the burden of all that you've been through. The

reason you haven't lost your mind, is because I've been carrying it with you the entire time. I refuse to leave you by yourself. You have never been without help."

I need to get out of this house. Maybe…

He felt around blindly, in search of his phone. Although his vision was perfect, he couldn't process anything he was seeing in front of him. He found his phone on the couch opposite of him, and scrolled through his contacts.

Ring, ring.

"Hello?" Esther's soft voice, floated through the speaker. It was almost enough to calm him.

"We need to talk. Can we meet?" There was a brief pause.

"I thought we were meeting?" She asked, her voice rose in pitch--a sign tat she was confused.

He shook his head quickly back and forth as if he was trying to convey the urgency of the situation. He knew that she couldn't see him, but maybe the action would help him figure out his words. He began pacing, one hand was anxiously pushing back his hair, consistently and frantically raking his fingers through it.

"No, I mean earlier." Another pause. In the absence of her voice, he heard other voices and an annoying beeping sound. "What are you doing right now?"

"I am at Kroger right now, grocery shopping. I'll be home in like twenty minutes. Meet me on the balcony?"

"No! No-I...I need to get as far away from this apartment as possible."

"Micah, is everything ok?"

"Not really," Micah said, his voice rising in pitch.

"Ok… Can I meet you at the diner in like, thirty minutes?" Micah nodded to himself. Thirty minutes? He could do thirty minutes.

"That sounds great, Esther. Thank you."

"No problemo," she mused.

He could almost hear the smile in her voice. If she truly knew that something was wrong with him, she didn't show it. She didn't ask. He didn't tell. When they hung up he practically ran to the bathroom, attempting to get to a somewhat decent state.

"Micah."

I'm ignoring You.

"As usual."

Still ignoring You.

"And yet, you keep answering Me."

Micah didn't respond but instead, began brushing his teeth. He spat into the sink, and wiped his mouth. His eyes wandered up to the mirror before him and his entire body became immobilized by his reflection. His eyes that four years ago were jubilant emeralds, were now two raging storms trapped within emerald casings. They were mirror images of the battle within. It was one thing to feel it, but another to see it. Every time he saw his reflection, all he saw was a battle weary young man.

NINE

He studied her carefully, analyzing every move she made. Her hair was wild and windblown from having the window rolled down while driving. She took her sunglasses off in one fluid motion and put them on top of her head, using it as a headband to hold the hair from her face. His analysis of her continued as she got out of her car and waltzed over to him. Her steps were gazelle like, graceful and light. The smile he was growing to adore, broke out on her face when their eyes met.

"Hey," she greeted. The corners of her lips turned downward as she took in his posture. He was tense, coiled up like a snake poised to strike. He smiled back at her, but it was feeble.

"Hi," he said. She gave him a warm one-armed hug. Her scent caught in the air between them and he inhaled it with the hope that calm in some way, shape, or form would find and overtake him. His body began to unfurl from its coil, but his mind was still in turmoil.

"I would ask how you are," she said. He waited for her to continue, but she didn't.

"Thank you for meeting me earlier than we planned," he said. She shrugged her shoulders and eyed him warily.

"It's not a problem, sounded like it was important. What's going on?" He stuck his hands in his pockets and gestured with his head towards the door.

"Let's go inside first, and get comfortable." She nodded in agreement. They sat in a booth located in the corner farthest from the door. She sat across from him and folded her hands on the table waiting patiently for him to speak.

But Micah couldn't speak. His eyes were focused on Esther's tiny hands. The God he'd hated, yet had denied the very existence of for the past few years, had just spoken to him. In fact, this God had been speaking to him for a while now. Not only did God speak to him, but He told him that He loved him. God didn't seem angry at him; he didn't chastise him for the times he'd got drunk, had sex, or gotten high. God had simply loved on Micah, and only chastised him for running away from that love.

What kind of God is this? Is He bipolar? First, He takes my parents, then He tells me He loves me?

No, it wasn't the first time that he'd encountered God. There was the voice he'd heard in Sheba's dorm, then that strange service he'd gone to. With all of his might and reasoning, he could not justify how Esther knew what she knew about him. His lack of explanation frustrated him to the point of simply filing the night away in a folder within his mind. He labeled this folder, "coincidence."

He could have easily brushed off the second encounter—the vision--as having hit his head too hard on the tile. Part of him contemplated accepting this God, but the bitterness in his heart continued to press its way to the forefront of his mind. A waitress, who Micah knew as Sonya, approached the table. She took their drink orders quickly and left.

"What's going on, Micah?" Esther asked after a few moments of silence.

"I don't know where to start," he told her honestly. He looked up at her briefly, and then shifted his gaze back on the table.

"What's going through your head currently?" She said. Sonya returned and placed their drinks on the table. "I'm not hungry yet, Micah. Are you?" Esther asked. He shook his head and took a deep breath. They thanked Sonya and when she was out of earshot Micah turned back to Esther.

"I think I'm going crazy."

"Oh?" She raised her eyebrow at him. "Can't wait to hear the reasoning behind this."

"I'm hearing," he leaned forward and cupped his hands around his mouth, "voices," he whispered.

"Eh?" She asked as she scrunched up her face. He rolled his eyes and looked around before repeating himself.

"Come again?" She said leaning forward. He repeated himself again, this time it was a little too loudly. She pressed her tongue to her cheek and leaned back in her seat. Oh, she had to be enjoying this. The very same thing he'd teased her about was now happening to him.

"And what are the voices saying?" She asked, smirking at him.

"Be serious please."

"I am," she reassured him. "Start from the beginning."

The waitress reappeared. She greeted them and told them if they needed anything they could just holler for her. When she was out of earshot again, Micah began his tale. He recounted every detail of his conversation with the One Whose Existence He Questioned. He mentioned the incident in Sheba's room, the vision he saw, and the dream he'd recently had about his death. She listened without interrupting, her eyes burdened with an expression that he couldn't identify. When he finished speaking, he sipped his water and refused to look at her.

"Well," she began. She placed her elbows on the table, folded her fingers, and rested her chin on her folded hands. "You are an idiot. The creator of the Universe tells you He loves you and you deny Him. Please explain this to me."

Micah flinched at her words. *Way to be sensitive, Ess.*

"You don't know what happened," he argued.

She sighed. That smirk of hers remained firmly in place.

"No, I don't." He hesitated. His eyes shot up to hers. She didn't say a word. Before he could stop himself, words poured out, "We were coming home from visiting mine and Rea's Grandparents. It was icy outside on the road." He swallowed hard, his Adam's apple bobbing up and down. "Long story short, we wrecked. They died, we didn't."

"I'm sorry," she whispered. She was no longer smirking, but rather she was staring at him with compassionate eyes--no pity, just pure compassion.

"Yeah. Me too." He took a sip of his drink. "We moved here when I turned eighteen to stay with our grandmother. She died a year later."

"You don't have any other relatives?" Micah shook his head. "I know that had to have been hard on you two. I'm very sorry to hear that."

"What's hard for me is understanding why a God who claims to love me would take away my parents and my grandmother."

"He gave you His answer. What makes you think I could tell you any different?" She reached across the table and took his hand. "Micah, I know and understand why you're mad at God. We may never know the reason why some things happen, but He never does anything or allows anything just for the fun of it. When He says that He loves us, He means it."

"You're defending Him." She shook her head at him.

"No I'm not. I'm telling you what I've learned. He wants to heal your hurt and be your comfort. You just have to let Him." Micah kept his eyes trained on her. How could she be so open to God allowing something like this to happen to someone? How could she be ok with it?

"Let me ask you something. If it was your parents that He took, would you feel the same way?"

Esther's face smoothed over, becoming void of any expression. "I don't know, maybe I'd be like you Micah," she admitted. "You seem to be under this impression that my life is all sunshine and roses and that's why I serve God. I guess you think that I was just born like this. "

Micah shrugged.

"More or less," he said. Esther scoffed. She stared down at the table, the wheels in her mind turning. Micah watched with interest as he wondered what was going on inside that head of hers.

"I grew up in church," she said finally. "I went through all the motions on Sundays and Wednesdays. My father was a pastor and he got up there every Sunday and taught the congregation about love, and the goodness of God. Yet when the service was over, he was the exact opposite," she trailed off and her eyes became distant. It was as if she was being transported to some distant land or taken back to a far-off memory. "I figured that if he couldn't make up his mind on what kind of God he served, I didn't stand a chance in really knowing God and I didn't really want to, so I gave up on the whole thing."

Micah's heart clenched with sympathy and understanding. If all that was true, how could she be so adamant about a God that would allow that to happen to her? How could she say that He was good, and that He was loving?

"I have been used and abused by church people, people that claimed to be representatives of God but they manipulated me, took advantage of me," she continued. "I remember wondering who would want to serve a God like that. Now, I can honestly say that I've learned not to blame the leader for what the followers do. God didn't have anything to do with how messed up my daddy was or how evil those church people were. God is not out to get us. The death of your parents is tragic, and I understand that you want someone to blame, but while you're spending your time and energy being mad at God, maybe you should consider the fact that you are still alive and so is Rea. I'm not saying dismiss the way you feel."

Micah placed his face into his hands. Her words, her story, her advice all barreled around in his mind. She gently pried his hands away from his face.

"Your feelings matter," she continued passionately. "You don't need me to tell you that your pain is justified, Micah. However, if you're going to place blame or cast judgement, make sure it goes to the right place." Esther sighed and looked around the restaurant before continuing. "Someone I once knew put it to me like this: as hard of a pill as this is to swallow, your loved ones don't belong to you. They never did. They belonged to God, and He wanted them back. It hurts, and it sucks, I know. Trust me, I know, but if I allow you to borrow something of mine, I'm eventually going to want it back. The time that I want it or need it back, isn't always going to be convenient for you. If it's something you love, then it will always be inconvenient."

"That doesn't still excuse—"

"God doesn't need an excuse to do anything. He is God. When things don't go our way, that truth really bites, but it is still the truth. He doesn't have to explain Himself to anyone. You can't blame God for everything that goes wrong, especially if you're not willing to give Him credit for everything that goes right."

"I need some time to think about it," Micah whispered. "None of this makes sense."

Esther shook her head as if she couldn't believe what she was hearing and sat back in her seat.

"I came here to talk about this with you because I need to know I'm not crazy, and since you hear voices all the time I figured you'd know a thing or two about this," Micah continued.

Again, Esther shook her head.

"That's not entirely true, Micah and you know it. You know that there is a God but you're so mad at Him you try to deny it. You know that if you admit it you're going to have to do something about it, and let go of all the anger and bitterness."

"I'm not bitter, " Micah said.

Esther continued on as if she hadn't heard him, "You are going to have to come to the point, Micah, that you're done making up excuses, you're done running and you are willing to give it all to Him. There's nothing that I can do to help you, especially not if you're unwilling to help yourself. You know the truth. Now do something. I have two words for you: Getcho' life. Literally!"

"How did you decide?" He asked as he intertwined his fingers and sat them on the table. "How did you come to your realization about God not being responsible for your dad." She was quiet for a moment, her face contorted into an expression of deep thought.

"I hit rock bottom and I realized that life is short. I also realized that He was worth every sacrifice that I was going to have to make to serve Him. I had a million reasons to walk away but He gave me one excellent reason to stick around."

"And what was that?"

"Him. I got to know the real *Him.* I got to know His love and He literally loved me back to life, back to restoration, back to wholeness…He was it for me."

"Well, you seem like you've got it all figured out," he murmured. Esther shook her head.

"Not even close. I'm just learning to not resist the process. There are many things that I need to work on."

"Like accepting who you claim that you are," he said.

"What? I haven't claimed any-"

"I saw the way you reacted when I called you a prophetess in public. You freaked out, hardcore."

"Yes, that," she whispered. "But we're not here to talk about me today, we can reserve that for another time. Like I was saying, once you know His love there's nothing like it." She cleared her throat. There was a story behind those eyes, a mystery. Micah was beginning to realize that she'd only given him the bare minimum of what she went through.

"I used to think that I knew Him."

"Then you got mad," she added. He nodded.

"Then I got mad."

"And thick headed." She giggled, then sipped her drink.

"I got angry and came to the exact same conclusion that you did—who would want to serve a God like that? One that kills His own people." Micah sighed. "It was easier to pretend He didn't exist, than deal with the reality that someone who claimed to love me would hurt me like that. What makes you so different from me?"

"Not a thing," Esther sang. "I got to know Him for myself."

"Now you sound like one of those old church mothers."

"Hmm…I've had enough heartbreak to last me a lifetime Micah Williams, but I have experienced a joy much greater than all of it. I met Jesus. I know I sound like an old church mother, but they're telling the truth Micah. You've got to know Him for yourself. I cannot tell you who He is and expect you to take my word for it. Go find out for yourself."

"Thank you."

"For what? Telling you what you already know Micah? Please. You don't need to thank me for that. It's my pleasure." She gulped down the rest of her drink and then looked at Micah. "You should come to my church Sunday, bring Rea," she suggested. Micah smirked.

"Your church?"

"Yes, *my* church," she sassed. "The place I go to worship? I think you'd like it."

Micah laughed. "Anything is better than the church I'm going to."

She took a piece of ice in her mouth and began crunching on it. She swallowed before answering. "They let you into a church?"

"Play nice," he said.

She grinned at him. "Oh I am. I think I've been there once or twice, when I first started visiting churches in the area. Vernon Rush right? They seem nice." She shrugged.

"Seem is the key word," he said, snickering. "A lot of those people have their place in Hell."

"So do you," she quipped. "And me too, if we don't get right."

"Bull," he muttered.

"Excuse me?" She raised her eyebrow at him. The only sign of her not being truly angry at his comment was the right side of her lip, as it was curved upwards to produce a mocking smirk.

"Nothing, beautiful."

"That's what I thought. Don't you go judging those people, Micah. We've all got issues." He dismissed her statement with a wave of his hand.

"Well anyways, I'll think about it," he relented.

"Service starts at eleven. Be there or be square." He snorted at her childishness, watching in amusement as she made a square with her index fingers and thumbs.

"I said I'd think about it, not that I'd go." She opened her mouth to protest but he stopped her by putting a finger to her lips. "I said I'd think about it—"

Her lips are soft… he thought to himself. He left his finger and his gaze there, perhaps a little longer than he should have. His eyes flickered up to her eyes, only to see that they weren't watching him with the strange expression that he'd half expected. Instead, her eyes were trained on his lips as well.

"Right," she replied. "Please remove your finger from my lips, I don't know where they've been." She smirked at him, as he immediately removed his finger. Even he had to admit, that was a little creepy, but her coy smile assured him that everything was fine.

Whatever excuse he'd intended to come up with for not visiting her church, was fading away. He was now motivated by true desire. He didn't know what this was going to turn into between the two of them, but Crystal's analysis of his dreams seemed like a pretty decent ending to him. Even though he hated his dreams most of the time, he couldn't deny their accuracy. Proof of that was sitting before him, sipping on a sprite looking lost in thought. She was staring at the table, eyes wide and unfocused. Perhaps he was overreacting, but her actions made him nervous. Was she getting something from the voices in her head? Was she having a vision?

"Quarter for your thoughts?" He asked. He laid one hand on the table, allowing his fingers to drum on its smooth chestnut surface. He shifted in his seat, waiting for her response. She remained lost in thought as if she hadn't heard him. "Ess?" She looked up startled.

"Huh?" Her eyes jumped to his, brown meeting green again in a beautiful impasse. He cleared his throat, refusing to allow himself to be lost in the brilliance of her eyes.

"You zoned out for a minute, you ok?"

Her lips turned up for a split second before she responded. "Yeah."

"You sure?" She huffed and nodded.

"I'm fine, just spaced out a little." She smirked. "You can stop looking so scared Micah. Just because I zone out for a bit doesn't mean I'm reading your mail and anyways, I thought that sentiment called for a penny, not a quarter." He looked down and laughed. She'd caught him, dead on even.

"Trust me, nobody's cared and for the record, I think your thoughts are more valuable than any penny." He winked at her and waited for her to swoon. She didn't. When he looked up at her again she was still sporting that signature smirk of hers. She didn't seem the least bit impressed.

"So they're worth a whole twenty-four cents more? Cute. Lame, but cute. I'll give you points for originality and effort."

"Can't a friend compliment a friend?" Her smirk minutely dropped. Had he not been paying close attention to her he probably wouldn't have noticed it.

"Yeah, and it's my duty as your friend to tell you how lame that compliment was." He laughed boisterously causing her to emit a small giggle.

"Fair," he admitted. His attempt at flirting was a bit lame, he was well aware of that, but he'd seen it work with a few other girls. Why was it that even though he knew she was different, he kept using his same parlor tricks with her? Although it hadn't gotten the reaction he'd hoped for, he did get a good laugh out of it, they both did. Neither of them noticed the waitress approaching the table.

"Do y'all want anything else?" Sonya asked, startling Esther and Micah.

"No. Thanks, Sonya. Just the check please," Micah said sweetly.

Esther held out her hand to stop him and said, "Sonya, do you know anyone named Jason?"

Micah tilted his head to the side in confusion.

What the hell? He knew Jason. Jason was Sonya's older brother; he was strung out on drugs. How would Esther know Jason?

"Jason's my brother…" Sonya said stammering. She wiped her hands on her apron. "Why?" Esther smiled up at her brilliantly.

It was a comforting smile, Micah realized. It was the same smile that she gave to the little boy the night he'd first seen her prophesy. It was a smile that just screamed 'It's going to be alright.'

"This is going to sound really weird, strange even, but God just spoke to me about Jason," Esther said.

Sonya raised an eyebrow skeptically and put a hand on her hip.

"God?"

"Yes. God," Esther replied simply, unfazed by Sonya's attitude. "He says that Jason, is coming home and that he is coming home sober and that once He gets a hold of Jason, he will never touch another drop of alcohol, he will never even look at another drug again in his life. God is going to give him a marvelous testimony Sonya. You just watch and see." Sonya covered her mouth, as tears began to flow down her cheeks.

"How did you…?" Esther shrugged.

"Not me, God. He speaks, I repeat. Simple." She took another sip of her drink. "Just keep praying for him. He'll be alright."

Sonya nodded. Micah supposed it was all she could do.

"Why would God do that?" Sonya finally murmured. "I haven't been to church in…I don't know how long."

"It's not about you," Esther replied softly. "It's about His love *for* you."

"Always about him," Micah muttered.

Esther flashed him another one of her dazzling smiles.

"You may think God is selfish because it's always about Him," Esther said. "When you make it all about Him, He makes it all about you. The cool thing is that no matter what we do, we can never match up to what He does for us. That my friends, is a fact. Make it about Him, He'll make it about you. Remember, He sent Jesus for us so that we could be with Him in Glory for eternity. What Father wants to live without His children right? Everyone wins." She shrugged and sipped her drink again. "And Quan is getting a new job."

Micah tilted his head to the side in confusion.

"Quan?" He asked.

"My boyfriend…how—" Sonya began, "But…God…why would He? I know we ain't supposed to be living together and all that but—"

"His kindness is intended to turn you away from your sin, believe me this is not a go-pass to continue sinning. You gave your life to him at a young age and you became His daughter. Just because you're his child that ain't doing right, doesn't make you any less of His child."

Esther was quiet for a moment. "Hey, can we pray?" She asked finally.

Sonya nodded and Micah watched in amazement as Esther, still seated, took Sonya's hand. Right there, in the middle of the restaurant Esther began to pray. Her prayer wasn't loud and eloquent. It was simple and had he seen that from across the restaurant, he would have thought they were simply talking.

"Micah." The sound of God's voice caused Micah's breathing to hitch.

You again.

"This is what I want to do with You," God said. Pray? Pray in front of people? No. There was no way.

Ha. You're funny. You know, I tried that once…the whole serving You thing? Didn't really work out. Do You mind reeling Your daughter in a bit?

"When you see her doing My work, think of it as looking into a mirror."

A mirror? What? You mean I'm gonna be like that? Ha. Funny. You're funny.

As Esther prayed, Micah looked around and began to grow uneasy under the gazes of the people in the restaurant. People were beginning to take notice. His face began to grow hot and he pulled out his cell phone scrolling through his texts hoping to find something to distract himself. He did. He found a group text between Jay, Sheba, and a few other people that he didn't know very well. A group text meant that a night out was soon to come.

Burke's tomorrow night? -Sheba.

Aaabsolutely! -Donovan

Time? - Jay

10-Sheba

Meet you there- Micah

Micah wanna pick me up? XD- Jay

I guess worrisome. Worried that wifey will find out? - Micah

I'm grown! -Jay

Sure XD- Micah

Oh, so you can respond to the group text but not to me? - Sheba

Micah rolled his eyes. *Exactly,* he thought. Esther looked over at him when she finished praying. Micah quickly put his phone away.

"Hey, I don't mean to be like…weird or whatever, but can I please have some fries or something? I'm hungry." Esther said through her laughter. That in turn caused Sonya to laugh as well. *It's kind of late for you to not be weird Ess.*

"No you're fine!" Sonya reassured. "Just fries? Nothing else?"

Esther put a finger to her chin and thought for a moment.

"Well since you asked…can I have a slice of that sweet potato pie please…ooh make that two slices?" Esther said as her eyes grew wide with excitement.

Sonya nodded with a genuine smile on her face, despite her still falling tears, as she wrote down her order.

"Anything for you, Micah?" Sonya asked as she wiped her face with her free hand.

"A burger, please and fries. No lettuce or pickles." She took his order and then gave one final nod.

"I'll put those in for you guys," Micah thanked her and she left.

"Excited much?" Micah asked.

Esther leaned forward on her elbows. "I love food," she explained. "Don't you?"

Micah laughed before nodding, "Yeah."

A comfortable silence passed between them before Micah finally asked, "So, you do this a lot?"

"What?" Esther stared at him, confused. Finally, it started to sink in. "Oh that thing with Sonya?" Micah nodded. "I guess." She shrugged. "It happens anywhere. God wants to speak to people. He's always speaking."

"And you," he said gesturing to her. "Are His messenger, so to speak?"

"Yes sir. You are looking at an employee of Heaven's postal services." She grinned.

"Why are you so nonchalant about it?" He asked. "It's like it's nothing to you." His curiosity was eating away at him, and like always, he needed some answers.

"I'd never say that it's nothing. Speaking with God is always a privilege. Not many people hear the audible voice of God, especially not often. Yet, He speaks to me and I to Him, just like you and I are talking right now, like…" She waved her hand around as if she were trying to conjure up the right word. "Friends."

"Hm."

Friends…I hate the friend zone.

"Yep and what do you expect? Should I hoop after everything I say? Should I scream? Shout? It's not a show; it's not entertainment. It's just God being God. I'm just thankful to be a part of His work."

"You sound like a commercial ad," Micah said. "I'm waiting for you to say, *for two easy payments of nineteen-ninety-nine we'll send you salvation in a bottle.*"

Esther snickered.

"I could have made it big in Hollywood, jerk."

Micah laughed in response. A few moments later, he shifted in his seat and pursed his lips.

"So they do this…" He looked at the ceiling as he searched for the correct word.

"Prophesying? Words of knowledge? Prayer?"

"Yes, that. They do that at your church?" He asked.

"Yes, quite often. I can see why you're hesitant about it, but don't worry, we won't make you drink the Kool-Aid or anything."

"Hesitant?"

"Yep."

"What was that? Did you just pick up on my hesitance by tapping into," he paused to insert his air quotations, "the prophetic realms or some other BS like that?" She rolled her eyes and leaned forward so that she was propping herself up on her elbows.

"Nope, it's called psychology. It's written on your face. Seriously Micah, half of these people that call themselves prophets just need to go get their degrees in psychology and sociology and call it a day."

Micah took a sip of his drink before asking, "Why is that?"

"Because they can read you like a book. They definitely know what to say to get your goat. Watch this." She closed her eyes, took a deep breath and then released it. She opened her eyes, stared at him for a moment and then squinted at him. She held her hand out toward him, fingers slightly bent. Micah had seen many preacher's make that hand gesture. It usually came right before they said something super deep, or said something "mic drop" worthy. "God sees your struggle, it's an internal battle that you're fighting. He says that you are a pillar of strength, and that you will have a car that's fully paid for." Micah crossed his arms and leaned back.

"And how did you get all that?" He smirked.

"Well, clearly you aren't struggling financially. Look at you, Nautica? John Varvatos…c'mon Micah. It's not hard to figure out that you're pretty well off. Which, by the way, I've been meaning to ask you how you're able to afford that. As for the pillar of strength thing, look at you. You've got the whole 'Oh look at me I'm a strong guy' attitude and hey, you have a strong chin. It was worth a shot. As far as the car thing. Your car isn't paid for, maybe…I don't know. That one was kind of a stretch but it could be a very generalized statement. Of course, if you pay your car payment your car will be paid for. Duh!"

Micah guffawed at her antics. Her large hand gestures and over dramatic facial expressions made what she was saying all though true, seem pretty hilarious.

Sonya returned a few moments later, with their food. As she sat it down she thanked Esther.

"Food is on the house guys," Sonya said. Before either could protest, she turned and walked away. Micah stared after her strangely. Esther had already begun eating her sweet potato pie.

"Maybe I should take you out to eat with me more often. You want to go see a movie or something after this?" He asked.

"Depends," she said, watching him pensively. "What movie?"

Micah shrugged.

"Whatever your little heart desires," he said, grinning.

TEN

"The moment they kissed at the end was classic. It was definitely a Hallmark moment," Esther gushed.

Micah rolled his eyes at Esther as they walked through the parking lot of the movie theatre. He was glad that she'd enjoyed herself. In all honesty, he'd enjoyed the movie as well, but he'd never tell her that. He griped and groaned about seeing the chick flick that she chose and she would never let him live it down if he told her that he actually ended up enjoying it.

"If you say so," he said.

Esther whirled around to face him.

"I do say so," she said.

He lifted his hands, palms facing outward.

"Alrighty then."

He held open the theatre door for her and they walked side-by-side into the chilly night air.

"Well what do you think about it?" she challenged.

He shrugged his shoulders.

"Meh," he said, shrugging his shoulders again.

"You're kind of a jerk, you know that?" She said, grinning.

"Is that why you won't date me?" The playful atmosphere almost instantly disappeared. "Never mind, forget I mentioned it." He paused in the middle of the parking lot, staring into her chocolate diamond eyes. "I was just playing." She squeezed his arm reassuringly, in response. He sighed bouncing his knees and looking around until he finally he blurted, "Ok maybe I wasn't. Look, I can tell you like me."

"Oh?" She said, crossing her arms.

"Yeah, *Oh*. Ess, you won't even give me a chance."

"Why are you so insistent on this? We both know I'm not your type." He huffed in frustration. He knew about the dreams she'd been having, but he'd never told her his. Was now really the appropriate time? What would she say?

"I know that, Esther Wickers. I'm well aware of the fact that you're weird, scary even! I'd like to get to know you some more. There's something about you that draws me to you. I don't even like relationships, but I want one with you."

"Maybe it's not me you're drawn to."

He furrowed his eyebrows and glared down at her small frame.

"What is that supposed to mean?" He asked. She sighed.

"Nothing, it's just…if you want to get to know me, then be my friend Micah." She sighed. "We can't be anything more than that. The most important thing in my life means nothing to you. Tell me how that can work out?"

"People do it all the time."

"I'm not those people."

"What about the dreams you've been having? I've had some too."

Esther rolled her eyes, then looked away as she said, "Dreams aren't always given by God. Some are fueled by your subconscious. If you're about to tell me that you had some stellar out of this world dream about me and that's what's driving you to pursue me, don't. It's not helping your case."

"But I've had dreams before Esther and they've come true."

Esther's eyebrows shot up to her tiny widow's peak.

"What do you mean?" Micah nodded.

"I had a dream before my parents died in the accident. I brushed it off as just a dream until it happened. I also dreamt of you, before I knew you. Is that subconscious?" He challenged.

"What other things have you dreamed about?" She said.

Micah shrugged. "Lately, not much. I keep seeing my best friend in the hospital and my own funeral, but…"

"You're in a dangerous place, Micah," she said. "You know the truth, and have known for a while and yet you still refuse to do anything about it. You live opposite of what you know to be true. That's dangerous."

A heavy silence passed between them. What exactly was he supposed to *do* with that kind of information?

"You said that."

"It's not going to get better until you make a decision to change."

"And here I thought things were going so well."

"I'm being serious."

"I know you are. Look, can we change the subject? I'm sorry I brought up the whole dating thing. If you want to be friends, we can be friends ok? I wasn't expecting you to go all deep, dark, and serious with me," Micah said, clasping his hands together.

It's a damn turn on and turn off all at the same time. He fumed mentally. Esther stared at him for a few moments and then sighed.

"Fine, but we're not done talking about this ok?"

He smirked. "Oh you wouldn't be you if we were."

"I'll see you later, Micah. You still owe me for that popcorn you spilled!" She said as she got into her car.

Micah rolled his eyes. "I owe you nothing."

Esther stuck out her tongue at him and shut her door.

"Sunday, eleven a.m.!" She yelled through her rolled down window.

"I'll pray about it. Isn't that what you Christians say when you really just wanna say no?" He joked as she pulled out of her parking spot.

"See you and Rea on Sunday!" She yelled, then drove off before he could respond.

"Yeah sure," he said as he shoved his hands into his jeans pockets, "Whatever."

***

Sunday morning raised a lot more hell than Micah had anticipated. Rea sat on his bed with an amused smile on her face, waiting as her brother fussed over what to wear. There were clothes strewn all over Micah's large bed room.

"What do you wear to a psycho church?" He asked finally. Rea rolled her eyes.

"Wear what you usually do. Or… you could ask Esther." He froze, then glared at his younger sister.

"I am not about to call her and ask her what to wear. I just don't want to go in there looking like a fool," he admitted.

"Too late." Rea said as she pulled herself off of the bed and raced to her brother's side. "Here, let me help bone head." She sifted through the few clothes that still remained on hangers and found a pair of khaki pants and a nice light blue button up shirt. "There. Hurry up, we're going to be late. My face is already beat and you still aren't even dressed." Micah rolled his eyes but smiled in spite of himself.

Thirty minutes later, they pulled into the parking lot of Siani Church. Micah's eyes slanted as he looked at the building before them. It was an old office building. He got out of the car slowly, hoping that by taking his time, he'd miss the entire service.

"This can't be it," he murmured as he shut his door. Rea appeared beside him. She stared wide eyed at the building and then looked back at the GPS app on her phone.

"This is it," she whispered. Her voice mirrored her brother's shock.

The music pouring out of the building confirmed their location. Micah wasn't sure what to expect from a church that was inside of an old office building, he'd never even heard of something like that. With his sister on his arm, Micah reached for the door handle. As he began to open it, a short, balding man stopped him. Micah read the nameplate on the man's shirt that read: usher.

Peering through the glass door, he saw that the inside of the building had indeed been transformed into that of a sanctuary. Rather than ornate cushioned pews, there were chairs and a stage that sat in the front of the room. There was a single podium and no chairs on the platform. Chill bumps began to form on his arm as he saw someone stand before the small crowd of people with a microphone in hand. He didn't recognize the person, but he did recognize presence that entered the room when the person began to pray.

"Woah," Rea marveled. Micah only nodded in agreement. It was a far cry from the church that he'd been going to for the past twenty-two years of his life. When the individual's prayer was finished, Micah was escorted into the church by the usher just as another person was getting up to take the mic.

There's only like thirty people in here, why do I need an usher? He thought.

After Micah took his seat, his eyes scanned the room in search of Esther, and found her. She was standing a few rows in front of him.

*It is unholy to be that fine, that is of the devil…*He mused as he took in her appearance.

She was modest in dress, at least he thought so, as she sported a stark white dress. It wasn't skin tight, but it flattered her shapely figure. On her feet, she wore a pair of black pumps. Her hair was in the wild, curly afro that she usually wore.

When the person on stage finished their prayer, a young man

took the platform. Behind him a group of six—two men and four women—took their places behind their appropriate microphone stands. *No choir?*

Micah's gaze returned to Esther, who was sitting next to a young woman he didn't recognize. Rea wasted no time in gathering her things and scrambling up to where Esther was seated. When Esther noticed Rea's presence, she stood and greeted her with a strong embrace. As she hugged Rea, she looked around the room. When her eyes met Micah's, that jewel-like smile appeared on her face. With one hand, Esther motioned for him to come up there with her. He took a moment to assess the consequences, rubbing his chin as he considered what the worst outcome could be. He didn't like being in the front, mostly because he didn't like people and he didn't want to be seen. On the other hand, it was Esther who'd invited him.

That was another thing he loved about Esther. She did all she could to make people feel like they belonged, even if they didn't. She was warm and welcoming with everyone, and seeing her treat his sister and others that way only added to his high opinion of her. She hadn't exactly been so warm with him in the beginning, but he couldn't blame her. She was exceptionally kind to him considering his contrary attitude.

Well, I'll have Rea up there.

He did as she requested.

The atmosphere of worship in the sanctuary was unlike anything he'd felt in a very long time. What was he feeling? He himself was unsure. He did know that the congregation's response of lifting their hands, and crying out to their God in admiration interested him. Even the praise team seemed lost in their worship and praise.

He'd visited a few other churches in the area before and occasionally his church would have visitors for their annual days. He'd seen people lift their hands, and cry during *worship* but there was always something missing. It seemed like they were just going through the motions or that the service itself had been rehearsed. Those thoughts had only been speculations at the time, but they were confirmed when he'd seen those same people acting out in the store, or other public places. Rare were the occurrences of true worship from sincere hearts that he'd seen. As much as he tried to block out the memories, most of those occurrences took place in his bed room.

Seven years ago:

Fifteen-year-old Micah sat alone on his bed, tears streaming down his face as he composed new melodies by the inspiration of the Holy Spirit. At that moment, a peace settled upon him unlike anything he'd ever experienced. His earlier worries dissipated; under the weight of this peace all of his fears and cares bowed. The very depths of his heart cried out to this God that he sang about every Sunday, the God he prayed to faithfully, the God he loved. The melodies transformed from a new and unfamiliar heavenly song into a familiar tune. The words from the song he'd listened to a thousand times, poured from his lips like liquid truth. Praises flowed from his heart continuously, emerging through the words of the song. He threw his head back, and took lifted his fingers from the keyboard. In silence he sat, in awe of God's presence.

Micah placed a hand on his chest, which ached in longing from the memory. It had been a long time since he'd allowed his mind to wander back to that bittersweet place.

For the first time in about two years, he felt the pain of God's absence. In his heart, he'd been carrying a deep yet dull, pain. It was different than the razor-sharp pain he felt when he thought of his parents. Until today, that dull pain had been unidentifiable. It was the emptiness, the loss of no longer feeling God's presence. Micah knew what true worship looked like and even though he didn't want to be there, the sincerity was refreshing.

A familiar melody began to flow from the speakers. He recognized the fast-paced music and runs from his own church that formed what was known as, "shouting music." *Here they go…* he thought. Although the urge to roll his eyes was strong, he resisted.

It's not time yet, he thought to himself as he leaned forward and rested his knees on his elbows. *They played the shout track too soon…they just started service! They should have stayed in that worship song just a little longer and the— what the hell do I care?* He wasn't the minister of music here, worship leader, or even a member of this church. He didn't even really consider himself Christian. So why should he care? He pulled out his cellphone from his pocket and began scrolling on social media. Like all the other services he'd attended, he simply spectated. He could imitate those people in his sleep. The best imitations came when he was bored. He could play the part with the best of them and they would never know the difference.

After the shout music, produced via track, finally stopped and the minister approached the stage, Micah actually poised himself to pay attention. The minister looked young, in Micah's opinion--perhaps in his early twenties. He didn't have on a suit. In fact, he had on black skinny jeans, a graphic tee, and a black suit jacket. He had long well-kept dreads and a light complexion.

Skinny jeans...on the platform? You're kidding. What the hell kind of church is this? Micah looked around, hoping to gauge the reactions of the church members. No one seemed the least bit bothered by this minister's appearance. *Is this normal?*

"Praise the Lord everybody!" He began.

Oh my God. He sounds like he's sixty! Micah thought.

"Praise the Lord," the congregants replied.

"I wanna talk for a few minutes with you guys from the subject of, there's only one," the minister continued.

"He's really good," Esther whispered to Rea.

"And he's not bad looking either," Rea replied flirtatiously.

Having overheard their conversation, Micah gagged. *Looks like a punk to me,* he thought. Seeing Esther nod in agreeance with Rea's statement caused that unwanted feeling of envy to rise within him and he hated it.

"Just wait until he starts actually preaching," Esther said.

Again, Micah rolled his eyes, but nonetheless, listened closely. How well could a person so close to their age preach?

"There's only one way," the minister began, "and that way is Jesus." The minister waited for the congregants to finish clapping and saying. "Amen" before he continued, "Although some people would disagree, we can't make it without Him. There's only one Savior and that is Jesus. There's also only one *you.* No one else can be you, but you. Listen carefully to what I'm saying. You were created for a purpose. You were created with a destiny. Jeremiah 29:11 says that God knows the thoughts and plans that He has for you, they are for good and not evil. He is not out to get you!"

From the corner of his eye Micah could see Rea nodding as she took notes, every once and a while she would look at what Esther was writing and copy it.

Great, they're bonding over notetaking. Sensational.

"You may not understand everything that's happened in your life thus far, and that's ok. Just know that it's working for your good. Excuse me—if you love God, it's working for your good."

Despite Micah's flash feelings of jealousy, he could sense the sincerity in the young minister's voice. Micah could relate. He could understand where the minister was coming from, and no matter how hard he tried to fight it, he was inspired by it. To even think that their

God had plans for him was interesting. Of course, those plans were probably God-Centered; after all, He did always make things about Himself.

"Those plans are for you to prosper, live and not die," the minister continued. "Those plans do not include sleeping with women, plural, men; but if the Lord wills, a wife."

Of their own accord, Micah's eyes drifted toward Esther. After a few moments of watching Esther, he quickly diverted his attention back to the minister.

"It doesn't include getting drunk and getting high. Contrary to popular belief, those things won't solve your problems, and they don't lead to a better life," the minister continued.

May not solve my problems but it sure does make me feel better about 'em. Micah thought with a smirk.

"The eventual end is destruction. You can run all you want, but I guarantee that you'll get tired and when you do, God will be waiting."

"Amen," Esther murmured.

Micah could feel Esther's him, but he refused to look in her direction to find out if his suspicions were correct. Why would she be looking at him? He wasn't sure whether to feel offended or not.

After service, Micah gave Esther no opportunities to make introductions. He gave her a quick hug, and after prying Rea away from her, they made their way to his car. That altar call was strange. Those *people*--ministers, as they'd been called, were strange. The way they'd poured the oil onto their hands and began to pray for the people individually at altar call was a foreign concept to him. He was used to seeing the deacons put out chairs, and wait for people to come up and sit in them at invitation or better yet, he was used to everyone gathering and holding hands at the altar for altar call. What were these people doing? He'd heard Jay jokingly "speak in tongues" multiple times, and he'd seen people at his church do the same while they were shouting, or when the preacher got too excited. Part of him wanted to laugh when he saw it, the other part of him—which was significantly smaller—was curious. Yet, here they were at this small church, speaking in tongues and laying hands. He could sense the power behind it.

Their mysterious garbled tongue, which they believed to be heavenly was if nothing else, confusing to him. What power could be locked up behind a few lines of gibberish? He remembered hearing one of the ministers instruct the congregation to "pray in their heavenly language." Was that the same as the tongues he'd heard of before? Or were those separate? That same presence he felt when he'd been at the altar that Wednesday evening and when he walked into Mt. Siani church that morning, was present when they began *praying* in their unintelligible language. He watched a woman fall backwards into the arms of an altar worker. She was out cold. The minister that had been praying for her, had barely touched her. *Was that what I looked like?* He thought. The thought of how ridiculous he must have looked mortified him. A young woman, less than half his size had laid him out on the floor. *Impossible.*

He hadn't even received a program when he walked through the door, nor had he been asked to stand up and introduce himself to everyone present. He'd simply been greeted by smiling strangers, and then taken a seat. It was an odd feeling, to see everyone so *free*. It was as if the congregation gave no thought to their appearance, or the time for that matter. They weren't concerned with following a program. They were concerned about following their God. Although Micah was pretty desperate to get home, he was taken aback by the fact that they weren't. Their…*attitude* had invited in that presence. He'd watched the atmosphere shift from strange, to extremely strange within the first song the worship team sang. As strange as it all was, he felt so desperate for it. He'd experienced it before, many years ago when he was alone with God.

That's why he had to leave. The moment that the young minister finished preaching, they opened the altar, and that time at the altar led into another session of worship. The worst part was that Micah couldn't even make fun of them for it. He couldn't joke about how funny they looked when they were shouting and running all over the sanctuary like children hyped up on sugar. Rather, they'd been a people hyped up on the presence of God and Micah knew that. *Knowing and believing are two different things,* He reasoned. *These people are hyped up on emotions. Once it wears off they'll realize how pointless this all is. Watch. Just watch.*

***

"It was alright," Micah said as he watched Rea flit about the kitchen. She was experimenting with recipes, *again.* He placed the phone on the kitchen counter and pressed the speakerphone button.

"Just alright?" Esther asked. Micah shrugged, even though he knew that she couldn't see him. Rea paused, then turned around to give her brother a pointed look. He shooed her away with one hand.

"Yeah, just alright. I mean it was cool or whatever," He said, tapping his fingers on the counter. He hated the fact that he couldn't see her facial expressions. He imagined her raising her eyebrows at him like she always did, or her giving him that signature coy smile of hers.

"To each their own I guess. Am I on speaker phone?" She asked.

"Yep."

"Great, is Rea around?"

"I'm right here!" Rea said loudly as she turned on the stove.

"What did you think of church today Rea? Your blockhead brother gave me no details."

"I can still hear you," Micah grunted.

"Good, that was the point," Esther quipped.

Rea giggled at their exchange.

"I loved it. You guys are so different than the church that we go to."

"So I've heard," Esther said nonchalantly.

"You were right about that guy. He was a really good preacher. He made it really easy to understand," Rea said.

Immediately, Micah rolled his eyes. So the guy was inspirational, *big whoop*. Micah could give him that much, but he wasn't worth all of their praise. Micah grabbed a water bottle from the refrigerator and began drinking it in large gulps. Nope. Definitely not worth their praise.

"I told you! He's an associate minister. His name is Henry. We go way back. We're actually from the same hometown," Esther said.

"Is that bae?" Rea asked jokingly.

Micah choked on his water, as Rea smirked at him. *That little…*

"No. Just friends."

"What? Is he not holy enough for you either?" Micah teased.

Esther snorted.

"As if. The boy is anointed and he's a total sweetheart. He's a real man of God and a good friend to me."

"Ignore him," said Rea. "He's just jealous."

Micah glowered at her.

"Ok, that's enough," he said. Micah grabbed his phone from the table and turned off the speaker phone. He put it to his ear as he walked to his room. "Make sure you wash those dishes when you're done Rea!" He called over his shoulder.

"So when are we hanging out again?" He asked.

"I can meet you on the balcony in five," she said.

"No, I mean, like on a friend date, but...I would like to meet you out there later."

"Ohhhh. Um…" Esther paused. "I dunno," she said finally, her tone hopeful and light. "Whenever you're free I suppose. Rea and I talked about having a movie day or something. Hey! We could do that! The three of us, we could all get together and watch movies this weekend."

"Sounds like a plan." Micah grinned. "Just as long as it's not one of those *War Room* or Compass of God movies."

"It's *God's Compass* and deal. We can just watch *Left Behind*, she quipped.

"Then you can leave me behind because I'm not trying to watch that wack-ass Christian horror movie," he protested. He'd heard of it, he even watched it with Rea once, but the feeling of dread he'd contracted from it was enough to convince him to never watch it again.

"It's only scary if you believe it—and before you say you don't, it's not a horror movie, so if you call it that, then that must mean that it horrified you."

"Whatever."

"Esther one, Mop Head zero!"

"Mop head?" He imagined her smirk growing into a large grin that would reveal her perfect set of pearly whites. "Ok, Curly Q. You're on." He threw himself on his bed and stared up at the ceiling, an easy smile resting on his face. "I'm just interested to see whether or not you can go a whole fifteen minutes without preaching to me. This could be fun."

***

That Friday night Esther accepted Rea's invitation to hang out at her apartment. Micah, Rea, and Esther were seated on the couch, dressed in their pajamas. Rea was wedged between Micah and Esther, with her head on Micah's shoulder. The evening had already been filled with laughter and fun but Micah was holding his breath, waiting for something—anything, to go wrong.

"I'm honestly loving this onesie," Rea said between giggles.

"Awww thanks!" Esther exclaimed. She got up to model her onesie. It was dark blue, with bright yellow stars.

"I think," Micah began."You look like a walking rendition of *Starry Night.*"

Rea covered her mouth with one hand to silence her laughter and slapped her brother on the arm with the other. Esther's lips tightened into a thin line as her eyes enlarged and she inhaled deeply.

"You are *such* a jerk!" Esther exclaimed before laughing and throwing a decorative couch pillow at Micah.

In truth, Micah thought that she looked adorable in her onesie. With her hair wild and untamed, she seemed carefree and child-like.

"I'm kidding," said Micah as he attempted to control his laughter.

"Still a jerk," Rea added.

"I know that's right," Esther sassed. "I look good." She gave him the evil eye as she made her way back to her seat on the couch

"So, what are we watching?" Micah asked, desperate to change the subject.

"Well," Esther began, "I brought *Left Behind*, *Phantom of the Opera*, *Titanic*—"

"Now hold on," Micah interrupted, holding up his hand. "What did I tell you on the phone about these movie choices?" Micah whined like a petulant child as he gestured to the stack of DVDs.

Esther shrugged, unfazed by the whining, stomping feet and swinging arms that accompanied Micah's temper tantrum. "Must have slipped my mind. What do you guys have?"

"I say we watch Phantom," Rea suggested.

Micah wrinkled his nose.

Secretly he found the movie to be bearable; the score was ingenious. On a family vacation to New York, he saw the Broadway production and loved it. He still listened to the soundtrack at times, but watching it all the way through with two women was a little more than he thought he could bear at the moment. Rea was a crybaby when it came to movies, and Micah didn't really do tears. He had no idea what Esther would do, but he supposed that as long as *Titanic* was no longer on the table, he could deal with it.

"Sure," he said, lying his head back on the couch.

"Try not to look so excited Micah," Esther said.

Micah chuckled. "Is it that obvious?"

"I mean…yeah," said Rea, sitting up to take the movie from Esther's hands.

Esther's stomach growled loudly, sounding more like a monster from a horror film than a natural bodily function. Micah guffawed.

"Esther…was that your stomach?" Rea asked between giggles.

"Maybe," Esther said as she covered her stomach with her hands. She looked down for a moment, then laughed along with the two of them.

"Well, that's my cue to order pizza, I guess," Micah said.

"Let me run back to my apartment and get some cash," said Esther. She began to stand but Micah stopped her.

"No, I've got it."

"You sure?" Esther asked.

Micah laughed at her obvious discomfort, her face crumpled in disapproval.

"I'm positive, you're a guest."

"I mean it's no big deal."

"Ess," he said, placing his hand on top of hers, "I've got it." Esther's eyes immediately went to his hand. Although sitting beneath her gaze made him self-conscious, he refused to move it. Her eyes traveled upwards until they met his, leaving third-degree burns on his arms from the fire within them. Rea cleared her throat causing Esther to immediately look away. Micah however, kept his eyes on her face.

"Ok," Esther said. "Fine, but next time I'm buying."

"Micah?"

"Huh?" He looked to his sister, who'd called out his name.

Esther was picking at her nails, seeming to avoid his gaze at all costs.

"Can you hurry up and call the pizza guy? *I'm* hungry *too*," Rea whined. "I'm gonna make popcorn because my stomach is eating my back." She jumped to her feet and stomped off toward the kitchen cabinet.

Esther put her hand over her mouth to stop her laughter but failed.

"Did you really just say your stomach is eating your back?" Esther said, unable to hide her amusement.

"Yeah," Rea said shrugging indifferently.

Esther shook her head as slight giggles still escaped every few seconds. Micah threw Rea a questioning glance, but decided to change the topic rather than comment.

"We typically get pepperoni. What do you like?" said Micah as he rose to his feet.

Esther shrugged. "I can rock with pepperoni."

"You sure?" He asked. He wanted her to be comfortable. She seemed like the type of person who would agree with the majority just for the sake of being polite in this sort of situation.

Esther nodded.

"Ok. Let me go find my wallet." Micah walked up to the kitchen counter, looking and scanned over the area. There was nothing there but a glass bowl filled with fruit. "Hmm."

He could have sworn that he put it there. After a few minutes of searching he found it sitting on his night stand.

"Found it," he said, walking back into the living room.

"Congrats. Now can you please order this food?" Rea whined.

Micah took in her childlike expression with a surprising endearment. He loved moments like this with his sister. Although it was annoying at times, her behavior made him grateful that she was ok. It reminded him of simpler times, and reassured him that despite all they've been through, they'd be ok. That *Rea would be ok*. "Sure," he said.

As Micah made the call to order pizza, his phone began to vibrate profusely and Sheba's name flashed on the screen. "Of course," he muttered.

"What?" Rea asked.

"Nothing, nothing."

Rea sat on the hardwood floors in front of the DVD player. She was holding the remote with one hand and pressing buttons, seemingly frustrated with her task.

"Please don't break the DVD player," he said.

He declined Sheba's call. Not ten seconds later, Sheba's name flashed on the screen again. And just like last time, sent her directly to voicemail. This time he was able to call the pizza place and place his order before she called him back, yet again. He declined her call. Micah took Rea's former seat in the middle of the couch next to Esther, stretching out both of his arms on the back of the couch.

"How long will the wait be?" Esther asked. She tucked her legs beneath herself, her knees facing outward, as she leaned on the arm of the couch.

"They said about thirty minutes," he replied nonchalantly. "Rea, I thought you were making popcorn."

"I have to fix this stupid thing first," she whined.

A systematic chain of buzzing noises erupted from Micah's back pocket. With a heavy sigh, he pulled out his phone again. Sheba was no longer calling him. Instead, she was texting him. Hesitating, he opened the texts, thankful that his read receipts were off.

`Answer your phone. –Sheba`

`I miss you. –Sheba`

`Tf is going on with you? –Sheba`

`I haven't seen you in weeks. –Sheba`

`I thought you were hanging out with us tonight? –Sheba`

As soon as he read the last text, she called again.

I should just turn this off...well no. If I did that, the pizza guy wouldn't be able to contact me. Micah sighed. *Please let these thirty minutes go by quickly.*

Half way through listening to Christine Daae sing "Think of Me," Micah received a phone call from an unknown caller. Simultaneously, there was a knock on the door.

"Finally!" Rea exclaimed.

Shaking his head, Micah answered the phone as he made his way to the door. "Hello?"

"Yeah this is Jacob with Carl's Pizza just wanted to let you know that your delivery time will be delayed due to the high level of demand tonight." Micah paused with his hand on the door knob.

"And why is that?"

"Game night. Sorry for the inconvenience but we should have it out to you in about another thirty minutes."

"Fan-freaking-tastic," Micah said as he hung up the phone.

As he opened the door, he cursed under his breath and looked away when he saw who was standing there.

Sheba.

She stood there--arms crossed, eyes fierce with anger and lips pressed together in a thin line.

"I knew you weren't busy," Sheba said as she tried to push past him.

"You're out of your mind if you think I'm about to let you just walk up in my apartment like you pay rent here," he said as he took a step to the side to block her path.

She took a step back, allowing Micah to fully assess her. She was clad in a skin-tight, black, strapless dress, and black pumps. She must have been on her way to the club.

"Why haven't you been answering my calls?"

"Micah? Who is that?" Rea asked.

Micah looked down to see Rea standing at his side with an indignant look on her face.

"I've been busy," Micah said to Sheba, his eyes narrowing. Sheba scoffed at his reply. "I don't have to explain myself to you," he continued.

Sheba stood on her toes and craned her neck to see inside the apartment. Micah stepped in front of her to block her view, as he knew what or rather who, she was looking for, but it was too late. One look at the girl on the couch and Sheba became livid. Sheba rocked backwards and planted her hands on her hips, eyes tearful, and lips turned up into a grievous snarl.

"Busy, huh? Busy screwing her?" Sheba asked in a disgusted tone as she gestured behind Micah.

Micah tore his eyes away from Sheba for a moment and looked down at his sister. "Rea, go and sit down Ok? Make sure the movie is paused. I'll be right back, I swear," Micah said softly.

Rea nodded and after giving Sheba the most menacing glare she could muster up, she walked away. Micah took a step outside and closed the door behind him. Sheba's eyes filled with angry tears. She bit the inside of her cheek as she refused to look at him.

"I told you to stay away from her, Micah," Sheba warned. "I'm gonna whoop her ass." She tried to walk past him again but he blocked her way.

"Why? I'm not your man Sheba. Grow up. I told you from the beginning this was nothing but casual sex. There's nothing going on between us. I've got a lot going on. I have a job, unlike you. I'm not obligated to call you back, nor am I obligated to text you. And you have the balls to show up at my apartment and try to run me? Hell nah, you need to leave."

Sheba's mouth fell open in disbelief.

"You're telling me to leave?"

"Yes, I am." Her mouth closed abruptly as her eyes widened, taking on a wild and almost crazy appearance.

"You'll come back," she said. An obnoxious snort followed. "You always do. You better be glad I have somewhere else to be otherwise I'd—"

"Bye, " Micah said, as he slammed the door shut abruptly.

The silence was deafening. He took a deep breath. *Inhale, exhale.*

Esther was sitting there, silent and expressionless. He didn't want to know what she was thinking. *Damn. Damn, damn, damn.* Rea sat next to her with her arms folded.

"Wel his night went to hell fast," he whispered.

Unsurprisingly, he had no idea how to fix it. He did the only thing he could think of, get as far away from her as possible. He quickly took a seat on the far end of the couch, doing everything he could to avoid looking at Esther.

"So..." he began, staring down at his hands.

"Tell your hoes to stay in their lane," said Rea coldly.

Micah's eyes immediately shot to Rea, whose expression was disgruntled as she crossed her arms and stared at the TV screen. Esther patted Rea on the leg reassuringly, but otherwise didn't react. *Why isn't she saying anything?*

There was another knock at the door, causing Micah's stomach to drop. *Does she not know how to take a hint?*

"I'll get it," Rea said. She ran to the door and threw it open before Micah could protest. She sighed in relief when she saw that it was Jacob, the pizza guy. "Thank God it's you. I'm starving."

ELEVEN

Micah leaned forward on Jay's desk, both palms flat against the oak wood as he relayed the recent events to his friend, "And then she shows up at my house, unannounced and we had it out. I ran into her on campus on Tuesday and some things happened and I'm scared to death for Esther to find out—Jay are you listening to me?"

It had been a few weeks since the incident with Sheba happened. Since then, his late-night talks on the balcony with Esther had come to an end. They passed each other some days without truly speaking. Some days they exchanged a smile. Other days, it was just a wave. Regardless, they began to see less and less of each other. Maybe it was for the best. He'd tried to do right for a little while, but, why should he? He knew they were destined for failure because her God was not on his radar.

Rea was now hooked on Esther's church and because he didn't want to have to deal with the devils of Vernon Rush church alone, he had no choice but to attend as well, or not go to church at all. The latter option didn't really seem that bad. It was awkward to see Esther on Wednesdays and Sundays. They were always cordial, but nothing was as it had been. He'd never tell her, but their Bible studies were interesting. He'd never heard the Bible from that perspective before. He'd never heard people pray that way before, he'd never…well he had never seen a lot of things that went on at Mt. Sinai Church. He asked Esther once, what the story behind the church's name was. She'd told him that she wasn't sure, but she imagined that it had something to do with Moses' encounter on the mountain top with God. She thought it was a fitting name, considering that every Sunday they had "crazy encounters with God." Those were her words, not Micah's.

Deep down, Micah agreed that there was "something at work" within that church. Something was different, and that's why he kept coming--the chill down his spine when he walked into the sanctuary, the strange movement he felt within the depths of his spirit during worship—even when the worship team was completely off or hit the wrong note. He was getting in too deep to continue to openly deny the existence of God, but the stubbornness he was born with prevailed. If he was going to keep up this pretense, he had to break away. So, he stopped attending and ran back to everything and *everyone* that was comfortable and safe. But just how safe was it?

He knew that he had no future with Sheba, but she was just like him. He could be himself around her. She provided everything that he needed right at that moment, and if he wanted to be in an actual relationship with her, all he had to do was say the word. There was nothing challenging about it. Being with Sheba was easy, at least it used to be. The stab of conviction in his heart became more painful every time he laid down with her and every time he drank with her.

Who was he kidding? Esther probably knew what he was doing and that's why she was keeping her distance from him. Or was he keeping his distance from her? He couldn't tell the difference anymore.

Jay sat at his desk, staring blankly at the wall, fidgeting. Micah was sitting on the desk, close enough to smack him if need be. The smack wasn't necessary, as Micah's question caught his attention.

"Yeah, yeah man."

"You alright?" Micah asked as he placed a hand on Jay's shoulder. Jay turned his office chair towards Micah and nodded.

"Yeah, I'm fine."

"You're lying."

"I'm good man."

"Jay, you know if you need anything—"

Jay slammed both hands down on the table. "Man, I said I'm good!"

Micah held up both hands and stood up. "I'm just trying to help you. You know what, you've probably been really stressed. Let's go out tonight. It'll take both of our minds off of our problems."

Jay shook his head. "I'm sorry man, I'm just…I don't think it's a good idea for us to go out tonight."

Micah folded his arms and his forehead wrinkled as confusion spread across his face. "Why not? You're always down to go out."

Jay's hands were shaking as he shuffled papers around his desk. "I just—I just have a lot of work to do and—"

"We're going out tonight," Micah said, his voice ringing with finality. "You can even pick the place," he offered with a shrug.

Jay hesitated and then nodded. "Yeah ok. Who all is coming?"

"Jason will be there, Sheba's going to be there…"

"Dang, you mean you hit that, again? You really *can't* let her go, can you? Thought you had a thing for…what's that girl's name? Esther?"

Micah sighed and dropped his folded arms.

"I do and I can when I choose to, but I need something to do with my time. Esther won't even consider the possibility of being with me."

"Probably because she knows you're a thottie thot thot thot," Jay said quietly, a small smile playing on his lips. Despite his attempt at keeping a low tone, he still spoke loud enough for Micah to hear.

Micah laughed and smacked Jay in the back of the neck.

"I am not! There's the Jay I know. See? Just the thought of going out tonight is already getting you right."

"I hope so."

***

"Jay, shut up!" Micah exclaimed.

Jay had been singing loudly and terribly for the past fifteen minutes and Micah was way past done. Maybe if he was as buzzed as Jay was, he wouldn't care as much. Jay laughed and threw an arm around Micah's shoulders.

The air whipped around them both, causing goosebumps to rise on Micah's arms. All he wanted to do was go home. He couldn't believe that their so-called friends had just *left* them at the bar. Sure, Jay was embarrassing while drunk but who didn't have their moments? It wasn't as if this was the first time they'd seen him drunk. Now, they stood outside waiting for their Uber driver to pick them up.

"Well, well, well…" Jay's eyes enlarged with terror as he gripped Micah's arm.

It took Micah a moment to register the voice, but Jay recognized it immediately.

"It's Shawn," Jay whispered.

Confusion and discomfort sparked within Micah as he heard the tremor in his friend's voice.

"There should be no problem, right? You paid him the other day," Micah whispered.

Jay took to looking anywhere other than Micah. His eyes became glued to the old and crusted gum on the concrete, then to his shoes. Micah's panicked expression soon faded into an intense glower as he looked from Jay to the quickly approaching Shawn.

"You didn't, did you? Please tell me that you paid him," Micah begged.

The fearful look in Jay's eyes and Shawn's dark expression told him everything he needed to know. He took in Shawn's appearance. He was muscular and tall with dreadlocks that were in desperate need of a re-twist. Shawn's hand was clenched around something that was situated between his pants and hip. Micah cursed as he realized what it was. He grabbed Jay's arm and looked him in the eyes.

"Run," Shawn commanded, smirking.

The two took off. Micah did everything in his power to keep his plastered friend, upright and moving. They didn't make it far. Just as they were about to cross the street a gun shot rang out, piercing the night air. He took a left turn down an alley hoping—two seconds away from praying—that it was the right turn.

It wasn't.

Micah reached the end of the alley way and took in a shaky breath when he saw the brick wall before him. Still grasping onto Jay's arm, he turned around but stopped when he saw who was blocking their path.

"Guess this means you don't have my money," Shawn taunted.

Jay leaned against the brick wall breathing heavily as Micah extended a non-threatening hand toward Shawn.

"Listen, Shawn we don't want any trouble."

Shawn sneered at Micah's attempt to placate him.

"This ain't got nothin' to do with you. Stay out of it."

Micah huffed. "I can't do that Shawn. You know that."

Shawn shrugged and drew his gun from its makeshift holster. "I got enough bullets for both you and him and they ain't choosy."

Micah narrowed his eyes. His life couldn't end here, not like this.

"Jay will pay you back your money. Right, Jay?" Micah said as he looked to his friend who merely nodded. He was shaking, much like the golden zils of a tambourine. "Jay!" Micah pleaded. Shawn cocked his gun and laughed.

"Man, I'll pay that punk," Jay slurred.

Shawn's eyes narrowed as he advanced on the two.

"On second thought, Jay shut up!" Micah exclaimed, his voice cracking in pure mortification and desperation. Now, was certainly not the time for Jay to be gaining liquid courage.

"Punk?" Shawn looked around, seemingly confused as to who Jay was talking to. "Man, I'll kill you!" he yelled. His nostrils flared as he pulled back his broad shoulders.

Micah turned to Shawn, his expression cautioning and pleading.

"He didn't mean that. He'll pay you back."

"I know he will. I gave him two months to get me my money. I extended his time twice. Now he's gonna pay me back, this time with his life."

Micah's body shook as his heart thudded against his rib cage. His mind swirled with ways to help his friend. None of them seemed good enough. His lips trembled as he opened his mouth to form words, and closed it again--nothing seemed like the right thing to say. Finally, he stammered out, "If you let me go to the ATM, I can—"

Jay help me out here, get your ass up and help me… Jay didn't even seem willing to fight for himself and here Micah was, pleading his case.

"Past time for that," Shawn growled. "Look at him, ain't said a word." He laughed. "He's gonna let you take a bullet for him I bet."

Micah looked over at his friend. Jay was gripping the wall behind him for dear life and shaking his head back and forth, murmuring to himself.

"Listen Shawn, you don't have to do this," Jay finally stuttered.

Shawn fired a shot in the air.

"You thought I was playing with you?" Shawn exclaimed. "I want my money."

Shawn fired another shot, but this time the bullet lodged itself within Jay's leg. Immediately, Jay yelped in pain and fell to the ground grabbing at his leg.

"That's $1,000 right there," said Shawn said, releasing a bitter laugh.

Micah bent down to aid his friend but froze when he looked up and found himself staring at Shawn's gun.

"Shawn, listen to me. I will get you the money," Micah said, as he lifted his hands in surrender.

How am I gonna get out of this? Fight or flight? He couldn't abandon Jay so flight was out of the question. Fighting was Micah's only option. He looked around searching for any possible exit, the only way out of this alley was to get through Shawn. *Maybe, I could surprise him--who am I kidding?*

Micah was strong, but he wasn't stronger than the piece of metal in Shawn's hand. Regardless of what Micah chose to do, he had a feeling he wouldn't be going home to Rea. If he didn't attempt to overpower Shawn, he'd still get shot because he'd be a witness to Jay's murder. He didn't have very many options, and none of them looked very good to him. His heart was pounding against his rib cage. The sound of it deafened him to any other noise.

It's now or never...

He raced towards his attacker, taking him down at the waist. Both men grunted as they hit the hard and chilly pavement, narrowly missing some of the shattered glass bottles that littered the alley floor. Shawn's weapon clattered to the ground a few feet away from the force of impact.

Thoughts of Rea and Esther whirled around in his mind as he grappled with Shawn. He thought back to all of the conversations he had with each of them about God; and finally, his mind traveled back to the moment that he walked down the aisle during service and accepted Christ. He was only six at the time, and amidst all of the hooping and hollering the church members did in celebration of his new life with Jesus, he'd walked down that aisle with such confidence, peace, and pride...

He remembered the Pastor's words before he'd even made the decision to walk down the aisle. The old, ashen faced man asked the congregation if they knew where they were going to go when they died. Micah had been taught what he needed to do in order to secure an eternity with Jesus, and leaped at the opportunity. He was more than happy to live for the God-Man who died for him.

But now he wasn't so sure how he'd answer the question. Throughout his life, he'd heard people argue over whether salvation could be lost, or how it was gained. He'd heard them debate over the validity of the principle of "Once saved, always saved." Regardless of what he believed regarding that, he knew that he wasn't in a very good position either way it went. If he was about to die anyway, what did he have to lose?

One hard punch to the face, threw Micah to the ground and gave Shawn adequate time to scramble towards his gun. Panic seized every part of Micah's being.

No. God! God…if You're there--, swear on everything I love if You let us get out of this, you can have my life. Please just let me make it home to Rea, she can't lose anyone else… He wasn't sure how far the prayer would get, or if God would be willing to answer it, but he had to at least try. He didn't have any other options. The two men scrambled to their feet. Shawn rose with gun in hand.

"You little..." he growled as he pointed the gun at Micah.

Micah could see the words forming on Shawn's lips but couldn't hear them. A brief moment passed in which black steel, met green eyes as Micah stared into the abyss that was the barrel of the gun. In that dark and dismal barrel, he saw his life--the life he was about to lose. Micah saw his sister's smiling face as he shut his eyes and braced himself for the brief moment of searing pain, and darkness that he was sure would follow.

Click.

The sound forced Micah's eyes open and caused all of the surrounding noises to flood into his ears. One sound, in particular although shrill and authoritative, put him at ease.

Are those sirens?

Click. Click.

Shawn pressed the trigger repeatedly, cursing loudly as the sound of police sirens filled the night. Micah was too stunned to realize what was truly going on.

"What the hell?!" Shawn exclaimed.

He threw the gun to the ground just as blue and red flashing lights lit up the alley way. As the gun hit the ground it went off. The sound of it pierced the night like an archer's well aimed arrow. The bullet pierced the dumpster across from them.

The police? What the--? Micah looked back over at his friend Jay, who lay bleeding, with a cell phone in hand. *Way to come through…* Micah thought as his body began to sag with relief and his eyes filled with tears. *I'm not dying tonight.*

His mind wandered back to the prayer he'd just briefly lifted. Two burly officers, exited their cars and forced Shawn's hands behind his back as Micah ran to Jay's aid. He was barely conscious on the ground.

"I'm never going drinking with you again," said Micah. Jay cracked a weak smile as Micah continued in a serious tone, "I am *so* deadass, Jay."

They answered the police officer's questions, and while Jay was being loaded into the ambulance, Micah was taken to the police station. As they drove away, Micah scoffed when he saw the Uber pull up in front of the bar. *Oh, now you want to show up.*

***

Micah counted it as a double miracle when he walked through the door that evening. He was at the station for a few hours, and was grateful that things went as smoothly as they did. His brain was a mess that night as he tossed and turned in his bed, unable to sleep.

. Why had he been spared? Why was he still alive? Why didn't the gun work? Was it jammed? The prayer he'd prayed that night weighed heavily on his mind. Had this God that he'd been so angry with, ignored, argued with, and denied so many times truly just saved his life? He couldn't understand it.

If God truly heard that prayer, then He'd heard that promise, and at this point, Micah was more than happy to honor it. He hardly ever made promises because he'd been known to break them in the past. Micah stared into the darkness that covered his bedroom. *Why?* The idea that God's love had been tried and proven true that night crossed his toiling mind. At that thought, peace washed over him like ocean waves-- powerful, strong, and refreshing. With his mind was finally clear, he drifted off to sleep.

TWELVE

"Ready!" Rea exclaimed. She stuck her head into her brother's bedroom and frowned.

She had no idea what had transpired the night before. All she knew was that her brother had come in late and he wasn't supposed to have been working that night. She'd stayed over at Mallory's until he got home and although questions were threatening to spill from her lips, she withheld them.

There was no phone call to indicate his late arrival. His clothes were wet and muddied, and the stench of alcohol seeped from his clothes. He was bruised up, and she could see the scrapes on his knees through his torn jeans. She'd simply hugged him, figuring that he wasn't in the mood to talk and then went to bed. However, despite what happened last night, she wasn't expecting to find him still in bed. He was resting peacefully, a slight smile on his lips.

"Micah!" She yelled.

Micah jolted upright instantly, eyes frantically searching about the room, "Who? What?!"

When he finally realized what was going on, he cursed loudly.

"Language!" Rea scolded.

He didn't grant her a second glance and threw the sheets off of himself as he shouted, "I'm late!"

"You think?" She asked, leaning against the door way with her arms folded across her chest.

"Long night, I'll explain later."

"Can't wait to hear it," she said as she waved him off.

"Leave! I have to shower!" He yelled.

"You're telling me…" Rea said smirking as she walked out and closed the door behind her.

Thirty minutes later they were on their way to Mt. Sianai.

Micah's first instinct when he arrived at Esther's church was to run. He remembered his promise, and although he wanted to be faithful in keeping it, he was still terrified. He'd been in this ring before. He'd been a servant of Christ and all the pain he endured had led him to this point of doubt and anger. Who was to say that he wouldn't be expected to endure that same pain again?

Micah took a seat in the back of the church and Rea beside him.

As Micah saw Esther in her usual spot upfront, all he felt was guilt. When Esther turned around and saw him, she smiled softly, but it wasn't the smile he was used to. This smile was too *polite*--neat even. Her eyes used to genuinely light up when she saw him and she would show all of her teeth, but now it was as if he was just another visitor. Worship began and her attention returned to the front. Everyone around him stood and began to worship, but he couldn't bring himself to even look the part. His guilt weighed upon him like an anchor, holding him to his seat as he grappled with himself.

In his Sunday school class as a child, he learned that God knew all things, including how many hairs are on your head. Of course, being who he was, Micah asked his teachers if God knew how many arm hairs everybody had. The teacher told him, "yes" and stressed the fact that God knew *everything* about *everyone.* Although that fact had seemed cool to Micah back then, it sort of terrified him now. That meant that every time that he smoked, God was there. Every time that he drank, God was there. Every time he laid down with someone, God was there.

Eiw.

God was present for everything he ever did and yet, when God spoke to him the other day, He didn't mention any of it. It was as if He had ignored it.

"I didn't ignore it. I died for it."

Micah jumped at the still, small voice. He hadn't heard that voice in a while and was beginning to actually believe that God had finally honored his request to be left alone.

I guess it was only a matter of time before you showed up again.

Micah, sat up straight in his chair, then leaned forward to rest his elbows against his knees. *You show up at weird times.*

"This is My House, where else would I be?"

Micah imagined God smirking at Him.

So you don't care about anything I've done?

"Oh I care about it all. I care, but it is as I said—I died for it. The hard part isn't gaining My forgiveness. The hard part is letting go and that will be because you don't know what I know about you."

And what would that be?

"That there is nothing in this world, or the next that could ever separate you from My love. You're too precious to give up."

Too precious? You do know that I even ran over someone's cat once?

"I was there."

I've dinged without the ring.

"I was there for that too."

Micah wrinkled his nose in response.

I liked it.

"I know."

I drink.

"I know."

That was present tense. I actually had a bit last night and it was amazing.

"I was there too, saved your life remember? I did catch the tense by the way."

I've lied.

"Nothing you can say or tell me will be new or come as a surprise to Me Micah. Come to Me. If you're worried about changing, don't. We do that together. It's Me and You Micah, as it always has been and always will be. Just say you will, and I'll do the rest."

Micah turned his head to his left to see Rea with her hands lifted and eyes closed. He sucked in a shaky breath knowing that he was now out of excuses, and out of time. He had to make a decision. After surviving last night, it shouldn't have been hard to make that choice, but a promise to serve the Lord would last a lifetime, not just one night.

The sound of an older man's voice drew his attention. Micah looked up to where the voice was coming from--the platform. The man was tall and lean, with kind, tear-filled eyes. Despite his tears, the man smiled warmly at the congregation. In the weeks before, Micah had only seen this man a few times. Brother Mark, is what they'd called him.

Brother Mark inhaled softly and the sound echoed through the speakers as he waited patiently for the music of praise and worship to settle, until only the soft instrumental music could be heard.

"As we were worshipping, I felt the Spirit of the Lord telling me to open the altar," he said. He lifted one of his hands as he continued speaking. "Oh church, I just feel that He's here and that's He's working on the hearts of some people in this room. So, I say to you, if God has been speaking to your heart, come. This altar is for you. We will pray with you and for you. There is no judgement here, only the love of Christ."

Micah's heart dropped into his stomach as the fear of rejection welled up within him. He was beginning to sweat when someone placed their hand on his shoulder, effectively breaking him from his stupor. Looking up from his lap, his eyes met Rea's smiling and reassuring face.

"I'll go with you," she whispered.

Micah looked over her shoulder to see Esther at the altar with a few other church members.

"Ok," Micah whispered. He took his sister's outstretched hand and blinked back tears before standing. *This is it…I guess…*

Everything seemed to move in slow motion and become a blur of color and sound around him as they made their way to the altar. It was crowded, and he instantly became worried. Perhaps he should have waited, or maybe he shouldn't have waited this long. Would they get to him? Would there be anything left for him? Was it crazy of him to worry that there wouldn't be enough *God* left for him? He needed a lot... *What am I supposed to do once I get there?* Micah thought as he inhaled deeply.

His eyes followed Brother Mark as he went from person to person, praying with them. Brother Mark made his way to another young woman, but suddenly stopped and looked in Micah's direction. Much to his surprise and confusion, Brother Mark walked away from her and Micah's heart beat sped up as he realized that Brother Mark was making his way over to *him*. He steeled himself for the onslaught of questions about why he needed prayer, but they never came.

"Son, I can tell that God is working on your heart," Brother Mark said as he stopped abruptly in front of Micah. All Micah could do was nod. "Rea?" Brother Mark began cheerfully.

Rea smiled brilliantly. "Yes sir. I'm here for moral support," she chirped. Her grip on her brother's hand became tighter and Micah squeezed back, thankful for her support.

Brother Mark nodded with a smile.

"So, how do I do this?" Micah asked, his voice shaking lightly. He cleared his throat, hoping to preserve at least a little bit of dignity and pride while doing this.

Micah didn't believe it was possible, but Mark's features lit up even more. Rather than the simple slight curve of his lips, the man's teeth were exposed from his large grin.

"Confess with your mouth and believe in your heart that Christ

Jesus is the Son of God and that He died for your sins and He rose from the dead," Brother Mark instructed.

Ah, seems simple enough.

Rea squeezed her brother's hand and took a step back.

"Jesus is the Son of God and He died for my sins," Micah confessed. Images of everything that he had ever done wrong flashed through his mind. He was unable to hold back the tears anymore; his eyes filled to the brim and spilled over. "And that He rose from the dead."

The man placed his hand on Micah's shoulder, and leaned in reassuringly, "Now open your heart to Him. I can outline a prayer for you to repeat or you can simply say what's on your heart. He'll hear either of them, they're both powerful and will get the job done," he said, smiling.

Micah squeezed his eyes shut. A tiny fragment of disbelief flickered within him—testing him. Oh and the unworthiness he felt! The shame and guilt from everything he'd ever done began to encompass him and he felt as though he might stop breathing. *What if I fail? What if I slide back into my old ways*? He'd already walked away from God once; if he did it a second time there would be no coming back. A peace filled him then, and those thoughts began to fade away. He knew deep down that after this prayer, there was no going back, and in that moment, surrounded by the peace and presence of God, he realized that he didn't *want* to go back.

"I-I'll pray," Micah whispered. He opened his mouth to speak but shut it again. "God," he began softly. Almost instantly, he could sense God's closeness. "God I'm sorry," Micah whispered. "I could stand here all day and still not finish giving you a list of all the things I've screwed up. I don't deserve Your grace, and I definitely don't deserve Your mercy or Your love but I've never been one to turn down gifts. I love free stuff, so I accept You Jesus. I've wasted so much time being angry at You and I'm sorry. Please forgive me." His voice cracked and his knees felt weak. "Please forgive me," he whispered brokenly. "I'm so sorry. Jesus please, please take me back." His words transformed into broken sobs. "Please take me back. In Jesus name, Amen," he whispered.

The man leaned in close to Micah's ear and whispered, "God says, 'I was there and I will honor every sacrifice. I saw the way they talked about you. I saw the way they criticized your hair and the music that I gave you. That's right, *I* gave you those melodies and those lyrics. *I* gave you the song in your heart and I loved every moment that you sang for Me. I am giving you a new song, and this time they will hear you. I've missed you, son. Surrender the hurt to Me, surrender the pain to Me, surrender all of your anger'. He says, 'I understand. I know that it hurt. I know that you did the very best that you could. Now let Me take it from here."

Micah had barely been able to stop crying long enough to hear those words and upon hearing them he became completely undone. He knew that he should have been embarrassed. He was a grown man, full-out weeping in front of everyone, but it didn't matter. Nothing else mattered at that moment. His knees gave out as sudden relief rushed through him. It was as though a huge weight had been lifted off of his shoulders. It was a weight he hadn't even realized that he'd been carrying, but he fully realized it's absence.

Mark quickly embraced Micah, and although Micah didn't know him, the embrace brought him a strange feeling of security. It was a tight hug, a fatherly hug--something Micah hadn't had in a long time.

"Come here moral support," Mark said as he beckoned to Rea, whose own glowing face was stained with tears.

She sank to the ground next to her brother, and threw her arms around him. He returned her embrace with everything in him.

"I told you it was ok to believe," she whispered gently.

"I never stopped believing he was real," Micah whispered through his tears. "I stopped believing that He was good."

"We've got a long way to go Micah," The Lord whispered in his ear. *"But we'll make it.*

***

"Micah!" Esther exclaimed as she raced towards him from her spot at the altar.

She threw her arms around him, her thin arms tightly circling his neck. "Geeze Ess, let me breath," he joked as he wrapped his arms around her waist.

When she pulled away, glowing and smiling, her hand remained on his shoulder.

"I'm *so* happy for you," she gushed. "This is great. What happened? What changed?" She asked.

Micah shrugged, scratched his chin, and said "I decided that I wanted to live."

His eyes bore into hers and he could see the joy sparkling in her brown eyes, making them appear lighter than usual.

"Amen," she whispered.

"I've got a long way to go," he said.

Micah released her hand and then shoved his fists in his pockets as he looked around the room, observing the genuine love and fellowship. From the moment that he'd left the altar he'd been embraced at least once by nearly everyone in the room.

"You don't have to go that way alone. Anything you need, I've got you," she vowed passionately, placing her hand on his shoulder.

The sincerity in her words burned a hole straight through Micah's newly cleansed heart. He nodded and smiled back at her.

"I've got you too," he said softly as they locked eyes.

"How do you feel?" She asked, looking away.

He paused for a moment, turning the words over in his mind. How *could* he describe it?

"Honestly? I feel like I've been dreaming this whole time and I just woke up."

Esther's smile grew.

"I know the feeling. It's amazing huh?"

Micah nodded. It did feel amazing. He had been under the impression that he was getting back at God by denying Him, but in truth he was only hurting himself. The peace he could have felt, the joy…

"Don't dwell on your past Micah. Don't think about what was or what could have been. I hold your future in My hand, and My plans for you are good," The Lord whispered.

Easier said than done.

Rea ran to Micah and embraced him, locking her arms around his waist.

"Rea," Esther mused. She took Rea in for a hug. "I'm so happy to see you, both of you. We have to celebrate."

An impish grin broke out over Rea's face.

"I'd love to, but can we eat at home? I don't want to go out," Rea said. Micah raised his eyebrows at her curiously.

"Sure. If that's fine with Ess."

His eyes never left his sister's seemingly innocent ones. Those jade eyes that mirrored his own were alight with mischief.

"Yeah, that sounds fine," Esther replied as she swept a piece of hair behind her ear and looked back and forth between the Micah and Rea.

Micah was still amazed by their relationship. Rea still hadn't let go of Esther. Rea liked people. She was very personable, but she didn't cling to people like that. Well, apart from Mallory and her family.

"I spent the night with my friend last night," Esther continued, "So she drove this morning. I can have her take me home."

Micah shook his head at her.

"That's not necessary. We can take you with us. Neighbors remember?" Micah offered.

Esther shifted from one foot to the other.

"Sure," she agreed.

Micah grinned.

"It's a date—it's *so* not a date, it's dinner," he corrected himself quickly and scratched the back of his neck as he gauged Esther's response.

She acted as if she hadn't heard the slip up, and only continued to smile at him before excusing herself to find her friend. Micah watched her retreat, missing her presence already.

"What are you up to Rea?" He asked, his eyes still on Esther's retreating form.

"Who me?" Rea asked, her voice rising in pitch.

Micah looked down at his sister and watched in amusement as her smile grew. "Yes, you."

Rea laughed and wrapped her arms around her brother's torso. "Wouldn't you like to know?" She quirked before taking a step back.

Brother Mark approached them slowly with a large and gentle smile on his face. He embraced Micah warmly.

"How do you feel?" He asked.

Micah shrugged, "Kinda great," he replied. To be honest, he was bursting at the seams, he feared he might explode with joy. He could only imagine what he truly looked like to everyone else.

Mark chuckled, "I never introduced myself, I'm Mark. I'm the Pastor here."

"Thank you, Mark. For everything," said Micah.

"That's *Brother* Mark; we're brothers now," Mark said as his smile enlarged.

"I guess we are," Micah said, returning Mark's smile. How long had it been since he'd called anyone that, and *meant* it? *Brother...*

"I see you've met Pastor Mark," Esther said brightly as she re-appeared at Micah's side. She gave Mark a one-armed hug. "He's awesome."

Micah nodded, "I can see that," he said. "Thank you again, Pastor--Brother Mark, for everything you did today."

Mark bowed his head. "Don't thank me, Micah," he said. "Just know that if there is anything you need, we can and are willing to help or at least point you in the direction of someone who can. Now that you're walking with the Lord Micah, it's very important that you keep up the faith, and learn about Him and grow. You are welcome to come to Bible studies, and come to Sunday school but don't think that just because you accepted Christ here that you are tied to this church. Any church home that will help you grow is good. You're not obligated to come here, but we'd love to have you here."

In all honesty, Micah *wanted* to be there. He wasn't too keen on the idea of going back to his other church. He loved this new place. He loved the freedom in this environment and the love that he felt when he walked in the door. The people at Esther's church, barely knew him and yet they loved him as though he'd been with them his entire life. Micah looked at his younger sister. She was staring at him, waiting for him to say something. He knew exactly what she wanted. *Stupid puppy dog eyes.*

"We've been here a few times. We'll be making a reappearance," he said finally.

Rea's eyes darkened and the expectation in her face dissipated in disappointment. Micah knew it was because she wanted to join, not simply visit. He'd watched her as she observed the services. She had never seemed so amazed or happy.

"Great! Well, I'll see you both soon and I'll see *you* Wednesday, Esther, " Mark said as he hugged all of them one last time before leaving.

"You ready?" Micah asked.

Esther nodded.

"Where are the keys?" Rea asked, holding out her hand.

Micah gave her an exasperated look. *What is up with her today?*

"Don't drive off with my car," he warned her as he fished around in his pocket. Once he found his keys, he placed them in her hand and glared at her playfully. She rolled her eyes.

"Yeah, yeah, yeah. I'll be in the car," Rea replied flippantly as she danced away from them, whistling loudly.

Micah scratched his head and looked at Esther. "Thank you," he said as they walked to the car.

She snapped her head towards him with a confused expression on her face. "For what?" She asked.

"For not giving up on me," he whispered.

He held the door open for her and led her to the car.

"Micah," she began.

"Ssh. Just say you're welcome," he pleaded.

She glared at him. The glare was ineffective, for he could see the amusement dancing in her eyes.

"Fine. You're welcome," she conceded, "But it wasn't me."

He threw his hands up in the air in playful enragement and then opened the passenger side door for her.

"Don't you know how to take a compliment? It's not hard I promise."

She shrugged, then got inside his car.

"Sure," she said as she winked at him and shut the door. Micah rolled his eyes as he walked around to the driver's side. When he started the car, she laughed at his sour expression. "You could always just tell me I'm pretty," she teased. Micah shook his head. "Why?" She asked.

"Because you're beautiful." He refused to look at Esther but could feel his eyes on him. Those eyes, like arrows were piercing him. "…and you'll probably say that I should complement the Creator because He made you."

She snorted at his comment and flipped her hair.

"I'm all for giving Him what He's due, but honey, *I* did this highlight and contour today. *I* labored on these eyebrows. Hashtag, eyebrows on fleek."

Rea howled with laughter from the backseat as Micah stared at Esther incredulously.

"You drew those on?!" He exclaimed.

Esther rolled her eyes, then swatted him on the arm.

"No," she said as she wrinkled her nose, "I filled them in."

He grinned before admitting. "When I first heard you praying on the balcony, I thought you were going to be some weird, ashy, skirt to the ankles, every-inch-of-your-body-covered type of--"

"Ashy?!" Esther exclaimed in disgust as she placed her hand over her chest. "Honey, anointed *doesn't* mean dusty. I can be saved and saucy. A *moisturized* minister--"

"But," Micah continued, unfazed by her interjection. "I was pleasantly surprised."

With wide eyes Esther continued, "And again I say, anointed doesn't mean dusty. I can still be a believer that blends and a Christian that conceals. Oil is in the Bible, there is no reason for me to be ashy. And the people of God said…"

"Amen!" Rea finished as she laughed.

"Amen!" Esther said.

Micah rolled his eyes. "Still didn't say thank you," he grumbled.

"Thank you," Esther said smirking.

"Women," Micah said jokingly, as he shook his head.

When they arrived at the house Micah opened the door for Esther and helped her out. Rea went on ahead, leaving the two of them in the car.

"How can I thank you?" Micah asked.

"For?" Micah shrugged.

"What I said earlier." Esther rolled her eyes. "If you keep doing that, your eyes will get stuck like that," he teased.

"You don't have to thank me," she said. "I didn't do anything. I was just following orders."

"I didn't give my life to Christ again, to be with you…or try to anyways. I did it because I needed to, because I need Him."

He felt silly having to say it aloud, but he wanted to make sure that she knew--that everyone knew, he was in this for the long haul.

Esther raised an eyebrow at him.

"I know and that," she said. "And that is why I'm happy."

"But that doesn't change the fact that I want to thank you for the impact you've had on me. Let me take you out to dinner, a real one this time? It can be as friends…just friends. I think that's what I need right now."

Esther's nodded appreciatively.

"I think so too," she whispered. "I think I can make some time for you," she joked.

Micah's cheeks began to burn. He hadn't realized that he'd started smiling.

"Great. Until then," he said as he scooped her up in his arms. "I know your feet hurt. This is my temporary thank you."

Esther squealed at the sudden movement.

"My feet do *not* hurt," she insisted as she laughed.

Micah looked at her skeptically.

"Girl, you were gettin' it in those heels. I was worried for a minute that you might fall during that praise break."

Esther threw her head back and laughed loudly and obnoxiously. It seemed that there hadn't just been a weight lifted off of his shoulders, but also off of hers as well. Micah mounted the stairs carefully with her in his arms, images of him carrying her over the threshold of a new house flashed through his mind. He was grateful when her voice snapped him out of it,

"What can I say? For Jesus I'm willing to break my heel…and eat the carpet," she joked as he sat her down outside of his front door.

Suddenly, she froze. Micah stared at her expectantly.

"What's wrong?" He asked as he opened the door.

"Nothing, nothing."

After they stepped inside, Esther used his shoulder as a crutch as she took off her shoes.

"I thought your feet weren't hurting," he quipped, crossing his arms.

Esther shrugged again.

"They're not. I'm just trying to be a respectful house guest." She sat them down beside the door and then smiled at him, rubbing her hands together excitedly. "Let's eat. I'm starved."

***

"So, that's where you're headed now?" Jay asked skeptically. Micah nodded and gathered his things from the hospital chair. "That's fine. Wifey will be here soon. I won't waste away alone."

Micah narrowed his eyes at his over dramatic friend. After eating with Esther and Rea, he'd bustled over to the hospital to see his friend. He hadn't planned to stay long—just an hour or so; but judging by the way the visit had been going for the past few minutes, Micah was convinced he wouldn't make it to an hour.

"Right," Micah said, sighing.

"You mean to tell me that the girl that you were creeped out by invited you to her church, you got saved and y'all had dinner and now y'all are finna go hang out?"

Micah nodded.

"And that's all y'all are finna do? Netflix, no chill?" Micah glared at his friend and let out a large huff.

"Really, Jay?"

"You've gone soft."

Micah cut his eyes at him.

"Hey, lay off, ok? I asked her to teach me some stuff. She knows a lot and it's been a while since I picked up a Bible. I don't exactly know where to start."

Jay shot him a disbelieving look. Six years ago Micah could confidently quote scripture, but now he wasn't so sure who God *truly* was anymore. He was determined to find out, to know God just as intimately, if not more than he had back then.

"So she's like your mentor?" Micah nodded, causing Jay to snort. "Well, I'm happy for you, man. The devil thought he had you, but you ran."

Micah was unsure of where Jay's sarcasm was coming from. Shouldn't Jay have been happy for him? Why was he being like this?

"What's your problem? You say you're happy for me, but you've done nothing but antagonize me since I got here."

Jay sighed and shook his head.

"You almost died a couple of days ago, Micah. The reality is that you got scared and now you're trying to get right with God. We both know it won't last. Besides, I've been trying to get you to come to church for years."

Micah stared at his friend incredulously. His skin burned with anger and his heart clenched.

Did this man get shot in the leg or the head?

"Why are you coming at me like this?" Micah asked through clenched teeth.

"Because you rolled up in here thinking you were better than me, talking about how church was and how you just felt God's love, and *blah, blah, blah, blah*. Just a few weeks ago, you were saying how all of this stuff was fake!" Jay fumed.

"How is that me saying that I'm better than you? I'm so confused right now."

Shouldn't Jay friend have been happy for him? Jay, more than anyone else. It was true, Jay had been trying to get Micah to come to church with him for years, but did it matter what church he went to, as long as he'd met God? Wasn't that what it was all about anyway? This conversation didn't even feel real.

"I've been a Christian all my life and I never came at you with all this stuff. You too holy for everybody now."

"How? Is it because I said I wasn't going to do anything with Esther? Because I want to study the Bible? Shouldn't you be happy about that?! And what does you being a Christian your whole life have to do with me?"

"Because I know when someone's full of it, and you are right now. I'll give it about two weeks. I'm not new to this Jesus thing, I'm true to it," Jay said sharply, beating his fist against his chest one hard time.

Micah leaned forward, eyes wide in disbelief.

"Jay! Your life is messy as hell-*heck*! I didn't say a word about anything you did, the jokes you made, or the way you acted because I didn't care. You were just like every other Christian I'd ever met. *You* were fake. I'm visiting you in the hospital right now because you got mixed up with a drug dealer, but you're livin' right and I'm wrong? Ok," Micah said throwing himself back against the chair and lifting up his palms.

Jay glared at him, his nostrils flaring in rage.

"I *know* you ain't trynna come at me about how to live."

"You lived no different than me and I wasn't even a Christian! The only difference between the two of us is that I was honest about my mess. So why would I want to go to church with you? If I wanted hypocrisy and bull crap, I could have gotten that at my own church!"

"The only thing different is that ol' girl has a rack and a vagina."

Micah stood up quickly, knocking over the hospital chair he was sitting in.

"Stop! Do you know how stupid you sound right now? Esther has been consistent since day one! The moment she stepped into my life she changed it. It wasn't because she was so amazing. It was because she wasn't straddling the fence. I've never chosen a woman over you Jay but I'm warning you, keep her name out of your mouth."

"Man, screw that. When she drops ya' ass don't say nothing to me. She didn't even want you before this and now y'all are all buddy buddy because you got saved? Ain't nothing real about that."

"You don't know the first thing about being real Jay, and you don't know anything about our *friendship*."

Micah grabbed his jacket and started to walk towards the door. As he reached for the handle, he paused. Micah turned around and *really* looked at him. His friend had lost weight in the past couple of weeks, and as he laid there washed out by the bright lights of the hospital room, Micah contracted the strangest feeling of Deja vu. *I saw this, in my dream…*This revelation slightly curbed his anger, but when the realization faded, the rage returned.

"You know what?" Micah paused and ran his hand over his chin. "I don't even understand how you can sit here and act like this. We almost died the other night. I mean, do you even remember what happened? Or were you too out of it?"

"I told you I had it handled," Jay said icily.

"Didn't look like it to me. Shawn almost shot me *and* you."

"Because you got involved."

Micah reeled back. What was he supposed to have done? Was he supposed to have let Shawn kill him? Aside from the fact that he couldn't let his best friend die. If Shawn *had* killed Jay, who was to say that Shawn wouldn't have turned the gun on him? *Maybe I shoulda' just left his ass…* Micah shook his head to clear the thought from his mind.

"You're my friend. I wasn't just going to let you die in that alley! It was your stupidity and loose mouth that got him all riled up anyway," Micah said simply.

"I didn't ask you to do that for me! Don't you think I feel bad that you got dragged into it? My family was in danger, *you* were in danger and all because of me." Jay sighed and looked around the room exasperatedly. "Micah, I'm sorry. Is that what you wanted to hear? I messed up." Micah sighed. He was furious with Jay's actions. He'd not only lied to him, but he endangered the both of them. "Stop judging me, ok?" Jay said. "Not all of us have it as easy as you do."

"Easy?!" Micah yelled.

"No disrespect," Jay began. Micah snorted. Now he wanted to talk about not being disrespectful. "It sucks that your parents died and everything, but you don't have any other legit problems!"

Without another word Micah left the room. His entire body was shaking with rage. *That mother f--* Micah caught himself. The whole not cursing thing was going to be a bit of a challenge. *He really brought up my parents…* Micah thought in disbelief.

He stormed out into the parking lot and quickly found his vehicle. *Calm down. Just calm down,* Micah thought as he climbed inside and slammed the door.

He drove around town for a while with his music blasting., trying to calm himself before he arrived at home. If he didn't keep it together, Rea would be asking questions, and he wasn't ready to answer any just yet. He didn't want to lie either. He was pretty sure that was a sin. Then again, if Rea saw his appearance when he came in last night and didn't ask, maybe she'd keep quiet this time. When he pulled into his parking space, he inhaled and exhaled repeatedly. He *never* would have expected that from Jay--his supposed best friend. Maybe he was just unstable from the night before. Or maybe, he just wasn't the person that Micah thought he was.

Figures, Micah thought.

"*Do not become bitter, Micah,*" God whispered to Him. "*He has his own way to go. Some people are seasonal. They serve their purpose and then they leave."*

"That may be, doesn't change the way it makes me feel though," he said with a shrug. "I expected him to be happy for me," he murmured as he mounted the stairs.

"*In his heart he is Micah, but he has a lot of issues that he has to work on for himself. Pray for him."*

Micah nodded as he raised his hand to knock on Esther's door. She was out of breath as she pulled open the door and she smiled up at him. Micah returned the smile, but soon frowned when he realized that it wasn't the smile he was used to. Normally, she would greet him with a smile that showed all of her teeth, today her smile didn't stretch that far and she had dark circles under her red, puffy eyes.

"Hey," she said, her voice cracking.

"Esther are you ok?" He asked.

"I will be," she said as she leaned against the doorpost. "What's up?"

He ran his eyes quickly over her disheveled form. She was dressed in a burgundy jogging suit. The jacket was zipped up all the way and her hair was falling out of the messy bun she had it in. She looked disheveled and distraught.

"I just needed to talk," he murmured. "But I think you probably need to talk more than I do."

"No, no. It's fine. Meet me outside on the balcony in like twenty minutes ok?"

"Sur—"

"Great."

She closed the door quickly before he had the chance to say anything further. Dumbfounded, Micah took a step back. *Ok?* He made his way into his apartment and knocked on his sister's door.

"Rea, I'm home."

"Ok!" She responded. "Wait! Don't go anywhere, " she yelled as she threw open her bedroom door and walked out.

"How is Jay doing?" She asked.

He was unsure of what to say. Should he mention the physical state or rather, the *mental* state of his friend? Should he mention their blow out?

"Good," he said simply. "He'll be out soon."

Rea nodded. Micah had given her the bare minimum after Sunday's service, saying that there had been some kind of accident. She did her best to try him for more information, but he wouldn't budge. He didn't want to lie to her, so this was his only option. She'd finally conceded, and with a resigned sigh, she promised to pray for him.

Rea wrapped her arms around him. Her short stature causing her face to meet his chest. Micah returned her embrace tightly.

"I'm proud of you," she said.

"Thank you."

"Love you."

Micah kissed the top of her head. "Love you too. Now, enough of this mushy stuff."

She pulled away from him, and stared at him for a moment with a small smile on her face. Tears glistened in her eyes.

"I'm gonna go shower," she said.

"Ok," said Micah.

Rea gave him one last hug before retreating to her room. Micah grabbed a bottle of water from the refrigerator, then made his way to the balcony and took a seat in one of the chairs. True to her word, Esther came out a few minutes later, looking as good as new. There was no evidence of their earlier encounter.

"Hi, friend," she said cheerfully. "I would have thought you'd have taken a nap after dinner."

Micah laughed.

Briefly he debated telling her about where he'd been, but he hadn't even told her about the fact that he'd nearly died a few nights before. He wasn't sure how long he'd keep that to himself, but he knew that it would at least stay a secret for that night.

"Nah. I had to run an errand," he said. Esther nodded. "Why did you want to talk out here?"

"We haven't been out here in awhile; we haven't really talked in a while either." Micah scratched the back of his neck.

"Yeah about that…"

"Tell her the truth," The Lord whispered.

"You don't have to explain yourself, Micah," Esther said, shrugging her shoulders. "It's none of my business."

"It kinda is."

Esther leaned forward, but otherwise gave no other physical response. Her facial expression was smooth and blank. He couldn't read her.

"How so?" She asked. Micah sighed and ran his hands down his face. "It's ok, Micah. You can talk to me."

Why are my eyes watering? Must have gotten something in my eye. Micah didn't want to think about what he did. He knew it would hurt her. He was fully aware of her feelings towards him, and he admired her restraint. Esther refused to admit that she had feelings for him aloud, but he could see it in the way she looked at him, and he felt it in how long their hugs lasted. Even when he refused to succumb to God's call, he had to admit that *her* steadfastness was inspiring.

"During the weeks that we didn't talk…I was with Sheba."

Esther looked down at her hands and leaned back.

"What does that have to do with me?" She murmured.

His heart twisted as he watched her facial expression glaze over with indifference. He knew that look all too well, as he'd put on that face many times himself.

"I was running from God, from you, from everything and so I went back to her because she was safe and she was what I knew and she was easy—"

Esther shook her head.

"You don't have to tell me about this, Micah. We're not together, I'm your friend."

"Yes, but you believed in me."

"Micah…"

"No let me finish. You and I were close and I made it clear to you that I had some feelings for you but I pushed you away because I felt ashamed of what I did, which is weird, because I hadn't felt that sort of conviction in a while. Esther, you carry Christ in you and I have an obligation as someone who now claims to love Jesus, to treat you as such."

Esther squinted her eyes at him.

"Micah, I—"

"Nope, still not done. I care about you Esther—a lot, and you know how much I love my sister. If someone did to my sister what I did to you, I'd be pissed. I'm sorry that I disrespected you and I kind of missed having you around. You may not feel like I wronged you, but I do and I'm sorry for that."

Esther sighed, and then smiled at him. This time her smile was genuine. Her eyes twinkled.

"I forgive you, Micah, but I still don't feel like you have to apologize to me."

"I'd hug you, but..."

"You'll get your chance." She paused, seemingly weighing her words. "And for the record…I missed you too." There was an easy and comfortable silence that passed between them before Esther spoke again, "Was that what you came to my door for?" She asked.

"I wanted to ask for your help. I want to start studying the Word, and I need someone to help me figure out where to start."

She smirked at him,"Do you still have that list I gave you?"

He grimaced. "I'm not sure."

"Well, if you don't have it, I suggest that you start at the beginning."

Micah's eyebrows drew together. He was perplexed by her idea.

"What do Sunday School stories have to do with my life right now?"

"They have everything to do with it, Micah. You want to know God better, right?" Micah nodded. "Then you start from where we first get to meet Him. By we, I mean Man. The love of God for Man starts from the very beginning of the Bible." Micah's confusion only grew. Questions bounced around in his head, and he found himself unable to decide which to ask first. "Micah, why were we created?" She asked.

He shrugged.

"For His amusement and entertainment?" He offered sarcastically.

"No." She giggled. "Although, I'm sure we are pretty entertaining to watch." She mused. "He created us for His glory and to have a relationship with us."

"But weren't the angels, like, I don't know. Weren't they here before us?" He leaned forward in his chair. Esther shifted so that she could tuck one of her legs beneath her.

"Yes. They were here before us. From my understanding, God loves them a great deal, but He didn't make them as He made us. He wanted to have a relationship with Man. He wanted someone to love Him freely. He wanted us to choose to love Him. He made us in His image, and in His likeness. He has emotions like we do, He's intelligent, the gift of free will, I could go on and on. Micah, we were made to love and be loved by the only One who can truly relate to us. That's why the beginning is important. It's crazy, huh?"

Dumbfounded Micah sat back in his patio chair.

"Crazy doesn't even begin to cover it." They were silent for a moment, not staring at anything in particular, both lost in their own thoughts. "That's the dopest perspective I've ever heard on Genesis."

"I mean the Bible itself is pretty dope," Esther agreed.

Micah guffawed.

"What?" She asked, sitting up straight in her chair.

"No, don't say dope. You can't say that word." He clutched his stomach that was now aching because of how hard he was laughing. Esther rolled her eyes. "It's just not your thing, Ess. Stick to what you know."

She crossed her arms and pouted.

"I can be cool," she protested.

"Right… I think I'm gonna go for a drive later on. Wanna come?"

"I would, but I have a paper to finish." Micah nodded. "That's technically what I should be doing right now."

"Well, please don't let me keep you from being a good student."

He smirked. She smiled.

"I'm not in a rush."

"That's a first," he said. Esther stretched and yawned. "Sleepy already?"

"A little but, I just wanted you to know that I'm really proud of you, Micah and I am really happy for you. I know I said that earlier but, you should know that your salvation doesn't change my perception of you."

Micah's eyebrows furrowed. Esther took her hair down from her bun and shook her head to loosen its shape.

"What do you mean?" He asked.

"I mean that we were good friends before you were saved Micah. Yes, you've given your life to Christ but that doesn't mean that the goofy, sarcastic, and fun side of you has to leave. I tried too hard when I first got saved to play the part. I just want to encourage you to be who God made you, don't try to do God's work for Him. Remember, He wants to get rid of the bad in us, not the things that make us unique." She sighed and fiddled with a few strands of her hair. "I guess what I'm saying is that, the fire you have inside of you is not supposed to die out now. It's just supposed to burn for a different purpose." Micah stared at her, absorbing all that she was saying, trying to read between the lines of what she meant.

"Don't over analyze it," Holy Spirit whispered. *"Take this for what it is."*

"Ok," he said aloud. "Thank you, Esther."

"You're welcome."

The two lingered in silence for a while longer, allowing the sun to set and fade into darkness. In the past, he'd never been able to sit in silence and be at peace. There was no need to fill the space, or make an awkward conversation. Micah broke the silence first,

"Are you ever going to tell me what was wrong with you earlier today?" Esther took a deep breath.

"I just…it's a long story." She exhaled, blowing a stray curl out of her face.

"Give me the short version."

"Just having some issues with my family," she murmured. Maybe it was stupid of him, but he had just never assumed that Esther would have problems. "Long standing issues, but I'm honestly fine," she said with a smile. He studied her face, noticing how this particular smile was different from all the others. It was sad, resigned.

"No, you're not," he murmured. "Esther, you don't have to be so put together all the time."

"I know." She looked down at her hands, and sniffed. "Guess it's a habit. Not everyone you meet can handle your humanity."

"But I can."

Esther nodded, her eyes wandering around in the dark.

"I know, I should go finish my paper," she said, standing up.

Micah followed suit.

"Esther, wait," said Micah softly.

"Yeah?"

He wanted to press the issue further but thought it best to let it go. She would share when she was ready.

"Have a goodnight."

With an awkward wave, Esther retreated back to her apartment. Micah waited for a moment longer before going inside. When he entered, he tapped on Rea's door.

"Going out for a minute, I'll be back soon!"

"Ok!" She replied. "Be careful."

"Always."

Micah was smiling as he pulled out of the apartment complex. *God, I know what you told me earlier but I'm confused. Jay was supposed to be my friend—my best friend. He says he believes in you. If that's true, then why did he do this?*

"He doesn't know Me. He knows of Me," God gently whispered.

Micah rested his head upon his elbow that was resting against the car door as he drove.

And what exactly does that mean?

"Get to know Me and see."

Micah snorted. He was beginning to wonder if God's M.O. was sarcasm and vagueness.

What exactly is that supposed to mean?

"The more time that you spend with Me Micah, the more you become like Me in your thinking and your actions."

Micah drummed his fingers against the steering wheel as he waited impatiently for the light to turn green. He watched all of the cars pass by him, zooming back and forth.

Is what Esther said true? His question was newly formed.

"Yes," was His simple reply. *"I created you, Micah, with all of the love in My heart. Love is your purpose."*

Warmth flooded Micah's body as he realized the truth behind God's words. There was no denying it, no arguing with it. He was beginning to see that God's love, just was. There was no rhyme or reason to it. His love was so perplexing, exhilarating, and warming that he didn't want to question it any more. He just wanted to be grateful for it, but he couldn't help *but* to question God's love. Why would a holy God, love an unholy man like himself?

"No one is perfect, Micah."

Except You.

"Yes, I didn't give My Son for just you Micah. I gave Him for the world, because everyone would need Him so that they could be perfect, as I am perfect. That is why He is accessible to all mankind."

You have an answer for everything, don't You? Micah replied whilst chewing on his bottom lip. There was no response. *Maybe not. Ok, I was just kidding.*

"Happy now?" God asked.

Micah rolled his eyes but couldn't stop grinning. He'd never expected for God to be like this. For the past few years of His life the idea of a loving God had withered away within Him. Had someone told him, he never would have believed that God would be someone with a sense of humor, someone who truly knew Him, someone who really loved Him.

Just wait til I screw something up… Insecurity began to rear its malevolent head, challenging what he was finally understanding to be true.

"Don't worry, I've made provisions," He said.

Micah pictured in his mind what he believed God would look like. He pictured long brown locks and meaningful eyes—perhaps blue or brown. Upon His face he pictured a grin, one that was reassuring and almost teasing. No, God wasn't anything like what he expected. He backed into his parking spot at the apartment complex. He turned off his car and sat alone in the darkness, staring at nothing. He was overwhelmed by racing thoughts.

First, there was Esther. He'd never been in denial about his feelings toward her but he knew that perhaps a relationship wasn't the best idea for him right now. *Well, that was presumptuous. Who said she wanted to be in a relationship with you?* He shook his head. That was true. As far as he knew, the attraction was one-sided. He thought back to the moment they shared earlier. When he suggested that friendship was the best thing for him, her face lit up.

She wasn't the easiest woman to understand, but then, she wasn't like other women. She was a gem. A rarity. She was one that he couldn't ever hope to deserve, but he couldn't help it…he wanted her.

I'd do just about anything to have her. He sighed.

Right now, he needed to focus. His attention needed to be on his walk with God. He had an overwhelming desire to learn the Word and develop an intimate relationship with God. *No point in worrying about a relationship with a girl that I can never have anyway.*

"Never say never Micah," Elohim whispered.

That's not funny.

"I'm not laughing."

Micah opened the car door and walked towards his apartment. He immediately went to his sister's room, with the intent of simply checking to see if she needed anything before he went to bed. The scene before him, sent a chill through his entire body. His eyes filled with tears as joy, that he'd never expected to feel, coursed through his body like veins rushing blood to his heart. This reaction was different from the last time he'd seen his sister in this position.

His younger sister sat cross-legged on her bed. In her lap was a worn, black leather Bible. Her head was bowed, as she spoke in a low tone. She was praying--she was praying for him. Tears coursed down her cheeks as the fervor of the prayer covered her entire being.

"…thank You, God, for saving Micah. I pray God that this is for real. Call him forth as a man of God," she prayed.

Pride began to well up within his heart. The realization that he'd actually tried to deter her from this path tore at his heart, but he quickly pushed the thought from his mind.

Things are going to be different now.

THIRTEEN

The next few months passed rapidly and Micah was amazed at how quickly he'd grown and how much things had changed. He and Jay apologized to each other for the argument they had. Despite their apologies they were unable to restore their friendship to its former glory. There still remained an unaddressed chasm between the two. Although Jay apologized for his harsh words, Micah still believed that Jay honestly meant what he'd said. In the meantime, Micah made new friends.

It was December now, and Micah had opted to have a small gathering with friends from church at his apartment. Rea called it a Christmas party, but Micah said that it was too small to be considered a party. He and Esther had been spending a lot more time together and he was convinced that he had a shot with her. He never would have imagined how quickly his life had changed, how quickly *he* had changed.

Although God had become his primary focus, he was still having a hard time kicking some old habits. Cursing was one of them.

As he helped Rea decorate the apartment, he thought back to his conversation with Esther about cursing.

"It's not in the Bible," he'd said with a smirk.

She'd merely rolled her eyes and shrugged saying,

"Did you find that answer on Google? The Word does say not to let any unwholesome talk come out of your mouth, the f-bomb doesn't exactly classify as wholesome now does it?" She paused and eyed him smugly. "And besides," she continued, "how can I tell you're different from the world if you cuss like they do?" Micah took a moment to think about it for a moment before he conceded.

"Point taken."

She'd laughed at him, she knew she'd win the argument from the beginning. That was Esther—a know-it-all. The more he was around her, the more her knowledge of the Bible surprised him.

Their conversations about the Word ran deeper than he'd ever thought they could. They discussed some of the same stories he'd heard when he was a child from a different point of view. There were things that he'd forgotten that he knew about the Bible; things that he'd learned in Sunday school, or the stupid little conventions that his church made him attend as a child. She was fearless in her faith, or at least that's how she seemed. She was not afraid to argue her point and he loved that about her.

Loved.

That was a strong word. He shuddered at the thought. He had seen that word abused, and he'd been an abuser of the Word in the past. It wasn't until he actually came to the Lord, that he truly understood its meaning and power. God's love for mankind was unending and all-consuming and Micah was consumed. He'd been consumed by the fires of a passion so deep and so fervent that he often felt overwhelmed. He was desperate to learn anything he could about Christ. More than anything on earth, he wanted to know God. Love was the first of many things that he learned after coming to Christ.

He knew he still had a long way to go, but day-by-day the anger dissipated and the weight on his heart lifted. He'd been frustrated with himself many a time for falling into some of his old ways, but God would always remind him that it was He who changes hearts. The amount of prophetic dreams he was having increased. Although he didn't always understand the dreams, he was quick to ask for help in interpreting them. He was grateful and his heart was full from all of the support that he'd gained.

It was that support that drew Micah to Siani. He and Rea officially left Vernon Rush shortly after his salvation. They had no ill feelings toward the church, but wanted to go where they felt comfortable and for them that was Mt. Siani. As new congregants, they rarely missed Bible study and if Micah had to miss, it was because of work. Things were normal until Jay returned to work. Jay was more than happy to assert his position as Micah's boss rather than his friend. Sometimes he gave him more work to do than everyone else, and other times he would cut Micah's hours. Every time Micah thought about it, he became angry. He wasn't as angry over his treatment at work, as he was with the fact that their friendship was now in shambles.

Micah was stringing garland over the fireplace when the Lord began to whisper to him. *"Remember what I told you Micah. Sometimes, people are in your life for a season. People come and go."* Micah sighed. The sound of his Father's voice soothed him, but the words He spoke unnerved him. Would he really have to let go of Jay? *"I didn't say that his season in your life was up Micah. Just know that there's a purpose for everything that happens. Some things aren't for you to know, and some things you will understand in time."* Although Micah was wounded by Jay's behavior, he was appeased by God's response, at least for the time being.

To have been friends with Jay for so long, and have their friendship torn in two over something like that seemed ridiculous to him. Maybe it wasn't just the argument that had bothered Micah. Maybe it was the fact that when Micah defended Jay, Jay didn't even attempt to defend himself. Then after Micah tried to defend him, Jay attacked him. If anyone was going to be angry out of the two of them, it should have been Micah. That's how Micah saw it, at least. He was going to allow Micah to take the heat for him. *I guess that sounds familiar.* He shook his head and returned to streaming the garland until Rea entered the room.

"Micah!" Rea skipped into the living room, her Santa hat planted firmly on her head despite the wild curls beneath it.

"Yeah?" He finished with the last of the garland and turned to face his sister. She was vibrating with excitement. Rea loved Christmas despite the fact that it was only the two of them celebrating every year. No holiday was really ever the same. Some years, they'd go out of town just for a change of scenery. Overjoyed with this change of tide, Rea couldn't wait to see what this year would be like. She knew that Esther would play some part in it. She'd already begun to think of her as an older sister and that sense of family she'd been longing for was satiated when the trio got together.

"When is everyone supposed to get here?" Micah looked at his wrist watch. It was just turning five o'clock.

"Give them about thirty more minutes."

She rolled her eyes. He chuckled at her impatience

"Why don't you ask Mallory to come over earlier so that you guys can hang out or something? She can keep you occupied." Rea's face fell at the mention of her best friend's name. She began wringing her fingers and stared at the floor, her downcast expression showing that her mind was filling with negative thoughts. Micah frowned at his sister's new disposition.

"What happened?" Rea shrugged.

"Mallory and I don't really…" Rea sighed. "Well, we're not really friends anymore." Micah froze.

"It's the apocalypse," he muttered.

"Be serious, please."

"I am." He stuffed his hands in his pockets. He waited patiently for her to say something, anything. "What happened?" He walked over to his sister and put his arm around her.

"She just doesn't like me anymore, I guess. She doesn't talk to Stephanie anymore either."

He wasn't buying it. Those girls had been friends for years. There was no way that their friendship could have just ended. He looked at his sister apologetically and promised her that they weren't finished with their conversation.

"Coming!" He yelled. He opened the door and beamed at the young woman in front of him. She was bundled up in her winter wear from head to toe. He stepped back to allow her inside.

"Ess, you're early." He frowned when he noticed the plastic Walmart bags in her hands. "And I told you that you didn't have to bring anything."

She rolled her eyes and shoved her bags into his hands.

"Boy, please. I didn't have to bring this, I chose to. I was already out." Uninterested in arguing with her, Micah smirked.

"I'll take your coat for you," he offered.

She smiled at him and allowed him to help her out of her blue pea coat. She removed her knitted toboggan and took a look around. When her eyes landed on him, she looked at him inquisitively.

"What are you smirking at?" She asked.

His smirk remained firmly in place as he replied, "Nothing, beautiful." She pushed him playfully and took her bags from him.

"Is Rea home?" Micah snorted as he hung her coat on one of the mounted hooks near the door.

"She wouldn't miss this for the world, especially if you're here. Maybe you can talk to her. She's having a bit of friend trouble--girl stuff I guess," he explained.

He put an arm around her shoulders and guided her into the living room. His eyes widened in surprise when she wrapped her arm around his waist. He looked down at her with those wide eyes, unable to truly believe that she was reciprocating his affections. It wasn't uncommon for him to show some sign of affection toward her; a hug that lasted a little too long, a lingering touch of hands, a casual arm around her shoulders, but it was rare that she returned his subtle advances.

Her curly hair had been straightened and fell down her back in loose curls. Despite the vast amount of flyways and cow licks she'd acquired from her hat, she was still beautiful. There wasn't a drop of makeup on her apart from the burgundy lipstick she sported. He'd expected her to dress up, but he was pleasantly surprised to see her dressed in jeans and a wine long sleeved sweater. He was hesitant to take in her full appearance, knowing that his mind would wander, and he knew that after the first wayward thought settled, he'd be no good from that point on.

Esther wasted no time enveloping Rea in a hug as soon as she saw her. Before they spotted each other, Rea had been seated on the couch, playing with her cell phone.

"Hey, Rea," she greeted.

Rea smiled.

"Hey."

"What's wrong?" She asked.

Ever since she'd left Vernon Rush Church, Mallory had begun distancing herself from her and Stephanie. At the time, Rea had let it go, deeming it as something temporary. However, as the days went by, Mallory began talking to her less and less. Mallory had also taken to hanging out with a different crowd--one that had begun teasing Rea and Stephanie at school. Esther listened intently, as Rea recounted these events. When Rea finished, Esther pulled her into another hug while Micah watched, seething. His skin was reddened with anger and his arms were crossed tightly over his broad chest.

"That's so stupid," he fumed. "You guys have been friends for so long..."

The words God had spoken to him earlier came to mind and he paused allowing their real meaning to sink in. *Ah I get it. I see what You did there God.*

"Rea, I wanna tell you something that God told me today," Micah said.

Rea looked up at her older brother, her eyes were glistening with unshed tears. He could tell she was doing her best to hold back the tears but it wouldn't be long before those tears spilled over. Micah cleared his throat and shuffled from one foot to another. Esther smiled at him as she ran her fingers through Rea's hair.

"He told me that people come into your life for a season, and when their season is up, you just have to let them go. He also told me that everything happens for a reason. I know you and Mallory were good friends Rea, but sometimes even our good friends can hold us back from what God has for us in the future." A vague sense of pride rose up within him. He wasn't sure where that last part had come from, but was pleased that it came out.

"See, you didn't need my help," Esther said.

"Guess not," Micah admitted with a smirk.

"Rea, your brother is right. Pray for her, but don't hold on to what God may be trying to push out of your life. Let her go. Love her from a distance. As for those people who are teasing you, I know what that's like; trust me. It's like having a target on your back or something. As a Christian, you're going to get made fun of, it's inevitable. Jesus was hated and we will be too; it comes with the territory. Don't let it get to you. It's not because there's anything wrong with you, or because you did anything wrong. It's actually the opposite. So, dry your eyes and every time they make fun of you, just remember that you're doing something right."

Rea nodded.

"Now, don't I feel like a parent?" Micah muttered.

He remembered having these kinds of talks with his father, who always sounded so wise. He always knew the right thing to say. And listening to Esther talk to Rea in such a calm, wise, and comforting fashion reminded him of the way his mother spoke to him when he was upset. *We'd make a pretty great team.* He kicked himself, as the thought crossed his mind. He had no business thinking about that but he couldn't help it. He'd have to try harder. *Some help here God would be nice.* He was met with silence. *I know You can hear me.* Again, there was no response. *Hardy Har Har.*

"So..." Esther began whilst looking around the room appreciatively, "Nice decorations. Which leads me to the question of what you two do around here for Christmas."

Micah shrugged before replying, "It depends," he said nonchalantly. "I think this year we're going to stay home."

Esther's eyebrows furrowed.

"By yourselves?" She asked, her voice rising in disbelief.

Rea nodded. "We don't have any other family."

Esther sat in silence for a moment, lost in her own world.

"Hm. Do you cook, Micah? Rea?"

"Not really. I mean I like to cook but I'm not the best at it," Rea answered.

Esther nodded and silence filled the room again. Esther's phone went off. She glanced down at the caller ID and sighed.

"Is there somewhere I can take this call privately?"

"You can use my room," Rea said.

"Thanks," Esther said. She answered her phone as she walked toward Rea's room. Whether she realized it or not, Esther left the bedroom door slightly cracked enabling them to hear more than they probably should have.

"Yes, Mom." Pause. "No, I…" Esther sighed in frustration.

Micah felt a little guilty. He didn't want to intrude on her private conversation, but if he moved any closer to close the bedroom door—even if it was just to close it—he was worried that she might feel embarrassed. It wasn't like he was *trying* to eavesdrop.

"No, Mom, can—can you just put Nana on the phone please." Esther's voice cracked and thickened. "Mom, we've been through this!"

Micah flinched before sharing a look of confusion with Rea. Both of their faces scrunched up as they continued to listen to Esther's phone conversation.

"Did Esther ever tell you anything about her family?" Rea asked quietly.

"Not a whole lot. I've asked her about it before, but she seemed pretty closed off about it," Micah said.

"Well, something is going on," Rea said, folding her arms.

"I know," Micah agreed. "Hey, come help me set up this food."

Rea nodded and followed him into the kitchen. There wasn't much to be done. The chili was finished so all they had left to do was put the food out onto the counter. It wouldn't take long, but at least busying himself in the kitchen would put some distance between himself and Esther's conversation.

It wasn't that he was not concerned about Esther's family issues. He understood that every family had their problems, and Esther's family was no differen.. She'd talk about when she was ready.

Maybe I should let her know that she can talk to me...Micah thought as he opened up a package of paper plates. *But she should already know that...right?*

The kitchen itself, smelled sweet. A mixture of different scents like vanilla and pumpkin bread overtook the entire apartment. Micah and Rea had just finished putting out the desserts, which consisted of pumpkin bread, red velvet cake and various other sweets that Rea had made onto the counter, when Esther entered the kitchen. She leaned against the refrigerator, as Micah asked Rea where she'd come up with the ideas for her Christmas inspired foods.

"Pinterest," she replied with a smirk. "It's a girl's best friend.

Rea caught sight of Esther as she entered the kitchen quietly with reddened eyes and a tight smile. Rea saw through it, but refused to call her out on it. She simply went to hug her, then motioned for Micah to join them.

"I won't ask," Micah whispered as he embraced Rea and Esther tightly. "But we're here."

"Thank you," Esther whispered.

Guests began arriving shortly after their group hug broke apart. Amidst the first group guests, were Pastor Mark with his wife Tammi, Fallon, Jennifer--one of the teenagers from the church that Rea befriended, and Jasper. Jasper was a student at the University that Esther and Micah attended. Micah recognized him from his English class when he saw him one Wednesday night. Jasper was new to the faith, much like him in many ways, and both of them had become spiritual sons to Mark.

Micah was now leaning against the kitchen counter, watching as everyone became wrapped up in their own private conversations. Rea had taken over ushering in guests, the count now totaling about twenty.

From a distance, he watched his sister laugh and talk with Jennifer, who'd taken to helping Rea greet new guests. In Mallory's absence, Rea had gained a new friend. He should have noticed the change. He should have noticed the fact that she never asked to hang out with Mallory anymore. How did he miss it? He noticed Jennifer's name coming up a lot more and she spent the night there a lot, but he'd never thought that he needed to be concerned about Rea's friendship with Mallory.

"Hey," said Jasper as he approached Micah. Jasper was about six-two with cropped brown hair, and eyes the same greenish color of the Dead Sea.

"Hey. Enjoying the party?" Micah asked

Jasper shrugged indifferently before responding. "It's cool. I just don't usually like to be around people that much. I'm working on it. This--this is nice though." He gestured to the people positioned throughout the apartment. Some laughed, while others engaged in deep conversations. Esther danced up to the two of them. Her heavily improved attitude was contagious. It was good to see a genuine smile on her face after the tears she'd just shed. She hugged Jasper and then came to stand by Micah.

"Hey, Jazz," she said.

Jasper smiled slightly at her. She was bubbling over with energy, and he couldn't blame her. The positive and warm feelings of comradery and genuine love were intoxicating.

"Hey, Esther," Jazz said. He leaned against the kitchen counter beside Micah.

"You guys having fun yet?" She asked. "I asked Rea to put some music on ten minutes ago and—" She paused as the sound of, "Winter Wonderland" filled the space. "Never mind." She smiled at the two men, who shared knowing looks. "What?"

"Nothing."

Esther huffed at Micah's response. "I'm going to pretend like you didn't just lie to me. After all, God is watching you." She squinted her eyes at him, causing all of them to laugh.

"Yeah, well. It's just that you can never keep still," Micah admitted.

"Hard to do when you're happy," Esther admitted gleefully.

"I dunno. Jazz, I'm pretty happy. You?" Micah said as he looked over at his friend with a lazy smile.

"Yep, I'm just *overflowing* with joy," Jasper said casually.

"Whatever," Esther said. She looked over her shoulder to see Pastor Mark and his wife dancing to the music. The man couldn't dance to save his life. He was moving this way and that, taking a few steps forward and backward, while waving his arms, always close to catching the beat but ultimately always missing it. Seeing him do that while in his ugly Christmas sweater only made him look that much more hilarious. "Wanna dance?" Micah scratched his head.

"Umm…"

"I was talking to Jasper," Esther said. She stuck her tongue out at Micah, then grabbed Jasper by the arm. *Poor guy doesn't have a chance.* Micah thought.

He laughed at Jasper's desperate expression as Esther pulled him away.

"Help me!" Jasper mouthed.

Their living room area was already the ideal space for a get together. The apartment itself, being spacious already, provided a good amount of room. However, Micah wanted to ensure that everyone was comfortable, so he'd pushed the couch back against the wall, clearing out a large open area that was perfect for dancing.

Jasper was awkward. There was no doubt about that. Esther had been instrumental in bringing him out of his shell. When Jasper first arrived at Mt. Sinai, he refused to talk to anyone, but Esther was persistent in becoming his friend.

"He needs one," she'd told Micah.

Micah took Esther's words to heart and began to talk to Jasper as well. They became fast friends. Brother Mark had even asked Micah to pray over Jasper a few times. Of course, Micah immediately declined, but the Holy Spirit's conviction soon changed his answer.

Esther danced around Jasper, ignoring his lack of rhythm. She finally took pity on him and allowed him to retreat back to the kitchen area.

"She's something else," Jasper said, shaking his head as he exhaled in relief.

Micah and Jasper watched Esther as she danced with her friend Fallon, the two spinning each other around goofily. The people around them laughed at them. Rea eventually got up to join them.

"Yeah, she is." He grabbed a red solo cup from the counter and poured some eggnog into it. He took a sip of it, and when he pulled the cup away from his lips he saw Jasper's knowing smirk.

"What is it Jazz?" Micah sipped his drink as he waited for Jazz's response.

"Don't *'What is it Jazz'* me. Anybody can see that you and Esther have something going on."

"That would be why she asked *you* to dance," Micah said. He rolled his eyes and took another sip of his drink.

Jasper chuckled. "You jealous?"

"Um, no. That's ridiculous," Micah said.

"You said it and you don't even believe it. Don't worry, I'll set you guys up. Got any mistletoe?"

Micah smacked Jasper on the arm. "Seriously, Jazz?"

"What's the hold up?" Jasper asked. "Why don't you just ask her out?" Micah shook his head.

"I did that when I first met her. She didn't want to. We hung out a few times, but she strictly friend-zoned me."

"You weren't saved then were you?" Jasper crossed his arms. Again, Micah shook his head. "But you are now…do you think that's the reason that she wouldn't date you?"

"I think there's honestly more to it than that. Esther wasn't stupid. She knew I was still messing with my ex. I don't blame her, and I wasn't exactly nice to her when I met her either." Micah gave Jasper a brief run-down of his first meeting with Esther, all the while watching the young woman in question dance with his sister.

"Wow," Jasper said. "That's…"

"Ridiculous, I know. She was my proof." He looked down at the eggnog in his cup and swirled it around. "Besides, I don't know that a relationship is a good idea for me right now. I don't want to get distracted."

Jasper shrugged and folded his arms.

"That's between you and God bro, but I honestly don't think that's what would happen with the two of you."

Micah groaned. "Don't you have something better to do than get on my nerve—"

"Do you ever think about it?"

"What?" Micah asked, putting his cup on the counter.

"I mean, you said you couldn't stop messing around with your ex. Do you still want to mess with her?" Micah scratched the back of his neck.

"Well, yeah, sometimes. It's hard to quit something you're used to." Jasper chuckled as he continued. "But overall, no. No. I don't want her. I know the price and I'm not willing to pay it."

"Ok." Jasper looked away, seemingly lost in thought.

"What? Did you think you were the only one?" Micah laughed.

Jasper shrugged. "Kinda. Some of the people at church seem to have it so…right? Like, they have it all figured out--your girlfriend included."

Micah glared at him.

"She's not my girlfriend, Jazz, and don't be so hard on yourself. I've been feeling that way for a while too. I especially felt that way when I met Esther, but I honestly don't believe they have it all figured out. Esther will tell you up front that she doesn't have her life together. No one's perfect but sometimes it certainly does feel like it."

"I just wish that someone would say that. You know? I'm not saying they should tell all their business, but I mean…I just wish…I don't know."

Micah smiled reassuringly at him before patting him on the shoulder.

"You wish they'd just be transparent. You wish they'd just be human."

Jasper nodded. "Exactly."

"Well buddy, they are. No one's trying to fake it. Some people are just a little farther along in this walk than we are."

Wow, where did that come from?

Micah had never confessed to feeling inadequate or out of place amongst their museum of perfect spiritual people, to anyone. He'd alluded to it while talking to Esther but never made a big deal out of it. He didn't mention his struggles, the fact that sometimes late at night his finger would hover over Sheba's name in his phone. He never talked about the bittersweet emotion he felt when he deleted the messages she sent him—the sweetness of victory over his flesh and the bitterness of losing to his spirit. No one had shared that part with him when he got saved at a young age, but he knew sort of what to expect when he rededicated his life to Christ.

Jasper, however, didn't. His parents converted to Islam from Christianity when he was ten. Jasper never really bought into any religion, until he heard the Gospel in its simplest form from a friend of his. He bought into Christianity the relationship, not the religion.

"Hey Micah? Who's your friend?"

Micah tensed at the question. The sound of her voice drove him to dig his nails into the palms of his hands.

Jesus, say it ain't so… He thought squeezing his eyes shut. He could have sworn he heard Jasper curse, then quickly apologize.

Slowly Micah opened his eyes and exhaled. When he turned around his nails bit deeper into his flesh. Sheba stood there with one hand on her hip, arrogant as ever. With a smirk firmly in place, she wiggled her fingers at him. Her sweater dress clung to every curve. Her high heeled boots clacked against the hardwood floors as she took a few steps closer to him. In days past, perhaps he could have appreciated her appearance without discomfort. In fact, he would have been more than appreciative of her appearance. She was attractive, but she was also dangerous--the way a shaken-up coke bottle beside a brand new laptop could relieve thirst and destroy your day. He began to sweat. *My God, who turned up the heat? I think I'm going to be sick.* Micah swallowed hard as every nerve stood on end. There was no way this was going to end well.

"How did you get in?" He asked.

"Your sister let me in."

His stomach turned as he took in her smug expression. The way her lips turned slightly up at the corners vexed him. *I know she's lying.*

Rea appeared at his side, seemingly out of nowhere with a fierce scowl on her face.

"I tried to tell her that now wasn't a good time, but she pressed her way," said Rea fuming.

"It's ok, Rea," Micah said, standing up straight with his arms folded and his face impassive.

Should he kick her out or try to reason with her? In his heart, he knew that reasoning with Sheba was next to impossible.

"What are you doing here, Sheba?"

"I was hurt that I didn't receive an invitation." She folded her arms and matched Micah's tense posture. "Heard that you got all churched. Welcome to the club. I'm *so* happy for you." She smirked. "That would explain why you haven't responded to any of my texts or phone calls—you've been avoiding me."

"Micah, I think we should—" Jasper's suggestion was interrupted by Sheba's sharp tone.

"We're talking," she said, glaring darkly at Jasper.

"It's all you," Jasper said as he clasped Micah on the shoulder. He walked away quickly. It was for the best--Jasper had a temper, and dealing with Sheba was a disaster waiting to happen.

"If you wanted a freaky church girl, all you had to do was dial my number. You didn't have to get all involved with that girl. Once a hoe always a hoe, I don't care how saved she claims to be."

"Don't talk about her like that." Yes, Sheba knew how to press his buttons. Disrespecting the people he loved and cared about was one of those buttons. She was not merely pressing his buttons, she was banging on them.

"Ooh, protective, are we? You just tell her to watch her back." Sheba's tone was light, but held a sinister undertone that made Micah's skin crawl. Her warning was accompanied by a devilish smile.

"He doesn't have to tell me," Esther said calmly. "I'm right here."

The sound of her voice caused Micah to jump. She was walking towards them, Jasper looming behind her. Mentally Micah made a note to either thank or strangle Jasper later. That would all depend on how this showdown turned out.

Micah opened his mouth to speak, but God stopped him. *"Watch."*

Sheba glared at her and bit the inside of her cheek. "He was mine first." She took a step toward Esther.

"God's actually. I'm not arguing with you over Micah, Sheba. That's not my place, and your relationship or non-relationship with him isn't really my business. The two of you can sort that out; but while you do that, I ask that you'd keep my name out of your mouth."

"And who's gonna make me?"

Esther smirked, easily piercing through Sheba's combative demeanor.

"If you're going to threaten me, Sheba, you better be prepared to back it up," Esther murmured. "Try the egg nog, I hear it's good." She grabbed a red solo cup from the counter, poured herself a drink and then walked past Sheba who was now fuming.

Rea placed a hand over her mouth to keep from laughing. Micah watched Esther walk away with wide eyes. Not once did she raise her voice, but in his opinion, her clap-back was epic. If he knew Esther as well as he thought he did, he knew that there were indeed some intense emotions raging behind those chocolate brown eyes.

"What she said. Cookies are good too," Micah said.

He walked away quickly, not giving Sheba any time to respond. Rea followed quickly behind him.

They made their way across the room to the large, ornate Christmas tree that was covered in gold and red garland, and ornaments of various shapes and sizes. There were a few gifts under the tree, about four or five. Micah took this opportunity to spoil his younger sister, so the rest of her gifts were hidden away in his room. Esther leaned against the wall talking to Fallon. She seemed calm enough. She was smiling and laughing as if the incident with Sheba had never happened. Esther took a sip of her drink, then wrinkled her nose.

"Yuck," she said.

Her voice was easier to discern the closer he got to her. Fallon laughed at her friend.

"Don't like the eggnog?" Micah asked, with his hands in the pockets of his dark denim jeans. Esther shook her head and peered down at the contents of her cup with disgust.

"I forgot how much I hate this stuff." She made a few disgusted faces, each of them causing Micah's smile to enlarge.

"Listen Esther, I'm sorry about Sheba," he said. "I didn't invite her."

"Who?" Esther tilted her head to the side, eyes wide with feigned confusion.

"She—oh I see what you did there." He smirked.

Esther placed her hand on his arm. "You can't control the actions of other people, and that girl doesn't bother me. Ain't that just like the devil?"

Micah laughed.

"How much did you hear?" He asked.

"The part where she called me a hoe and then threatened me. I find it funny that she has my number but won't call to threaten me. She simply tells you, and you know why?" She said, leaning forward.

"Why?" Micah asked as he leaned in to meet her.

"She ain't 'bout that life," said Esther. She leaned back and took another sip of her drink as Micah laughed. "And that's one of the reasons, I can't be worried about her."

"One of the reasons?"

"Vengeance is mine saith the Lord,"she mused.

"Oh, right."

"Hi, Micah," Fallon said, drawing Micah's attention. Micah smiled at her, slightly embarrassed. He hadn't meant to ignore her.

"It's good to see you again, Fallon."

Fallon looked at Esther and then back to Micah before replying mischievously. "You too. It's good to see both of you…here…together…" She eyed Micah and Esther with a look that suggested she was up to no good.

She really wants us together, huh? Looks like we have a fan base already.

"Fallon! Enough, please!" Esther begged.

Fallon rolled her eyes.

"Girl, bye. Just remember the safest sex is no sex. Holiness is still right." Fallon did her best interpretation of an old church mother, complete with the stern glare and imaginary fan.

"I'm walking away now," Esther said. She was doing her best to hold in her laughter but it wasn't working. As she began to walk away,

Fallon grabbed her arm and pulled her back.

"You stay, I'll leave." Fallon looked between the two of them again, then smirked and walked away.

"I'm sorry about her…" Esther began. Micah waved off her comment.

"No worries."

"Micah…" Rea sang his name in a way that indicated that she was about to cause some trouble.

He turned to see her standing next to Jason, who was holding mistletoe in his hand.

"Rea!" He exclaimed.

Rea shrugged.

"Don't say I never did anything for you," Jasper whispered as he held the mistletoe over Esther and Micah's heads..

Esther's eyes were practically bulging out of her head and Micah's expression was no better. His palms began to sweat.

"Oh c'mon!" Jennifer said cheekily. "Can't be that bad."

"This is peer pressure!" Micah exclaimed, looking around the room anxiously.

"Fine," Esther conceded, crossing her arms.

"Fine?" Micah said, eyes widening.

Esther crossed her arms and smiled teasingly at him.

"Yes, fine. Kiss me, on the cheek."

She tapped her cheek with her index finger. *Dang…* He thought. *Better than nothing…* He supposed. He leaned forward and gave her a soft peck on the cheek.

"Happy?" He asked his sister.

She looked just as disappointed as he felt. Dryly she replied, "Ecstatic."

FOURTEEN

Four days, thirteen hours and twenty-five minutes had passed since Esther left to visit her family for the holidays. He decided that he was going to make the most of his Christmas break. Every day, he pulled out his keyboard and stared at its ebony and ivory keys, before returning it to its prior location—underneath the bed—otherwise untouched. Micah was determined that this time, he was going to play. This time he was going to *at least* touch a key. It had been so long since he'd played… Would he even remember how to? Yes, it was ingrained in his being--his very core. He asked for a keyboard when he was seven and learned to play by ear. Once his parents discovered his talent, they immediately enrolled him in piano lessons to sharpen his gifts. He was deemed as nothing short of a young prodigy.

Now here he was fifteen years later, afraid to even touch a key. What would his mother say if she saw him now? Would she be ashamed? Would she tell him that she was wasting the money she spent on piano lessons, or would she tell him that he was wasting himself?

Micah sat on his bed in front of the black and silver Yamaha. Very slowly, he reached out to touch the keys. What was he so afraid of? If he got back into music…that meant he was going to open himself up again. Well, he didn't have to tell anyone. This could just be between him and God. *Right God? This is between us.*

He was met with silence.

Micah huffed and placed both hands on the keys. He tried playing a simple C-chord and succeeded. He played a mindless tune, to get a feel for it again. *I should try a song,* he thought. *What was that song…what was the song momma loved so much? Balm something…Balm in Gilead. I'm just going to try it and if I screw it up, I just screw it up. No one is here but me and Rea…* He turned the volume down on his keyboard, took a deep breath, exhaled, and then played the first chord.

"Is there a balm in Gilead?" His voice cracked. He cleared his throat and then tried again. "My soul is sick, my heart is broken, who is this Balm in Gilead? Who is the salve for the sin sick soul? They call Him Jesus. They call Him Savior…"

His fingers danced over the keys a little while longer and before he knew it, he'd made his way through the entire song. By the time he played the final key he had tears in his eyes. How he'd missed this; the feeling of fire coursing through him as he played not just for his own entertainment, but in an effort to please the King of His Heart. He felt as if God was truly standing in front of Him, smiling at him, encouraging him to continue. Micah wiped his nose briefly and then went back to playing.

"Play the song I gave you," God commanded. His voice was full of excitement, and in that moment, he realized how much God truly loved his worship. *"Go on."* He urged. The melody immediately returned to Micah's mind, and he set his fingers to the keys quickly repeating the melody he was hearing. *"Record it."* God said. Micah pressed the recording feature on his keyboard immediately.

How could he have ever forfeited this feeling? This intimacy he found in worship…and not corporate worship, but an intimate time that he hadn't even intended to occur. This moment, where he was pouring out his heart through song, was a moment he was truly touching the heart of God. He hadn't intended for this to happen, but God clearly did.

"It is because you said yes," God said.

"I don't have lyrics for this," Micah murmured.

"You will soon," God answered. An infectious grin broke out over Micah's face as the song changed once again, to something more upbeat.

He broke out in laughter as the joy of the Lord truly began to fill him. He sang the words to this familiar song, "Joy" written by Vashawn Mitchell, one of his favorite artists. This song had never been truer to him than in that very moment. He stood to his feet, continuing to play but allowing himself to truly get lost in it.

His smile grew even larger when he heard a quiet soprano voice harmonize with him. He turned his head to the door. Rea was standing there, a large smile on her face as they sang together. When they sang the song to its completion, they stood in complete silence.

"You should tell Mark," she whispered.

"No, I—I can't." Rea placed her hand on her brother's arm. He'd yet to remove his fingers from the keys.

"Yes, you can. I won't tell him, don't worry but I think you should. Just think about it," she said.

Micah nodded. He knew the church had been looking for a musician, and their worship leader—Daniel—claimed that he had been called to ministry in another place—at least that's what he'd told everyone. That didn't exactly sit right with him, but whatever. Daniel still had a few more months with them. Rea patted him gently on the arm.

"It's good to have you back." She sighed. "You may think that I don't remember you leading worship at the church when you were younger, but I do. Anyone could see that you were called to this. Just let God show you what to do. If God's taking suggestions, then I suggest that He suggests, that you join the praise team. Keep practicing," she said with a smirk.

Micah nodded, not quite knowing what to say to that. He wasn't sure what Mark would say if he found out about his gift. Mark wasn't only the Pastor, but he also was his friend and mentor. Maybe Rea was right.

"I'll think about it," he said.

Rea nodded and left, closing the door behind her. He played all through the evening, late into the night. He fell asleep, face on the keyboard.

Five and a half years ago:

"God is..." Micah's eyelids began to droop as he rehearsed the song for what felt like thirtieth time. "He is th—" A yawn interrupted the sweet melody. The door to his bedroom cracked open.

"Alright, time to give it a rest."

Micah's lip turned up slightly to form a tired smile. He turned toward the door and through drooping eyelids, saw his mother leaning against the door jam. She was smiling at him. He liked to think it was a smile of pride and endearment. Lyla Williams, with blazing brilliant emerald eyes and bouncing brown coils, pushed herself off of the door jam. Slowly, she made her way over to Micah's queen-sized bed and sat down. She eyed the gray Yamaha upon it's stand in front of Micah. He still hadn't moved his hands from the keys, but his eyes were on her.

"I'm so close, Mom, there's just this one part in the chorus I need to get down."

Lyla shook her head. "I know, baby. You'll get it, but you're going to need to be well-rested to do it."

Micah nodded.

"I don't know why I even bother," he admitted quietly.

Lyla placed her hand on him. "What do you mean, baby?" She asked as she began to rub soothing circles on his back.

"No matter how much time and dedication I put in to this ministry, I'm always getting into trouble for something. Something is always wrong."

"Don't you pay any attention to Mother Wilks," Lyla said sternly. "She's a hateful old woman, and you can't stop doing what God told you to do on account of someone else."

"But mom—"

"Mm. No sir. You have a gift, Micah. You are what this ministry needs. Have you noticed that she's the only person criticizing you?"

Micah shrugged.

"I mean, she's the only one who says anything. All those other women that she sits with, look at me like I ran over one of their eighty-five cats. She's not the only one that has a problem with me, Mom."

"There's a few that don't like you, but the masses think otherwise."

Micah stared down at the beautiful mix of alabaster and black keys.

"I heard you and dad talking," he admitted.

"Did you now?"

"Yeah."

"And what did you hear?"

"Why is Mother Wilks so evil? What is it that she has against me? Dad's pretty mad from what I heard, said she has a whole bunch of men's shoes under her bed. I'm assuming that means she's a hoe."

Lyla sat stunned at first but then soon erupted into laughter.

"Yes," she said between giggles. "That's exactly what that means."

"Sounds about right--hypocrite. It was probably the entire deacon board." The venom in his voice immediately caused Lyla to stop laughing.

"Micah—"

"No, mom. I'm sick of this. First, it was the songs I picked, then she didn't like the arrangement of the doxology that I did, and now it's my hair. She's going to talk about my hair, but she cut hers and she's a low-key thot! She's got her ears pierced, and the list goes on and on! Why am I a problem? In her eyes I can't do anything right. I know you said not to worry about her, and I wouldn't care about her feelings if Pastor wasn't always agreeing with her." Lyla sighed and ran her fingers through her son's tight ringlets, her fingers getting tangled every now and again.

"I agree." She exhaled deeply. "It is wrong. Your father and I have talked to Pastor already but he ain't tryina' hear us. Johnetta Wilks is this church's greatest investor."

"So? We have money too. If all this is balanced on a hefty tithe, then why aren't we being considered?"

"Well, in addition to that money, she has quite a bit of influence. If she walks out, half the church will too."

"Well so? If they walk out over that then they shouldn't be there to begin with."

"I agree."

"So why are we still there? Why do we even bother coming to that church? Every time I go, I get torn down." His eyes stung and glistened with unshed tears.

"How do you feel when you're singing and playing?"

"Close to God," he responded immediately.

"And you have issues with how many people in the church?"

"Just two." He sighed, already aware of where this conversation was going.

"So you're gonna let two people run you off?"

"Ma, there are other churches!" He exclaimed. He turned around to face her

wide and understanding eyes.

"I know. Trust me baby I do, but if the remnant leaves, who will fight for the ministry? There are good people in this church Micah, and the Pastor is just as human as we are. Promise me something."

"Depends." Upon seeing his mother's serious look, Micah quickly back tracked. "Kidding, what do you need?"

"Promise me, you won't walk away before God says it's time. Pray, and if He says it's ok, then I will take you anywhere in the city until we find you a good church home. If He says to stay, then despite how much you don't want to, promise me you'll stay. No matter what happens, stay."

"Ok. I promise."

"And one more thing."

"Anything."

"Promise me that you won't give up on the gift God has given you. Baby, you're something special and that's why you're going through this. If the enemy can shut you up and sit you down, he will win. Don't let him win, stay in the good fight." She placed her hand on his cheek and stared into his jade eyes intently. Micah nodded.

"Ok."

That had continued for another year, until he put down the microphone and stepped away from his piano after his parents died. If he got back into music ministry, whether be it praise team or musician, who was to say that the same thing wouldn't happen to him? Who was to say that he now had the ability to truly stick it out? Suppose this was a repeat of his past…Then again, he wasn't the same person that he was back then.

He loved God back then, truly he did but, if he was being honest with himself, he didn't stay in the ministry just for God. Over the years, his heart grew cold towards the ministry he was a part of. Nothing seemed to get better. He would feel the atmosphere shift and then hit a wall for whatever reason. Sunday after Sunday, he went home disappointed and angry despite everyone's compliments and Facebook statuses about how great the church service was. As a result, he ended up staying out of obligation and for the promise he made to his mother. After he moved, he was unable to keep that promise, even if he wanted to.

***

It was awkward going to church without Esther there. He'd never been there without her. She was the one who brought him there, so to be going without her seemed… wrong. At altar call, Micah went up for prayer, thinking that perhaps a prophetic word was what he needed. He didn't want to reveal information that he was supposed to keep quiet. So, he stood there with his hands raised and eyes closed. His prayer was that God would clarify and confirm what he needed to do. For the past week, he'd prayed and heard no response. Maybe his spiritual ears were clogged?

The person that came to pray for Micah was not who he would have chosen for himself. He had nothing against the man, but he'd heard him pray before. His name was James and his prayers were very basic. What Micah needed was a word from God, not some general, cover-all prayer. Perhaps his thinking was a little wrong and off, as he wasn't exactly the best at praying either. His prayers were also short, sweet, and to the point.

James told Micah to lift his hands and Micah did so hesitantly. James began to pray, "Father God, I just--I just come to You um, right now for Micah. God, I don't know what He needs but I pray that you would meet him at the point of his need. Um, Micah this might sound really strange but, in the spirit I see music notes around you. God says, I didn't give you that gift to keep all to yourself. I will teach you what you need to know. I will show you what to do. I don't know if that means anything to you Micah, but I know that God said it and I pray that if it doesn't make any sense now, that it will make sense later."

James couldn't have been more than thirty-five. He was tall, and in Micah's opinion, goofy looking. He had a huge gap between his teeth, and often came to church in jeans and a plaid shirt, and yet, God had just used James to speak into his life. Micah swallowed hard, immense conviction filling his heart. *Ok, God, I'm sorry. I shouldn't have judged him.*

"It makes perfect sense," Micah said.

James' face lit up as he grinned.

"Great! Whatever that gift is, we need it here, brother." He placed his hand on Micah's shoulder. "God bless you, brother."

"You too, Bro," Micah said.

He gave James a brief hug and made his way back to his seat.

From across the room, he locked eyes with Pastor Mark. They were definitely going to have a conversation.

After service while Rea went around talking to everyone, Micah made his way over to Brother Mark.

"Hey, Brother Mark," he greeted.

"Hey, son, " he said.

He embraced Micah tightly, and then let him go. Micah fiddled with the hem of his sweater.

"What's on your mind Micah?" Mark asked, smiling knowingly.

"I just wanted to share something with you."

"Ok, I'm listening."

Micah stuffed his hands in his pockets as he admitted softly, "I can play the piano and I sing."

Mark smiled widely at him before responding in a light tone, "I know."

"You know? What do you mean you know?" Micah exclaimed. He pulled his hands out of his pockets and stared at Mark incredulously, his eyebrows kissing his hairline.

"Well, I had a feeling. I want you to go pray about this but, I think you'd make a good addition to our praise team. Right now, Daniel is training them to lead worship. He's going to be letting them lead until he leaves. That way, while we're looking for a new worship leader, we have some people to lead." Micah nodded. "He may want you on the keys though. I mean don't get me wrong, these tracks are great but…" Micah nodded.

"Ok, I'll pray about it."

"I can tell this was a big step for you, " said Mark as he crossed his arms.

"Yeah, it was. It was Rea's idea."

"It was a good one."

"I'm starting to think so too," Micah said smiling. "Well, I better get going. I think Rea's about ready to leave." He said. He glanced over Mark's shoulder and saw Rea waving goodbye to a few of her friends. It warmed his heart to see her so happy. Although she'd lost one friend, she gained many more in return.

"Ok. Call me later and we'll talk about this some more," he said. Micah nodded. Mark gave him one last smile, then walked away.

***

"That's great Micah! I'm so happy for you!" Esther exclaimed. Her eyes were large and full of mirth. They were dancing at the news. "The praise team…that's awesome!" Micah smiled back at his phone screen, thankful for video chatting. "Hold on one second," she said holding up her finger in the camera, then put the phone down. The view of a vaulted ceiling filled the screen. In the background, he could hear Esther yelling at, what sounded like kids.

"Sit down somewhere!" She yelled. Micah laughed.

"You sound like someone's mother," he said when she returned to the phone. She laughed and shrugged.

"So I've been told. Now back to you and this praise team business! I can't believe you actually joined it! I hate that I'm going to miss your first Sunday on the team."

She stuck out her rose-colored lips and crossed her arms.

"Oh, stop pouting, you'll have plenty of time to see me sing."

"I know, but still. I'd like to be there. I don't even think I realized that you sing."

"I didn't until a week ago," he admitted. "I stopped doing gospel when my parents died and I gave up music altogether when my grandmother passed. I was planning to go to school for music but I changed my major."

Micah adjusted a few things on the coffee table in front of him, refusing to look at Esther.

"What about now?" He looked up and saw her smiling softly at him.

"Now…" He took a deep breath and exhaled with puffed cheeks.

"I'm going to get back to the music. I don't know about changing my major or anything like that—"

"Well, you're undecided, aren't you?" She asked. Micah nodded. "You're going to have to pick something. You're about to be a Super Senior."

"So are you," he joked.

"I never planned to be a fifth-year student…" She shook her head. "I need some fifth-year funding."

Micah nodded. He hadn't forgotten that others were not as fortunate as him, but he didn't think about it often. He never thought about it when it came to Esther. She always seemed well put together, and she never complained so he never had a reason to think that she was having any sort of financial problems. She was able to afford the same apartment that he did and he automatically assumed that the girl was well-off.

"Well, I'm sure there's scholarships for that."

Esther nodded before looking over her shoulder and then back at him.

"You're right. I just applied for a few this week but hey, I have to go. We're about to eat and my twin cousins are about to get in trouble."

"Ok, we'll talk soon?" He asked.

"Of course. Have fun at rehearsal tonight!" She said.

Micah ended the call with the promise of texting her later. No matter how much they texted or called, it never felt like enough. He *missed* her presence.

"Guess, I better get to rehearsal," he murmured, grabbing his coat from the arm of the couch and standing to his feet. After shouting his plans to Rea, he quickly made his way out the door.

FIFTEEN

"Ok, start from the bridge. Say, He's great!" Daniel instructed as he threw his hand up in the air, signaling the praise team to immediately begin singing.

Daniel was a short man who was known for wearing large framed glasses and blazers. It was clear that Daniel had been raised in a church where traditional gospel music was celebrated, as well as newer music. His favorite thing to teach his praise team, was jazzed up versions of hymns.

Micah smiled as he sang the song he'd only learned twenty minutes ago with confidence.

This was his fourth rehearsal and he felt right at home. After talking to Daniel four weeks ago, he was immediately welcomed with open arms. To his amazement, Daniel didn't want Micah on the keys. Daniel wanted Micah on a mic. Micah ended up sharing a microphone with the only other tenor, Rodney.

"Uh, excuse me Sopranos," Daniel shook his head as he cut

them off. "Jesus be a fence…" he murmured in exasperation. "Latricia, how can you be flat and sharp at the same time? Is that even possible? I think you made that note up. What is that, *flarp*?"

Everyone laughed as Latricia smirked at her friend.

"The same way that you can match and not match at the same time every Sunday, just disrespecting the whole color wheel," she said, placing a hand on her hip.

Daniel chuckled. "Whatever. This is you all's note."

He hummed the note for them to hear, and then cued them to come in. Micah watched him with rapt fascination. Was this how he used to look when he was leading rehearsals?

"Nope, something is still off," Daniel said. He ran his hands over his face. "Here, I'm finna record y'all and maybe someone can tell me what's off."

Daniel recorded them as they sang that part for what felt like the fiftieth time that night. He had them gather around. Micah hung towards the back, wanting nothing more than to observe. As soon as Micah heard the recording, he immediately knew what the problem was. *Should I say anything though*? He wondered. He was still new. No one would want to hear from him. Yes, they were like family but everyone was nice until you crossed over into their lane. He should know…

"Anybody?" Daniel asked. He looked around the circle. The

two altos: Maggie and Cora shook their heads, and the sopranos, Latricia and Cami did the same.

"Micah? Rodney?"

Rodney immediately shook his head and held up his hands.

"I think it's the tenors," Maggie said jokingly.

Micah rolled his eyes.

"Micah? What do you think?" Daniel asked.

Micah rubbed the back of his neck and grimaced. "I think…" Lord knows how he hated being put on the spot, "I think that the altos—no shade—are a little flat. They come in from that one part," Micah sang the part to illustrate his point. "And it makes them stay flat throughout that whole part so even though the sopranos were sharp, I think that the altos were low-key—no pun intended—flat the whole time, like a half step flat."

Daniel looked at him, eyes wide, and mouth a gape. Everyone else looked at him with similar expressions, all except Maggie. Maggie glared at him playfully and was the first to speak.

"Dang Micah, I was just playing. You didn't have to do us like that."

Micah laughed nervously.

"Sorry, I mean—I could definitely be wrong here. This is just my personal theory."

"Let's test it," Daniel said excitedly. "Give them their note Micah and let's see how it goes." Micah nodded and gave them the correct starting pitch and qued them. Micah and Daniel both smiled when they realized that Micah's theory had been correct. After the song was over, Daniel clasped Micah on the shoulder.

"You were right! That was dope," Daniel said. "Thank you."

"It's no big deal," Micah said, his face beaming. "I used to work with the youth choir a few years ago."

"That's right, you told me that. I shouldn't be surprised that you were able to fix the issue so quickly. You *are* a musician." Micah shrugged.

"Just recently got back into it."

"Well, I can't tell." Micah grinned.

"This is just the beginning," Adonai said. *"Just wait."*

When he got home, he went on for about an hour to Rea, telling her how happy he was that he'd made the right decision in joining the praise team. When he finally allowed Rea to go to bed—as he'd kept her up with his talking—he called Esther. He was more than a little disappointed when she didn't answer, as he hadn't heard from her in a few days. He knew that she was probably spending time with her family, or asleep. Or maybe she just didn't feel like answering the phone; she was in no way obligated to answer every time he called. That night, Micah went to bed smiling. The joy of being used in the ministry that he was created for settled on him.

-----ONE WEEK LATER----

For the first time in a long time, Micah woke up inundated in sweat. It was about four a.m. Sunday morning, and it was still dark outside. Only the ghost of streetlights crept through his closed blinds. The dream that haunted him the night before was still fresh in his mind. In his dream, he'd seen Esther sleeping peacefully on the ground at the hitch point of a cross road; to his right stood Pastor Mark. Mark had grabbed Micah's shoulder and turned him around so that they could look each other in the eye.

"Choose," he'd demanded.

Those words were still ringing in his ears as he forced himself to lay back down on the bed and take several deep breaths. He reminded himself that he was no longer there, and that he had no decisions to make. Perhaps the dream was inspired by his growing worry for Esther. He'd tried calling her for the past few days, but got no response. There was no text, no returned calls. He brushed it off time and time again, saying that she was with her family but in his heart, he knew that something was wrong. That just wasn't like her. Maybe he was just being obsessive? She hadn't been on Snapchat or Facebook or Instagram. Maybe she was fasting from her phone? Perhaps, she needed a break from the social world?

He tried to soothe himself with these thoughts, but as Mark's command continued to repeat and run wild through the confines of his mind, his heart beat accelerated. He didn't need help interpreting that dream. He was going to have to make a decision and soon and whatever decision he was going to make had something to do with Esther.

He wasn't the best at making decisions--his past was evidence of that. What if he had to choose between Esther and God? What if God was calling Micah to separate from her? It would be hard…but, if he had to do it, he would. Immediately, he dropped to his knees. The need and desire to inquire of his Heavenly Father overcame him.

"I'm going to ask you to trust Me," Adonai replied.

"Of course," Micah vowed. "Of course."

"That is the decision you're going to have to make."

Micah looked up, confused.

"I've already made my decision. I'm going to trust You, no matter what." The uneasiness Micah felt in the pit of his stomach indicated that something was coming that would test his declaration of unwavering faith.

If that wasn't the case, then God wouldn't have made such a big deal about it, right? He stood up and looked over at his phone, it was sitting on his night stand. It began vibrating loudly and it was the only noise he could hear at that moment above his pounding heart. When he saw Mark's name flash on the screen, his heart stopped.

"Jesus," Micah whispered breathlessly. He didn't want to answer the phone, but if Mark was calling this early then whatever he was calling about had to be important. It seemed that he was going to have to make his decision sooner than he thought. With shaky hands, he answered the phone.

"H-Hello." His voice was trembling, and he did his best to swallow despite how thick his throat felt.

"Micah? I'm sorry to call you so early."

"It's ok. I was up anyway," Micah said. Micah scratched his head, nervously. He took a seat on his bed as he waited for Mark to continue.

Mark sighed before asking, "Are you sitting down?"

Micah's heart fell into his stomach as his entire body tensed. No one said that unless extremely bad news or extremely good news was coming, and he was willing to bet everything he had that this news was not good.

"Um...y-yeah. Yeah, I'm sitting down."

"Listen, I'm sorry to tell you this, I know how close you and

Esther had gotten over the past few months but…"

"But what?" Micah exclaimed.

"Esther's been in a car accident."

Sitting down didn't help. He felt as if the floor, the bed, everything that was holding him up had fallen from beneath him.

"Micah? Micah are you still there?" Mark's frantic voice came through the speaker of his phone.

"W-what?" Micah whispered. His eyes were stinging with tears. Not again. Not again.

"Esther's been in a car accident, her grandmother just called me. She was on her way to visit a friend and she just—"

"I…I don't want to hear what happened. Is she ok?" Micah asked. His free hand found its way into his bronze curls.

"She's alive, but comatose. It was a pretty bad accident Micah. She could have been killed on impact."

Comatose? Coma…comatose….

"I probably should have waited until after service to tell you," He continued, "but I knew they were going to bring it up and I didn't want you to be caught off guard. I knew this would probably hit home for you." His voice trailed off. "With what happened to…

Micah scoffed. *Probably?*

"Yeah. Th-thank you. Thank you for telling me."

"We're going to be praying for her. She's going to be alright."

"How do you know that?" Micah said. His eyes were burning as he attempted to hold back his tears. "She may never wake up."

"Because I trust God." *Trust God.* "You can choose to let fear overcome you, or you can overcome fear with faith and watch God fight this battle, not just for you but for Esther. We know that whatever happens, she's safe with Him."

Micah nodded although Mark couldn't see it. Tears finally broke free as sobs followed. Quickly, he subdued it by biting his fist. *She's not dead. There's a chance that she could make it, right? She'll be fine, right?.*

"What a way to start the new year," Micah said between shaky breaths.

The first Sunday of the new year would be one spent praying for one of the most instrumental people in his new life, to live.

"Yes, God is already showing His hand. The doctors said she wouldn't make it through the first night. She made it, and she's stable. God's got this under control. I know that's easy to say, and not necessarily easy to hear or believe, but He's able Micah. She's going to be fine."

"How long has she been there?"

"About a week. Her grandmother just got my information from

her friend, Thomas."

Again, Micah nodded. His dream finally made sense. He had a choice—he could either run away and become bitter or he could choose to have faith and stand his ground. Not even five minutes ago, he declared that he would trust God no matter what, but he didn't realize that "no matter what" would entail this.

Numbly, Micah listened to Mark pray. He was so numb that he couldn't even form an 'Amen'.

"Trust Me," Elohim whispered.

Micah nodded quickly, tears falling down his face. Yes, he was glad that she was alive but all of this felt too familiar. The phone call, the fear, the emptiness—he'd been through it all before.

They hung up a few minutes later and Micah lay in his bed, staring at the ceiling, unsure of what to pray. There were still so many things that could go wrong.

He told Rea what happened when she woke up, and her reaction was not at all what he expected. She was so calm and peaceful.

"She's gonna be ok, Micah, " she'd told him. "Can we go see her?" She asked. "School starts next week. I wanna spend a few days seeing her."

"Of course."

His response was automatic, but on the inside, he was terrified.

What would she look like when he saw her? He hadn't allowed Mark to explain the extent of her injuries to him and he still didn't want to know. He just wanted to know that she would wake up, and be healed. Better yet, he wanted all of this to be a dream.

"We can leave after service," he said.

Rea nodded and immediately started packing. Micah took in a deep breath, nodding to himself.

Why were they going to service again? That was the last place he wanted to be, but God was his only hope. God was all that he had and he decided that he was going to worship with his whole heart. He was going to lay on the altar until his knees hurt and petition God to spare this young woman's life.

When they arrived at church, Daniel was the first to greet Micah and Rea.

"Hey! Y'all ready to give God some glory on today?" He clapped his hands together, a huge smile on his face. When Micah and Rea didn't laugh or smile, apprehension washed over Daniel's face. "What's wrong?"

"You didn't hear? Esther's been in a car accident," Rea said.

The moment those words left her mouth, Micah's heart clenched. It was as if hearing the words in the light of day, out in the open, made them more real. *I can't do this.*

"Aww man. Weren't you guys really close to her?" Daniel asked. His eyebrows furrowed in concern as he placed his hands on his hips.

"Yes. We *are*, said Rea.

It took everything in Micah not to snap on Daniel for speaking about Esther as if she'd passed. Yes, Micah realized that it probably wasn't intentional, but the biting reality of the possibility that she would have to be referred to in past tense, broke his heart.

"I'm sorry. What happened?"

"We're not sure. She was visiting a friend and then…" Rea trailed off, looking down at her shoes. "I don't know. I'm hoping Brother Mark can tell us some more info."

Daniel nodded. Throughout the whole exchange, Micah kept his eyes on the floor.

"Don't worship Me today out of fear Micah, worship Me out of faith," God whispered.

Micah nodded to himself.

"Micah?" Daniel asked.

"Yes?" Micah said quickly. His head snapped up and judging by the looks on both Rea and Daniel's faces, this was not the first time his name had been called.

"You ok? Do you need to sit out today?"

Micah hesitated. He knew that he'd vowed to worship God with his whole heart today, but he could do that from the pew. As much as he wanted to do that, he couldn't.

"I'll be fine," Micah said. Daniel patted him on the shoulder and nodded. He sighed.

"Let's go pray." He herded Micah away from Rea, and to the other praise team members.

It was the hardest Sunday of his life, the biggest press he'd ever endured. Every time he opened his mouth to sing, flashbacks, crossed through his mind. He sang through them. When the church corporately prayed for Esther, his heart leapt at the possibility of her survival. Surely, if a whole church was praying for her, God would heal her. He stood on the platform praying silently with his eyes shut as tightly as he could.

"Even if you were the only one praying, I'd heal her. I'd do the work because you asked in My name and you believed. One man, nearly saved a city with his prayers. Consider My servant Abraham. Do you remember the story?"

Yes. He prayed that you wouldn't destroy Sodom, but you did anyway. Is that supposed to be comforting?

"You're forgetting something, Micah."

And what is that?

"He petitioned Me in prayer. He asked that I would spare the city, in the

event that I find some righteous people in the city."

And you didn't find them…

"No. I would have spared the entire city Micah, for the sake of the righteous. As it is written, those who are born of Me are the righteousness of Me. Had there been but ten, had there been but five, I would have spared the city for their sake. If one man's prayers, one man's petition caused Me to reconsider destroying an entire city, imagine what your prayers could do. The prayers of the righteous availeth much."

That's good for the righteous ones.

"You are My righteousness."

What does that even mean, God?

"You are an example of My mercy and My grace. You are a walking example of My love. You are My hands and feet in the earth. You are My heart. You are in right standing with Me."

You act as if I'm up there with Mark or somebody.

"You are all equal to Me. My love is not merit based. The moment you committed your life to Me, you became My righteousness. You were placed into right standing with Me. Your prayers availeth much. Every time you read that verse, I want you to read it aloud saying, 'My prayers availeth much'."

Floored, tears sprang to Micah's eyes. He sank to his knees. He briefly registered a hand on him, another voice praying for him in tongues. He knew that he'd been forgiven of his sins, but to be called the Righteousness of God…

I am not the person I was when I was sixteen or even eighteen.

"Good," said God. *"I want you to be better. You were closest to Me at sixteen-years-old, but I didn't pursue you so that you could revert back to who you used to be. That sixteen-year-old boy was not meant to stay in that one place forever. Your destiny is to go from glory to glory and there will be a higher glory after this."*

At altar call, Micah came forward immediately, knowing that the altar was where he needed to be. Pastor Mark prayed with him fervently. He prayed that Micah would submit to the process and that he would trust God in spite of how things looked. He prayed that Micah would not hide because of his fear. He spoke life into him, and Micah received what Mark spoke as best he could.

***

Pacing in the waiting room of Red River Hospital was practically torture for Micah. Rea was sitting in a chair, watching people come in and out of the metal double doors. Just beyond those doors was Esther Wickers' unconscious, and more than likely broken and battered body. Could he see her like that?

He had no idea what he was walking into; perhaps he should have allowed Mark to explain. Mark attempted to tell Micah all of the details twice, that morning when he'd first called, and again after service. Mark called Esther's Grandmother with the intent of only getting her hospital room number, but she insisted on meeting Micah and Rea. Apparently, Esther had been talking about them quite a bit to her grandmother. So, there they stood in the waiting room, waiting for Elnora Wickers to meet them there.

They'd driven nearly six hours to get to Esther's hometown. That six hour drive was mostly silent, and Micah prayed most of the way. He allowed Rea to control the radio. She eventually plugged up her cell phone to the USB port and played her music the rest of the way. She finally fell asleep about half-way through the trip, and that was good because he wanted to be left alone in his thoughts. One sentiment that Mark told him, while he was on the altar resonated in his mind:

"You don't have to beg."

He'd read about sonship, embracing God's love, and the benefits he now had as His son, but reading and believing were two separate things. He believed in adoption, yes. He believed that God had forgiven His sins, yes. But, believing that he was of a royal priesthood, believing that he could ask what he would of God and receive it, was truly stretching his faith. Oh, how he wanted to believe! He desired more than anything to see himself the way that God saw him.

Micah sighed and ran his fingers through his hair. He'd long since taken it out of its original bun. He wanted to demand that someone tell him what her room number was. Better yet, he wanted to go find it himself. He'd find it, eventually. Had he not been pressured to meet up with Esther's family at the hospital, he would have done so. Now, he was subjected to their time table.

"Micah look," Rea said. Micah looked toward the sliding doors of the entrance.

He sighed when he saw a short woman walking inside. Beside her was a taller woman, with a bob hair-cut. The shorter woman seemed like she was well into her sixties, the younger woman, in her thirties. The older woman looked around the waiting room. Her expression was neutral and calm, while the younger woman's face was turned up in what looked to be disgust.

Oh boy.

He'd bet his right arm that she was Esther's mother. He recognized that expression as the same one Esther made after drinking eggnog. When the older woman caught sight of him, she smiled and after nudging the other woman she hurried over to him. Micah stuck one hand in his pocket as Rea came to his side.

"Hello," the elderly woman greeted.

"Hi," Micah replied.

"You must be Micah," she said warmly, "Is this beautiful young lady your sister? Rea?"

Rea smiled gratefully at the older woman and dipped her head a little in embarrassment.

"Yes ma'am I am," Rea said.

"It's nice to meet you, Mrs. Wickers," Micah said. He extended his hand to her, but she rejected the hand and pulled him in for a tight hug instead.

"I've heard a lot about you, young man," she whispered.

"All good I hope."

"Not at first, but now, nothing but great things." Mrs. Wickers pulled back from him. "Strapping young man, so handsome."

Micah's smile was small, but his heart was pricked by her words. He wished his own grandmother had been like that; the pain of her passing flashed within his heart.

"Thank you."

"And please, both of you call me Nana Wickers," she said as she pulled Rea in for a hug.

The other woman—who Micah suspected was Esther's mother—looked on in annoyance. Her arms were crossed and her facial expression was sour, with a wrinkled nose and icy eyes.

"This is my daughter, Esther's mother, Chariese."

Micah extended his hand to Chariese and she took it hesitantly. Had it been any other time, he would have been offended, but given the circumstances, he wasn't exactly in the 'meeting and greeting' mood either.

"It's nice to meet you," Rea said. She shook Chariese's hand as well. "I don't mean to rush you or be rude, but can we see Esther?" She asked. He couldn't have said it better himself.

"Of course," Nana Wickers replied. She led them through the double doors and down the dim hallway.

The walls were a pale mint green. The smell of the hospital—which Micah hadn't registered—now filled his nose and made his stomach churn. Patients passed him, some looked worse than others, but all of them looked miserable. The group made a sharp turn down a hallway and Nana finally stopped at a door. It was closed, and for that he was grateful. He needed a moment, but he refused to walk away.

"Now, she's in pretty rough shape. Don't feel bad if you have to leave. I did the first time I saw her, believe it or not, she actually looks a little better," Nana said.

For the first time, Micah could see the effect of this tragedy on her face. She'd aged well, with few wrinkles and blemishes; but her eyes were burdened with circles and filling with tears.

Micah and Rea could not respond verbally, neither of them knowing exactly what to say. Nana opened the door, she and Chariese went in first.

"God help me," Micah murmured as he walked in.

His hand was clutching Rea's tightly. The sight before him brought tears to his eyes. Esther Wickers' pin straight hair was pulled into a bun on top of her head, giving onlookers a perfect view of her face. Her normally golden and glowing skin was pale. Her left cheek was bruised and tiny cuts littered both of her cheeks. A breathing tube was down her throat, and her leg was suspended.

"Hey baby, told you we wouldn't be gone long," Nana said. She took a seat in the chair next to her and took Esther's tiny hand in hers. "We brought some people to see you. Micah and Rea are here, you were right, he's cute." Chariese snorted.

"This is ridiculous," she said.

Her voice was venomous, startling Micah. He recognized that tone, it was the product of deeply rooted bitterness. Chariese threw up her hands and walked out. Micah's gaze immediately shifted to the floor. Rea, struck with surprise, took a step towards Esther's unconscious form. She took another step, until she was standing right by Esther.

"It's ok. If you want to hold her hand you can," Nana Wickers said. "Don't mind Chariese. She's not good at coping. I keep telling her that Esther is gonna be fine, our baby girl is strong and that we have God on our side, but she's not trying to hear me. Go 'head and sit down in one of those chairs."

As Micah looked around the room for a chair, he noticed the absurd amount of floral arrangements and teddy bears. Nana noticed Micah's gaze and said, "People from the church."

Micah nodded. *Had to be her home church,* he thought. Rea had already located a chair for herself and pulled it up to the bedside. Micah took a seat in a chair by the window. It was the farthest from her, but still gave him an unobstructed view of her. He was afraid to get close, afraid that he'd break her or mess something up if he but touched her. This was not how things were supposed to go. She didn't deserve this.

"You can talk to her. I imagine she'll hear what you're saying," Nana said. Rea looked up at the older woman with tears in her eyes, clinging to her every word. "I talk to her every day."

Rea didn't hesitate. She looked down at Esther and smiled, despite the tears budding in her eyes. "Ok…um…Hey Ess. It's me, Rea! Micah and I drove six hours to come see you." Rea took Esther's hand in hers and bit her lip as she struggled to hold back tears. "It was the most boring ride ever."

Nana smiled at Rea, then turned her gaze to Micah. His eyes were wide as he took in the scene before him. His own eyes stung with tears but he refused to shed them.

There was no smile on Esther's face, no laughter. There was no sarcastic expression or glare to reprimand his stupid behavior. She was emotionless, seemingly breathless…nearly lifeless. He kept waiting for her to pop-up and tell them that this was just a prank. He swore to himself that he wouldn't even get mad. He'd just be grateful that she was ok.

Rea looked at her brother. Her eyebrows raised, with expectation.

"Tell her, Micah," Rea urged.

He opened his mouth to speak, but no words came out.He tried once more, and still no words came out. He stood up and walked out of the room.

Rea had been unconscious the entire time they'd been transported to the hospital after the accident that took their parents.

But he was awake.

He saw their lifeless bodies. He'd seen what death looked like, and Esther's pale body seemed a little too close to it. She was too still for his comfort. He leaned against the wall, and slid down. He took a deep breath.

God, I need your help.

This woman, who'd become nothing short of his closest friend over the past few months, was now one step away from death. Yes, he knew what God had told him earlier that day. Yes, he knew what everyone at church was telling him; and yes, he knew that he should have faith that God would heal her, but believing that was an entirely different story.

SIXTEEN

"Where are you staying?" Nana Wickers asked. Nana Wickers, Micah and Rea joined Chariese in the waiting room.

"We have a hotel room for the next few days," Rea said.

Micah nodded in confirmation, not trusting his voice. Part of him was slightly embarrassed at his episode.

"That's not necessary. You all can stay with us," Nana offered.

Chariese glared at her mother incredulously. "Mama!"

Nana Wickers silenced her with a look so stern that Micah nearly recoiled. Esther had mentioned before that she had some family issues, and he was beginning to wonder just how deep those issues were. Chariese rolled her eyes.

"Please, excuse my daughter, we'd be more than happy to have you all stay." Rea looked up at Micah questioningly.

"We appreciate it, but we'd hate to put you out," he said. His voice came out scratchy, as if he hadn't spoken in days.

"At least come over for dinner before you turn me down."

He looked away from her, wondering why in the world was she being so hospitable to two people she'd never met. He could see, then, where Esther had gotten her kindness and hospitable spirit from. Still, he wondered how she could be so welcoming, so open with two perfect strangers.

When he looked at her again, he understood. As he looked at her closely, he could see that her smile was desperate; behind those delightful chocolate eyes there was so much pain. She needed them to come, to fill the void she was suffering through while her granddaughter was lying in the hospital.

"Alright, " Micah murmured.

Rea jumped up and down, then grasped Micah's arm in appreciation.

"Good!" Nana Wickers exclaimed with genuine excitement, as the crow's feet around her eyes crinkled even the more. "You can follow me home. Do you like chili?"

"Yes ma'am!" Rea said. Her entire face lit up at the prospect of having decent chili again. Neither of them had eaten some good, home cooked chili since their grandmother died. They walked out into the chilly night air together, all of them masking their pain in different ways. Knowing his sister, she would eat her weight in chili to avoid thinking about everything she just saw. He would try to do the same.

***

The next morning saw Micah sitting by Esther's bed side. He'd cancelled their hotel reservation at Rea's request, and they were staying with Esther's grandmother. He snuck away early that morning. Rea wanted to stay and talk with Nana Wickers and while he was leery about leaving her alone with this woman, he knew deep down that she wouldn't hurt his sister. Esther spoke very highly of her grandmother in their conversations. She hadn't said much about her mother and now he could understand why. Her mother was an icy woman. Her brown eyes—the same color as Esther's and Nana Wicker's eyes—were harsh, and cold. Looking at her, it became clear to Micah that life had beaten Chariese down one too many times.

He stared down at Esther's unmoving body. The soft hissing sound of the ventilator filled his ears, only slightly louder than the sound of his own thunderous heartbeat.

"Talk to her," God whispered.

What should I say?

"Whatever is on your mind."

Micah nodded. He sighed and took her tiny hand in his, intertwining her slender fingers with his own.

"Hey Ess." He paused, and had the situation not made him feel so pathetic he would have laughed. He'd truly paused as if she was going to respond to him. "It's me, Micah." Briefly he permitted himself to imagine what her response would be. She would probably say something like,

"No duh."

Micah cleared his throat.

"I'm sorry that this happened to you. You deserve better than this. I don't know if you realized that I was here yesterday. It kind of bothers me to see you like this so I couldn't stay. I don't know if you can hear me, they say I should speak to you as if you can. God even told me I should talk to you, so I guess that means you can hear me, right? Or maybe He thinks it will be therapeutic." Micah took a deep breath. "I'm going to try to have a little bit more faith, ok? Everyone keeps saying that you're going to be fine. I want to believe that, but I've been here before…you know, waiting and on the verge of losing the ones you love. I don't want you to think I'm giving up on you, or God but this really, really sucks right now. This sucks. You aren't supposed to be like this, you don't deserve this."

"There's more at work here than what you see Micah," Elohim whispered. *"You will understand in time."*

Micah had no words, and therefore no real answer, but in his heart he heard the words to a song that his mother used to play on the radio all the time. He grew to love it and sometimes, he'd even play it with the choir.

"Will you trust Me?" God asked. *"It's ok to be angry, it's ok to be upset. This hurts you, I know, but in spite of the pain I need you to trust me."*

Micah nodded and lowered his head. He placed his forehead on the side of the bed, his hair falling on either side of his face, shielding him from the world.

His heart, although broken, swelled as he sang softly to himself. The song writer had been onto something when he wrote that song. He sang the song all the way through, his voice barely rising above a whisper.

He wasn't concerned about hitting the right notes or doing any fancy runs. He was merely concerned about allowing the words to minister to him. Could he—would he, trust God? In spite of all that He'd been through, could he truly trust God? He believed God was good and that God was healing the broken pieces of his heart, but there still remained a shattered piece or two within him that cried out for him to run the opposite direction and forfeit all that he'd worked for and accomplished with God.

But despite that broken piece, his spirit cried out for restoration and healing—not just for Esther's physical body, but for his own heart, and spirit. Would God leave him in pieces for ever, or would God finally finish this healing?

He knew that deliverance was instant for some people. Some people are healed in the very moment they cry out and others receive their healing and deliverance with time. Why couldn't he have been one of the instant ones? Why couldn't he move past that stupid, burdensome, place of hurt and put all of his trust in God?

Pain gave way to frustration, and gently, the Spirit of the Lord whispered to him, *"This is the place you need to come to Me from. Your pain and frustration won't scare Me off. Come to Me with these real and raw emotions, this frustration, and this pain. That's what I need you to surrender to Me and until you do, you will never be able to trust me fully."*

"God, I want to pray for you to heal her but I don't believe that You will. It bothers me, because I know You're the only one who is able. I want to believe that You want to heal her, and that You want to heal me but for some reason, I just keep ending up in the same cycle. I need You! I hear You talking but I don't see You working. You talk to me in riddles that I don't always understand, You show me dreams of things that I can do *nothing* about, You tell me that You will answer my prayers but You won't give me the faith that I ask for. I know that I can't ask You for anything and expect to receive it without faith. So how exactly is this supposed to work? I don't want to fail. I'm scared to go back."

Immediately, God's presence manifested in the room. The hairs on the back of Micah's neck stood up and his entire body froze in shock. He recognized the presence, and instead of feeling guilty for his emotions, or as if he should apologize for being upset, he felt validated. He felt the weight of someone's hand on his shoulder. He didn't need a Bible commentary to tell him Who was now beside him. A reverential fear washed over him. He looked up. All he saw was a washed-out hospital room, bright lights and a closed door, but he knew that someone was there.

"Ask what you will of Me Micah. I am here. I have always been here, but you now know beyond a shadow of a doubt that I am here. You have not always been able to feel My hand upon your shoulder or Me standing beside you but this is where I have always been. I told My disciples that if they had faith the size of a mustard seed, they could move a mountain. Your faith grows with every trial and every test. You have all the faith you need. Trust is not a concept that you sit and wonder about. It's not a subject to be debated, or a text that you have to exegete. It is moving when I say 'move'. So far, you have been obedient to Me Micah, that shows Me that you trust Me."

So, trusting God was not something he had to debate within himself about? He didn't have to make some large statement of faith?

"Stand," The Lord commanded. Slowly, Micah complied. He never let go of Esther's hand, and God's hand never left Micah's shoulder. *"Will the floor fall from beneath your feet?"*

"No," Micah answered immediately.

"How do you know?"

"It looks sturdy." Immediately, Micah understood the point that Jesus was making. He'd stood without thinking, he never even thought of the floor possibly falling from beneath his feet. He took for granted every step he took on that ugly-tiled-floor. As silly as it sounded, he trusted the floor. "It's never, not held me up," Micah murmured.

"Exactly. The reason you feel like you can't trust Me is because you feel like I have not held you up in the past Micah. I have always held you up. You are still standing, you are still walking. I have not allowed you to fall through. This hand on your shoulder has always been there. Even when you didn't want to deal with Me, I watched you. I was still walking with you. I understood your pain Micah. Although you walked away from Me, I never walked away from you. Revelation brings light and light destroys darkness every time."

This is what everyone was talking about when they said that You're faithful. Micah thought.

"*Yes. Allow this revelation of My presence and love in your life to pierce through the darkness that the enemy has tried to fill your heart with by lying to you about who I am and what I will and won't do for you.*"

Micah nodded, not knowing what else to say but,"Yes Lord."

He hadn't thought this to be possible, but he felt as if God was truly smiling at him. He allowed this new revelation to pour through his heart, chasing out the darkest parts and bringing truth to combat the lie of the Enemy.

"*Stay free,*" Jesus said. "*You are free, when you allow My truth to pierce through the lie and pull down the stronghold, but the responsibility is now on you to stay free. The Enemy will return to you, to lie to you but immediately you must combat his lie with truth. Don't even engage in any further arguments or discussions. Cut it down immediately, do not allow it to take root.*"

Micah nodded vigorously.

"Yes."

"Now, ask of Me what you will and if it is in accordance with My will, that will I do."

"Your will?" Micah murmured. "What if she's not meant to live? What if that—"

"The more you learn of Me the more you will learn of My will. You will learn that My will is not for anyone to perish. I came to give each of you an abundant life. Again, I say, ask what you will."

"Jesus, please…wake Esther up. Heal her. Leave no trace of this accident on her." Micah said.

His confidence became unwavering although his voice said otherwise. There was a tremor in his voice that he didn't even recognize. He never felt God's presence leave, but Jesus grew silent. There was no witty comment, no sort of acknowledgement that God had heard him. Apart from the sound of the heart rate monitor and ventilator, there was only silence, just as there had been in his bed room a little over four years ago. This time he didn't need a response, he simply knew that God had heard his prayer.

FOUR MONTHS LATER

Micah stood on the platform with a microphone in hand. No way had he thought he'd be leading a song, let alone worship. Four months had slowly gone by and there was still no change in Esther's condition. He wasn't going to kid himself. After the first week or so, he'd contemplated giving up. God had instructed him on how to pray for Esther's healing, and for her family. He started every prayer with a statement of faith, proclaiming that God was able to do exceedingly and abundantly above all he could ask or think. He would proclaim that he did in fact trust and believe God. He'd truly taken to heart what Jesus had told him in that hospital room;

"Learn of Me."

Those words ignited a flame within his spirit that would not be quenched until he truly came to know everything about the character of Christ. He wanted to know everything about Jesus. Who was he truly? He wanted to know who he was for himself, so that if Jesus ever posed the question: "Who do you say that I am?" to him again, he'd have an answer. He was making a list of all the things that he'd learned about Christ: Healer, Deliverer, friend, Chief Cornerstone that the builders rejected, Balm in Gilead. He had a scriptural reference for every single one of them.

When Micah had gotten the call from Daniel on Friday, he didn't even flinch. Daniel entrusted him with the task of leading worship while he dealt with a family emergency. While he wasn't terrified to lead, he had been a little miffed that he hadn't been able to make his trip to see Esther that weekend.

Micah and Rea had journeyed to Esther's home town every weekend to visit her. While there wasn't much change, Micah remained by her side as much as he could, praying for her and talking to her. He looked forward to it, he knew that one of those visits would be the one in which she would open those pretty brown eyes of hers and walk out of that hospital. He'd become close with Nana Wickers, and called her at least once a week to check on her and to check on Esther.

"Micah what are we singing?" Latricia asked from her place behind her microphone, with her hands on her hips. She wasn't even attempting to conceal her attitude. Although he was fine with being chosen for this opportunity, not everyone was. Sound check was going to be a little difficult.

He told her the song list, unfazed by her attitude. He tapped the microphone and signaled the sound man, Chad, to begin checking mics.

"Why aren't we singing Spirit Break Out? We rehearsed it," she asked.

His first reaction was to say, "Because I said we're not," but he didn't, he held it in because he knew that would only cause more problems.

Instead he replied, "There's still a possibility that we may sing it." She sucked her teeth but Micah ignored her. "Ok, let's circle up for prayer."

***

Service began with fervent prayer. As Micah and the praise team took to the platform after the prayer, Micah scanned the sanctuary for Pastor Mark. He always had an encouraging smile to offer while the praise team was singing and he kind of needed that today. Micah prayed quietly in the Holy Ghost as he looked about the room. Mark was nowhere in sight.

"Stay focused," Adonai instructed.

Micah nodded and began to worship "God You are worthy," he whispered. "God, I praise You. God, I magnify You." He threw his head back, eyes closed and relished in the presence of God.

When the prayer was over, Micah tightly gripped the microphone he'd gotten from Chenelle, the woman who'd been praying.

"How many of you know that God is able?" Micah paused as he waited for the crowd's response. "Oh, come on, how many of you truly know that God is able?" He was met with a loud chorus of 'Amens'.

"How many of you believe God to do something awesome in your life? How many of you know that He's incredible and invincible?"

He nodded to the sound man and immediately the track started. As Micah began to sing the song, he could feel the anointing resting on him, propelling him forward as he sang with all of his heart and all of his soul and all of his strength. He wasn't just ministering to them, he was ministering to himself.

"God is! God is able to do anything if we but ask!" he exclaimed.

The music climaxed and he signaled the rest of the praise team to come in.

"Sing, He's an able God!" Micah sang as he signaled the praise team to come in. They echoed him as he followed up with another, "He's able!"

He could feel his body bending backwards as the sound flowed from his body. That one part of the song seemed to last forever, and he was ok with it.

"Somebody ought to declare it, He's able! And because He's able, it's easy to believe God," he said as the music slowed as the second song began,

Micah sang the first verse and chorus with tears in his eyes. He leaned back as he belted the notes from his innermost being. By the end of the song, Micah was barely able to contain himself. He jumped once, and twice, in an attempt to release some of what he was feeling. The desperate need to release a cry of praise and to give God more than he'd ever given Him before in worship filled him. Now, he now truly understood what it meant to believe God.

"*Look, Micah,*" God said.

Micah looked up immediately towards the door, and could not hold back the tears that stung his eyes when he saw Pastor Mark walk through the door, hand in hand with Esther. Her doe-eyes eyes were wide and searching, despite her curly hair falling in her face. Even at a distance, he could see the tears welling up in her eyes. She was fully awake, fully aware, and she walked with a slight limp but she seemed to be an entirely different woman than the one he'd seen a week ago. Her wild hair was free, and she was dressed in jeans and nice, light blue blouse. He was sure there was a story behind this. He had a million questions; *Why didn't they tell him that she was awake? How long had she been awake? How was she here? Why was she here?* But none of them mattered in that moment.

Micah surrendered complete control over his own limbs. He began to dance before the Lord, thanking God without a second thought. Micah had never shouted before. In the past, he'd often watched the older people at his former church shout and he'd laughed at them. He never could understand why they got so happy and seemed to lose themselves in praise; but now he understood. God was worthy, God is worthy, and praising Him should be as easy as breathing simply because God is worthy. Micah barely registered the shouting music, a blend of fast paced keyboard runs and hard percussion, beginning to play. He'd already lost himself in his praise.

As people noticed Esther's arrival, the praise grew more intense. God had answered their prayers and a regular praise just wouldn't suffice. Some of the congregants immediately raced to hug her, one of them being Rea. Others took one look and broke out into a shout, or a jump, some even a sprint. They'd all heard about her coma, they'd all been praying, and to see her walking and breathing on her own and smiling was a true miracle among them.

When Micah finally stopped dancing, he put the microphone to his lips, then pulled it away just as quickly. No words could fall from his lips, he bent over with his hands on his knees. He wasn't surprised that God had done it, but God didn't have to do it, and the realization that God did hear and answer not just prayers in general, but *his* prayers, washed over him like a tidal wave. God *was* a good Father.

Esther wasted no time in giving God praise and thanks. She couldn't dance the way she wanted to, that much was apparent, but she lifted her hands and she shouted her praises unto God. Esther couldn't run, but Rea took her hand and together they walked around the church both shouting their thanks.

You are great at surprises. Micah thought as he stood there with hands raised, watching in complete and utter amazement.

"And here You were upset with Me for not allowing you to come see her. It would have been a waste of time and gas. Didn't you ask Me for complete healing for Esther?" God asked.

Micah's eyebrows furrowed in confusion.

Yes God I did. She's walking with a limp, but that's ok. At least she's awake.

"I will complete the work. Look again."

Micah watched closely as Esther and Rea continued to walk. Tammi, Mark's wife, had joined them along with a few other women. With every step Esther took, her steps became stronger. Eventually, there was no limp and he clearly was not the only one that noticed. Pastor Mark lifted his hands with a radiant smile, firmly in place.

You did it God. Micah thought. *After all the time I spent fighting You and running from You, You did this. Thank You. Thank You so much.*

***

"I saw you killin' it up there," Esther said as she smiled up at Micah.

She sat back on the couch, Micah to her left with his arm around her shoulders and Rea to her right. After service ended, she retreated back to Micah and Rea's apartment to spend some time with them while her mother and grandmother went shopping at a nearby mall.

"Oh please," Micah scoffed. Esther elbowed him.

"Learn to take a compliment. You did well, Mr. Williams." She smiled at him. Her twinkling eyes locked with his.

"Are you trying to throw shade?" He asked.

He suspected that she was referring to the conversation they'd had months ago about her inability to take a compliment. Esther laughed.

"No, but my grandma says a hurt dog will holler. Are you trying to give me a taste of my own medicine?"

Micah shook his head, then pulled her close and kissed her forehead. There was no strange hospital smell on her, no tubes obstructing his view or keeping them apart. His best friend, the young woman of his dreams, the proof he'd asked for, was now in his arms again.

"When did you wake up?" Rea asked.

"A few days ago. My family is here in town. They're hanging with some other family members who live in the area to give me some time with you guys. They're going to take me back home for a little while. I think the accident really scared them," Esther murmured as she looked down at her hands and interlocked her slender fingers.

"Scared me too," Micah whispered.

"Me three," Rea said.

"I thought you were going to die," Micah confessed.

"I know. I heard everything that you all said. I was afraid, because I was aware of it all, but couldn't respond. I couldn't move, I couldn't do anything but listen. I could hear everything you guys were saying and I want you both to know that I love you and I appreciate you all being there for me the way that you did. You didn't have to make the drive every weekend to see me."

Micah gulped. So she *did* hear everything, including the secrets that he'd shared with her and yet prayed that she wouldn't hear or remember.

"You don't have to thank us for that, we love you Ess," Rea said.

Esther smiled at Rea and gave her a friendly, side hug. "Some of us more than others," Rea murmured.

Esther stiffened.

"I'm sure that would be terrifying," Micah said with a glare. He couldn't believe Rea was actually trying to bring that up. "You know, not being able to respond."

"Yes," Esther said.

Micah's tensed body relaxed a little as he realized she was going to let Rea's comment go. He was going to have a talk with Rea later about her timing and "jokes."

"Is your family always that hospitable?" He asked.

Esther chuckled. "You mean Nana? Yes. She likes you a lot."

Micah smirked. *Score one with the family.*

"So, you're staying with her?" He asked.

Esther nodded.

"Just for a little while. The doctors proclaimed my case to be a miracle. All of my internal damage was healed. The only thing remaining was that limp that God actually healed today." She paused for a moment before continuing, "I think they just want to keep an eye on me though, to see if this healing will stick I guess. I don't mind. Due to the fact that I was in a coma during the time classes started, school isn't exactly a possibility at the moment."

"We'll miss you," Micah said softly. His stomach tightened and he could already feel the sting associated with the loss of her presence. How could she just up and leave him again? After he'd just gotten her back, he wasn't exactly ok with her leaving again, but what could he say?

"I'll miss you guys too, but there's always video chatting and stuff. This won't be the last you see of me. This is only temporary."

"Still not the same," Rea said.

"I know," Esther said, sighing. "I know."

"When do you leave?" Micah asked.

"Tomorrow, so we better make the most of our time together," Esther said. She laid her head on Micah's shoulder and took Rea's hand in hers. "We can start by talking about Micah's footwork on that shout he was doing today. I never thought I'd see the day,"

"Shut up Esther," Micah said with a laugh.

Esther sat up and stuck her tongue out at him before playfully saying, "I love you too."

***

Micah sat outside on the balcony as the chilly night air enveloped him. He looked to his left and tried his best not to be disappointed in the fact that there was no one on that balcony. Esther had left an hour or so ago, he could hear them all laughing and talking next door. He knew she needed to be around her family. But, he wanted to be around her too. He'd come so close to losing her, and in doing so, he was more anxious than ever to completely break down whatever wall was keeping them from actually being together.

"Not now," God whispered.

I mean I'd obviously give it a few weeks God, she's been through a lot, but I'm so much closer to You now and I think that everything with Sheba has been resolved, I think that—

"Not now, and no. Everything with Sheba has not been resolved."

I haven't heard from her. I think she's gotten the picture.

"That doesn't mean that you won't hear from her. Ever heard of a soul tie?" Micah sighed.

Maybe once or twice.

"Deal with that, trust Me, and I will direct you from there."

Ok. I'll trust You.

His answer, although given begrudgingly was a true statement. He had to trust in God's timing. God had just done something wondrous for him that day, not just for him but for Esther and her family. The least he could do was be obedient.

"Not now, does not mean no. Pursue Me, and I will tell you when it's time to pursue her." Micah nodded.

She was my proof wasn't she?

"Yes. Micah if there is a prophet among the unbelievers, the unbeliever will be convicted and he will be called into account, the secrets of his heart will be disclosed and he will worship Me. He will know that I'm truly among you." Micah tilted his head.

I've heard that somewhere before. That sounds really familiar.

"It's in My Word. I gave you that dream of Esther nearly five years ago, giving you various prophetic dreams along the way. While unwrapping the gift within you, I prepared you for her arrival."

But why her? Couldn't you have used anybody else?

"Of course, I could have, but you were a sign to her also. Please understand, loving My Prophetess, loving My cherished daughter, was not the goal Micah. It was for the both of you to learn and see the extent of My love and to free your heart, so that you could love Me in return."

Micah scratched the newly budded stubble on his chin.

Wait, I'm confused.

Father God laughed, causing Micah to smile.

"You're not confused. You're overthinking it. Son there is much that you don't know, but you will learn in time."

What could she have possibly gained by knowing me? She pushed me, she led me back to You. What could I have ever done for her?

"You will see, in time."

And here You go again with these riddles, why can't You just tell me Abba?

"Because it's not yet time for you to know these things. Let Me do My job." Micah nodded and then yawned.

Ok, ok. Whatever You want God. It's Me and You. We're in this together.

"Yes we are."

***

Nana Wickers had invited Rea and Micah to have breakfast with them before they hit the road. Needless to say, that the relationship they'd developed with Esther's grandmother was not going to be a temporary one. Esther wasn't in the least bit surprised to find out about their relationship. They all now stood outside beside Nana Wickers' white Buick.

Esther gave Rea a tight hug, rubbing her back gently in soothing circles as she held her. Rea pulled back with tears in her eyes.

"I'm glad that I met you," Rea said.

"I'm glad that I met you too. Why do you say that like we're saying goodbye?" Esther asked, trying to hold back tears of her own.

"Because I almost had to."

Esther pulled Rea in for another hug and squeezed her eyes shut to ward off the tears that were threatening to spill over.

"Well, you don't have to worry about that, Sis. I'll be back in a few weeks, the fall at the latest. You can always come visit."

Rea nodded as she pulled away.

Micah pulled his shoulders back and exhaled heavily as Esther walked over to him. From the corner of his eye, he could see Rea and Nana Wickers' saying their goodbyes.

"Hey, Mop Head," Esther said.

"Hey, Demented Orphan."

"I thought we agreed to never speak of that movie again!" She shrieked.

Micah shrugged.

"Whoops."

She laughed, and when she stopped he noticed the tears in her eyes. One spilled over.

"I'm going to miss you," Esther admitted.

Micah pulled her in for a hug immediately and rested his head on top of hers.

"I'm going to miss you too, Ess. Be careful, please. I need you to stay alive, ok?"

Esther chuckled as she pulled away.

"I'll do my best." She gave him a kiss on the cheek. "I heard every prayer you prayed aloud in that hospital room, and seeing you here…at this place with God, brings my heart so much joy. You are not the angry and bitter man that I met last year. I'm happy for you."

"Thank you," Micah whispered.

Seeing the immense joy in her eyes, made her words that much sweeter to him and after sparing one final hug, Esther got into the passenger seat of her grandmother's car.

Micah and Rea stood side-by-side as they watched them pull out of the parking lot. Esther continued to wave until she was out of view. Micah put an arm around Rea's shoulders.

"God answered my prayers," Rea murmured, her voice capturing the astonishment that her wide eyes held.

"What?" Micah said looking down at her. Rea kept her eyes ahead, watching the road that Esther and Nana Wicker's disappeared on.

"I prayed for such a long time that He would save you, and make you happy. He did that."

"Did you doubt that He would?" Micah asked with a smirk.

"Oh that's rich coming from you." Rea laughed. Micah rolled his eyes. "So what happens now?" She asked.

“Whatever God wills,” Micah said nonchalantly, shrugging his shoulders. He wrapped an arm around his sister and smiled. “I’m sure we’ll find out soon enough.”

REFERENCE SCRIPTURES

“Be perfect, therefore, as your heavenly Father is perfect.” Matthew 5:48

“But if an unbeliever or an inquirer comes in while everyone is prophesying, they are convicted of sin and are brought under judgement by all, as the secrets of their hearts are laid bare. So they will fall down and worship God, exclaiming, "God is really among you!" 1 Corinthians 14:24

“Confess your faults one to another, and pray one for another, that ye may be healed. The effectual fervent prayer of a righteous man availeth much.” James 5:16

Story of Abraham pleading for Sodom and Gomorrah Genesis 18:16-33

THINGS TO THINK ABOUT

Did you know that dreams are a form of communication between you and God? While not every dream is from Him, God definitely uses this avenue to communicate with us! That's so cool! Think of Joseph from Genesis 37. (pg. 10)

At some point or another, all of us have experienced or participated in hypocrisy. Unfortunately, the Church is famous for it. Micah allowed the pain of his experiences with the church to drive him away from God. However, Micah was not accountable to God for what church members did. He was accountable for himself. It's important to remember that churches are full of imperfect people and while hypocrisy is wrong, and church people (people in general) can be mean, you can't blame the Leader (God) for what His followers CHOOSE to do. Forgive. Heal. Be free. Be everything that God has ordained you to be. (pg. 41)

Fortune teller huh? Prophets are ***NOT*** fortune tellers. They're messengers. What they prophesy, discern, or speak ***SHOULD*** always come from God. There are many false prophets in the world today, but true prophets have a heart for God and His people. (pg. 86)

Have you ever tried to pull away from God because of how unworthy you felt? God wants you to do the opposite. Change only takes place in His presence, and it is impossible to please Him without Him. (pg. 90)

What are soul ties, and why are they important? (pg.179)

Ministry end at the church house. Consider your life. Are you obedient to the urging, nudging, directives of God? I know. It's easy to get caught up in your daily life, but if you're a believer you work a 24/7 job. Do your best to be attentive to what God is wanting to do in your life, and in the life of those around you on a daily basis. (pg. 240)

Micah said that he returned to Sheba and his old ways, because they were safe. Is there truly safety in sign? According to Romans 6:23, the wages of sin is death. Although certain aspects of our lives may be comfortable, they aren't always good for us. No one ever said that sin had to feel uncomfortable or wrong. In some cases, it initially feels better than doing the right thing. However, if you stick to what is right, it'll pay off in the long run. (pg. 281)

Jesus laid down His life for us when we weren't willing to even follow Him or accept his free gift. The Bible says that there is no greater love shown than when a man is willing to lay down his life for his friend. When Micah fights with Shawn he realizes that the might lose his life and everything that he has (just as Jesus left His home in glory). Despite this, he was still willing to risk it all for his friend. Nevertheless, as always, God came through and the enemy was defeated! This situation was bigger than God simply keeping Micah alive, it was about Him giving Micah a real, live, interactive demonstration of the gospel and the sacrifice of Christ. (pg. 291)

When you get saved old relationships will change. They will react to who you are becoming. For some people this is a positive experience, for others…not so much. Has this ever happened to you? Have you ever had friends switch up on you because you've decided to change your life for the better? Although it's painful, sometimes it is for the best. People that mean you no good, only want to keep you around if you remain in a negative space. If you want to do better sometimes you have to change your surroundings—people included. (pg. 316)

If you haven't made Christ your Lord and Savior, what's holding you back? Ultimately, it doesn't matter what you've done in your life, or how far you've gone away from God. My prayer is that after reading this book, you'll see that there is hope—not only hope, but a beautiful and bright future in Christ. You are dearly loved.

ABOUT THE AUTHOR

Anna-Stacia accepted Christ at the age of six and has been seeking the Lord ever since. Her hope is that this book has encouraged and edified you as members of the Body of Christ. If you are unsaved, her hope is that this book will show you the mercy of God, the heart of God and that restoration is available and truly possible.

Like me on Facebook and follow me Instagram!

Facebook: Anna-Stacia D. Haley

Instagram: anna_stacia31

www.ingramcontent.com/pod-product-compliance
Lightning Source LLC
Chambersburg PA
CBHW060541310726
48982CB00009B/1331/J

* 9 7 8 1 7 3 3 4 6 3 6 0 7 *